PRAISE FOR

HUNTER'S SALVATION

"One of the best tales in a series that always achieves high marks . . . An excellent thriller."
—*Midwest Book Review*

HUNTERS: HEART AND SOUL

"Some of the best erotic romantic fantasies on the market. Walker's world is vibrantly alive with this pair."
—*The Best Reviews*

HUNTING THE HUNTER

"Action, sex, savvy writing, and characters with larger-than-life personalities that you will not soon forget are where Ms. Walker's talents lie, and she delivered all that and more . . . This is a flawless five-rose paranormal novel and one that every lover of things that go bump in the night will be howling about after they read it . . . Do not walk! Run to get your copy today!"
—*A Romance Review*

"An exhilarating romantic fantasy filled with suspense and . . . star-crossed love . . . Action-packed."
—*Midwest Book Review*

"Fast-paced and very readable . . . Titillating."
—*The Romance Reader*

"Action-packed, with intriguing characters and a very erotic punch, *Hunting the Hunter* had me from page one. Thoroughly enjoyable with a great hero and a story line you can sink your teeth into, this book is a winner. A very good read!"
—*Fresh Fiction*

"Another promising voice is joining the paranormal genre by bringing her own take on the ever-evolving vampire myth. Walker has set up the bones of an interesting world and populated it with some intriguing characters. Hopefully, there will be a sequel that ties together more threads and divulges more details."
—*Romantic Times*

Books by Shiloh Walker

HUNTING THE HUNTER
HUNTERS: HEART AND SOUL
HUNTER'S SALVATION
THROUGH THE VEIL

THE MISSING
FRAGILE

Anthologies

HOT SPELL
(with Emma Holly, Lora Leigh, and Meljean Brook)

PRIVATE PLACES
(with Robin Schone, Claudia Dain, and Allyson James)

FRAGILE

SHILOH WALKER

BERKLEY SENSATION, NEW YORK

THE BERKLEY PUBLISHING GROUP
Published by the Penguin Group
Penguin Group (USA) Inc.
375 Hudson Street, New York, New York 10014, USA
Penguin Group (Canada), 90 Eglinton Avenue East, Suite 700, Toronto, Ontario M4P 2Y3, Canada
(a division of Pearson Penguin Canada Inc.)
Penguin Books Ltd., 80 Strand, London WC2R 0RL, England
Penguin Group Ireland, 25 St. Stephen's Green, Dublin 2, Ireland (a division of Penguin Books Ltd.)
Penguin Group (Australia), 250 Camberwell Road, Camberwell, Victoria 3124, Australia
(a division of Pearson Australia Group Pty. Ltd.)
Penguin Books India Pvt. Ltd., 11 Community Centre, Panchsheel Park, New Delhi—110 017, India
Penguin Group (NZ), 67 Apollo Drive, Rosedale, North Shore 0632, New Zealand
(a division of Pearson New Zealand Ltd.)
Penguin Books (South Africa) (Pty.) Ltd., 24 Sturdee Avenue, Rosebank, Johannesburg 2196,
South Africa

Penguin Books Ltd., Registered Offices: 80 Strand, London WC2R 0RL, England

This book is an original publication of The Berkley Publishing Group.

This is a work of fiction. Names, characters, places, and incidents either are the product of the author's imagination or are used fictitiously, and any resemblance to actual persons, living or dead, business establishments, events, or locales is entirely coincidental. The publisher does not have any control over and does not assume any responsibility for author or third-party websites or their content.

PRINTING HISTORY
Berkley Sensation trade paperback edition / February 2009

Library of Congress Cataloging-in-Publication Data

Walker, Shiloh.
    Fragile / Shiloh Walker.—Berkley Sensation trade pbk. ed.
        p. cm.
    ISBN 978-0-425-22579-0
    1. Veterans—Fiction.   2. Social workers—Fiction.   I. Title
    PS3623.A35958F73 2009
    813'.6—dc22
                                            2008045434

PRINTED IN THE UNITED STATES OF AMERICA

10   9   8   7   6   5   4   3   2   1

FRAGILE

ONE

MAD.

That was the first thing that Luke Rafferty thought as he gazed at the face across from him.

Mad. And scared.

It was seriously *weird* looking at that face, seeing eyes that looked just like his, hair the same color. A mirror, sort of. An angry, scared mirror.

Dad had told him his brother's name was Quinn, had told him that their mom had taken Quinn from the hospital when they'd been babies. For eleven years, Luke hadn't known he had a brother. His dad never told him.

Then, a few days ago, while Luke had been helping Dad and a couple of the hands with a new horse they'd gotten, Janie, their housekeeper, had come rushing outside, her eyes wide, worried. She'd whispered something to Dad that Luke hadn't heard. Dad had looked at him for just a second. Something had shone in his eyes . . . something like hope.

Then dismay.

Without saying anything, Patrick had gone in the house with orders for Luke to keep helping with the horse.

An hour later, Patrick had sought Luke out and told him a story he could hardly believe. That he had a twin—a twin brother that their mother had taken from the hospital when they were only two days old. She'd abandoned Luke, although Dad hadn't used that word. But that's what she had done.

Left one brother, taken the other.

And now she was dead. Luke had often wondered about his mom, but whenever he'd asked about her, his father would just give him a sad smile and say, "Your mama wasn't a happy woman, Luke."

"*Did she love me?*" Luke had asked that, so often. When his father could evade him, he had. But other times, he'd simply sigh and either pick Luke up when he'd been small, or just wrap an arm around his shoulders as he'd gotten bigger. Then, in that sad, soft voice, he would say, "Luke, this is hard for you to understand. But not everybody is capable of love. Some people just don't have it in them."

Yeah. That had hurt. But his dad loved him. Eventually he'd stopped asking . . . because she'd stopped mattering so much to him. On the rare times he did think about her, it was to wonder what she was like, where she was . . . if she was any happier. If he'd ever meet her.

Now he'd never know anything about her, never would, because she was dead . . . dead, and the brother Luke hadn't known about was coming to live with them.

Twins. This was all so warped, having a brother he never knew existed.

But at the same time—and Luke wouldn't admit it to anybody, not even his dad—but at the same time, when his dad had told him about Quinn, some part of Luke had *known*.

He inched a little farther into the room, eying Quinn with curiosity, nervous excitement, and confusion. It was all turning his stomach into a *mess*. Their father, Patrick Rafferty, stood close to Quinn, and there was a look on his face that made Luke's belly feel all weird.

Although he tried to hide it, Dad looked like he was feeling the same anger, the same fear as Quinn. And sad. Luke didn't know if he'd ever seen Dad look that sad before.

Luke frowned, and that was when Quinn saw him.

Those gray eyes, so like Luke's, narrowed, and his lip curled. "What the fuck are *you* looking at?" Quinn sneered.

Luke's eyes widened, and unconsciously, he glanced at his dad. Patrick sighed and reached up, rubbed a hand over the back of his neck. Something about the way he looked just then made Luke think this wasn't anything that surprised Dad. Yeah, *Luke* was surprised. He wouldn't ever say that around his dad. The few times he had said it, it had been at school, with friends. But in front of his dad?

"Quinn, I'm getting tired of telling you that I don't allow that sort of talk coming from a child of mine."

Luke's surprise faded away into something else as Quinn flinched, almost like the man had raised his voice—or a fist. Without knowing how he knew, Luke realized that was exactly what Quinn expected. For Dad to hit him. Followed by that realization was a bizarre sense of resignation, and Luke almost heard the words ripple through his mind: *So what else is new?* Trying to think beyond all the stuff coming at him, Luke focused on Quinn as the boy turned and faced their father with a sneer. "Yeah, and I don't give a fuck." Then he raised his chin.

Luke blinked, startled. It was like Quinn was *daring* their dad to do something.

Patrick's eyes narrowed. "Boy, you are going to learn some respect."

Quinn laughed. It was an ugly, almost painful laugh, and Luke flinched at the sound of it. "How you going to make me do that, old man? Beat it into me?" Quinn shrugged as though he didn't give a damn what the answer was. "Won't be the first time."

The anger came on Luke before he understood what Quinn was saying. Pissed off, so damn pissed off that he couldn't think for it. *"Beat it into me . . . won't be the first time."*

All of a sudden, that anger in Dad's voice, in his eyes, made sense. The fear that Luke somehow knew was inside his twin made sense.

Out of the blue, Luke remembered his dad saying, *"Your mama wasn't a happy woman, Luke."* Not happy. She'd hit Quinn, and somehow, Luke knew it wasn't just a smack on the butt.

Patrick stood across from Quinn, a helpless look on his face. He closed his eyes, and Luke could all but hear his voice as Dad silently counted to ten. Before he reached it, though, Luke took a step forward, drawing Quinn's attention to him. "Dad doesn't hit people."

Quinn's lip curled up in that challenging, ugly sneer. "Yeah, right. Why don't you mind your own fucking business?"

Luke stiffened, his face flushing a hot red. Dad spun away, swearing under his breath, and then his eyes cut to Luke. "Luke, why don't you go out to the stables, see if you can help the boys for a while?"

Quinn laughed. "Yeah, you don't want him to see you hit me."

"Luke, get out to the stables. Now."

"My dad doesn't hit," Luke snapped. He shoved his hands into his pockets and glared at his brother. Planting his feet where he was, he did something he rarely did: disobeyed a direct order from his father and stood there, facing his brother and trying to think past the disgust and the disbelief rocking through him.

"Shit." Quinn shoved a hand through his hair, and when he did, Luke saw something on his skinny arm.

A bruise. Big, yellowed, fading. It wrapped all the way around his arm, like he'd been grabbed.

Seeing where Luke was looking, Quinn flushed red, but instead of looking away, he got that challenging look on his face again. In an unconscious mirror of his brother, he shoved his hands in his pockets and planted his legs wide apart. Lifting his chin, he smirked at Luke and said, "What the fuck is your problem?"

"What's *yours*?" Luke replied. From the corner of his eye, he could see his dad, and he was half expecting a hand to close around his neck as his dad forcibly walked him out of the room.

But Patrick Rafferty was silent.

And when Quinn abruptly took off, stalking out of the room, Dad gave Luke a curious look. Kind of wondering, thinking. Patrick was the thinking type. He talked slow, he was slow to anger, and he didn't bother wasting breath on words that weren't needed. The look on his face now was the same one he'd give a horse when he was deciding whether to buy: measuring, weighing, debating.

Finally, a faint smile tugged at his lips. "I've been trying to get through to him for a while now and not having much luck. Maybe you should go talk to him."

In that moment, Luke felt strangely adult. Almost old. Without saying a word, he nodded, and then he left the room. He didn't even have to look for Quinn. Somehow, his feet led him right to his brother, out in the backyard, behind the old utility shed, sitting with his back braced against it as he scratched at an ugly scab on one elbow.

"She hit you, didn't she?" Luke said, settling on the ground across from his brother.

Quinn tensed, and for a minute, Luke thought he was going to take off again. But instead, he just shrugged and muttered, "What the hell. Does it matter?"

"Because it ain't right."

"You really think I'm gonna believe that your old man never hit you?"

"He's *your* old man, too, Quinn." Then he shook his head. "I'm not going to lie and say he's never spanked me. But the last time he did was a couple years ago when he caught me getting into the gun cabinet."

Quinn's eyes widened. For a minute, he actually looked like a kid, like some boy that Luke would run into at school, instead of some angry, pissed-off punk. "Gun cabinet?"

Luke laughed. "Yeah, a gun cabinet. This is a ranch, not the city."

"What were you—?" Then he clamped his mouth shut, like he hadn't even realized he was asking something.

But Luke answered anyway. He shrugged and shifted around so that he had his legs drawn up in front of him. Resting his elbows on his knees, he answered, "I wasn't really doing anything. I just . . . Dad had been showing me how to hold the shotgun, how to clean it and stuff, and I wanted to see if I could do it without his help."

"And when he caught you, he beat the shit of you," Quinn finished, shaking his head like he wasn't surprised.

"No." Luke waited until Quinn looked back at him. "He turned me over his knee and spanked my butt a few times. Sent me to my room. Came upstairs later and gave me one of his talking-tos."

Quinn blinked. Squirmed around. Luke got the impression that Quinn *wanted* to believe him, but couldn't.

Softly, Luke said, "Decent people don't beat their kids, Quinn."

Again, that derisive, disbelieving smirk . . . but this time, Luke felt something else. Faint. Just barely able to make sense of it. But Quinn wanted to believe.

Twenty Years Later

"WHEN you shipping out?"

"End of the week." Luke glanced away from the window, meeting Jeb Gray's gaze. Jeb was an ugly bastard. Rangers had to keep their hair short, but most of them just kept it buzzed. Jeb shaved his hair completely off. His bald head was swarthy and dark. Should he ever let his hair grow long enough, it would be black. He had dark skin, but it didn't come from the sun. He'd probably been born looking like he'd spent months out in the desert.

Jeb's nose had been broken twice in the three years they'd been working together, and there was a scar bisecting the left half of his face. Starting just above the outer corner of the eyebrow, it slanted down toward his jaw. He'd barely missed being blinded in his left eye.

Yeah, Jeb Gray was an ugly one, all right. But he was one of Luke's best friends, and there were few men Luke trusted the same way he trusted Jeb. More than most, Jeb would probably understand some of the mess going on inside Luke's head right then. Luke Rafferty had been in the army from the time he graduated high school, as had Jeb. They'd been in basic together, gone into the Rangers together, had sweated and bled together.

It was all they knew.

Well, maybe not all; Luke knew there was a world out there where people didn't bleed, sweat, and die for their job. Where they had a life outside the job. And that mess was the part Jeb probably wouldn't understand, because Jeb was the job. If it had been Jeb injured, he'd be fighting tooth and nail to get back in the unit.

But Luke was actually ready to go, busted-up left leg and all. Looking down, he studied the leg in question. He could bear weight on it. Just barely. He could walk—with a cane. But the army was sending him to the best rehab hospital around, and Luke was going to leave the damned hospital with the ability to walk on his own two feet, with no help.

Jeb gave a low whistle. "That soon, huh? You okay with it?"

With a faint smile, Luke asked, "Do I have any choice?"

A smile curled Jeb's lips, and he replied, "Well, logically, yeah, you do. You don't have to leave, you know. Why the hell you want to leave before you know . . ." Then his eyes dropped to Luke's leg. Jeb had been there when Luke was injured; he knew how severe the damage was. "They said you wouldn't walk, Luke. Now they say you can't come back here. Prove 'em wrong."

"*Prove 'em wrong.*" If it was as simple as all that, if getting back into the unit was all that mattered to Luke, then he would do just that—or he'd die trying. Funny thing had happened on that last op in Afghanistan when those bullets had ripped through his leg: Luke had laid there on the ground, cold as ice, even though it was hot as Hades, and he'd realized he just might die without knowing anything more.

Blood, death, patching his buddies back up when they got injured, dealing with drug dealers, playing nursemaid to injured hostages while he and the rest of the team tried to get the innocent people safe before all hell rained down: it wasn't a life he regretted choosing. But if he kept on going, if by some small miracle he could get back into the unit—and that chance was small, as in microscopic—even if that happened, Luke wasn't so sure he liked the way his life was playing out in front of him at this point.

He was no longer so sure he wanted this to be the rest of his life. Even when he had served out his usefulness on an active Ranger team, even if he went on to train new recruits, ten, twenty, thirty years down the road, he wanted to look back and see something besides the army.

"If you're having second thoughts, now's the time to say something," Jeb said, misjudging Luke's thoughtful silence. "Maybe Tony could pull some strings . . ."

Tony Malone, their CO, stood across the room. "You're wasting your breath. I already tried."

Luke turned away from the window. It was a slow, painful journey, but he moved better with the cane now than he had last week. And in a few more weeks, maybe a month, he'd try walking without the damn thing.

"I'm not having second thoughts," he said, concentrating on the chair less than eight feet away. Six feet. Four. *Shit,* he thought disgustedly as he realized he was all but gasping for air. By the time he was able to sit down, he was covered with sweat and mentally questioning whether he'd be able to walk without that cane all that soon. Closing his eyes, Luke leaned his head back. His breathing calmed as he waited for the pain in his leg to ease a little.

"You sure?"

Cracking an eye open, he glanced at Jeb. "Do I really look like I can come back, Jeb? It ain't happening." Then he shrugged. "Besides, I think . . . I think I'm done, man. I'm done with this."

He was done, and he was good with that. He hadn't thought he would be. A year ago—hell, six months ago—had this happened, Luke would have thought he'd be fighting a medical discharge with everything he had in him.

Instead, he was cool with it. Hated the busted leg, but was cool with the discharge.

"Liar." Quinn stood by the door, one foot braced on the wall. Throughout the conversation, Quinn had been quietly watching everything with cynical eyes.

Luke looked across the room at his brother and said, "Yeah, I'm gonna miss you, too, Quinn." The two of them were identical, from the wheat blond hair, to their gray eyes, to their size-twelve feet. Identical twins, but they hadn't even met until they were eleven years old.

Born in the middle of an ugly divorce, it was probably safe to say they'd been born into warfare, although Quinn had definitely gotten the raw end of the deal. Their mother had been drinking, and drinking hard, throughout most of the pregnancy and had made it clear to everybody she met she didn't want the two brats she carried inside her. Not that Luke's father had ever said such a thing. No, Patrick Rafferty hadn't ever said a harsh word against the woman, although Luke knew his old man had plenty of them trapped inside him.

From what Luke could piece together, it had been a miracle Luke and Quinn had been born functional. As it was, Luke had been born with breathing problems and couldn't leave the hospital until he was nearly a month old. His dad liked to tease him that he'd been born smaller than most, and apparently it pissed Luke off, because within a few months, he'd grown like a weed, and by the time he was ready for school, he stood a head and a half taller than the other kids. A natural athleticism combined with the stubborn streak he'd been born with made it hard to believe he'd once been forced to let a machine do his breathing for him.

Quinn hadn't had as much trouble at birth, though. If he had, maybe she wouldn't have taken him.

Being born too soon had saved Luke from a very unhappy life, although now he had to live with the guilt of knowing his twin had been suffering while Luke grew up happy and loved.

Thirty-one years ago, hospitals didn't have the precautions against child abductions that they did now. Their mother had taken Quinn from the neonatal nursery and walked out just as easy as could be. Their father's attempts to find the newborn were unsuccessful, and Luke had grown up never knowing about his twin.

Quinn wasn't big on talking about his childhood. Luke didn't know much, but what little he knew wasn't good. Annie Rafferty hadn't been a good mother, not when she was carrying them and not after she'd given birth. Luke, the baby she abandoned, ended up better off than his twin.

He could still remember how pathetically thin Quinn had been when they went to Toledo to get him. Annie had died of alcohol poisoning; if she hadn't, Luke may never have gotten to meet his twin. His other half . . .

Quinn's lips quirked in a faint smile. But he didn't say anything. Quinn never said more than he needed to. He didn't have to. Luke knew what was going through his twin's mind. Quinn wouldn't ever leave the army. He was in it for life, and he couldn't understand how Luke was taking his medical discharge as well as he was.

Luke understood. Quinn had to be here. It wasn't just all he knew: it was all he wanted. He loved what he did. It was one of the few things in life that Quinn could totally commit to—and Luke meant very few. Sometimes, he suspected this life was the *only* thing Quinn could commit to. He lived and breathed it.

For a while, Luke had been the same way, not the commiting part, but loving the life, loving the job. But it hadn't ever defined him the way it defined Quinn.

Even though they had been separated the first eleven years of their life, they did have that weird bond so many twins had. They loved the same kind of foods; they were both adrenaline junkies; they went for the same kind of women.

But for every similarity, there were differences.

Luke was quick to laugh, quick to tease; Quinn rarely laughed and seldom smiled. Most jokes rarely struck him as funny. When they weren't on the job, Luke hit parties, went to movies, had one date lined up right after the other. Quinn would rather be on an op, and his downtime was spent in a small, two-room efficiency apartment on the base, usually just sitting in silence, almost like he was waiting.

Luke always had that weird feeling around Quinn, like his twin was waiting—waiting for an op, maybe. That was the only time Quinn really seemed alive sometimes—didn't matter if they were parachuting down into some war zone, slipping undetected through the rain forest on yet another battle in the unending war against drugs—that was when Quinn came to life.

The rest of the time, the quieter brother seemed more like a damned robot, even to his own twin. As much as Luke loved Quinn, there were times when Luke felt he didn't know the man at all.

Even after nearly four years in the unit, Quinn rarely spoke to anybody besides his brother unless it was required. He was just so damned isolated.

Luke's leaving the army also meant leaving his brother, to some extent.

But Luke was tired.

Tired of this life. Yeah, he liked the adrenaline rush. He liked knowing he was doing a job few others could do. A field medic in the Rangers, he'd saved the lives of his buddies more times than he could count. He'd loved it. But he'd also seen more blood than he wanted, and too much of it had come from innocent, helpless victims. He'd lost two friends. He'd spent too much time in hellholes, and there were things he had seen that were starting to keep him awake at night.

"Wish you'd reconsider leaving."

Luke didn't bother looking at Tony. His CO had made that more than clear. Nobody seemed to want to him to leave. None of them could seem to understand he was through, and it really didn't have much to do with his injury.

The injury had just forced him to acknowledge things a little sooner.

"I'm not a teacher. I don't want to be a teacher."

"You can't leave it behind as easy as that, Luke. You don't want to teach, don't teach. But this is your life. You can't just walk away."

"Wanna bet?" Luke shook his head. "I know you guys don't get it, but I don't want this anymore."

Quietly, Tony asked, "What do you want?"

"I don't know," Luke murmured. "But it's not this."

Off to the side, Quinn watched him with unreadable eyes. Luke met that level gaze for a minute and then looked away. He didn't know what was worse: his twin's unspoken censure, or the guilt because he didn't feel at all bad for leaving his twin behind.

TWO

Six Years Later

THE early spring rain came down in an ugly, cold drizzle. Fitting, Luke guessed, as he stood by the graveside and listened to the minister's voice drone on and on.

The gleaming black case held the remains of Sergeant Adam Murphy, one of Luke's friends from the unit. The rest of the unit was gathered around in their finest, various ribbons and medals decorating their uniforms.

Luke stood in the rain wearing a black suit he seldom wore and a topcoat that didn't block the chill in the air. It had little to do with temperature, though, and everything to do with the fact that he had to watch another friend get buried.

You weren't able to leave it behind after all, he brooded. Adam's wife of three years sat across from him with a blank, dazed look on her face. She still hadn't managed to process what had happened; it would take a while, Luke knew from experience. Even when a person was familiar with death, even when they'd had it happen close to home before, it wasn't something a body ever got used to.

The funeral ended as the flag adorning Adam's coffin was folded and given to Leah Murphy. She accepted it without really seeming to realize what she was doing. That dazed, shocked look on her face had both the doctor and the friend inside Luke concerned. He glanced at the older woman sitting next to Leah. It was her mother; he remembered meeting her at the wedding.

The men standing beside Luke were mostly friends from the unit, guys he'd bled with, laughed with. There were too many new faces, four new members of the unit in all, and only one of them was at all familiar to Luke.

The rest of them were strangers, and Luke knew within a matter of weeks, there'd be another new face, one to replace Adam.

Luke had only met one of them, Brandon, three years earlier when Adam had gotten married. Back then, Brandon had still been considered new, the guy who'd been brought in to fill Luke's place. Brandon. Brandon Lashley, Luke thought, even as he wondered why in the hell it mattered who the man was.

Typical human reaction, he knew, thinking about little details to avoid thinking about the big, ugly ones. Like the coffin being lowered into the ground. He glanced at his brother and murmured, "I'll be back in a minute."

Quinn didn't respond, just kept staring at the grave.

Working his way through the mourners, Luke reached Leah's side. She gave him a wan smile and held out her hand. It was cold, clammy. She was pale as death. "Hello, Luke. I'm glad you could come."

He squeezed her hand gently. "Of course I came." He dipped his head and kissed her cheek. "Is there anything we can do?"

Leah shook her head, tried to give him a smile, and failed. "No. I just . . . I think I should go home. Rest." She glanced to the lady at her side and murmured, "Mama's staying with me for a while."

"Good. That's good. You don't need to be alone right now."

"Alone." She closed her eyes, pressed her lips together. Her lashes lifted, and he saw the gleam of tears in there and silently cursed himself. But then she gave a watery little laugh. "I'm not going to be alone, Luke."

She squeezed his fingers and then took her hand back, laid it on her belly. "I just found out a few weeks ago I am pregnant." Her smiled wobbled and faded. "I hadn't told Adam, wanted to wait until he was home for a while. I . . . I didn't want to worry him. I was afraid he'd worry, and then something bad . . ." She sighed, passed a hand over her eyes. "But something bad happened anyway, and now he won't ever know he was going to be a daddy."

Her voice broke, and her mother stepped up, wrapped an arm around her daughter's shoulders. "Come on, sweetie. Let's get you home. We have to take care of that little baby now, right?"

Feeling like a helpless ass, Luke stood there watching as the women walked away. "Shit."

A hand came up, rested on his shoulder, and he glanced back to meet the grim blue gaze of his former CO. Tony looked like hell, his uniform not quite fitting right, like he'd lost weight. Too much of it. The guy was big, built like a linebacker, not just muscled, but broad and tall. But he had a gaunt look to his face, and the grief in his eyes had him looking a good twenty years older.

"She's pregnant," Luke said.

The men gathered around them reacted in different ways, some swearing low and ugly, others, like Quinn, remaining as silent as death. "Now that is a son of a bitch for you," Jeb swore. He glanced in the direction of Leah and her mom, his dark eyes unreadable. "Fucking unfair."

Fucking unfair. Yeah, that about summed it up.

An hour later found five of them, Tony, Jeb, Brandon, Quinn, and Luke, at Tony's small apartment in Fort Benning.

"Am I why the others didn't come?" Luke asked as he followed Tony into the living room, stripping off his soaked coat.

Tony shrugged. "I dunno. Told them they were welcome to come, but maybe they wanted to give us a while first. We were all with Adam the longest."

Part of Luke was grateful, even though he felt bad. People needed to be with friends in times like this, but he knew he wouldn't have felt as comfortable if the newer guys had been around. Weird enough having Lashley there, even though the two men had met before.

Luke's flight home wasn't until the following morning, and he needed the time with his friends. "You can't leave it behind as easy as that," Tony had said six years ago when Luke left the army behind.

In a way, Tony had been right. Luke had left the unit, but he was still a part of it. Enough a part of it that nobody but Lashley thought twice when Luke asked what had gone wrong, how Adam had ended up dead.

"Not really anything we can go into detail about," Lashley had said, only to be countered by Jeb's harsh laugh.

"Hell, Bran, he ain't asking for a write-up."

Lashley gave Luke a respectful nod, said softly, "I know he was your friend, but you're not—"

Tony cut him off. "Not what? Not with us anymore? You can't leave it behind as easy as that, kid. Luke wants to know the ugly story about how some bastard betrayed us, fine. Keeps me awake at night, and I have no problems sharing if he wants the same problem." His voice got harsher and harsher with each word, until he finally turned around and stomped out of the room.

"He's taking it hard," Jeb said softly.

Luke glanced at him. "Friend dies, you can't expect him not to."

Jeb shrugged. "It's more than just a friend, Luke. Tony's in charge; one of us gets hurt, gets killed, he feels responsible."

Luke wanted to respond, wanted to say it wasn't Tony's fault, that Tony wasn't responsible. In his gut, he knew it was true. But in his soul, he knew he'd feel the guilt the same as Tony if their places were switched.

In the end, it was Quinn who explained, in short, terse terms, reciting the main facts in a flat, emotionless voice. He didn't tell Luke everything, and Luke knew there were things he wouldn't ever know, not unless Quinn filled him in.

Tony's willingness to share his insomnia was only going to get

Luke a few highlights, no specifics. Neither Jeb nor Tony would share too much, and Luke hadn't expected anything beyond that.

"Somebody sold us out. Somebody who knew where we were coming in, where we were going. All of it. They had to; otherwise they never would have been able to lay that fucking trap."

"Damned miracle we ain't all dead," Jeb said softly.

Brandon snorted. "Miracles have nothing to do with it. Pure blind luck, that and because Quinn got through to us when he did."

Quinn's face was unreadable, his eyes turbulent and cold. "Fuck you, Lashley."

Lashley blinked and then scowled at Quinn's back as the other man stalked out of the living room. Luke heard the front door slam before he even managed to get on his feet.

"What in the hell did I say?" Brandon demanded as Jeb sent him a withering look.

Luke grabbed his coat, headed for the front door. Jeb intercepted him. "You might want to leave him alone for a while, Luke."

Luke lifted a brow. "You might want to get out of my way, Jeb."

Jeb scowled and scrubbed a hand over his face. He'd shaved that morning, but already there was thick stubble darkening his craggy face. "Luke, Adam wasn't the only one to get killed on this. There was a woman . . ."

He glanced over his shoulder, as if to make sure nobody else was listening. Lowering his voice, he murmured, "We had somebody feeding us information, a woman we've worked with before. They caught her, beat the hell out of her, raped her, killed her. Quinn found her when he . . ." his voice trailed off, and then he shook his head. "Quinn found her, Luke. And he never said anything, but I think he had feelings for her. He's blaming himself."

* * *

LUKE found Quinn in his cramped apartment two miles away, soaked to the bone from the rain and sitting on the floor in the living room. He still wore his Class A uniform, the tie askew, jacket unbuttoned. His head rested against the couch, and he didn't stir, even when Luke flicked on the lights and came to sit down beside him.

"You regret leaving?" Quinn asked after a while.

Luke shook his head, replied softly, "No." He shrugged restlessly, his eyes roaming over the bare walls of the apartment. No pictures, no calendars, nothing but bare, white walls. Empty. "I miss you. Sometimes the guys. But I don't regret leaving."

Quinn closed his eyes. "I'm glad you're gone. Today, saying bye to Adam, I kept thinking if you'd stayed, it could have been you we'd been burying. Four of us, man, four of us gone, and I keep thinking I'm damn glad my brother ain't with us anymore."

Luke snorted. "Yeah, and I keep worrying I'll get a knock on my door. I don't want to bury you, Quinn."

"You won't." There was an odd edge to his voice, and Luke glanced over, saw a weird light glittering in his brother's eyes. "Dying's too easy. I don't ever get the easy way."

"Jeb said a woman got killed."

Quinn jerked like somebody had stabbed him with a branding iron. Coming off the ground in one fast move, he crossed the room in long, erratic strides, coming to a stop by the wall, where he braced his hands against it and lowered his head. "Don't, Luke. I—I can't . . ." His voice broke.

Grief swamped him, all but broke him. Luke could feel it radiating off his twin, could feel the echo of it swarming through him as he slowly stood. Quinn edged away as he heard Luke coming, spun around, and gave him a wild-eyed stare.

"Leave it alone, damn it," he snarled. "Get the hell away from me."

Luke shook his head. "You know I can't. You want to get mad, go ahead. But I'm not leaving."

Quinn abruptly sagged to his knees. Luke settled down beside him, and as Quinn started to cry, Luke slid an arm around his twin's shoulders, felt the sting of tears burn his own eyes.

For the longest time, there was no sound but Quinn's low, harsh sobs. Then they faded away to erratic, unsteady breaths . . . and then silence.

"You find what you're looking for, Luke? Did you ever find it?"

"No. Not yet."

"Even though you ain't found it yet, you still glad you got out?"

Luke smiled a little. "I couldn't find it where I was, Quinn. And yeah, I'm still glad."

"Ever figure out what it is?"

Shrugging, Luke said, "A life, I guess. Some kind of normal life."

"No such thing. You and me know that."

"Maybe not, but what I have now is closer to normal than what I did have."

Quinn sighed, lifted his head. He stared around the empty apartment, and like Luke, his gaze seemed to linger on the bare walls. Slowly, as though it hurt every muscle in his body to do it, he stood up. "Not all of us deserve normal. Not all of us need it. Hell, some of us couldn't manage normal with a handbook full of instructions."

"You don't want a normal life, Quinn, there's nothing wrong with that," Luke said. He started to stand, grimaced as his left leg tried to stiffen up on him.

Quinn made an odd noise, half-caught between a laugh and a sob. "I don't know what I want, Luke. Even if it walked in front of me, I probably wouldn't figure it out until it was too late."

He slid Luke a sidelong look. "You're quicker about that sort of thing than I am. Always have been. When you find what you want, don't be too late in figuring it out."

THREE

July

*J*UNKIE *whore.*
     Useless little bitch. You're nothing. White trash.
     Staring at the house, she felt time spin away, and it was like she
was the kid hiding in that hellhole, unknowingly waiting for somebody to save her before it was too late. For just a few seconds, she
was helpless, scared, and hungry, dying inside, little by little.
     But then she shook it off and jerked herself out of the past.
     One more time, Devon Manning said silently. *You can go one
more.* It was a game she played with herself. How much misery
could she heap on herself before she decided she'd had enough?
     I can do this, she told herself. *I can do it just one more time.* It
was the same game she'd played yesterday, last week, last year. Tomorrow, she'd do it again. Just one more time. And again, the day
after that, and the day after that; for as long as she could, she'd keep
playing the little mental game and putting one foot after the other,
one heartbreak after the other.
     Because even though the heartbreaks were massive, often, and
gut-wrenching, there were bright moments. Reuniting a kid with his

mom after she finally managed to get straight. Placing a foster child with a family he'd love, who would love him, a real family. Seeing some of the teens she looked out for finally figure out there were better things in life than drugs or gangs and watching them find themselves.

The victories didn't always outweigh the losses, but they made the losses more bearable.

Devon had been told, and more than once, she didn't look old enough or strong enough to be in the profession she'd chosen. At twenty-six, she was certainly old enough, but she often wondered if they weren't right about the strength part.

So many nights, she went home feeling empty and useless, convinced nothing she'd done had made a difference, and nothing ever would.

Then she'd get a call that an adoption for one of her foster kids had finally gone through. Or she'd watch as one of the parents she dealt with worked her way through night school just to make something of herself so she could take better care of her kids.

Those were the reasons she kept on doing this, and one of those happy things would happen in the end for this one, too. She couldn't quit. Couldn't give up.

I can do this. Just one more time.

So once more, she stood in front of a squalid, run-down apartment and braced herself for what she might find inside. Physically, Devon didn't look like much. She was a slender woman, almost too slender, but no matter how much she tried to put on weight, she couldn't ever do it. Of course, half the time, the crap she saw in her job killed her appetite. She bordered on too skinny, but she didn't see it changing anytime soon. If she were a little taller, it wouldn't be so bad. Devon probably would enjoy that sexy, willowy look so many taller, equally slender women managed. But she was barely five feet four, and she looked more like a waif than anything else.

Her eyes were hazel, set in a pale face that would never tan, her hair a nondescript reddish brown. It was wildly curly, thick, and a pain in the tail to manage. There had been a time when she'd longed for that straight, sleek look that was oh so popular, but unless she wanted to spend an hour or so a day washing, drying, and then flat-ironing out the curls, it wasn't going to happen. So instead, she kept it pulled back from her face in either a tight knot or a braid. Anything else took too much time.

Same for makeup. Technically, her job was a nine-to-five, but it rarely worked out that way, and after nine, ten, and twelve hours on her feet, any makeup she might have put on would have been worn off, so she rarely bothered with makeup, either.

No, Devon knew she didn't look like much, but she hadn't let it stop her before, and she wasn't going to let it stop her now, either.

This place reminded her too much of that little hellhole where she had lived for two months, alone, back when she'd still been a teenager.

Devon figured she should count herself lucky. She'd been thirteen when her aunt threw her out, and she'd already been a junkie. Flopping in an abandoned house and avoiding the dealers and the johns, Devon had been wondering how she'd get money for her next fix and hoping people would just leave her alone.

But then the lady showed up at the door. Eden, Devon's own personal guardian angel.

In the back of her head, she could hear Eden's hoarse, raspy laugh. *"Baby, I ain't nobody's angel,"* Eden had said to Devon—and more than once.

She desperately wished Eden was around for some advice, a little comfort—even a swift kick in the ass would work. But Eden had retired four months ago, and she was living the high life out in Vegas with a rich widower a good twelve years younger.

Still, Eden didn't have to be there for Devon to know how she would respond. *Girl, get your ass in gear and get in there. There's a kid who needs you. You focus on her and not on the hell that's around you. Because, make no mistake, the hell she's in is worse. You know, because you've been where she is.*

Focus on the kid. It was what had gotten her through before, and she knew it would keep doing just that.

How much longer am I going to keep this up? Devon thought. *Just one more time,* she told herself, perpetuating the mental game. But the rational part of her head, the part that wasn't cringing in disgust, already knew the answer.

Devon would keep going until she just couldn't go anymore. Because that was all she could do. Eden had probably asked herself the same thing, over and over. If Eden had given up before she found Devon, Devon wouldn't be here.

There was no way she was going to miss out on a chance to help somebody the way Eden had helped her.

Devon stared up at the ramshackle, filthy house. It was a squat two-story that looked like it had been split into eight little apartments. The front lawn was littered with garbage, cigarette butts, and other stuff Devon didn't want to look at too closely.

"You okay?"

Devon looked over her shoulder at Officer Wayland Bennett and nodded. "Let's get this over with."

If she thought the outside of the house had prepared her for the inside . . . well, it wasn't the first time she'd been wrong. Wouldn't be the last. The inside of Shayla Reynolds's home smelled of rotting food, unwashed flesh, and filth Devon couldn't even begin to guess at.

Devon knew she had probably seen worse, but she couldn't remember when. What really sucked was that there was a little girl here, all alone, and God only knew how long she'd been here.

There weren't many places for a child to hide. Less than seven hundred square feet, it boasted a whopping two rooms. The main room served as bedroom, kitchen, and living room. The sofa bed, tucked into a recessed alcove along the back wall, was open, the mattress bare and covered with stains better left unidentified. On the mattress was an open pizza box, and Devon figured it was a good week old. It looked like mold was forming in the crust.

There were only two doors in the entire place. The entryway where Devon and Officer Bennett stood, and then the other one, on the back wall. Devon assumed it was the bathroom. So far, it didn't look like the little girl was anywhere in the main room, so hopefully she'd find her in the bathroom.

Bingo. When Devon pushed the door open, she saw the shower curtain shift. It rustled a little, and when she called out, a pair of big blue eyes peeped around the edge to look at her.

* * *

"Man, can you believe we actually signed up for this?"

Luke smiled a little as he heard two of the newest interns moaning over their coffee. He'd asked himself that question more than once during his residency, and yeah, even now after he'd been on staff at Rudding Memorial for the past year.

It had been worse during residency, though. It could make or break a doctor. Working twenty-four hours, forty-eight hours straight, longer, sometimes. Catching a fifteen-minute nap and living on chips and pretzels and whatever else could be found in the vending machine. No, his residency definitely had not been the highlight of his life, but it had been worth it.

Luke hadn't gone into medicine for the money. Of course, the money was nice. But he'd done it for the challenge. Every day brought a different one, although sometimes the only challenge was to keep from laughing at some of the stupid shit he saw.

Like the nineteen-year-old mother who had brought her two-year-old child in, complaining that the medicine they'd given her daughter to help control the vomiting had actually made it worse. Turned out the mom had been making the poor kid eat the suppositories, and when they explained, again, how to administer the medicine, the mom had freaked out.

Dealing with mothers who thought a temperature of 99.6 meant the kid had Asian bird flu or that a headache was a sure, definite sign of meningitis. Or worse, dealing with the kids who were taken away from their parents or found wandering in the streets, malnourished, abused, and all but broken inside.

Broken bones when some genius figured a chair was a good enough replacement for a ladder or lacerations when the kitchen knife slipped—they often made up a lot of the patients they took care of at Rudding Memorial. They weren't the most fun, but they were part and parcel.

Not every patient coming through those doors was bleeding from twenty different lacerations and drowning in his own blood. Which was a good thing. Working in the ER was a rush; it was no surprise Luke had gravitated to the medical field once he'd finished his rehab six years ago.

He'd started on the courses he'd need to go from field medic to physician while he was still recovering in the hospital. He'd finished medical school in record time, and his residency had landed him here.

He hadn't planned on staying. Rudding Memorial wasn't a bad place to work, but he hadn't planned on staying in Kentucky. He'd planned on going back home; he missed his dad, he missed the ranch, and he missed Wyoming. But there was something about this place. He just couldn't leave.

The place got into his system. Working the ER got into his system. He wouldn't have found anything quite like this anywhere near his father's ranch in Wyoming. Yeah, there were ERs in Wyoming, but the nearest big city was sixty-three miles away from the ranch. There was no logical reason he couldn't find a hospital in Cheyenne.

But he didn't want to.

He liked Kentucky. The rolling green hills and white painted fences, the huge horse farms and the little towns. The place just felt like home.

Rudding Memorial was just off the I-75 in Lexington. Not too far from the University of Kentucky. They saw their share of drunk drivers, college pranks gone bad, and just the normal senseless things humans did to themselves and one another.

Unfortunately, they also saw their share of the cruel things humans could do to one another. His shift last night had started with the exam of a rape victim, followed by an attempt to save the life of a pregnant mother who'd been hit by a drunk driver while she was crossing the street. The mother had gone into premature labor and had died on the table shortly after delivering her baby boy, nearly two months early.

The baby was probably going to be okay, but he'd grow up never knowing his mother. As Luke had tucked him into the incubator, he'd bent over the little guy and whispered, "You'll do okay, man. I came early, and all I had was my dad, and I made it just fine."

Still, it had been depressing as hell to escort the grieving father to the baby's side. Luke hadn't been able to resist sizing the guy up, and he'd liked what he'd seen: a guy fighting to hold it together when all he wanted to do was break—and then the awe in his eyes as he'd stared at his son. Yeah, that little guy would be okay.

Sometimes, life really did suck, and yeah, sometimes, he still had a hard time believing he'd willingly signed up for this. But he had no plans of giving it up for something a little less stressful, a little less heartbreaking.

Glancing up from the workstation, Luke caught a glimpse of dark red hair just before a woman disappeared around the corner.

Wouldn't you know . . . Luke's very own heartbreaker was here again.

"*You find what you're looking for, Luke?*" For some weird reason, Quinn's question from months earlier popped into his head.

Yeah, he had a feeling he might have finally found it, but he hadn't managed to go after it yet. His heart skipped a beat or two as he recognized Devon Manning, and automatically, he ran a hand through his hair.

Catching himself, he grimaced in disgust. He was coming off the end of a long-ass rotation, and he'd slept in the doctors' lounge last night. Looked it, too. He kept meaning to find a clean pair of scrubs and get a shower, but every time it looked like he'd have more than ten minutes, some other emergency came up. Or he had a chance to grab a cup of coffee and a rather tasteless vending machine sandwich. The food would win over cleaning up; he could clean up later, but if he didn't eat, he'd be useless.

It had been nearly a good four hours since he'd had a chance to sit down for longer than five minutes. The hours he'd pulled were definitely going to show. Clothes wrinkled, in desperate need of a shave and a good five hours of sleep—at least—there was no way Luke could hope to look any more presentable than he already did.

That really sucked, because there was no way he wasn't going to hunt down Devon.

"Here, Luke. This one is yours. I can't do another abused kid tonight." His boss and sometimes friend, Dr. Dwight Howell, came up and deposited a chart on top of the pile in front of Luke. So much for tracking Devon down.

That pile was already reaching epic proportions, and he scowled as the stack started to list to the left. He caught them before the charts could topple over, and he straightened the stack automatically before looking at the name and skimming the nursing notes.

Dehydrated, abandoned; despite the disgust curdling in his gut, a faint smile curved his lips. Escorted in by social worker Devon Manning.

A few minutes later, though, he decided it was a pretty shitty trade. Unfortunately, seeing Devon with a case like this wasn't ever good. His young patient, Ellie Reynolds, was four years old, small for her age, and she had the oldest eyes he'd ever seen. She had the same bitter acceptance in her eyes that he had seen on battlefields.

Her mother had left her alone in the house while she was out "working." Prostituting—Shayla Reynolds had been arrested four times, and each time, her child went into foster care. Each time, she'd gotten Ellie back.

There wouldn't be a fifth time. Shayla's last john had beaten her to death, literally. If the cop responding hadn't recognized Shayla's battered body, Luke didn't want to think about how long Ellie might have stayed hidden in her apartment.

"Hey there, pretty girl," Luke murmured as he sat on the wheeled stool in front of his silent patient.

Luke wasn't naive. He knew what kind of bad shit happened in the world, and he wasn't afraid to face it. Coming into this field, he'd known it wasn't going to be a cakewalk. But he hadn't necessarily expected it to be harder than what he'd walked away from. The carnage, the cruelty, the thousands of battles happening in the world the average citizen knew nothing about, it was rough. He'd loved being a Ranger, but he'd seen stuff that could break a strong man.

This job was no different. In some ways, it was even harder, because in a war, he expected to see the ugly side of human nature. He'd gone into the army, and the Rangers, because he wanted to make a difference somewhere in the world.

In places like Iraq, Afghanistan, and Colombia, people knew bad shit was going to happen. Here, in his home country—he couldn't quite explain it. He knew it, yeah, but actually seeing it was different. What people did to their own flesh and blood. Even to total strangers. And the kids were the hardest.

Logically, considering the shit his mom had put Quinn through, Luke should have been a little more prepared. But then again, he doubted anything could have prepared him for the sad little girl in front of him.

"Can you open your mouth for me, Miz Ellie?" he asked gently. She did so obediently and without making a sound or moving an inch. He wished she'd cry. There was something so completely messed up with a four-year-old little girl sitting as still as death while a doctor probed and prodded at her.

And she continued to do it throughout the entire exam. When the nurse drew blood, she didn't even blink. When he laid her down and did the required physical exam, probing her belly, checking her genitalia for signs of molestation, she simply lay there like a little doll.

By the time Luke had finished his exam, he was wondering if she could talk.

Devon Manning stood at Ellie's side and smoothed a hand down the girl's tangled, filthy hair. "You're a brave girl, aren't you, Ellie?"

Finally, some kind of response. She flicked a glance up at Devon and then looked back down at the floor.

"I'll be back in as soon as I can," Luke said softly. Unable to resist, he reached up to touch the little girl's face, but she froze. She didn't move, flinch, or pull away; she reacted the same way a wild animal would, retreating inside herself, as though if she were still enough, quiet enough, he wouldn't see her. Sighing, Luke let his hand fall to the side, and he left the exam room.

"Poor baby," Sarah Hensley said. A registered nurse with a friendly, freckled face, Sarah was more likely to laugh than cry, more likely to defend than attack. But when Luke glanced down at her, she had a mama bear look on her face. There was an angry light in her eyes, and she met his gaze and said, "That girl's mama needs to burn in hell."

Flipping through the rest of the chart, Luke murmured his agreement. "According to the report, she's probably doing just that right now. Her john beat her to death a few days ago. Kid's been alone in their apartment for God only knows how long."

"That poor baby doesn't look like she's had a good meal in weeks. Longer."

Luke glanced at her. "Maybe you should see about getting her something to eat. Some chicken nuggets or something from the cafeteria."

Sarah smiled. "And maybe some ice cream. Ice cream always makes my kids feel better."

An hour later, Luke went through the lab work on Ellie. He'd wanted to get to it before this, but another trauma came in, and he'd been called in to assist with that.

His legs felt leaden as he walked to the room where Ellie and Devon waited. Seeing that small, sad face was hell. Before he opened the door, he took a deep breath and counted to ten. Didn't help. He still had an ugly little knot in his chest, and he didn't know whether he wanted to snarl and break something or just cuddle the little girl against his chest and promise nobody would ever hurt her again.

Ellie Reynolds and the other little kids like her were going to break his heart all right.

* * *

ELLIE was a heartbreaker; that was for sure. Devon Manning got her heart broken on a regular basis, but Ellie was going to be a memorable one. Right then, Ellie lay on the bed, curled into a tight ball, sleeping like she hadn't slept in a week.

Easing up from the hard stool by the bed, Devon watched Ellie's face for a minute to make sure she wouldn't wake, and then she started to pace the small confines of the exam room.

Small, scared, and scarred, Ellie was a sad little thing, but it wasn't too late for her. She was only four years old, and half of her life had been spent in the care of foster parents, foster parents who loved her. One set of foster parents, the Parkers, really stood out in Devon's mind, and if she had anything to do with it, Ellie was going to go back to those people.

Hell, Ellie shouldn't have ever been removed from them. Devon knew the courts had good intentions, but the road to hell and all that. Putting that child back with her strung-out mama who had no desire to stay sober, it all translated to one thing: a BFM.

Big fucking mistake.

Unfortunately, she saw a lot of them in her line of work. This one, though, it was going to end all right. She'd damn well see to it. Poor Ellie wouldn't realize it now, and she may never realize it, but her mother dying was the best thing ever to happen to her.

"Will she be okay?"

Devon turned and looked at the doctor. He stood at the doorway, staring at Ellie with grim eyes.

Now there was another heartbreaker. Sexy and absolutely mouth-watering. Dr. Lucas Rafferty hadn't shaved in a couple of days, and his clothes were so damned rumpled, she figured he'd been sleeping in them. Heavy-lidded gray eyes, creases carved into the hard lines of his face, and a long, rangy build, he looked more like a warrior than a doctor.

Devon had been drooling over him from afar for weeks, but this was one of the few times she'd actually had any direct contact with him without a third party.

Ellie's soft snores drifted through the room, reminding Devon there was a third party—she was just sound asleep.

Forcing her attention away from the sexy doctor and back to the little girl, Devon hoped he couldn't see the hot flush on her cheeks. "You're the doctor. Shouldn't I be asking you that?"

Dr. Rafferty cocked a brow at her. "Physically, yes, she'll be fine. I'm more worried about the rest of her. You've been doing this awhile."

A sad smile curved Devon's lips up. Yes, she had been doing this awhile. Devon didn't just work for Social Services; she'd been in the system. Briefly, thank God. Sometimes she liked to think her life really began when Eden found her.

All the time before that? She preferred to think of it as somebody else's life or a nightmare. Her parents had died in a car wreck when she was three, and Devon had ended up going to live with her mother's sister. Aunt Cyndi hadn't been too bad, at first. She'd sure loved spending the money that should have been used to care for Devon. Then the money ran out. There was a trust fund set aside for Devon, but Cyndi couldn't touch it. It was meant for Devon and Devon alone. Used to living the good life, Cyndi wasn't going to go back to scraping by.

Cyndi ended up finding herself a rich man to marry, and she wasn't overly picky. Boyd Chancellor came into Devon's life when she was nine. He started molesting her within four months of marrying her aunt. He raped her the night she turned eleven, and it had continued until she was thirteen.

"A birthday present—you're a big girl now . . ." Shame, shock, and horror had kept Devon silent. Drugs were the easy outlet. Until she started getting in trouble, skipping school, and then she got caught stealing. She ended up in juvenile court, and that led to community service and therapy.

A sharp-eyed therapist pieced together what had been happening to Devon, and Boyd landed in jail. Devon had landed out on her ass. Cyndi accused her of seducing her husband, and she beat the shit out of Devon before dragging her ward out of the house and leaving her on the wraparound front porch in front of the house that had been built with money from Devon's rapist.

"Don't you ever come back here."

Yeah, that was the life she preferred not to think about. Life really started with Eden, then with the Mannings. Eden, with her wiry gray hair, overbright lipstick, and oversized plastic-framed eyeglasses probably didn't fit anybody's idea of salvation. Completely, without a doubt, Eden had saved her. For that, Devon thanked God every single day. Now she did her best to save other kids, like Eden had saved her.

Moving to stand by Ellie's side, she stroked the little girl's dirty gold curls. They were matted, tangled, and filthy. The girl looked like she hadn't had a bath in months, and that was entirely possible. She needed to get the girl cleaned up before they did much else.

Without warning, Ellie awoke, lying on the narrow bed and staring up at Devon. The look in her eyes wrapped a fist around Devon's heart. She swallowed the knot in her throat and forced herself to smile.

"Hi there, pretty girl. Nice nap?" she asked gently as Ellie sat up. Forcing herself to smile, she glanced over at Luke and said, "Ellie is going to be fine; aren't you, sweetie?"

Ellie didn't so much as blink.

Devon didn't let that slow her down. Ellie was young. She was sweet, she was scared, and she needed love. That was all. Devon was going to make sure she got it. Looking back at Dr. Rafferty, she said, "She's going to be fine."

He stared into her eyes for a long moment, and then he nodded. "I'm going to hold you to that. One of the nurses is going to come in, clean her up some."

He turned, and as he walked away, Devon didn't once stare at his butt. She might have glanced once or twice, but hey, that wasn't staring, right?

Looking back down at Ellie, she pushed the girl's tangled, filthy hair back from her face. "What do you say, pretty lady? You feel like getting cleaned up a little? Then I'll take you to see somebody special. Somebody who misses you."

The little girl looked down. She didn't say a word, but she reached out a small hand and laid it on Devon's forearm. Lightly. One second passed, then another. When Ellie started to stroke Devon's arm the way she'd stroke a kitten's fur, tears formed in Devon's eyes. She blinked them away and murmured, "That's a girl."

* * *

STANDING in the driveway, Devon stared at her car and swore. She had a staff meeting in forty minutes, and she was already running behind. Getting downtown in anything under thirty minutes would be a miracle, and she hadn't even eaten breakfast.

The coffee she'd guzzled when she realized she'd overslept had her wired, and now, the bagel she'd been wanting from Panera Bread wasn't going to happen. She needed something in her belly besides the caffeine, but more than that, she needed a ride to work.

And somebody to change her damn tire or fix the flat or whatever in the hell somebody did when the tires didn't have air. How fricking strange was that? The two tires on the driver's side were completely flat, and she knew they hadn't been when she went inside last night.

Hitching up her pants a little, she crouched down beside the front tire and eyed it, although she had no idea was she was looking for. Even if she saw a nail or something, she wouldn't know how to fix it. Anything mechanical, automotive, or electrical was out of her range of expertise. Well, unless it involved changing a lightbulb, flipping a blown fuse, or putting gas in the car. That, she could manage. But she hadn't even managed to hang up a picture straight when she moved into her own place three years earlier.

Her adoptive father, Reece Manning, had done all of that for her, trying not to laugh as he studied her dismal attempts to hang a few pictures up on the wall. Those dismal attempts had ended up requiring some drywall work and a gallon of paint. She stared at the tire for another minute and then pulled out her cell phone.

A familiar voice answered, "Hey, sweetheart. If you're calling to cancel dinner this Sunday, you'd better think again. Your mother will skin me."

"Hi, Daddy," she said, smiling despite herself. "I have a flat tire. Actually . . . two."

She heard the concern in his voice. "You're not stranded anywhere, are you?"

"No. Hadn't even left for work—and now I'm going to be late."

"I could be there—"

She interrupted quickly. "I'll find a ride, but I wanted to know if you could come out and take a look. I'd hate to have to pay a tow truck." And that immediately led to a lecture on why she should have AAA. She listened, nice, polite, and obedient—for the first thirty seconds. And then she interrupted, "Dad, I'm sorry, but I'm running late for a meeting, and if I don't want to get fired, I need to get a ride."

Getting that ride took a couple of phone calls and a bribe of cookies. Her coworker Noelle McIntosh wheedled some cookies out of Devon in exchange for a ride, and by the time they got to work, the meeting was already under way.

Following the oh-so-fun staff meeting was a meeting with a

child just recently assigned to her. He was there with his dad, and within three minutes flat, Devon knew these two males were going to be a pain in the ass. Tim Wilder didn't want to be there, his dad didn't want to be there, but more than some, those two needed to be there. Anger management was just the tip of the iceberg for Tim.

Amazingly, though, as rough as the day started out, it actually got better. She spent half the morning in court, grinning with pride as one of her clients stood before the judge. After two years on probation, two years of hard work, and a lot of arguments on both sides, Sloan Chapman was being released from probation. In another three weeks, Sloan turned eighteen, and he was joining the navy. His juvie record would be sealed, and he'd have a fresh start.

And Devon had one more of the little successes that kept her going.

By the time Noelle dropped her off at home, Devon had almost forgotten about the car and her promise to call AAA. The note on her kitchen counter had her grinning.

Happy early birthday, Devon.

That made her smile. Her birthday wasn't for another seven months.

Since I figured you'd forget, again, I went ahead and got you signed up with AAA. Aired up your tires. They were just flat. Must have been a slow leak, although it's kind of weird having two at once.

Don't forget dinner Sunday. And you owe me some cookies.

It was lying next to the list she'd made up while waiting for Noelle. He must have seen the ingredients for the cookies on the notepad.

After a few days passed, she'd forgotten about the tires.

FOUR

"I kept my word."

He was mouthwatering. Six feet, lean, and sexy, sleekly muscled, like a panther. Heavy-lidded gray eyes and closely cropped wheat blond hair. He kept it almost brutally short. But she thought it might curl if he let it grow long enough.

When Luke lifted his head to look at her, there was a faint smile on his mouth. His very, very sexy mouth. Devon could picture herself kissing it. She could picture herself moving to him and pressing against him, rising up on her toes and covering that mouth with hers and kissing that sardonic smile away.

He quirked a brow at her, and instead of reaching for him like she wanted to, Devon reached into her purse and pulled out her wallet. She pulled out the snapshot of Ellie and held it out to him. "I've been carrying that around for a few weeks."

His eyes dropped down, and Devon watched as his smile softened. "The little heartbreaker," he murmured. He stroked the edge of the picture with his finger. "She looks wonderful."

"She is wonderful." Under the guise of studying the picture,

Devon stepped close enough to him that she could feel the heat of his body and smell his scent. Woodsy. Dark. Sexy. She looked down at the picture and tried to focus on it. Ellie did look wonderful. "The last time she was in the system, she stayed with this family. They loved her. She loved them."

"I can see that." The picture showed Ellie hugging Rob Parker with both arms, her eyes sparkling. She was laughing. "She going to be able to stay with them for a while?"

Devon tipped her head back and smiled at him. "A good long while. They're adopting her. There's no father listed on her birth certificate, and nobody has been able to find any suitable next of kin. The only family member is an uncle who has a history of sexual abuse. No question of whether or not he can take her."

He started to give the picture back to her, and Devon shook her head. "It's for you. We all need reminders of the happy endings with these kinds of things."

His gaze met hers, and Devon felt her heart start doing a weird little rumba inside her chest. The heat inside her belly didn't completely take her by surprise.

She hadn't closed herself off from men. She'd dated; she had even thought she was in love once with a guy she'd dated off and on throughout college. Of course, the two times she'd attempted to develop any sort of sexual relationship with him, it had been a disaster. She'd been attracted to the guy—seriously attracted—but she couldn't move past her issues.

After the second failed attempt, Devon had broken up with him, and last she heard, he was engaged.

She wasn't a stranger to heat; that didn't completely shock her. What surprised her was the intensity of it. Devon knew nothing could have prepared her for this. It was like wildfire. It rippled through her, and she knew he felt it, too. She saw it in his eyes, in the odd tension that suddenly took over his body. Their gazes held for a long moment that seemed to stretch out into forever, and then his gaze dropped to her mouth. Devon started to sway closer. The cell phone at her waist started ringing, and the moment shattered. Devon blinked, felt blood rush to her cheeks, and she stepped back. *Whoa . . .*

He said her name, but Devon forced herself to smile. With that bright, false smile on her face, she looked down at her watch and said, "Wow. Look at the time . . ." She spun on her heel and headed down the hall, as fast as she possibly could.

Whoa . . . She fumbled for her cell phone, but by the time her clumsy fingers managed to flip it over, the call had already gone into voice mail. Just as well, because the only coherent thought in her brain was . . . *Whoa . . .*

* * *

DAMN.

Luke leaned against the wall and watched as Devon Manning disappeared. She moved fast for such a skinny thing. She smelled good, too. Soft, sweet, clean. Almost too soft for the life he knew she lived.

He hadn't seen her since the day she'd brought Ellie in, and Luke figured that was almost two months ago. That job of hers had to be hell. He didn't know how she did it. Yeah, he saw some shit cases around here, but they weren't everything. Since she was a social worker, he had to wonder how many happy endings she saw.

Certainly weren't a lot of happy moments when she showed up in the ER. As much as he liked seeing her, Luke had learned fairly early on seeing a social worker usually meant the ER would be treating some abused child, a battered woman, a strung-out teen. Either that, or the ER had been forced to call Social Services, and those times weren't exactly fun, either.

And none of it was very conducive to romance.

Pretty much from the first time he'd seen her five or six months ago, he'd wanted to ask her out. There just didn't ever seem to be a good time for it. Before Ellie, the last time she'd come in, it had been because one of her cases, a mom addicted to meth, had beat the crap out of her daughter. Hadn't been a good time then, either.

Studying the picture, he realized the perfect opportunity had been in front of him, but he'd been too slow to react, and once more, she slid away. He could still see her, walking down the hallway, her head bent, fiddling with that damn phone.

Shoving away from the wall, Luke headed toward her.

There wasn't going to be a better time. He could at least try to get her phone number. But he never made it. His own phone started to ring, and he grabbed it, swearing as he read the display.

So much for getting her number. He slid the picture of Ellie into his pocket and tossed back the rest of his coffee. Back into the trenches.

*   *   *

BY the time his shift ended, Luke had been cried on, yelled at, bled on, kicked at, and stepped on. At least the only body fluids were blood and tears. Some shifts, he spent an hour in the shower and still didn't feel clean. Today wasn't so bad. He'd been prepared for the worst when he had first seen Devon Manning. But whatever case she'd been in for couldn't have been a bad one, or all the nurses would have been buzzing over it. He hadn't heard anything through the grapevine.

It had been a long week, and he had three precious days in a row off. Three whole days. He didn't have to be back at work until seven Sunday night, and he was going to enjoy it. Luke was dead tired, but considering this was the first night he'd had off in nearly a week, thanks to staffing shortages, going home was not what he had on his list of things to do. At least not yet. He wanted a real meal he didn't have to cook, and he wouldn't mind a few drinks. Company wouldn't be a bad thing, either, but when he tried to think of some-body to call, the only face that came to mind belonged to Devon Manning.

But he hadn't been able to get her number before he got called back to the ER, and by the time he had a few spare minutes, she was long gone.

Luke didn't even know if she lived in the city or not. More and more people were commuting back and forth to Lexington for work. Some even made the hour and change drive between Lexington and Louisville, although he doubted a social worker would work that far out. Most of them had to take turns working on call, and somebody living an hour away wasn't going to be able to get on scene quick enough.

Luke could get the number. Had been tempted a time or two. If he wanted to breach some codes of ethics, he could get it from the hospital, but he wasn't too sure that would be the best way to go about asking her out.

Hell, he could find the number on his own, if he wanted. Wouldn't really take much, even if she was unlisted. He hadn't been the computer genius of his unit, but he knew his way around the Web. An unlisted phone number might be a little harder for the average civilian to get, but Luke wasn't an average civilian.

Somehow he suspected the lady wouldn't like him getting her home number using anything other than the normal methods—like asking her.

"Then why in the hell didn't you just ask her?" he muttered as he headed for the parking garage. Should haves, would haves, and what ifs—they all added up to jack.

Next time, he told himself. He'd get it next time. He'd seen that responding heat in her eyes. She'd backed off quick, real quick, but he knew what he'd seen. If her damn phone hadn't gone off, if he had taken a minute to concentrate on something beyond the fact that she'd been standing close enough for him to smell the soft, faint scent of lotion that clung to her skin, he could have had been having dinner with the pretty social worker, seeing if he couldn't coax a smile or two out of her.

Or maybe he was going to have that chance after all, Luke

realized an hour later. He stood at the bar of a popular steakhouse and watched as Devon made her way through the crowd. She kept a careful distance between herself and all the people around her. Pretty amazing. She managed to work her way through the tightly packed bodies without bumping into a soul.

Something about that extreme caution touched off a warning signal in Luke's head, but he brushed it off. He'd get her number, and he was going to sit down with her and talk about something other than cigarette burns, malnourished toddlers, and spiral fractures.

Forcing his way through the crunch of bodies surrounding the bar, Luke intercepted her right before she slid onto a barstool. "Miz Devon."

She jerked away, blinked owlishly like she didn't recognize him, then a smile curved her lips. "Dr. Rafferty."

Luke glanced down at the plain white button-down he wore. "I'm not wearing scrubs, a lab coat, or a stethoscope. It's Luke." He glanced around and saw that nobody seemed to be waiting for her. "You here alone?"

"Yeah. Came to do some shopping, and I got hungry. I was just going to have a burger or something at the bar."

He nodded toward a couple vacating a bar table. "Me, too. Wanna join me?"

Devon glanced at the table and then back up at him. That caution he'd glimpsed earlier made a brief appearance, and he knew she was going to say no. Already disappointed, Luke started groping for something to say to change her mind. The little girl, Ellie. Yeah, they could talk about Ellie, right? Or her job, maybe. Something.

But before he had even formulated one coaxing, convincing argument, she gave him a smile. "Sure."

Relief had him grinning like a fool, and he reached up, closing his fingers around her elbow. She went stiff for a second, but he didn't even notice. He was too busy reveling in the warm, soft feel of her skin. Soft as satin. Warm. Over the smoke in the air, he could smell her. That scent, sweet and female, went straight to his head and made him think about things he really didn't need to be thinking about, not unless he wanted to scare her away before they even managed to order an appetizer.

She always smelled so good, something warm, summery—sort of like honeysuckle. What was it? Some kind of lotion? Lotion—yeah, something she'd slick on when she climbed out of the shower . . . slick it on wet, bare skin . . . shit.

You're into self-torment, he thought, grateful for the noise and the crowd pressing in around them. It gave him at least a minute to get a grip and focus as they made their way to the now-vacant table.

A couple of college boys came rushing up to grab the table as Devon started to sit down, and Luke shifted his body, putting it between them and the table. "Hey," one of the kids said, shoving at Luke's shoulder.

Luke gave him a look over his shoulder. "Table's taken, kid."

The hand on his shoulder tightened. Luke dropped a look to the hand, and then back up. Twenty-two, tops, Luke figured. Had the clean-cut, all-American college kid look going, and he was about as dumb as a box of rocks.

He saw Devon's face from the corner of his eye and swore silently, about ready to just let the moron and his friends have the table. But one of the guy's buddies had a little more sense and grabbed his friend, pushing him toward a couple of open seats at the bar.

Sliding into the booth across from her, they were both quiet as a busboy appeared out of the crowd and cleaned up the table. "I've seen fights break out over less than a table in this place," Devon said. "This close to the campus, half the people in here are probably college kids."

"I wouldn't have gotten into a fight over a table," he said.

Devon smirked. "No. But you would have gotten into a fight when you punched him because you didn't like him shoving you." Then she grinned, her nose wrinkling a little. "Fortunately, the kid with him looked like he had half a brain."

She gave him an easy smile and leaned forward so she didn't have to shout. Luke did the same, and it brought him close enough that he could see the highlights in her hair; Devon had the prettiest hair he'd ever seen. A russet sort of red, but there were also strands of gold, strands of brown. If she had somebody doing that to her hair, they were worth every penny. He wished she wouldn't wear it up all the time. Instead of the complicated twist she normally wore, she had it piled up on her head with a clip, curly little corkscrews springing out all over the place. Luke wanted to lean forward, take the clip out, and watch it fall around her shoulders. Then he could bury his face in it, see if it was as soft as it looked.

Instead, he just forced himself to smile.

She glanced around. "I keep forgetting how busy this place is. You'd think on Thursday night, it wouldn't be so bad."

Luke shrugged and glanced at the TV. "Football. And being so close to the campus."

Devon grimaced. "Man, don't say the *F* word. Fall's coming, and that means half this town will have lost its mind within the next few weeks."

"Not into sports, huh?"

She grinned. "Not the kind you have to watch on TV. I don't mind going and watching a live game, but on TV? Just doesn't appeal to me as much."

"So if you're not into sports, what are you into?"

They were interrupted before she could answer as a waitress appeared at the table. She had matte black hair, a nose ring, and what looked like a dog collar around her neck. The pseudo-goth might have worked okay, except her voice was too cheerful and her face too animated as she recited the drink specials.

"I'll just have a Diet Coke," Devon said.

Luke asked for a Bud Light and then looked back at Devon as the waitress disappeared. He smiled. "My first night off in almost a week. You don't mind, do you?"

She shook her head. "Why should I?"

He shrugged. Normally, he wouldn't have bothered asking, but he had been watching Devon for a while, and now that he actually had her outside the hospital, he didn't want to blow it. If that meant bypassing a beer or two, he could handle that. "So if you're not here to watch football, why are you here?"

Devon scanned the crowd and then shot him a grin. "You, being a guy and all, might not have noticed that outside this steakhouse with the loud TVs, wonderful wings, and cold beer, there's this nifty thing called a mall. There are lots of stores: bookstores, music stores, shoe stores, stores where you can buy all sorts of girly stuff like lotion and clothes."

Luke grinned at her. "So you're shopping?"

"The coming of fall also means end-of-the-season clearance." She rolled her eyes. "I just spent half of next week's paycheck, and I haven't even gotten it yet. I'm kind of bad about that." She shot him a small grin and shrugged. "I have an addictive personality."

Crooking a brow at her, Luke repeated, "An addictive personality. Addicted to what?"

Devon smiled. "Oh, all sorts of things. Books. Girly stuff like lotion. Shoes—oh, man, shoes. I love shoes."

He craned his head around a little and glanced under the table. She had on a pair of glittery, strappy heels. Pretty feet, too. Her toenails were red. He hadn't ever thought that he was the foot fetish type, but Luke had an overpowering desire to see her wearing those shoes—just the shoes. That simple thought was enough to heat his blood to boiling point, and Luke's jeans were suddenly a little too tight. Straightening up, he forced a smile. "I like those."

When she stuck her foot out from under the table to look at one of her feet, Luke almost groaned. The sparkly straps caught the faint light as she rotated her foot one way and then the other. The bones of her ankle and foot looked incredibly delicate. Luke had the urge to climb out of the booth and catch her pretty foot in his hand.

Nibble on her instep. Kiss his way up over her ankle, over her calf, her thigh . . . she had on a long denim skirt that stopped just above her ankles, and he could see himself pushing it up as he went.

Damn it, Luke, you keep this up, and you're going to end up trying to have her on the damn table. No. Not the table. Damn table would be too damned cramped to lay her down on. Maybe one of the barstools, yeah . . . That would work. Sitting on one of them, pulling her onto his lap, and pushing that skirt up, pushing her underwear out of the way . . .

He groaned and sat back. Under the confines of his jeans, his erection was forced into a damn uncomfortable position. Slumping in his chair, he met Devon's gaze as she looked up from her shoes. "Spoils of war," she said, winking at him. "Found them on the clearance table a few stores down from here, and I had to try them on. Once I did, I couldn't take them off."

"So how long have you been an addict?"

Totally innocent question. But she didn't react in an innocent way, and Luke felt his stomach sink as her lids flickered, and she glanced away evasively. Luke was no psych major, and he'd only taken the courses required to get his medical degree, but he had a bad feeling he recognized the look on her face.

Guilt. Shame.

Over a shoe addiction?

Not.

Well, hell.

* * *

FORTY-FIVE minutes later, Devon gave Luke a strained smile as he walked her out to the car. Dinner had taken forever to get served, and she'd eaten a burger that tasted like sawdust. Something she'd said had made him pull back.

She wasn't under any illusions about what it had been, either.

The addict comment. She'd looked guilty. Hell, she was guilty, but not over a serious love of shoes. Those few years during her teens had left a mark on her, and although she dealt with her problem better than most people could expect, she knew the flaw was still there. She still had to fight the urges, and she still had to live with the guilt.

She hadn't been quick enough to come back with the appropriate teasing response to his teasing question, and he'd seen her guilt.

Luke was a smart guy—seemed like the expected thing, him being a doctor, but it wasn't just the book smarts. She'd met plenty of doctors who were dumber than a doornail when it came to people. Not Luke. He saw beneath the surface, and he read people as easily as some of those doctors could read a chart.

He'd seen below her surface, had read her, and now he'd gone and formed an opinion on something he didn't know jack about. The friendly flirtation hadn't stopped, but she'd recognized the difference. She'd tried to ignore it, but the more she thought about it, the more it pissed her off.

Abruptly, she stopped and turned to look at him.

"You don't need to walk me to my car," she said in a flat voice, not bothering to keep up the friendly, casual attitude he'd used throughout their meal.

His gray eyes slid sideways, met hers. "It's not a problem."

Folding her arms over her chest, she said, "It is for me."

Luke turned to face her. "Okay. What exactly is the problem?"

"Oh, please." She rolled her eyes and just barely managed to keep from sneering at him. "You don't know me, you know."

He cocked a brow and gave her a puzzled look. "Considering this is the first time we've spent more than twenty minutes together, I'd think that's kind of to be expected."

Her smile felt damned bitter, so she couldn't imagine how it looked. "Yes. So it's kind of weird you think you can go and make assumptions about me based on a couple of casual comments."

Tilting his head to the side, he shrugged. "Not sure where you're going with this, Devon."

This time she didn't bother wiping the sneer off her face.

Grabbing the sleeve of her jacket, she rolled up the cuff, baring the faint scars on the inside of her arm. The faint scars were more than a decade old, and they'd faded considerably, but at this point, she knew they wouldn't ever fade away completely. The needle tracks had been infected, and that infection, combined with her serious malnutrition and the drug addiction, had landed her in the hospital for a week after Eden had found her.

In truth, she was glad she still had them. They served as a reminder for her, a reminder of where she'd come from—that she'd lived on her own for six long months and done whatever she could to survive and feed her habit. They reminded her she wasn't alone anymore, that she'd overcome that addiction.

More, they served as a reminder that she wouldn't ever let herself go back to that hell again.

"I haven't touched any kind of drug in thirteen years. I don't even take Tylenol. When I was in a car wreck a few years ago, I wouldn't let them give me anything for the pain, and I just suffered through it." Turning her arm up, she exposed the scars marking the inside of her right arm. "I got hooked on drugs when I was eleven. When I was thirteen, a social worker picked me up. I ended up in the system, and a couple of people who gave a damn helped me get straight. I've been clean for close to thirteen damn years, and I don't need your judgmental attitude over it." With harsh, jerky motions, she shoved her sleeve back down and turned on her heel. She could hear him behind her, and the tension in the air was palpable.

"Devon . . ."

Digging her keys out of her purse, she sent him a scathing glance. The streetlight overhead fell across his face, highlighting the angles and hollows, revealing his turbulent eyes. She recognized guilt pretty well herself. "Save it, slick. You want to spend your time with some lily-white, perfect example of humanity, more power to you."

She thumbed a button on her key fob. The lock made a quiet snick as it unlocked, and she reached for the door, but a hand came over her shoulder, keeping the door closed. Panic flared its ugly head, and she turned around, edging away from him so he didn't have her pinned between the car and his body. "Can you hold on a minute?" he asked quietly.

Cocking a brow at him, Devon said, "I don't really see any point in that. I've got some unpleasant history in my life; I'm aware of that. Some bad shit happened, and I didn't know how to handle it. Ended up making some majorly bad choices and some majorly bad mistakes. I know that, and I can deal. I'm also aware there are people who will jump to conclusions about me. I can deal with that, too." A little sad, a little wistful, she murmured, "But I didn't really expect it from you. My mistake."

"No. It's mine." He blew out a breath and scrubbed his hands over his face. "Look, can we just wind the clock back a little? Let me try this again? Honestly, I'm usually not the judgmental type. It just . . . hell, Devon, this threw me for a loop. You just seem so . . . I dunno, steady."

"I am steady. But when I was a kid, not so much. Crap, Luke, how many kids do you know who are rock-steady? I was just a little more screwed up than the average teenager." *Okay, a lot more screwed up. But that's beside the point,* she thought sullenly.

"I'm sorry." He said it softly, with enough sincerity to punch through her anger. He reached up. Instinctively, she tensed, and then she cursed silently as something else appeared in his gaze: speculation.

Devon felt herself shying away from him. Her emotional scars weren't buried all that deep, and she didn't want him seeing those particular wounds.

Most guys weren't going to notice it when a woman tensed up just a little. But most guys wouldn't have picked up on the tiny little slip earlier and put two and two together. Actually, it was more like he had put together two plus some unknown integer and come up with the right answer with no other help from her. Because she sure as hell hadn't given him much more than that.

Interpersonal algebra, wonderful. As hot as this guy was, and as much as she found herself thinking about him, it suddenly dawned on her that he was a complication she didn't want or need. Devon decided it had been easier, even if it had hurt, when he had jumped to the mostly wrong conclusion about her.

This was worse, seeing that measuring look in his eyes and knowing he had probably guessed a little more about her than she really wanted him knowing. Considering how damn insightful he'd just proven himself to be, Devon made up her mind right then and there: Dr. Luke Rafferty was just too damn complicated.

Keeping her voice brusque, she said, "Fine. Now can you please move? I'm tired." And she was, dog tired and ready to go home and collapse. Except she had work waiting for her, reports she hadn't finished and cases she needed to review. But Devon suspected she wasn't going to be able to focus on any of it. Not now. She was going to be too busy sulking over the sexy doctor, his too-quick mind, and his damned assumptions.

"Devon, look at me."

She didn't want to. But there was something so gentle, so compelling about his voice. Reluctantly, she turned her head and met his eyes. The harsh white light of the streetlamp made his eyes almost colorless, but there was no denying the intensity of his gaze. "Don't write me off," he murmured.

Too late, she thought sourly. *Too fricking insightful*, she thought again. Just more proof of why she didn't need that man in her life.

Those eyes of hers showed too much and not enough, all at the same time, Luke decided. He could tell, just by looking at her, that all she wanted to do was kiss his sorry ass good-bye. But there were also unspoken secrets, a guardedness that made him want to smash down the walls she'd erected.

"Don't write me off," he murmured again, and he had to close his hands into fists to keep from reaching for her. Luke couldn't remember ever wanting to touch a woman as much as he wanted to touch Devon in that moment, but she held herself so stiffly, so rigidly. She was still pissed, and he couldn't blame her. Plus, he couldn't forget those brief moments when he'd glimpsed some deep fear inside her eyes.

"I screwed up. I'm sorry. It's just . . . hell, Devon." Luke wanted to kick himself. Badly. There had to be something he could say that would undo this mess—there just had to be. He hadn't mistaken the heat that had flared between them earlier, and in those few brief moments before he'd made an ass of himself, he'd felt something deeper than heat.

Luke didn't put much stock in it when people claimed some instant connection, something beyond physical attraction, but he'd felt something earlier, and he'd thought she had, too.

Then he went and made what he'd thought was a logical assumption. Although he hadn't said anything, he'd mentally started distancing himself. Luke thought he'd been pretty subtle about it, but obviously not, because Devon had been damned aware of what he was doing—and why.

The marks on her arm were old, years old. Other than those few faint scars that probably happened when the needle tracks got infected, the skin of her forearms was smooth and unmarked. When she'd said she was clean, he'd never once doubted her. That righteous indignation could be faked, he guessed, but she wasn't faking it.

Which meant he'd been backing away from a woman he was nuts about all because of some mistakes she'd made when she was a kid. But he'd be damned if he'd let that be the end. Not when they hadn't really even had a beginning.

"Devon . . ."

She averted her eyes. "Luke, don't. Just . . . don't, okay? Just let it go."

Cautious, keeping his movements slow, he moved a little closer. "I dunno. I'm going to have a hard time doing that, you see, because I think about you pretty much all the time. I go to work hoping I'll see you, and then I feel bad because, usually, I only see you when something bad has happened to one of your kids. I've been wanting to ask you out pretty much since I first met you, and now I finally got you outside of work, I go and screw it up."

The smile on her mouth looked forced, even to him. "I'd just take it as a sign, then. You and me wouldn't last through one date."

"Yes. We would."

He couldn't not touch her at that point. Closing the distance between them, he murmured, "I'm going to kiss you. And I haven't been this nervous about kissing a girl since I played seven minutes in heaven when I was in sixth grade."

Her hand came up, pressed against his chest. "Not a good idea."

"Not doing it would be an even worse idea," he argued. Reaching up, he covered her hand with his, stroked his thumb up and down the inside of her wrist. "Come on, Devon . . . Can you tell me you haven't ever thought about this, not even once?"

Averting her head, she said, "That's not the point."

Luke was quiet for a second and then he murmured, "So one dumb-ass mistake on my part, and you're going to totally write this off?"

"There's nothing to write off, Luke. We haven't even had a single date."

A grin crooked his lips upward, and he said, "My point, exactly." *Screw being nervous,* he decided. Dipping his head, he covered her lips, and it took less than a second to realize Devon Manning was every bit as sweet as he'd suspected.

Under his mouth, her lips were soft and full, and her taste was sweet, damn near addictive. On some level, Luke did understand addiction.

He was an adrenaline junkie, and that was every bit as addictive as a drug. But Devon? Man, the taste of her could easily beat that. Screw skydiving. Just kissing Devon Manning got his blood pumping like nothing he'd ever felt before. Cupping her chin in his hand, he angled her head to the side and deepened the kiss.

He waited for her to pull away. The hesitation, the caution he'd expected was there, but she didn't pull away. Luke ached to pull her closer against him, to deepen the contact. Through their clothes, he could feel the heat of her body, and he already knew how silken, soft her skin was. He needed to feel more.

Ached to feel more.

Her body all but vibrated against his, with heat, with hunger—and with hesitation. Luke would be damned if he caused her a second's fear, so instead of pushing for more, instead of sliding his hands under her shirt, instead of letting them roam over the denim covered curves of her hips and butt, he touched only her chin and jaw, his fingers spread wide and holding her still for his kiss. His other hand, he kept clenched in a fist at his side.

Devon swayed closer. Luke felt the last of his control slipping away, and he either had to take more—or stop. Luke went with stopping, slowly pulling away so he could stare at her. "There's something here, Devon. You can't tell me you don't feel it."

They were still standing close, so close he felt her breath whisper against his mouth as she sighed. "I've got enough complications just with my day-to-day life, Luke. I've got a bad feeling you're a complication I don't need."

"Actually," he murmured, catching her hand and lifting it to his lips. He pressed a kiss to the inside of her palm and watched her from under his lashes. "I think I'm exactly the kind of complication you do need."

A slow, almost reluctant smile curved her lips. "You're pretty damn full of yourself," she said quietly.

Luke shrugged. "Not so much. I just know what I see. You've got sad eyes, Devon. You look like a woman who spends way too much time alone. You look like a woman who doesn't smile enough. Whatever is complicating your life, it isn't making you happy."

She eased away, and the caution he'd been waiting for finally appeared, darkening her eyes. "Complications aren't there to make you happy."

"The good ones should. Not every complication has to be the

bad kind," he murmured. Some of her hair had slipped free from her clip, and Luke reached up, caught one thick lock. It was every bit as soft as he'd thought it would be, and it curled around his fingers. He wanted to pull that clip out of her hair and see all those long curls fall around her shoulders and her back—wanted to see her naked with all that hair spread out on his pillow. But he just rubbed the curl between his fingers and watched her face. "Sometimes the best things in life come from complications."

"Really?" Devon asked, smirking. "All the complications I've had in my life have pretty much sucked. I haven't yet had one bring me much of anything but trouble or grief." Her voice was flat and vacant, her eyes little more than a void.

His heart clenched inside his chest. "Then give me a chance to show you just how much fun a complication can be," he said, keeping his voice light and easy. "Let me show you I'm really not an asshole."

It was sheer stupidity that made her agree. It had to be. Because Devon couldn't think of any other reason she would grudgingly say okay. Or any other reason she'd give him her phone number.

She started digging in her purse, looking for the black day planner she carried around for notes, reminders, and her million appointments. But it wasn't in there. Weird . . . That organizer went everywhere with her. Glancing at him from the corner of her eye, she said, "I can't find anything to write on. You got a piece of paper?"

"No. But I don't need it. Just tell me."

Feeling just a little snarky, she thought spitefully, *That works. With any luck, you'll lose it.* But as she repeated her number, she had a feeling she'd be hearing from him.

Very soon.

Yet as disgruntled as she was, when he dipped his head to kiss her again, she felt her heart skip a beat or two. When he traced the outline of her lips with his tongue, it skipped a few more beats. As Luke deepened the kiss, slanting his mouth over hers and pushing his tongue inside her mouth, she thought her heart just might stop altogether.

Then he put his hands on her. Gently. One resting on the curve of her waist, the other cupping the back of her head, and her heart went into overtime, slamming away merrily within her chest. The taste of him, the feel of him, the strength and the warmth . . . damn, she'd gone so many years without this and never thought she was missing out on all that much.

She'd been wrong.

Easing a little closer, she opened her mouth a little wider and leaned into him. His body was long, muscled, and lanky. Restless, she circled her hips against his. Something powerful, demanding, moved through her. She dug her fingers into his arms—

And then he was gone, pulling away so abruptly, she wobbled a little. She was hot, hungry, and off balance. Her head buzzed from the heat of him, the taste of him. Blinking, she looked at him.

He reached up, brushed his fingers over her lips, and then turned her around, nudged her to her car. "I'll call you," he murmured against her ear.

A little dazed, she climbed into her car and ended up sitting there for a good five minutes. Devon might have sat there even longer if she hadn't glanced out the window and seen him standing under a streetlight five feet away, watching her.

Shoving her key into the ignition, she started the car and pulled away without looking at him again. Of course, it didn't matter if she looked at him again or not; the sight of him, how he'd looked at her, his eyes hungry, intent, was imprinted on her memory.

Just like the taste of him.

Just like the feel of him.

"A complication . . ." she mumbled as she hit the highway and headed home.

Trying not to think about anything, especially Luke, she finished the drive with her brain on automatic. Her home was in an older part of town, a rather quaint, cottage-style house that she never would have been able to afford on her own. But years earlier after taking Devon off the streets and placing her with a home, Eden had done some investigating and found out about the trust fund Devon would inherit when she turned eighteen. Divided into several large sums of money, some of it had been a graduation present, some had been designated for college, and when she graduated from college, she'd received the rest of it.

Devon, always the practical type, had used the money as a down payment for this house. She'd seen it and fallen in love. Parking in the driveway, she grabbed her purse and found her house key before she climbed out of the car.

Habit had her checking around her as she climbed out, and she walked up to the front door quickly. It was a nice, quiet neighborhood, and nothing ever really happened here, but Devon had learned caution the hard way.

She frowned as she neared the porch and noticed the light was out.

The house's lights, including the porch lights, were on a timer. The outdoor lights went on at dusk and off at dawn. Opening the front door, she let the light spill out onto the porch while she peered up at the porch light. Rising up on her toes, she twisted the bulb and then squinted as the light flared.

Retreating back into the house, she closed and locked the door. There were a million things she needed to do: case reviews, paperwork, some laundry, finding her missing planner, but instead, she went straight to bed.

And she dreamed of Luke.

* * *

"YOU'RE dodging me."

Devon had slipped out of the room long enough to get a Coke from the vending machines, and she'd been pretty sure Luke wasn't working that day. After all, she hadn't seen him when she brought Dana Watson in after the fifteen-year-old's john had beaten the shit out of her, and Luke seemed to have some sixth sense when it came to her. She stepped a foot inside the ER, and he knew.

So when he hadn't tracked her down in the first thirty minutes, she figured she'd gotten lucky. At least a little lucky, relatively speaking. She'd spent the past week searching for her missing planner, and it never showed up. Up until today, she'd been doing okay, but then she'd been late to court, she'd been late to a staff meeting, and then she'd gotten the call about Dana.

Not a good day. At that particular moment, she couldn't really say if seeing Luke was going to improve things or make them worse. The pessimist in her decided it was going to make things much worse.

Yeah, so what if she'd told him she'd . . . how'd he put it? She smothered a grin as she remembered: *Let me show you I'm not really an asshole.*

She knew that. He was a decent guy; he'd just jumped to the conclusion a lot of other people had made. Granted, they'd had a lot more information before they'd made their jump. He was just quicker than the rest.

But he made her so damn nervous.

Yeah, he sure as hell would add a complication, and the guy made her smile, so she could imagine he would add some variety to the complications she was used to. Devon was a coward, though. She had no problem admitting it, either.

"You going to turn around and look at me?" Luke asked.

Eventually she was going to have to move away from the vending machine, and if she didn't get her Diet Coke fix, she was going to be in sorry shape. At least she had a good excuse. Devon only had a minute or two while the nurses were helping Dana to the bathroom. Once they got back, she'd have to get in there. Slowly, she turned around, and looking at him hit her with that familiar intensity.

As usual, he had a heavy growth of stubble on his face, and she figured he'd probably been pulling another one of those unending shifts. His hair was growing out, she mused. If it got much longer, it would curl over his forehead.

The thought of running her fingers through his hair was enough to have her squirming uncomfortably and blushing furiously. "Sorry. I was distracted."

"Yeah, I know what that's like. I get distracted pretty much every damn time I see you, hear you, or think about you. But you didn't answer me."

Devon cocked a brow. "I turned around to look at you, didn't I?"

"That wasn't the question."

Scowling, she thought back. Understanding dawned, and she shrugged. "Well, that wasn't really a question. You just made a comment, said I was dodging you."

Luke grinned. "Okay, you wanna be literal? Devon, are you avoiding me?"

Damn, where in the hell is an interruption when you need one? she thought irritably. A sardonic little voice in her head said, *Chicken.* To that voice, Devon thought back, *Damn right.*

She'd meant it when she told Luke Rafferty he was a complication she didn't need in her life. She'd meant it, even though she wished she wasn't such a fricking coward. Devon just didn't know if she was ready to handle the ups and downs that came with anything more than a casual friendship. Casual friendships—that was all she had. And it was damn lonely, too.

Then you need to do something about it.

Before she could talk herself out of it, she looked Luke square in the eye and said, "Yeah, I've been dodging you."

He blinked, a little taken aback by her honest response. "Do I take that to mean you changed your mind?" he asked, his gray eyes narrowing on her face.

"I don't know. Yes. No—" Devon blew out a breath, feeling like a fool. And a coward. Damn it, she liked this guy. He was funny, he made her smile, and the way he was with kids just totally melted her heart. But she was too much of a coward to do anything about it. Shuffling her feet, she shoved her hands into the pockets of her blazer and said, "Yes, I'd changed my mind. Then I changed it back. Right now I'm kind of caught in the in-between."

Luke reached up, brushed a strand of her hair away from her face. His hand lingered, and Devon could have sworn electricity jumped between them, just from that simple touch. He felt it, too. She could see it in the way his eyes darkened, the way he hissed in a breath. His body changed, too, tensing, and from the corner of her eye, she could see his other hand close into a fist. The hand that had brushed her hair back from her face slid backward, curving around her neck. "We really shouldn't keep ignoring this, Devon. It's not going away."

She glanced up and down the hall, but it didn't seem as though anybody had even noticed them. Softly, she said, "I don't think I'm the type for anything casual, Luke. But I'm a mess. You need to know that. I can't do casual, but I don't know if I can handle *not* casual, either."

Reaching up with his free hand, he braced it on the vending machine at her back, leaning in. His long, rangy body seemed to surround her, and she waited for the panic to kick in. A guy couldn't stand this close to her without making her freak out—at least on the inside. She'd learned how to bury that fear so it wasn't so readily apparent. Weakness attracted predators, and Devon had learned how to hide her weaknesses.

But the panic never really came. Her heart skipped a beat or two, and her breath seemed to lodge in her throat for just a second, but she didn't feel the urge to tear away from him screaming, either.

Big step for her.

"You're never going to know if you don't give it a chance," he murmured. "Give us a chance. But since we're being honest here, you probably need to know I don't think of casual when I see you."

A smile tugged at the edge of her lips. "So what do you think when you see me?" she asked curiously.

"You. Just you." His head dipped, his lips just a breath away.

The sound of a crying baby intruded, and Luke stiffened, pulled back. A rueful grin curved his mouth, and he muttered, "Damn the timing." He straightened and stood there, watching her with those intense, insightful eyes. "Have dinner with me tonight."

Bad idea! the cautious part of her brain screeched.

But for once, the other voice was louder, and Devon found herself replying, "I'd love to."

FIVE

LUKE knew he'd been this nervous before.

Patching up a buddy under a hail of gunfire. Disarming a bomb. Carrying a crying, screaming hostage away from a building as it exploded behind them. Delivering a baby while the mother was in the middle of a heart attack—done that, too, and that kind of situation could get dicey fast. Yeah, he'd been nervous before. Intense situations weren't anything new to him.

But he was pretty damn sure he hadn't ever been this nervous just about taking a woman out.

Of course, Devon wasn't just any woman. He'd known that the first time he'd seen her. The first time he'd met her had been after he'd been forced to call Social Services because a patient's mom refused to stop breastfeeding her baby—and the mom had been doing some serious drugs. Devon had come in, two cops trailing along behind her, and she had taken the baby, gently but firmly telling the mom that unless she got clean, she wouldn't get her baby back.

The woman had lunged at Devon, and Devon hadn't even blinked. The woman had nerves of steel. She was also soft and sweet, and she smelled better than he'd thought any woman could smell. And Luke was partial to the feminine, delicate scent of a lady. Those big, green gold eyes pulled him in every time, and he suspected he could get lost in them.

Lost in her.

"I don't think I'm the type for anything casual, Luke." Hell, if she had any inkling how decidedly not casual he felt about her, she just might run away screaming. She might end up doing that anyway.

He knew he made her nervous and that wasn't helping his state of mind, either.

Another minute ticked by as he sat in her driveway, brooding and feeling like a fool. *You going to go get her or just sit out here?*

"Sitting right here sounds pretty good," he muttered.

His cell phone started to vibrate, the sound of Don Henley crooning out the first words of "Hotel California" filling the air. He grabbed at the distraction with a rush of relief that left him feeling even more a coward.

The number on the readout was a familiar one, and he flipped open the phone and said, "Hey, Quinn."

"Hey back. Might be coming into town in a day or two. You got room for me?"

"Always." He leaned his head back and wondered what his twin would think if he told Quinn he was sitting in the driveway of a woman and scared to death to go knock on her door.

Apparently he didn't need to say anything. "You're off about something. What's going on?" Quinn asked.

"Off?" Luke laughed a little. Yeah. He was off, to put it mildly. "I'm getting ready to go out on a date. Sitting in the driveway of the lady's house."

"Am I keeping you?"

Luke shook his head. It never occurred to him to feel stupid doing that in a phone conversation, not with Quinn. Quinn would know.

"Okay, so if it ain't me, what's the problem?"

"The woman," Luke replied, blowing out a harsh breath.

"Well, I have to assume you like her, or you wouldn't still be sitting in her driveway. So what's the deal?"

Still unable to figure out exactly how to explain that he was scared to death of a woman who stood five foot four and probably didn't weigh 110 pounds soaking wet, Luke was quiet for so long Quinn ended up laughing on the other end of the line.

"Get your ass out of the car, Luke. It ain't like she's going to bite—and if she does, you'd like it anyway. Seeing as how you've got your head in a mess about some lady, I might hold off coming in for a while."

"You don't need to do that—"

Quinn snorted. "Trust me, I don't need to see you mooning over a woman, either. As entertaining as it might be for a few minutes, it would get old fast for me." Then Quinn disconnected, and Luke threw the phone down on the console.

"What in the hell am I getting into?" he muttered. But he turned off the car and climbed out, his long body unfolding. Rubbing a hand over his jaw, he grimaced as he felt the stubble. He'd shaved that morning, but maybe he should have shaved before he picked her up.

At least his clothes were something other than worn, wrinkled, or bloodstained scrubs.

He lingered by the car for another minute, ran his hand through his hair, and basically just tried to get a grip. Then he started thinking about just what he'd like to grip, and the need inside him boiled back up to the surface.

One little slip of a woman, and she'd made him feel like an awkward, gawky teenage boy. Blowing out a breath, he muttered, "Enough, already."

Resolute, he headed up the old-fashioned brick sidewalk. It was edged on either side by a narrow strip of flowers. They bloomed in a riot of colors, and beyond the flowers, the lawn was a rich, deep shade of green. She put a lot of time into the house; that was for certain.

It was a pretty house, an old-fashioned stone cottage with a sloping roof, a porch about the size of a postage stamp, and stained glass windows on either side of the oak door. He rang the doorbell, and the door opened so fast, he had a feeling she must have seen him loitering out in the driveway like an idiot.

Damn. Feeling a little dumbstruck, he stood on the tiny porch and stared. Once more, her hair was pulled up, but instead of a knot or spilling out from one of those clips, she had pulled it into a loose ponytail, leaving a riot of curls falling down her back. Skinny, almost nonexistent straps held up a filmy dress that seemed to change color between green and gold as she moved aside and gestured inside. "You want to come in for a little while?"

Yeah. How about you show me your bedroom? he thought. It was a miracle he didn't actually say it out loud, because his brain wasn't functioning very well just then. No surprise, because it felt like all the blood had drained south. "Sure." *Good. You managed to say a word; now try a few more.*

"Nice house." *Oh, yeah. That's going to impress her.*

But she smiled, a wide, happy smile that brought out a dimple just to the left of her mouth. Luke felt his knees go just a little weak. That smile could lay a strong man out, he thought.

"Thanks. I love this place."

Dragging his attention away from her face took a lot of work, but he did. If he didn't, he'd just grab her and kiss her senseless. All over.

It was a cute house. He followed her into a living room painted a deep shade of red. It wasn't a huge space, but the high ceiling helped. High on the left wall there was a weird little open-aired window, and through it, he could see what looked like an upstairs hallway. A fireplace, the real kind, not some gas deal, took up the eastern wall. She had bookshelves galore, a decent-sized TV, and a plush ivory leather couch with fat, comfy-looking cushions. Flanking the fireplace was a huge chair and a table-sized ottoman. There was a book resting on the ottoman.

A smile curled his lips. He could picture her, real easy, sitting in that chair and reading while a fire blazed away next to her. Or better . . . forget the book, take her out of the chair, and lay her down on the floor in front of that fireplace. Not directly on the floor, though; the stones in front of the fireplace looked like slate, too damn hard for her pretty little body. A rug.

A nice, warm bearskin rug type of thing. Luke wasn't the bearskin-rug type, but he could see the appeal of that particular fantasy just then.

Focus on something besides getting her naked, he thought sourly. He had to; otherwise, it was going to be a long, uncomfortable evening. He crossed over and studied the titles on her bookshelves.

The Complete Encyclopedia of Serial Killers.

The History of Our Nation.

Lord of the Rings.

A slew of what looked like romances. A few fantasy and sci-fi books he'd read himself. And some mysteries. There were books by Stephen King, two or three different versions of the Bible, ten different books from The Complete Idiot's Guide series. He spied a couple of thinner books and started to laugh, reaching out to pull one off the shelves to stare at a familiar cover.

"*Bunnicula*?" he asked, as he turned to grin at her.

A smile teased the corners of her mouth, and she shrugged. "Hey, a vampire bunny has more appeal than you'd think."

Luke chuckled. "Yeah, I know. I had a copy of this when I was a kid. I read it to pieces."

"Then obviously, you have excellent taste."

"And you have very eclectic taste. You read all of these?"

Devon rolled her eyes. "Yeah. And these are just my keepers." She gestured to the hallway behind her. "I've got an office that has twice as many books in it, and most of those I haven't read yet."

"You're kidding."

Wrinkling her nose, she said, "No. I'm not. And that's probably a conservative estimate." An awkward silence fell. Devon broke it by giving him a rather forced-looking smile. "So, do you want a drink or should we just go?"

Instead of answering her, he caught a handful of her hair, combing his fingers through the wild curls. "You ever wear your hair down?"

"Ahhh . . . no. Not usually. Gets in the way."

"Way of what?"

How in the hell could she get turned on just from him fiddling with her hair? Devon wondered. But there was no mistaking it. She was definitely getting turned on, and the only thing he was doing was winding a curl around his finger and staring at her hair. "Everything. Gets in my face, gets hot." Grimacing, she added, "Plus I've had my share of parents or pissed-off kids pull my hair. Harder to do when I keep it put up."

"Hmmm."

He wasn't staring at her hair anymore. Devon's heart started to pound in her throat as his gaze fastened on her mouth. "I want to kiss you," he said softly.

A hot flush rushed to her cheeks. Staring into his sexy gray eyes, she murmured, "I'm fine with that." More than fine, actually. By the time he pressed his lips to hers, she was ready to beg for him to do just that. His lips were warm and so much softer than they looked as he nibbled her lower lip and then slid his tongue along the curve. She opened for him and slid her arms up over his shoulders.

But when she went to press against him, Luke eased back. Every instinct in his body was rumbling, and he was primed to take, take, take. If it wasn't Devon, that's exactly what he would have done. Staring at her, he cupped her cheek in his hand, swept his thumb across the satin-smooth skin. Her lips were swollen already, red from his, and as he stared at her, a soft, shaky little sigh drifted from her. In his arms, her body was hot and pliant, melting against his own, and there was no doubt he could have her.

He'd been eying her for months, and the past few weeks, they'd been dancing around each other, wanting just this. She wanted it every bit as much as he did.

But all those months of watching her, wanting her, Luke had come to know Devon Manning just enough to know he wanted to know more. A lot more. A few weeks, a few dates, a few rolls in the sheets, however much fun they'd be, it wasn't going to be enough for him. This was going somewhere, and until he had a good idea of where, he wasn't going to scare her off.

So instead of lowering his lips to hers and figuring out how to convince her out of that sexy little dress, he brushed a kiss across one bare shoulder. The scent of her flooded his head, hot woman and honeysuckle—damn, what a potent combination. "We better go."

* * *

DEVON wasn't a total incompetent when it came to men. Maybe a little inexperienced, but she was honest enough that she could admit she had more than a few personal hang-ups about sex. Considering what her aunt's pedophile husband had done to her, it wasn't a big surprise that she got a little wigged out when people intruded on her personal space.

Still, she did like men. A lot. She just hadn't found one she liked enough to consider trying to work past those hang-ups with sex, not until Luke.

Emotionally, she was mostly okay, and she occasionally went out on a casual date. But the problem with Luke was that nothing about him seemed casual. Not even for a moment. Devon had spent most of the day worrying herself sick, convinced he was either going to realize what a basket case she was, or that she'd be too nervous to manage any kind of coherent conversation.

But none of that happened.

Being with Luke was amazingly easy. Part of her had been braced for the fact that tonight wouldn't be much different from any other date, where she sat with a frozen smile and pretended she was enjoying herself—or maybe she would enjoy herself. Until he touched her. Then she'd freeze, panic, pull away, and totally freak him out.

It had happened before, and she always ended up feeling so damned pathetic. She wasn't looking forward to repeating the experience with Luke. But on a different level, she would have almost welcomed either of those happening. It would give her that much more reason to back away from him.

Devon didn't have to pretend to enjoy herself, and she didn't have to force herself to smile at him even once. The smiles, the laughter, they came so easily, it was like she'd known him most of her life.

When he touched her, she didn't feel that instinctive need to flinch away, and she found herself relaxing around him in a manner that was just not normal for her.

More than relaxing, she was enjoying herself. A lot. Devon hadn't laughed so hard in years. Maybe never. "You've got to be making that up," she accused.

He followed her up the walkway to her house, and she turned to see him giving her a wounded look. "Now, would I make up something like that? Hell, you've seen some of the Einsteins in the world. Why is it so surprising a woman would give a kid a suppository by mouth instead of the right way?"

She wrinkled her nose and shuddered. "Oh, gross."

Luke just shrugged. "Hey, you ought to hear some of the foreign-body stories I could tell you. And being in a college town? It's even worse."

Her brow creased. Leery, she repeated, "Foreign bodies?"

He grinned. "You probably don't want to know. People can do very, very bizarre things—and they don't even have the excuse of being a kid."

Now that, Devon understood. She'd had to go to many a home to speak with parents when their kids got hurt doing the normal kid thing. Kids did get hurt, and sometimes, kids hurt themselves in a purely innocent manner, but so often it made neighbors or teachers concerned. As unpleasant as it was, and as much as parents hated it, Devon would rather make those visits than visit the hospital because nobody reported the abuse.

That sobering thought had the smile on her face dying. A hand touched her lightly on the shoulder, a quick, innocuous touch. She looked at Luke to find him studying her. "Where did you go?"

Devon shrugged. "Just thinking. Kids—it's amazing what they can do. One minute they have you laughing, then you're ready to pull your hair out and scream, and then you just want to cry."

"I think you could use a few more of the laughing minutes." He lifted his hand, and Devon watched, mesmerized, as he caught a flyaway curl. Her hair was a thick, nearly unmanageable mass of curls. Usually she had it gelled and pulled back into some kind of submission, but at the end of the day the first thing she did was let it out of the twists, clips, and knots she used during the day. Loose, it hung halfway down her back. When it was wet, she could sit on it.

"I don't suppose you'd take your hair down, would you?" Luke asked, a little out of the blue.

She blinked, tipped back her head to see his face a little better. "Take it down?"

"Yeah." He continued to rub the curl back and forth between his fingers as he lifted his gaze to hers. His eyes were heavy-lidded, giving him a sleepy, sexy look that had her wanting to lean in and kiss him. "I have this thing for your hair."

A hot rush of blood flooded her cheeks. Slowly, she reached up and pulled out the stretchy band that held her hair up. The weight of it fell down around her shoulders, halfway down her back. "It's so long, it gets in my way," she said, shrugging self-consciously.

"It's gorgeous," he murmured. "I didn't know it was so long."

She watched as he caught a curl and wrapped it around his finger. Her mouth went dry, and she looked from his hands to his face to find him staring at her. "Man, I love these curls, Devon. There have been times when you come into the ER and your hair is trying to get free, and I wonder how you'd look with all this hair hanging down."

Devon opened her mouth, but the only thing she could say was, "Uh . . ." *Oh, don't you sound smart?* she thought sarcastically. She swallowed, and it sounded horribly loud. *Say something, Devon.* She needed to say something. But then Luke's gaze shifted to her mouth, and she couldn't think of a damn thing to say. Or a damn thing to do—except one thing.

There was one thing she wanted to do. She wanted to kiss him.

As she watched, his lips curved into a grin, and he murmured, "You're asking for trouble, looking at me like that, Devon."

She blinked. A sudden rush of courage flooded her, and she met his gaze with a smile of her own. "Am I? What kind of trouble?"

His hand came up, and he cupped her chin. That was the only place he touched her until he lowered his lips to hers. "This kind," he muttered, and then he kissed her. His mouth was warm on hers. He slid his tongue along her lower lip, and she pushed up onto her toes so she could lean into him. The hand cupping her face tightened a little. Devon opened her mouth. Luke groaned. His chest vibrated as the sound rumbled out of him.

Deep inside, that sexy, hungry sound made her ache.

Her heart skipped a beat or two when he laid a hand on her hip. He didn't do anything else, just rested it there, but she was excruciatingly aware of that heat burning through the thin layer of her dress. Luke deepened the kiss, taking it slow and easy—too slow, it seemed to Devon.

She burned for more. She wanted to feel his hands on her—all over her—and she wanted to touch him back. Her hands shook a little as she lifted them and rested them on his hips. The thin layer of his simple navy blue polo shirt was too much, and she eased her hands under it. Under it, his skin was warm, muscled, and smooth. He groaned again, and the hand cupping her chin slid around to the base of her neck, fisting in the tangle of curls. He arched her neck up and slanted his mouth more firmly against hers.

His tongue pushed inside her mouth, and the full taste of him hit like a nuclear blast. She wanted to rip his clothes away, and then her own. She wanted to explore the hard, muscled body, wanted to feel it against hers. Desperate to do just that, she pressed her body against his. The hand on her hip slid around her waist. He drew her close, their bodies aligning perfectly. So perfectly she could feel the hard-muscled planes of his chest, the length of his legs, and the thick ridge of his erection, pressed flat against her belly. Heat exploded through her, followed closely by a hunger unlike anything she'd ever known.

But the hunger was followed by fear.

It was nothing he did, nothing he said. Just one minute she was reveling in the feel of his hands on her body, and then she was battling the fear back into submission—or trying to. And failing. She felt his hand slip under one of the skinny straps at her shoulder. The heat and strength of his hand was no longer so enticing. She tensed, and as quick as that, Luke let her go. His hands smoothed down her sides, and then he stepped back. His lips lingered for just a moment before he lifted his head.

The fear in her eyes was enough to make him want to punch something. Luke had seen more than his share of battered women, battered kids; they all had the look in their eyes. Like they'd been kicked before, and they expected to be kicked again.

Seeing it in her eyes was harder, though. He'd pegged Devon as a fighter some time ago. She would have to be, to do the job she did. Bad thing about fighters, though, too often they were forged in fire. And the thought of what he suspected had made Devon into who she was . . .

The gut-deep suspicion wasn't just a suspicion anymore. He knew it. It was in the way she held herself, the way she moved, like an alert little cat, observing everything with wary, watchful eyes. What she'd revealed to him that night at the steakhouse, her drug addiction . . . What had she said?

"Some bad shit happened, and I didn't know how to handle it."

Oddly enough, he understood a hell of a lot better now, because he knew, without a doubt, his instincts had been right. Referring to it as "bad shit" was an understatement.

An ugly, black fury surged through him, and he had to fight to hide it from her. Somebody had hurt her, and he hated it. He was going to find out who it was, and if he didn't kill the bastard, it would be nothing short of a miracle.

She was staring at him with dark, unreadable eyes. He forced himself to smile, burying his anger down deep inside. Devon didn't need to see it. There was already enough anger and violence in her world. Touching his finger to her lower lip, he murmured, "You pack a punch."

Her cheeks flushed a soft pink.

Luke wanted to ask her if he could come inside. The thought of leaving her right now just wasn't tolerable, but coming inside, even if she wanted him to, was a bad idea. He wanted to hold her close, promise he'd protect her, promise he'd find whoever had hurt her.

It would be a bad idea all around, though. Especially when he was still so damned pissed off. He needed to get away from there before he exploded. Pissed as he was, as much as he needed to get away before he lost it, he couldn't leave. They saw each other often enough at Rudding, but it was too sporadic. He wasn't going to chance them going a couple weeks without seeing each other, and he wasn't going to count on Devon not getting antsy again and trying to dodge him.

"You got plans tomorrow night?"

"No."

Brushing her hair back from her face, he asked, "Maybe I could come over. We could go see a movie or something. Get a pizza."

She smiled, and that dimple made a brief appearance. "Sure."

Some of the tension inside his gut eased. Just a little. He wouldn't have to wait too long to see her again. Now he just had to get himself under control before it happened again.

Dipping his head once more, he brushed his lips against hers. "Sweet dreams, Devon."

Sweet dreams . . . Devon closed the door behind her and, unable to resist, watched his shadowy image through the stained glass as he headed back to his car.

Turning to press her back against the door, she felt a goofy, euphoric smile spread across her face. She felt—giddy. Yeah, that was the word.

Devon felt absolutely giddy. Her belly was jumping around, her heart banged against her rib cage with wild abandon, and she had all these weird little pains inside her. Her breasts felt heavy, her nipples were tight, and deep inside, there was a hollow, empty ache.

With a soft laugh, she pushed off the door and set the alarm system, and then she headed upstairs, stripping off her dress as she went, kicking her shoes off on the landing. Devon went through the routine of getting ready for bed, all with that silly smile on her face, and when she lay down a half hour later, she imagined she could still feel his lips on hers.

"*Sweet dreams,*" he'd whispered.

And they were sweet—all centered around him.

As she dreamed about Luke, smiling even in her sleep, somebody else was dreaming about her.

But in those dreams, there were no smiles. Until big, cruel hands closed around Devon's throat and she started to gasp for air, her face going red, her fingers clawing at his hands.

SIX

"I tried calling you last night, baby."

Devon glanced up over the island at her mother, unable to keep from grinning at the nosy expression on Liz Manning's face. "Oh?"

Liz reached across the island as Devon tried to filch a cookie, smacking the back of her hand lightly. "Let them cool off first." Then she smiled again. "Busy reading?"

"Actually, I was busy with a guy." It popped out of her mouth without her realizing how it sounded, and immediately, a brilliant blush turned her face red. Probably tomato red, Devon thought dismally. "Uh . . . not like that. We went to a movie."

Liz laughed. "Really?" This time when Devon tried to snatch a cookie, Liz let her, settling down on the stool and propping her elbows on the island. "Weren't you out with some guy a couple weeks ago?"

Mouth full of ooey, gooey chocolate chip, Devon nodded.

"Hmmmm." Devon's next attempt to grab a cookie resulted in Liz pulling the tray out of Devon's reach. "Same guy?"

Devon swallowed a bite of cookie and then replied dutifully, "Yes, Mom."

"Hmmmm."

Devon really hated that *hmmmm* sound. She suspected it was a mom sound, one moms across the globe made while they were trying to figure how to pry without sounding like they were prying.

Of course, Liz Manning had very few qualms about prying.

"Two dates with this guy, and you're just now telling me?"

Swallowing another bite of cookie, Devon said, "Actually it's more like five."

Liz's eyes widened. "Five dates?" Staring at her daughter, she tried to decide if she wanted to squeal with glee—silently, of course—or sulk. Five dates, and Devon hadn't mentioned him. But five dates. Devon hadn't dated the same guy more than once or twice, and she usually only went out on a real date a few times a year. The only serious romantic relationship Devon ever had was back in college, and it hadn't ended well.

Since then, a few sporadic dates here and there, and although Liz tried not to worry, it was hard.

After what Devon had been through before Reece and Liz found her, some scars were to be expected, but Devon was twenty-six years old. The one failed relationship back in college hadn't done much more than make Devon retreat even more.

And no matter how hard she tried, over the past year or two, Liz hadn't been able to keep from worrying. Studying Devon's eyes, she saw something there she couldn't remember seeing before.

Happiness: that giddy, head-over-heels-rush sort of happiness that came from being in love, or very close to it.

Whoever the guy was, Devon really liked him. And her Devon was a good judge of character. It was why she was so good at her job. Scooting the tray back to the middle of the table, Liz said, "Okay, so tell me about this guy."

"Geez, Mom." Devon rolled her eyes, squirmed around a little bit, and blushed.

Liz laughed. "Now, don't *geez, Mom* me. This is a mom moment . . . my baby finally finding some guy that makes her blush . . .
makes her smile." Her smile softened, got a bit sadder. "You have
no idea how much I've hoped and prayed you'd find just that."

Devon's blush deepened, but she forced a smile. Reaching out,
she took her mother's hand and squeezed. "Yeah, I do. You think I
don't see you worrying about me?"

With her free hand, Liz tucked a curl behind Devon's ear and
then cupped her cheek. "Of course you *see* it . . . but being aware of
it and actually understanding are different things. You know that."
Something dark moved through her eyes, there for only a moment
and then gone.

But Devon had seen that look before: fury, fury over what had
been done to Devon, over the hell Devon had gone through . . . a
hell she still had to cope with. "Mom . . . I'm okay."

Liz patted her cheek. "I know you're *okay*, baby. You're too
strong not to be. But I don't want you *okay*. I want you happy."

* * *

"DID I hear you right?"

On the other end of the phone, Quinn's voice was more than just
a little disbelieving. Luke rolled his eyes. "Yeah, you heard me right."

"Is this the girl you were moping about last month?" Quinn
asked.

Scowling, Luke replied, "I wasn't moping. But yeah, that was
her."

"If you weren't moping, I dunno what in the hell to call it. What
do you call sitting in some chick's driveway?"

"Thinking?" Luke offered helpfully.

Quinn snorted. "Yeah, you call it thinking, man. What's her
name again?"

"Devon." Lying back on his bed, Luke stared out the skylight
at the stars gleaming overhead and listened as his twin continued to
mutter and mumble something about getting his hearing checked.

"You're really serious. About some girl. One girl. One single girl."

"Woman, Quinn." Devon wasn't a girl, and she sure as hell wasn't just some girl. "And yes, I'm serious."

"Huh. Never would have thought to hear that from you." Quinn was quiet another minute, and then he asked, "So how long you been seeing her?"

"A little over a month. That night you called, it was our first date."

"A month. Only a month, and you're already that serious about her? Hell, why haven't you mentioned her until now?"

Luke had been putting this conversation off for a while now. Explaining Devon, a woman with a history of drug abuse, might not go over real well with Quinn, who'd grown up dealing with physical abuse coming from his strung-out mother.

Even though Devon's past was just that, some people would judge her; she'd been right about that. Luke was worried his twin might be one of them.

Right now, he didn't really want to tell anybody much about her, and part of it was just because he was still feeling his way through the minefield of a serious relationship. Even Quinn, whom he was closer to than any other soul on earth, seemed a lot harder than Luke would have expected.

Didn't help that Quinn had been more moody than normal lately. Usually Luke managed to talk to his twin a couple times a month, but lately, Quinn had been distant, even for him.

And that was saying a lot.

Not long after Adam had died, Quinn had left the army. For a while, he'd drifted through town every few months, never staying for more than a few days, and then without even letting Luke know he was leaving, he'd get it in his head to move on, and it would be weeks before Luke heard from him again. Leaving the army hadn't done much to help his twin, Luke didn't think. Quinn still seemed caught between fury and grief, and nothing Luke said or did seemed to help.

Quinn had always had issues connecting with people, always

had problems realizing that things he did or said had an impact on those around him. But since Adam's death, it was even more apparent. Luke wouldn't be surprised if Quinn fell off the radar. Every time they spoke, Luke was half-prepared for the fact that it may be months . . . longer . . . before he talked to Quinn again.

Luke hadn't ever learned any more about the op that had killed Adam or the mysterious girl whom Quinn still wouldn't talk about. That girl, whatever had happened to her, was at the root of Quinn's rage, but the man wouldn't talk about it.

Luke had been content to wait, figuring Quinn would talk when he was ready. But that time, so far, hadn't come. Quinn just remained disconnected, getting a little worse every time Luke saw him.

It was weird sometimes, the relationship Luke had with his brother. They were twins, and as such, they had their weird bond, but it wasn't what it should be. Quinn kept everybody at a distance, even his brother. Luke was closer to Quinn than most people, but Quinn wouldn't ever let anybody in entirely.

At least Luke wouldn't have thought so. Except in his gut, he knew the unknown woman had meant something to Quinn.

While Luke had flirted and romanced his way through high school, college, and half his adult life, Quinn had kept to himself, and now it seemed he'd lost the one woman he might have been interested in.

Still sounding a little disbelieving, Quinn asked, "You're serious about this girl you've only known a month?"

Luke rolled his eyes. "I've known her for longer than that, Quinn. We just now started going out, though."

"How come I'm just now hearing about her?"

There was an edge in Quinn's voice, one that actually caught Luke by surprise. Although Quinn cared about his brother, the everyday things of life hadn't ever much mattered. Small talk was a waste of time for Quinn, and unless it was connected to the job, Quinn considered almost everything small talk.

Luke winced, realizing he had unwittingly cut Quinn out.

Quinn had been cut out of too much, always the outsider, and getting it from his brother was a shitty deal, even if Luke seriously hadn't realized that it would matter that much to Quinn.

You're falling in love with her. He's not just your brother; he's your best friend . . . Why wouldn't it matter? The voice of his conscience spoke up, and guilt stirred.

He had very little doubt about the sincerity and depth of his feelings for Devon. He suspected her feelings ran just as deep, and if things moved the way Luke was starting to hope, there would be one more thing Quinn was cut off from.

Made no sense feeling guilty because he'd always been happier than Quinn and was getting ready to become even more so. But Luke couldn't put his life on hold because of Quinn.

"I dunno, Quinn. I just . . ." He sighed, closed his eyes. "I haven't been in this place before; still trying to figure it out. Not real sure how to handle it."

"I'm no expert, but I think you just keep doing it. There's no trick to handling life. You just live it." Quinn's voice, when he replied, was a little less edgy, almost understanding, and though Luke couldn't see his brother, he felt the understanding—and the envy. Without saying a word, Quinn got it.

"Going into psychology now that you're out of the army?" Luke asked, trying to force some humor into the tense silence.

"Shit, no." His words were derisive, but Luke could hear the faint smile in Quinn's voice. "What's it like?"

"What's it like?" Luke repeated.

"Yeah. This thing . . . with her. You love her?"

He shrugged restlessly. "Not real sure yet." *Liar.* Damn it, that voice of his conscience was getting annoying. Abruptly, Luke wished Quinn were there. Yeah, the guy wasn't much for talking, and he didn't mess with giving advice, but he knew how to listen. "Yeah . . . yeah, I think I do."

"So what's that like?"

Luke blinked, a little surprised by the question. Quinn . . . actually giving a damn about love? Curious about it? Might seem a little unfair to somebody that didn't know Quinn, but Luke knew how his twin was. Quinn didn't let himself care about too many people, and he liked it that way. He didn't want to care about people; if Luke and his dad weren't family, if Quinn hadn't had that bond with them, Luke doubted Quinn would have a soul in the world to truly call a friend, and he also suspected Quinn would be just fine with that.

Yet here he was . . . asking Luke what it was like to love somebody, and feeling envious. "I don't know that I can explain. I wake up, and I want to see her. I go to sleep, and I miss her, even if it's only been an hour since I saw her last. I think about her, wondering what's she doing, if she's had a bad day and if there's anything I can do to make it better."

"Sap." But there it was again, that undercurrent of envy. "Would I like her?"

And that was the crux of it. Two of the most important people in Luke's life, and there really weren't that many who mattered, and Luke wasn't sure how they'd handle each other.

Quinn came off as cold, uncaring, to most of the world.

Devon, with her scars both emotional and physical.

If they could work past their immediate hesitation, Luke suspected they'd get along just fine. But Luke suspected he knew how Quinn would react to Devon; the man seemed to have some instinct when it came to certain things: he sensed weakness, and Luke had no doubt how Quinn would peg Devon. He'd see a junkie, not a woman who'd overcome hell and heartbreak and battled an addiction as a child, but a junkie.

Compassion wasn't one of Quinn's strong points.

Of course, even as he thought that, Luke realized he'd been too damn quick to judge the woman for the actions of a troubled child. But his reaction would be nothing compared to Quinn's. And considering these two were the most important people in his life, Luke pretty much dreaded them meeting.

Although Quinn would probably keep his feelings to himself out of respect for Luke, Devon would pick up on Quinn's vibes the same way she picked up on Luke's that first near-disastrous night when he'd jumped to conclusions.

From there, it would only go downhill.

And Quinn, even under the best of circumstances, didn't like a whole lot of people. Seemed like even before it got started, there were already marks against her, as far as Quinn was concerned.

"I hope you'll like her," Luke finally replied as honestly as he could. "She means a lot to me. She's a good woman, has a good heart."

"I get the weird feeling there's shit you ain't telling me."

Luke rolled his eyes. "Yeah, well, some things are better explained in person, preferably over a couple of beers." In person—where Quinn couldn't hang up the phone the minute Luke tried to explain some things about Devon.

Quinn grunted. "Hell, if you're that serious about her, guess I need to meet her sooner or later." He paused a beat and then made one of his rare jokes. "Might as well be before the wedding."

Wedding . . . Luke's mouth went dry. "Uh, I didn't say anything about a wedding."

Yeah, maybe his thoughts had run down that road a few times, but just a few. They'd only been going out a little while, a month. Not long enough to be talking about weddings.

But even as part of his brain shied away, there was another part of him that didn't, a part of him that wondered what she'd look like dressed in white lace, a part of him that got all rabid with glee at the thought of being able to call her his.

"Yeah, you didn't say jack shit about a wedding, but I don't hear you laughing, either."

* * *

HANDS on his hips, Luke stood in Devon's backyard and stared at the dead skunk. Six weeks of dating, he was dying from sheer frustration, he spent more time jacking off in the shower now than he had in high school, but instead of necking with Devon, he was getting ready to bag up a dead skunk.

Devon stood just a few feet behind him, the collar of her shirt in her hand and held up over her nose. "What happened to it?"

Glancing at her, he grinned. "It died."

"Gee, really? And here I was thinking it was just sleeping," Devon replied tartly. "Man, I didn't realize they smelled that bad."

"Go on inside," he offered.

He managed to bag the thing without touching it, and before he tied the garbage bag shut, he looked it over a little but he didn't see any mark or injury on it. Frowning, he tied the bag shut and tossed in into the trash and then studied the backyard. She had a white picket fence around the yard, and there was definitely enough space the thing could have gotten between the pickets. Had it just come into her backyard to die?

The animal hadn't really looked old to him, but then again, Luke specialized in people, not animals. Although he'd worked with a few people who hadn't smelled much better than the skunk.

Heading into the house, he grimaced. The smell of skunk could permeate damn near everything, including skin and hair. Devon was at the counter, chopping up an onion with a fast, easy speed. "I don't suppose I could take a shower, could I?" he asked, careful not to get too close.

She wrinkled her nose at him. "I'd appreciate it if you would. You got any clothes in your car? I could wash those for you. Sorry, Luke, but you don't smell too sweet right now."

"Better be nice, or I'll come over there and hug you. Then you'll need a shower, too."

Stupid move, Luke, he thought as he left the kitchen and headed upstairs. Thinking of showers and Devon at the same time. Occupied with that torturous thought, he forgot to go outside for his gym bag. Inside her bathroom, he took a long look around and swore. Hell, this was going to be torture.

It smelled like Devon in there. He saw a black bra hanging on the doorknob. Hanging on a hook by the shower was a cotton robe, simple and white—and short—damn short. He could see her wearing that, the cotton clinging to her wet body, her hair hanging down her back.

"Shit."

His body sprang to attention as he reached out and took the robe, bringing it to his nose and breathing in. The sweet, warm scent of her had permeated the fabric, and he let it flood his senses. When he realized his mouth was actually watering all because he stood there smelling her robe, he put the robe back on the hook and started to strip.

Luke really didn't know how much more of this he could take. He was trying to take it slow, and he knew Devon didn't need him rushing her, but six weeks was a damn long time. Seemed like he'd spent most of those six weeks walking around with a hard-on, too, either because he was with Devon, he was thinking about Devon, or he had just walked away from her house after a hot and heavy make-out session.

He climbed into the shower stall, planning on taking a good, long, cold one so maybe the heat in his blood would cool, but standing in the shower, surrounded by the scent of her shampoo and her soap, Luke knew ice cubes could fall from the showerhead, and the second he looked at Devon, he'd be in the same shape he was in now.

Hard and damn near desperate for her.

So instead, he made the water warm, letting it slide over his skin like silk. Ducking his head under the spray, he scrubbed his hair, tormented himself as he breathed it in and imagined having Devon in there with him. Taking the mesh sponge looped over the wall-mounted rack, he squeezed some of her soap onto it and then scrubbed it over his body and imagined it was her hands moving over his body.

His erection jerked against his belly, hard and insistent. Putting the sponge up, he closed a soapy hand around his length and stroked. Up, down. Hissing out a breath between his teeth, he leaned his head back against the tile wall behind him and did it again. It was a sweet, painful pleasure, and standing there, surrounded by her scent, he could almost imagine he was with her, that her slim, soft weight pressed against his body, and that it was her riding him, instead of his own hand bringing him to completion. He could almost imagine the warm kiss of water was in fact her hands gliding over him.

Almost.

But not quite. Quicker and quicker, he stroked himself, lips peeling back from his teeth in a grimace of ecstasy, his heart pounding like he'd just parachuted into enemy territory. When he came, it was hard and fast—and empty. Swearing under his breath, he washed himself again, quicker this time, because the water was cooling.

Damn it, if he didn't have her soon, Luke suspected he just might lose his mind.

Then, as he dried off a few minutes later, he realized he was probably a little closer than he'd thought. He'd climbed into the shower and scrubbed himself clean from the skunk smell, but he'd left his gym bag out in the garage. He swore as he wrapped the dirty clothes in a towel to contain the smell. Then, with another towel wrapped around his hips, he left the bathroom and headed downstairs. Not wanting the smell to spread through the house any worse than it already had, he stopped by the small alcove off the garage where her washer and dryer sat. He dumped the clothes in, added some detergent—then a little more for good measure—before closing the lid.

"Hey . . ." Devon came around the corner and then stopped dead in her tracks. Her eyes widened, she slid her tongue out, licked her lips.

"Uh . . ."

The look that entered her eyes as she stared at him made it seem as though he hadn't just jacked off in her shower. His body reacted, blood draining south until his erection was throbbing under the cotton towel.

The towel started to slip, and he fisted the ends in his hand, anchoring it to his hip as he stared at her. Hoarsely, he said, "I forgot to grab my gym bag."

"Uh . . ."

Closing his eyes, Luke tried to block out the look on her face: hungry woman. "Devon, if you don't quit looking at me like that . . ."

There was a whisper of movement, but until she reached out and touched his chest, he hadn't realized she was moving closer. Closer to him, not away. He caught her wrist in his hands and opened his eyes, staring down at her. "Not a good idea, Devon," he said roughly.

She flexed her hand against his chest and looked up at him. Her eyes were serious as she asked, "Why not?" Leaning into him, she pressed her mouth to his chest and licked away a stray bead of water that had dripped off his hair.

The feel of her tongue on his flesh was hell. It was heaven. It was somewhere in between, and it was neither. Wrapping his arm around her waist, he jerked her against him. Through the thin material of her dress and the cotton of the towel, they could feel each other. Luke could feel her warmth and her softness, and Devon could feel the strength and hunger radiating off of Luke. "Because of this," he rasped, rocking his hips, cuddling his hard length against her belly and just barely managing to keep a rough growl behind his lips. "Because I want you so bad I can't think for it, and my control is pretty much shot."

Devon tugged against his restraining hold, and when he let go of her wrist, she trailed her hand down his chest, back up, smoothing over his shoulders, his face. Everywhere she could touch, it seemed, and she left behind a trail of fiery hot sensation that only made him burn even hotter. "Maybe you should stop trying to be in control so much," she suggested softly.

Her hand stroked back down, passing over his shoulders, his pecs, brushing against one flat nipple. Luke gritted his teeth and reminded himself he had good reasons for not rushing her into bed. Or up against a wall—hell, the floor under their feet would work just fine. Reasons—reasons for . . . oh, yeah. He had reasons for not rushing her. Reasons for staying in control. But for the life of him, with her leaning against his body and touching him with soft, smooth hands, he couldn't remember those reasons very well.

"You're not ready for this, Devon," he said gruffly, reaching up and capturing her wrists. Stopping those light, feathery touches before she totally destroyed any control he had left.

A smile flirted with the corners of her lips, and she leaned forward, pressed her lips to his chest. "I really don't think that's your call, is it?"

Then she stepped back. Luke had one second to breathe out a sigh of relief, but as he blew out a harsh, ragged breath, it turned to fire inside him. Hot, explosive fire—because Devon hadn't pulled back. She'd only stepped away enough to reach behind herself and tug down the zipper at the back of her dress.

It fell to her feet in a heap of red and white, and under it, she wore a strapless bra and a pair of underwear that must have been designed to drive a guy nuts. They were cut almost like a pair of men's boxers, but shorter—a lot shorter, and snug enough to cup the curves of her ass, the subtle flare of her hips.

"Devon . . ."

She smiled at him, stepped against him, and pressed herself against his chest. Her breasts, small, perfectly formed, and round, flattened against him. "Stop being so careful with me, Luke."

That was when he realized she knew. She knew why he had been so careful, knew why he had spent so much time trying to keep himself in control. Pushing up on her toes, she licked his lower lip and then murmured, "I won't break, Luke."

Blood roared in his ears. Need, throttled into submission for weeks, rumbled to the surface. Wrapping his arms around her waist, he hauled her against him and lifted her off her feet. Her body, soft, sleek, and delicate, pressed against his, and her knees came up, squeezing his hips. The towel didn't have a chance. It fell free from his hips, and when she started to rock against him, it slid to the floor so that now, the only thing separating them was the thin, almost nonexistent scrap of cloth between her legs.

"Bedroom?" he muttered, his voice gone harsh and tight from need.

Smiling, she pressed her mouth to his. "Not worried about a bedroom, Luke."

He swore, and this time, his voice cracked a little on the end. He was this close to turning, pressing her against a wall, and fucking her until they both collapsed. But common sense intervened, and he headed down the hall instead. His wallet was where he'd dropped it earlier, and inside was a rubber.

Just the one, although he did have a few more stashed in his car. He hadn't been planning on this happening, although hope sprang eternal, and thank God he was an optimist, because he would have been dying . . . Oh, shit, he was dying anyway, he thought, as Devon leaned forward and bit his earlobe. Her breasts pressed flat against his chest, and he could feel the silky rain between her thighs as she rocked against him.

Damn—yeah, screw the bedroom. The kitchen table would work just fine. It was solid oak, and when he laid her down on top of it, it had her hips at just the right height. Just the right height for him to sink to his knees in front of her and lean in, press his mouth to her core, and feast. Slick, wet, and sweet. He groaned at the taste of her and cupped her butt in his hands, hauling her closer.

Her thighs tightened around his head as she tried to bring her legs together. She tugged on his hair, and he glanced up at her, saw her face was pink with embarrassment.

He shook his head and muttered, "I need to, Devon. I've been dying to do this, to taste you like this and feel you come against my mouth." And that's exactly what he did, using lips, teeth, and tongue to bring her to the edge of orgasm, and once she was writhing and whimpering and screaming his name, he tore the rubber open, rolled it down his engorged flesh, and then he stood.

Leaning over her, he stared down at her flushed face. Their eyes locked as he pressed against her. The thin barrier of the rubber couldn't hide her heat, couldn't disguise the silky wet embrace of her sheath, yet it wasn't enough. Not nearly enough. He wanted her with no barriers, with nothing between them.

"Wrap your legs around me," he said gutturally as he bent over the table and slid his arms under her shoulders, bracing her body.

She shuddered under him as she lifted her thighs and slowly wrapped them around his waist. Pressing his forehead to hers, he asked, "You good?"

Her smile was all female, all sexual heat and promises. "Oh, I'm more than good. Make love to me, Luke. I'm dying . . ."

Slowly, he forged his way inside her, the silken tissues giving way and yielding to him. Wrapped around his engorged flesh, she was tight as a vise, sweet as sin, and soft as a kiss. Halfway inside her, he encountered resistance and lifted his head to look at her face. Her eyes had gone dark, and he could see the pain she tried to hide. Freeing one hand, he cupped her chin and murmured, "Just relax for me, baby. Relax . . . Open for me . . . Yeah . . . Fuck, just like that."

He talked her through it, murmuring soft, sexy words into her ear and scattering kisses across her face, her neck, and her shoulders, moving against her with slow, shallow thrusts until Devon thought she'd die if she didn't feel all of him. Rocking her hips upward, she tightened her thighs, tried to pull him deeper. Luke groaned, tensed against her—and then he rasped, "Fuck . . . Devon, please don't . . ." His voice faded off, and then he lunged, slamming into her with all the force of his lower body, taking her deep and hard. Harder, harder, until she threw back her head and screamed.

All the while he murmured against her ear, "Sorry, baby . . . Damn, you're sweet—you feel it, too, don't you, Devon? Shit, you do—fuck, you're coming for me, aren't you, baby? I feel it . . ."

He worked a hand between them, finding that small, sensitive bud of flesh, and touched her, fast, rough strokes that ricocheted through her lower body, centering in her womb, until she thought she'd explode. Arching into him, she screamed out his name.

She went flying. There were no other words to describe it as she seemed to explode out of her body, even as the pleasure washed over her, anchoring her.

Hard, fast, and breath-stealing, and when it was over, he was still moving on top of her, still hard, still muttering to her and praising her. Dazed, too weak and sated, her hands slid off his damp shoulders and smacked on the table. His spine bowed and he drove into her one final time, coming with a hoarse shout that bounced off the walls.

Her name, Devon thought. When he came, he shouted her name.

That was her last conscious thought before she drifted into a sweet, dark slumber.

* * *

LYING against his side, Devon circled Luke's flat, coppery nipple with her forefinger and watched as it drew tight under her touch. "How long have you known?"

One thing she loved about the guy, he didn't pretend not to understand a difficult question. Instead, he turned his head and kissed her crown. The arm around her back tightened. "Since our first date, the for real one, not when we ran into each other that night. But I suspected it then."

Lifting her head, she stared at him curiously. "How?"

He shrugged. Restless. For a minute he was quiet, and she let him be, figuring he was doing the same thing other people did when they learned she'd been raped as a child. Not too many people knew: Eden, her adopted parents, her boss, and a few close friends. Finding the words for something like that was way outside most people's comfort zone. "I've seen too many women who've been hurt like that not to recognize it."

She nodded. "Working the ER, I guess you do."

But Luke shook his head. "Not that. It's what I did before." Gently, he eased her away, and she watched as he sat up and pushed the sheet off his legs. His left leg was a mess from about midthigh down. There was a patchwork of old, healed scars, and she winced in sympathy as she touched the longest one. It was on the outside, starting about four inches above his knee and running halfway down his calf. It had a surgical neatness to it most of the other scars lacked.

"I was in the Rangers," he said softly. "Six years ago, I was injured while in South America." His eyes took on a far-off look, and he rubbed his hand against the scarred leg almost absently. "People will do really shitty things to one another, Devon. I saw some of the worst, or so I thought. But every year, it got a little worse, and it was getting to me. When I got injured, it was severe enough they would have put me at a desk or had me teach."

He glanced at her, shrugged. "I'm not a teacher, and if I'd wanted to ride a desk, I wouldn't have joined the army. So I took a medical discharge, went to medical school."

Shoving up onto her knees, she studied the scars. "I don't have a medical degree or anything, but this looks pretty bad."

Luke nodded and traced a finger down the longest scar. "They had to reconstruct my knee. I've got some steel pins in there that I'll have until I die. But hey, I can walk. I can run. I can work out, and it only hurts when I'm really exhausted or if it gets too cold."

Unable to resist, she bent down and pressed her lips to the scar.

Luke sighed raggedly, and then he slid a hand down her back, curving it over her ass. "Of course, all I'd have to do now is think of you, and I'd warm right up."

Grinning at him, she straightened and threw a leg over his hips. "I don't mind keeping you warm."

"Not warm," he grunted as he cupped her in his hand. "I'm hot—damn hot." Then his mouth twisted. "But I'm also out of rubbers. I only had the one on me. Rest are in the car."

Leaning, she kissed his chest. She hoped she wasn't about to make a fool of herself. Under her lashes, she stared at him. "I haven't ever done this with a guy. What happened . . ." Her voice trailed off, and then she swallowed, cleared her throat, before she tried again. "It happened when I was a kid and after, I had all the tests run. I'm about as clean as a baby."

One free hand came up to her hip, his fingers digging into her hip, and his lashes drooped low over his eyes. "I had to have them yearly in the army. Since then, I haven't been with too many women, and I had a life insurance physical done six months ago. I'm clean— and I haven't been with a woman since that blood test was drawn." He held her gaze as he slipped a hand between their bodies, sought out the hard, sensitive nub of flesh, watching as she shuddered and arched back. "But that's not really the only concern. Fuck knows, I'm crazy about you, but there are other considerations."

He started to pull back, but she reached down, wrapped her fingers around his wrist, and rocked against his hand. "I'm on the pill. Had to—female-type issues. So if it's pregnancy you're worried about, then I'm safe on that front, too."

"Fuck—" He plunged two fingers inside her and then pulled away so he could cup her hips and hold her steady as he rocked upward, grinding his aching length against her. "I'm a doctor, Devon. I really should know better than this."

She quirked a brow at him. "I sense a 'but' coming."

He swatted her rump and then stroked a hand down the soft curve. "I want you—completely. All the way. I want you with no barriers, with nothing between us," he murmured, leaning forward to press a kiss to the hollow of her throat. "But if I go skin to skin with you, Devon, it's going to be because we've got something serious here. No backing away. You ready for that?"

She wiggled against his hips. "If I wasn't serious, you wouldn't be in my bed doing what you're doing." Then she eased back. "But if you want—"

Devon didn't get another word out before he flipped her onto her back, split her thighs, and pushed inside, his entry unrelenting, his hard shaft forcing soft, swollen tissues to yield to him. His eyes bored into hers, his hands fisted in her hair, and he watched her face as he stroked deep. "I want just this," he rasped, staring at her from heavy-lidded eyes. "I want you. I want you all the time, and I want you in a thousand different ways, ways that would probably terrify you if I tried to explain."

A smile curved her lips and then it faded as a groan shimmered out of her when he circled his hips against hers. He felt huge, hard as iron and smooth as silk, as he pumped in and out. "I really don't scare all that easily, Luke."

Dipping his head, he kissed her roughly. "Don't tempt me, Devon. Shit—" His voice broke off, and he rotated his hips against her, laying a hand on her knee and sliding it upward until he could palm her ass. "You can't back out now, darlin'. You're mine now." He reiterated his words with a series of deep, hard thrusts. The sound of flesh slapping against flesh, the labored rhythm of their breathing filled the air. His fingers tightened on her bottom, and he muttered once more against her mouth, "You're mine."

Then the time for talking passed, and they stared into each other's eyes as he rode her hard, pushing her to the edge and then backing off, slowing his pace. His fingers dug into the soft, supple flesh of her hips, and he took her with a decided lack of gentleness, careful not to hurt her, but not easing up on his passion.

Devon loved it. Hoarse from screaming, she fisted her hands in his short hair and begged, pleaded—pleaded. She'd gone her entire adult life without really needing intimate contact—she might have wanted it, but she hadn't ever needed it with an intensity that overrode all thought and all desire. Not like this.

"Scream for me," he ordered gruffly, dipping his head and sinking his teeth into her lower lip. "Scream my name."

But she didn't have the breath to scream; she barely even had enough breath to remain conscious, it seemed, and when he slowed his thrusts and worked his hand between their bodies, what little breath she did have exploded out of her in a harsh moan. Climax hovered just in front of her, every bit as powerful, every bit as consuming as the first one. But he wouldn't let her reach it. Pushing her so close, and then backing off.

His voice, harsh and guttural, growled in her ear. "Scream, Devon. Scream my name."

A soft, strangled, "Luke," was all she could manage, but she raked her nails down his back and tried to pull him even closer. A slow, sensual smile curved his lips as he eased his weight off her body, settled on his knees between her splayed thighs. He slid his hands down her torso, cupping her breasts and plumping them together, pinching her nipples a little too tightly, pushing her a little too close to pain, yet it did have her arching against him as the fire inside her flared hotter.

Then he continued to stroke his hand down . . . down . . . down until he was stroking . . . oh, hell, right . . . there. A heated blush spread across her upper chest, up her neck, her face, and she squirmed under the intensity of his gaze. "I've thought about taking you like this," he said, his voice a low, sexy growl. "So often. Wondered how you'd taste, how you'd moan when I made you come."

She shuddered, caught between the seductive rumble of his voice and the teasing touch of his fingers between her thighs. With light, teasing strokes, he caressed her and all the while, he rocked his hips back and forth, the hot, hard flesh of his shaft stroking back and forth inside her sex, the thick head rubbing against one sensitized spot, pushing her farther, making her flesh draw tighter, until her entire existence narrowed down to him—just him. His fingers stroked and teased, his sex throbbed inside her, his eyes rapt on her face as he watched her.

Slowly, still watching her, he trailed his fingers up her body, leaving a damp trail up her torso, along her neck, until he could rub the lingering moisture onto her lips. Bending low over her, he muttered, "You're sweet." He licked her mouth and made an appreciative little growl that rumbled and vibrated through him.

Sweet—hell, that didn't even begin to describe her, Luke thought, sucking her lip into his mouth. The tight, silken clasp of her sex around him, the honeyed taste of her lips, it was mind-blowing. Breath-stealing. Hot-cold chills raced down his spine, and he knew he couldn't hold back any longer. Hooking his arms under her knees, he held her open, exposed. She was so tight, already so close to coming, he could feel in the minute, convulsive caresses of her sex, and then this time when he felt it coming on her, he let it come, let the explosion take her, and as it broke over her, the rhythmic milking sensations pulled him along with her, and he came, hard and powerful. She squeezed down around him, drawing it out, emptying him until he collapsed against her body with a groan.

Letting go of her legs, he slid his arms around her waist and remained there, enjoying the faint tremors still racking her body.

He cupped a hand around her breast and muttered, "Mine, Devon." The soft brush of his breath had her nipple puckering up tight, but he was too dazed to do anything but admire the pretty pink tip. Luke didn't even have the strength to shift over enough to kiss it. Exhausted, he felt himself slipping off. Gathering his strength, he lifted his head. "Crushing you. Need to move."

Her arms tightened around his shoulders. "Don't you dare."

So like that, their arms and legs tangled, his softening cock still sheathed in her sex, they fell asleep.

* * *

IT was late when he finally woke, late enough that the only light in the room was the silvered moonlight filtering through the curtains, but it was enough for Luke to see by as he pushed up on his elbow and studied Devon's face. She looked incredibly young when she slept, he decided, when the thin shield of eyelids hid those unsettling, insightful eyes away from the world.

World-weary eyes. Luke had a burning need to know exactly what had transpired to put that sad knowledge in her eyes. All of it, not just the bits he'd managed to piece together.

She'd tell him. Luke wouldn't let her not tell him. But not yet.

This was too new. As satisfied as he was, as complete as he felt lying there with her, Luke was under no illusions about their relationship. They were both guarded, private people who had fallen hard for the other. They had their secrets, their shadows, and some of those shadows could make things rocky.

So they could wait.

One thing that couldn't wait, though, was his stomach. They'd forgotten about dinner, and Luke could only be relieved Devon hadn't actually started cooking earlier. Unless the house had burned down around them, he doubted either of them would have noticed much.

Gently easing away from her body, he padded naked out of her room, heading downstairs. He paused by the washing machine and lifted the lid a scant inch before lowering it again. Those clothes might pretty much be trashed. The faint, cloying scent of skunk still lingered. Starting another wash cycle, he added more detergent and then left to find the towel he'd used earlier.

Hooking that around his hips, he headed outside for his gym bag, which was tucked in the trunk. Getting to it required a little more movement than he liked wearing nothing but a towel, but the thing stayed in place. Snagging the bag and pulling it closer, he unzipped it to check inside, then grinned. Damn, he'd even remembered to pack clean clothes, thank God. The bricks of the sidewalk and driveway felt chilly under his feet, and the night air wrapped around him in a cool embrace. He moved a little quicker, slinging the bag over his shoulder and locking the car before heading back up to the house.

On the porch, though, he paused. The skin on the back of his neck stood up and he felt . . . something.

Eyes. Watching him.

Slipping inside the house, he locked the door and did a quick walk-through, checking the other doors and windows before heading into the living room. The itchy, crawling sensation along his spine faded as he stood at the window, keeping to the shadows as he watched the street.

Nobody's watching you, man. Nobody around here gives a damn. Pushing a hand through his hair, he muttered, "You're getting paranoid."

Still, he remained there for a while, hidden in the shadows and watching the street. He stood there for nearly an hour, watching and waiting, but he never saw anybody move.

SEVEN

As much as he'd like to think otherwise, Luke wasn't the type to have issues with an overactive imagination. He didn't see monsters when they weren't there, or at least he never had before. It bothered him enough that he slept restlessly the rest of the night. Used to getting by on little amounts of sleep, when the alarm clock went off, he came awake easily. Devon, though, lifted a hand and batted at the clock and then burrowed in closer to Luke.

She lay on her side, and Luke lay behind her, his arm hooked around her narrow waist, her head tucked under his chin. "You need to wake up, sleepyhead," he murmured, stroking his hand up her side.

"Don't wanna." Her voice was hoarse and drowsy, a sexy little purr.

"Hmmm. I don't much like the idea of you getting up, either," he whispered, pushing up onto his elbow and dipping his head to kiss her shoulder.

She rolled onto her back and stared up at him, her eyes still half-closed and bleary with sleep. "You're really here."

Crooking a grin at her, Luke asked, "Did you expect me to disappear?"

Moving her shoulders in a shrug, Devon answered, "I dunno. Thought maybe I dreamed it." She pushed up onto her elbows, snagging the sheet and tucking it under her armpits. From the corner of her eye, she glanced at him, and he watched as a soft blush stained her cheeks pink. "Wouldn't be the first time I dreamed about you."

Hooking a finger in the sheet, he tugged it down, baring the delicate curves of her breasts. "You must really not want to get out of this bed," he teased, dipping his head and biting her lower lip gently. Then he shifted downward, closing his lips around one pink, pouting nipple.

"No . . . I really don't." Her words were a ragged little gasp. Her hands skimmed up over his shoulders and then fisted in his hair, urging him closer.

Closer sounded damn good to him. Working a hand between them, he grabbed the sheet and pulled it free so Devon's slight, nude body was pressed against his own. "I could get used to waking up next to you," he muttered. "Damn quick." Wedging a knee between her thighs, he settled his hips against hers. She was warm, soft, and wet as he pushed inside. And swollen—tighter than she'd been the night before. "Are you sore?" he asked gently.

Instead of answering, Devon slid her hands down his sides and closed her hands over his hips, pulling him tighter, closer. Lifting her face to his, she brushed her lips against his.

As the morning sun streamed in through gauzy white curtains, they lost themselves. The quiet of the room was broken by wordless moans and soft sighs. The slow, lazy beauty of the moment didn't last, though. Hunger rarely waited patiently, and this was no different. Slow and easy turned to hot, fast, and demanding. If he had been able to think, Luke would have worried he was pushing Devon too hard, too fast, but he couldn't think, and she was every bit as hungry as he was.

He could feel it as her nails raked across his shoulders, as she sank her teeth into his lip and bit him as she wrapped her legs around his hips and arched to meet every deep thrust. They came together, Devon screaming out his name while Luke buried his face in her hair.

*   *   *

THE soft, low sound of Luke's voice over the phone was a distraction Devon couldn't afford at the moment. Her desk was so overloaded, she couldn't even see the surface. She had three different court appearances scheduled for the afternoon, a couple of follow-ups to do, and, assuming she didn't get anything else dumped on her, she just might get home before dark.

But not by much.

Glancing toward the open-ended section of her cubicle, she said, "I'm not getting out of here anytime soon, Luke."

"So I'm not going to see you today, either, huh?" His voice had a weird undercurrent, one she couldn't quite put her finger on.

"I wish I could. If I had a little longer for lunch . . ."

"Or I could have called earlier," Luke said, his voice wry. "Everything going okay?"

Grimacing, Devon shot the work on her desk an evil look. "No. I think all my cases went and made like bunnies over the weekend. I swear, I don't remember this many files being on my desk when I left Friday."

"Happens to me every time I take a coffee break." On the other end of the phone, Luke blew out a sigh and forced himself to tell Devon bye. She responded, her voice soft and quiet, and then the phone went dead as it disconnected. Lowering the handset, he hung it up and moved to stand at the window. Arms crossed, he stood there brooding. It had been four nights since he'd seen Devon for longer than thirty minutes. Too damn long, in his opinion.

When he'd gotten off last night, he'd swung by her house. It had been late—nearly midnight. A shitty shift: several nurses and two of the doctors out with an early case of the flu had him hanging out a good three hours past the end of his shift, trying to catch up and help out a little. When he'd driven by her house, everything but her security lights had been out. Giving up on hopes of seeing her, he'd headed home.

He missed her way too much.

This seeing her once or twice a week, it just wasn't enough for him. The whisper of an idea formed in his mind, one he almost brushed aside.

It sucked, the way the past week had gone. Besides, it couldn't hurt to ask . . . right?

"Do it," he muttered. "Maybe you'll sleep better. Hey, what's the worst she can do? Say no?"

Before he could talk himself out of it again, he grabbed the phone and punched in her number. She answered with a breathless, "Luke, I'm on my way out."

"You got a spare key?"

She paused. The silence seemed to stretch on forever, and Luke shoved a hand through his hair and resisted the urge to start pacing the doctors' lounge. "I miss you," he said, keeping his voice level and low. Damn it, did he miss her. He didn't need to see her every day, although he'd sure as hell like to, but it had been almost a week since he'd seen her for any decent length of time, almost a week since he'd touched her. That was too damn long. "I'm not asking to move in or anything, but maybe while things are so crazy, I was thinking I could sleep over there every once in a while. See you in the morning before you go to work and stuff."

"Luke . . ." Her voice trailed off, and he could picture her face. She'd be standing there, chewing her lip and trying to figure out how to tell him no. His gut knotted.

The door to the doctors' lounge flew open, and Luke looked up, saw the grim look on the nurse's face. "We need you out here, Dr. Rafferty. Gunshot victim en route, age nine. ETA less than five minutes."

FRAGILE 101

Luke swore and then blew out a breath. "Look, forget I asked. I got to go. Sweet dreams, Devon."

* * *

DEVON climbed out of the car, her eyes scratchy with exhaustion and her head aching like a bitch. She was so damned tired, she just wanted curl up in bed and sleep for twelve hours straight. But instead of driving home after she'd finally finished up the day's paperwork, she had driven to the opposite side of town, parked her car, and was now walking on very sore feet toward the brightly lit Emergency Department of Rudding Memorial.

The doors slid open soundlessly, and the familiar scents of the ER washed over her as she headed inside. She spent way too much time in these places. Unwashed bodies, the scent of antiseptic, blood, death—no amount of cleaning could ever completely erase the stink of death, Devon suspected. It was like it saturated the walls, the floors, and the very air.

It was past eight. There were a few empty chairs in the waiting area, which probably meant they weren't having too chaotic a night. Swallowing, Devon shoved a hand into her pocket and closed her fingers around the key there. She did have a spare key, several actually. One at her neighbor's across the street and one for her parents, and one on a ring she kept inside her office desk.

If she thought about this too much, she might change her mind. Her stomach was all jittery even thinking about it. She was half-terrified, half-elated. First time she'd ever given her key to a guy, first time she'd ever had the opportunity, first time she'd been tempted. First time—that was the source of the terror and the elation. Devon was a master at keeping herself slightly distant from most people. She let very, very few people inside the walls she'd built around herself, and this was just one more step to letting Luke inside those walls.

One more step? Hell, Devon, he's already shoved the walls down and taken up residence.

Her mouth twisted in a grimace. Yeah, it was too late to keep him out now, which was why she was here with a recently made spare key. If she'd gone home to get the spare from her house, she would have thought about it too much.

Thought about it and maybe changed her mind. There was a big home improvement store a few exits up the interstate, and she'd dropped by there to get the copy made. While she waited, instead of thinking about that damned key and the reason she was getting it made, she'd called information and gotten the number for the chain restaurant across the street and placed a to-go order.

A couple of big, messy burgers and two orders of fries were currently in a brown sack, and the smell of the food wafted out to tease her nostrils as she headed for the triage desk. The nurse behind the glass window recognized her and slid the window open, giving Devon a friendly smile.

"Hi, Devon. I hadn't heard that one of yours had come in. Did you get paged?"

Shaking her head, Devon said, "No, Karen. Actually, I'm here to see Luke . . . Dr. Rafferty."

Karen's silvered brows went up. A grin flashed across her face. "Oh, really?" She closed the window, but through it, Devon could hear her talking as she called somebody over to sit at the window.

A minute later, the doors of the ER swung open, and Karen stood there, still grinning, her hands tucked inside a very, very bright orange scrub jacket with grinning black skulls all over it. "You getting ready for Halloween already, Karen?"

Karen laughed. "Yeah. Drives a couple of the doctors batty. There's one who just hates bright colors. I've got one that's neon green with little witch hats all over it. I'm saving that one to wear just on the days he's working." She gestured down the hall. "Dr. Rafferty's in the doctors' lounge, I think. Probably trying to scrounge up something decent from the vending machine."

The door to the doctors' lounge swung open before they reached it, and Luke came walking out, adjusting a long white coat. He glanced up, saw her—and both of them stopped dead in their tracks.

Slowly, that familiar, sexy little grin curled his lips, and he murmured, "Hey."

Swallowing against the nervous knot that had suddenly settled right in her throat, Devon smiled back. "Hey. Thought you might like something other than hospital food or chips from the vending machine." She lifted the bag, and Luke crossed the few feet separating them, took the bag, but instead of looking inside, he reached out, hooked his hand around the back of her neck, and pulled her against him.

Wolf whistles and cheers rose up around them as he covered her mouth with his, but Devon didn't hear any of it. Her heart was pounding in her ears, and her senses were full of Luke: the smell of him, the feel of him, the taste. Rising on her toes, she pressed against him, and he growled against her lips, then pulled back.

Blushing hotly, Devon buried her face against his chest as a couple of the nurses started to applaud. "Oh, geez."

Luke laughed. "Ignore them, Devon." Then he pulled away, sliding his hand down her arm to link their fingers.

Easier to do once Luke led her into the doctors' lounge and they settled down at a postage stamp–sized table. It was so damn small there wasn't room for them to both sit at it without their knees bumping underneath. Luke's solution was for him to place his legs outside of hers, squeezing in with his knees just slightly, just enough so she could feel him through the layers of his scrubs and her khakis.

He grinned at her and tore into the bag, popping a couple of fries in his mouth before he even unwrapped the burger. "Devon, you are an angel," he said.

Devon laughed. "I don't think bringing you a burger qualifies me for sainthood."

"Does in my book." He took a huge bite, followed by another. He was halfway done before Devon had even managed her first bite. "Man, I was starting to forget what real food tasted like."

Grinning at him, she said, "Obviously. Maybe I should have ordered you two."

He returned her grin. "Nah. I'll just finish off yours. Not like you'll eat more than half of it anyway."

"Just don't touch my fries," she warned him as she shook some salt out onto hers and searched through the discarded bag for ketchup.

They ate in companionable silence, and slowly, Devon managed to relax a little. A couple of doctors came in and out, but none stayed for more than a couple of minutes. True to his word, Luke finished up his burger, and about half of hers as she polished off her fries. He tried to steal one, and she smacked his hand. "Hands off my fries, slick," she said, grabbing the last two and popping them in her mouth.

"Greedy," Luke murmured. He grabbed a napkin and wiped his hands and mouth as he pushed back from the table. "Come here."

Devon glanced at the door but slid out of her chair, took the two steps necessary to walk around the table. Luke reached out and looped his arms around her waist, pulling her to stand between his legs. He rested his head against her belly, nuzzled her through her clothes. "Thanks for coming by."

Sliding a hand through his hair, Devon wrapped her arms around his head and held him. "You look exhausted."

"Hmmm. Bad shift," he murmured. He tipped his head back and stared at her through gold-tipped lashes. "Seeing you helps."

She eased back a little and slid her hand into her pocket. "I brought you something else," she said. She held the key out to him and bit her lower lip nervously.

Luke's eyes dropped to the key, then slid back up to her face. He said nothing, just reached out, took the key, and slid it into the breast pocket of his blue scrubs. Then he curved his hands over her waist, staring at her face. Slowly, he stood, his eyes never once moving away from hers as he pulled her in closer, leaned down, and pressed his lips to hers. He kissed her, deep, hard, all the while watching her.

Devon, unable to close her eyes, stared back at him, and by the time he lifted his head, a fine sweat had broken out all over her body, and her heart was racing like she'd just run a mile. "What if I decide to wake you up when I get there?" he asked, brushing his lips across her cheek.

With a shaky laugh, Devon replied, "After that, if you decide not to wake me up, I might get a little upset."

* * *

"You didn't have to get up," Devon murmured as Luke slid into the empty stool across from her. Although his eyes were heavy with sleep, he looked a lot more alert than she felt.

When he'd come to her bed early that morning, a little before one, she'd been awake. She'd woken up when she heard him pull into the driveway and had watched from her window as he climbed out of his Jeep and headed up her driveway. By the time they'd both gone to sleep, it was nearly two, but she'd gotten a little sleep before that.

He hadn't.

Shrugging, he said, "I'll lie back down in a little while, if you don't care." Leaning across the breakfast bar, he rubbed his mouth against hers. "I can always sleep. Can't always see you."

Damn. A kiss from him did more to clear the cobwebs from her brain than a cup of coffee. Grinning against his mouth, she said, "Can't argue with that logic."

"Useless arguing with me anyway. Hmmmm . . . come here." He closed his fingers around her wrist, tugged gently, until she slid down from her stool and circled the bar. Blood rushed to her cheeks as his gaze slid over her. The camisole and panties she wore seemed about as revealing as a teddy, and Devon wished she'd pulled some sweats or something on. "You're so damn pretty," he muttered, almost as if he could hear the self-doubts circling through her mind.

He closed his hands around her waist and lifted her. Reaching out, she braced her hands on his shoulders as he pulled her onto his lap so she straddled him. "Remember that night we ran into each other at the steakhouse?"

Cocking a brow, she asked, "Before or after you put your foot in your mouth?"

Luke dipped his head and nipped her lower lip. She squealed and jerked back, but he caught her head in his hands and then kissed her lower lip, gently, soothingly. "Smart-ass," he muttered. "Before. When we were trying to get a place to sit down, I remember looking at you and thinking how much I'd like to shove that long skirt you wore up to your waist and lay you flat on a table so I could have my way with you."

Devon wrinkled her nose. "Those tables are too damn skinny—and hard as a rock."

"Hmmm." He lowered his lips to her neck, and she shivered as he raked his teeth along the curve. "Yeah, I kind of figured that out, too. So I decided one of the barstools would work. I'd sit down, just like this, and put you onto my lap . . . just like this . . ."

She felt him tugging on her panties, and then he was pressing against her, pushing inside her. "Then I'd fuck you . . . just like this," Luke said hoarsely, lifting his head and staring into her eyes.

Molten steel—his eyes were as hot as molten steel as he watched her face. The muscles in his arms moved with easy, liquid grace as he guided her in a slow, steady rhythm like she weighed less than nothing. "You're so soft . . . so delicate," he rasped. "Am I hurting you?"

Devon's head fell back, and she moaned, arched closer. "No. Please don't stop . . ."

"Wrap your legs around me," he ordered, guiding first one leg, then the other around his hips.

Devon locked her ankles behind his back and started to rock against him. At first, he met her rhythm, but then he slowed, stopping altogether, letting her take over. *So damn pretty,* Luke thought. So soft, but so strong. She was delicate: delicately made, delicately curved, delicate, soft skin that would easily bruise. Yet she took him inside her, rode him with a sensual smile curving her lips, flexing her inner muscles around his shaft in a teasing caress.

Rising and falling against him, her hips circling, she draped her arms around his neck and dipped her head, pressing her brow to his. Her hair fell around them like a veil, blocking the world out so all he could see, all he could feel, was her.

His heart tripped a little as she slid one hand up to cup his cheek, cradling his face. Falling in love—he'd always imagined it would be a slow, lazy kind of drift. Lust was a crazy free fall, or so he'd thought. But he'd been wrong—and right.

Falling in love was, all at once, a slow, lazy little drift, like a feather circling down to the earth, that gentle drift into love happening over weeks or months—and a plummet off the edge of a cliff when you finally realized you weren't falling in love; you were already there. Maddening, terrifying, and exhilarating.

Luke had suspected she could do this to him, but he still hadn't been prepared for it. Wrapping his arms around her, he gave in, gave in to the needs of his body and a deeper need, a need that threatened to eclipse anything and everything else in his life.

EIGHT

IT wasn't a fast thing, and it wasn't really even intentional on Luke's part. But as the weeks rolled by, he found himself more or less living at Devon's house. It hadn't dawned on him just how much time he'd spent away from his own place until he went home to get some clothes for Thanksgiving dinner over at Devon's parents', and he saw the dust collecting everywhere.

He wasn't obsessively neat, but he wasn't big on dust or clutter, either, which translated to him cleaning up the small condo on a regular basis. Eying the fine coat of dust on his dresser, he thought back and tried to remember the last time he'd cleaned—and couldn't.

Well, that wasn't exactly right. He'd cleaned over the weekend, over at Devon's house. Scowling, he swiped a finger through the dust and then turned around and stared at his room.

He hadn't slept in his bed in over a week, and then it had only been for two nights, because he'd gone back to sleeping at Devon's place. Paying for a place he barely used made about as much sense as him not owning up to how he felt about Devon.

The cleaning junk was in the utility closet off the kitchen.

Tugging off the black sweater he'd pulled on over a T-shirt, he turned on some classic rock and set about spending the next hour or two cleaning his seriously neglected condo.

Halfway through, with the musty, closed-in smell replaced by the cleaning power of pine, he took a break and grabbed a bottle of water from the fridge. The fridge was about as neglected as the rest of the place: bottled water, a few cans of beer, some bologna and cheese, couple of eggs.

There was no bread in the house, no milk, next to nothing in the cabinets other than canned soup, peanut butter, and crackers. His belly rumbled, but he had plans that night with Devon that involved reservations, white tablecloths, and candlelight—followed by some wine, more candles, and a long, hot bath.

So instead of trying to put together something edible to go with his water, he flipped through the stack of mail that had been accumulating. He paid all his bills either online or through automatic withdrawals, so most of the junk was just that: junk. A glossy catalog caught his eye, and he found himself staring at a golden ring with one very shiny rock. Below the engagement band was a small picture, a woman with her arms thrown around some guy's neck and that shiny rock sparkling on her finger.

"You've gone crazy," Luke muttered to himself, rubbing his forehead.

He'd gone by the mall Monday before his shift started and found himself loitering in front of a jewelry store, staring at the rings, and now he was eying a jewelry catalog. "Pathetic."

Hell, he hadn't even told Devon he was in love with her. Luke wasn't really sure why he hadn't said it yet; it wasn't exactly that he was waiting to hear it from her first. If he waited for Devon to say it first, he suspected he'd be waiting a damn long time. Although she wasn't as shy as she first came off to be, she was guarded—very much so. He could even understand that. Devon would be the kind to take her time on damn near everything in life, and that was just how she was.

"Well, maybe not all the time," he said to himself. A grin curled his lips, and he shook his head.

She took her time, though. Anything important, she moved slow, weighed her options—sometimes for a little too long. That caution was a part of her, and Luke had a feeling it had something to do with why he hadn't told her how he felt yet.

He didn't want to spook her, scare her off. It wasn't something he wanted to risk, not considering how gone he was about her. Blowing out a breath, he flipped the catalog open, turning past the displays of engagement rings and wedding sets.

When he came to a picture of a single strand of pearls, he paused.

Luke wasn't much for gift giving. But he realized he did want to give her something. Just to do it. Just to see the look in her eyes and see that slow smile light up her face.

Mind made up, he flipped the catalog closed and tossed it in the trash along with the empty bottle of water. The rest of the junk mail ended up in the garbage can, too, and he finished cleaning the condo in record time. If he was lucky, he could avoid traffic, get to the mall, get back to Devon's, and be ready before she got home.

The phone at his belt started to vibrate as he locked up the condo behind him, a garment bag slung over his shoulder. He tugged it off the clip and read the display. He recognized the number, and under normal circumstances, he would not have felt a little irritated.

Opening the phone as he jogged down the steps, he said, "Hey, Jeb."

Jeb's raspy voice drawled back, "Long time, no hear, stranger. Thought you were going to keep in contact."

"Sorry," Luke said, although it wasn't exactly true. "Just been busy."

"Poking and prodding people take up that much time?"

"Nah, but having a life does." He unlocked the Jeep, tossing the garment bag over the passenger seat as he slid behind the wheel. "You remember a life, right? Football games, movies, women."

Jeb laughed. "I can get a woman when I need one. Movies are a waste of time, and I'd rather watch paint dry than sit and watch a football game, Rafferty."

Luke shifted the phone to handless, plugging it into the charger. "Yeah, my life's gotten so mundane it would probably put you to sleep."

"No doubt. Can't see how you put up with it."

Starting the car with a glance in the rearview mirror, Luke backed out of his parking spot. A smile spread across his face as he pictured Devon as she'd looked that morning when he'd joined her in the shower. Naked, wet, and so damn sexy—so damn his. "I muddle through somehow, Jeb."

Leaving the condo's parking lot, he joined the heavy flow of traffic on Nicholasville Road, heading toward the mall. The silence on the phone stretched out but he didn't do anything to lighten it. Jeb had called for a reason. Just like Devon, that guy moved about as slow as an ice age at times. He'd say whatever it was when he was good and ready.

"So . . . you talk to Quinn much?"

Something shifted in his Luke's gut. An odd undercurrent was there in Jeb's voice, something heavy, something not quite right. "Couple times a month. He's moving around a lot right now. At loose ends, I guess."

"Everything okay with him? He ain't answering when I call him."

Frowning, Luke said, "You know how Quinn is, Jeb. He talks when he wants to, and screw it the rest of the time."

Jeb's only response was a noncommittal grunt. A few more seconds ticked by, and then Jeb asked, "He ever tell you why he got out?"

"No, but he doesn't need to. Adam, the woman who died. He'd had enough. If he needs to tell me more, then he can do it when he's ready to. But I'm not holding my breath about that happening," Luke answered honestly. A little irritated, he said, "What's going on, Jeb? And don't tell me you called just to say hey. You've got some kind of agenda; I know you too well to believe otherwise."

On the other end of the line, Jeb sighed. "Look, I'm just kind of worried about Quinn, that's all. You had a reason to get out; you got hurt, and you were ready to leave. I get that. Losing Adam screwed Quinn up some. It hit all of us hard, always does. And the woman . . . Yeah, I know she had something to do with it, but still . . ." His voice trailed off, and when he spoke again, his voice was soft, worried. "Quinn just got it in his head one day he was done. Damn near a month since we buried Adam, there we were in the middle of a fucking war zone, and he decides, *That's it. I'm through.* I thought for a minute he was just going to bail right then and there."

"Quinn wouldn't do that."

"I wouldn't have thought so, bud. But you didn't see his face. I did. The rest of the team did. He hung in throughout that mission, and then he was just gone."

"You make it sound like he went AWOL or something. Chances are he'd been thinking this through for a while and just hadn't told anybody."

"Maybe." But there was a world of doubt in Jeb's voice. "I can't help but think the timing was sheer coincidence, sheer luck. If he'd gotten the idea in his head a few months earlier, I got a feeling he wouldn't have served out the rest of his time. He would have just left."

"No. He wouldn't."

"If you say so. Look . . . I'm just worried, okay? You know how it can get. All this shit, it gets damn heavy after a while, and I'd hate to think it got to Quinn."

"It got to all of us, Jeb. No way it couldn't."

The traffic was lighter than he'd expected, and he got to the mall in near record time, but instead of climbing out and heading inside, he sat there in his Jeep, brooding. A knot of worry formed in his gut as he thought back to his last conversation with Quinn—and all the ones before that.

"You know that ain't what I'm talking about, Luke," Jeb said, his voice soft, almost gentle.

Something ugly and hot moved through him, chased closely by denial. Quinn had some bad shit in his head, but he wasn't a bad guy. He was too strong for what Jeb was insinuating. He wouldn't break.

But . . . it was an insidious whisper inside his head and one Luke hated with a passion. In that moment, he hated Jeb, too, for putting it inside Luke. "He being watched?"

"Since the day he pulled out."

"And?"

"No *and*. Hell, if I had gotten answers that way, you think I'd be here yammering with you?" Jeb broke off, swore. "Look, I just want you aware, okay?"

Then Jeb disconnected, and Luke sat in the car, staring off into the distance without seeing a damn thing. *Aware of what . . . ?*

But the ugliest thing of all was that part of him already knew that answer.

No.

Shaking his head, he muttered it aloud. Quinn wasn't the easiest guy around, kept too much hidden inside; that was nothing new.

But he was a good man. Solid. Decent. Nothing Jeb said, nothing that had happened to Quinn was going to change the core of the guy. Jeb might seem to think Quinn had reached some breaking point, but Luke knew better. He knew his twin.

Still, he needed to hear his twin's voice. Needed to talk to him.

It took three rings for Quinn to answer, and when he did, his voice was soft, drowsy. "'Sup?"

"Nothing much. Just hadn't talked to you in a while . . ."

* * *

"WHAT'S wrong?"

It seemed to Devon that Luke had to force himself to look at her. The smile on his face seemed just as forced, and when he leaned across the table and took her hand, she couldn't brush aside the feeling he wasn't really there with her.

Not completely.

"Just some things on my mind," Luke said, linking their fingers.

"Is it work?"

He shook his head. "Nah." The thick fringe of his lashes drooped low over his eyes, shielding that soft, dove gray gaze. He took a deep breath, and she watched as he tipped his head back, rolled his shoulders, kind of like a prizefighter, getting ready to step into the ring. Then, bit by bit, the weird tension inside him seemed to fade away, and when he looked back at her, the smile on his face seemed a little more real, a little more natural. "I'm putting it away. I've got better things planned for tonight than brooding."

Devon squeezed his hand. "But you make such a sexy brooder," she teased.

His lids drooped low, giving him a sleepy look that only added to his appeal. "Really?"

The waiter appeared out of nowhere and left the bill, tucked inside a simple black leather folder. Luke slid a card out of his wallet and laid it with the bill, and as the waiter appeared once more to carry it off, he looked back at Devon. There was a grin on his face again, a secretive-looking one.

"I've got something for you," he said softly.

She jolted. A ridiculous pleasure spread through her, and she felt a foolish grin curling her lips. "Really?"

In response, he reached inside the black suit coat. He looked damned nice in a suit, Devon had noticed earlier, the simple lines following the long, lean muscles of his body. Very damned nice.

Her mouth went dry as he laid a burgundy velvet box on the table between them. It was long and slender, the kind that usually held jewelry. Her heart skipped a beat. Looking from the box up to his face, she reached out and took it. Her fingers shook a little as she picked it up, shook even more as she flipped it open.

Candlelight gleamed off the soft, creamy white pearls as she lifted the strand and stared at it.

"I know you don't wear much jewelry," Luke said softly. "But I wanted to give this to you anyway."

She rapidly blinked back tears. She was not going to cry. So what if it was the first gift she'd ever gotten from a guy? It wouldn't matter if a hundred men had given her gifts, either. Because this was from Luke. Her heart clenched, and her voice shook as she said quietly, "It's beautiful."

Luke slid out of his chair and moved around the table, taking the necklace from her. Reaching back, she pulled her hair aside so he could slip the pearls around her neck. They were cool against her skin at first, warming slowly. She flushed hot as Luke bent over the chair and whispered softly in her ear, "I want to see you wearing just that when we get home."

So that was why, less than an hour later, she stood in front of the fireplace, the crackling flames warming her skin as Luke slowly stripped her naked. Her knees went weak as he eased down the zipper at her back. The dress parted, cool air kissing her flesh. When he laid his hands on the shoulders of the dress and slid it off, Devon shivered.

As the dress drifted down to her feet, so did Luke, slowly kneeling in front of her and pressing his lips to her belly. Luke slid his hands around her back, unhooking her bra and tossing it to the floor. "I love the way you feel," he whispered. Nuzzling the skin of her belly, he added, "The way you smell. The way you taste."

Settling back on his heels, he stared up at her, laid his hands on her hips, hooking his thumbs in the low-slung waistband of her panties. "I really love the way you look wearing nothing but those pearls." He stripped her panties away and tossed them off to the side.

Devon blushed hotly. The look in his eyes was one of sheer want, sheer adoration. Having all that hot male scrutiny focused on her made her self-conscious. She started to lift her arm, having half a mind to cover herself, but then she forced her hands back down, made herself meet his eyes. "I'm too skinny, too short," she said.

Shaking his head, Luke leaned in, pressed a kiss to the soft skin between her breasts. "You're perfect. Delicate."

Snorting, she glanced down at her pale, slender body. Her breasts were too small, her hips as narrow as a boy's. "Delicate, yeah. I guess that describes me well enough."

He reached up, caught her breasts, plumped them in his hands. "Delicate . . . soft, sweet . . ." He breathed the last word against her flesh as he took one swollen nipple into his mouth. "I like delicate, Devon."

Skimming his calloused hands down her sides, he tugged her down until she straddled him. He stared at her through heavy-lidded eyes, rocking against her. "This is what you do to me, Devon. I look at you, and I hurt."

Arching back, she rubbed against him. His black trousers were too thick, too much a barrier. She could feel his heat, feel his hunger, but it wasn't enough. "I'm hurting, too. Stop teasing and make love to me," she demanded, and then she wrapped her arms around his neck and pulled him close, slanting her mouth across his.

Luke laughed against her lips. "Greedy and demanding, too. I love a demanding woman," he teased. Wrapping his arms around her waist, he rolled forward, pressing her back against the smooth stone floor, already warmed from the blazing fire. "The first time I saw this fireplace, I thought about doing this, making love to you here, seeing you in the firelight." Shoving up, he knelt between her thighs and said, "Only thing missing is a bearskin rug."

A startled giggle escaped her lips. "Bearskin rug? I'm hardly bearskin-rug-sex-fantasy material, Luke."

"Hmmm. Speak for yourself," he muttered, shifting down so he could sprawl between her legs. "I've had all sorts of sex fantasies about you, so I can guarantee the material is just fine." Dipping his head, he kissed her between her thighs and added hoarsely, "Damn fine."

Devon moaned as he nuzzled and licked the sensitive flesh. Fisting her hands in his hair, Devon rocked up to meet him. He pushed and teased, licked and nuzzled, until she was keening out his name and begging. When she hovered on the edge, he pulled away and stood up. Staring down at her, he started to undress. Slow, methodical movements, and all the while, his gaze bored into hers.

When he was naked, he came to her, kneeling between her thighs, sliding the flats of his hands up over her thighs, her hips, curving over her waist. "I need you," he whispered. "I need you so much it hurts."

His voice was hoarse, rough with emotion. It sent shivers down her spine and closed a fist around her heart. Lifting her arms, she waited wordlessly. Words were useless at that point; they couldn't describe her own painful need for him or the way he managed to soothe her and excite her at the same time. Words couldn't describe the way he eased the ache in her soul even as he created a whole different kind of ache.

And words couldn't describe the pleasure as he pushed inside, slowly, teasingly. Hooking his arms under hers, he cradled her head in his hands and angled her face up to meet his, their gazes locked.

Slowly, with an almost lazy grace, he made love to her. His lips brushed over her brow, along one cheekbone, down the curve of her neck, each gentle caress lasting only a few seconds before he'd lift his head so he could see her eyes once more, almost as if he couldn't stand not being able to see her as their bodies moved against each other. With the firelight flickering over them, turning their skin gold, their gazes remained locked.

As the climax started to break over her, Devon cried out, her lashes fluttering closed, and Luke slid a hand up, curved it over her neck, and angled her face toward his. "Look at me, Devon. Don't close your eyes."

Forcing her heavy lids to lift, she stared up at Luke, let him watch her as she came—and she watched him, watched as his face contorted in a sexy grimace, watched as he planted his hands on the ground by her head, arching into her and rasping out her name.

Even when it ended, and he rolled them onto their sides, they continued to gaze at each other's faces.

* * *

"Damn it, I don't know how I can still be hungry, but I am," Luke muttered, sliding the bag in Devon's lap a dirty look. Her mother had stuffed the two of them so full, Luke thought he just might pop. But the delicious smells coming from the bag of leftovers had his mouth watering. "She put any of the pumpkin pie in there?"

A smile on her lips, Devon said, "What little was left after you ate half the thing at dinner."

Luke grinned. "Hey, it was good."

"Mom's a good cook."

From the corner of his eye, he saw her rest her head back against the headrest. "Yeah, I noticed. They seem like pretty decent folks."

"They aren't decent. They're the best," Devon said softly, closing her eyes. She fell silent for a moment and then rolled her head on the headrest to look at him when he came to a stop at a red light. "They adopted me a few months before I turned fourteen."

He glanced at her.

She smiled. "Go ahead and ask, Luke."

"Ask what?"

"Whatever in the world it is that you want to ask," she answered. "Don't tell me there's nothing you're curious about."

The light turned green. As he pressed on the gas, he reached over and stroked her forearm. Through the thin silk of her shirt, he could just barely feel the faint, faded scars. "What led up to these? What happened to your real parents?"

"They are my real parents . . . just not my only ones," Devon said, her voice soft, a little sad. "I don't remember my birth parents much. They were killed when I was little. My mom's sister was appointed my guardian."

Devon's gut knotted as she tried to find a way to explain Cyndi. "She was okay. At first. My dad was an insurance salesman, pretty practical minded. Did well for himself and Mom, I think." A faint smile curled her lips. "I don't remember them much. Disney World, seeing Mickey Mouse. The beach. Happy times, but there aren't many memories." Swallowing the knot in her throat, she continued, "Mom and Dad had set aside a decent amount of money that was supposed to help provide for me. Food, clothes, all those little expenses that come with raising a child. But Aunt Cyndi liked the money. A lot. She went through it like mad, and by the time I was nine, it was all gone, everything except a trust fund set aside for when I turned eighteen. And I bet she tried to get at it anyway. She met this guy, Boyd Chancellor. He was loaded. He was also a sick son of a bitch. Started molesting me a few months after they got married. When I turned eleven, he raped me. It kept up for a few months. I was getting in trouble at school, stealing, started doing drugs."

Squeezing the words out took effort. She didn't want to do this. Didn't want to go there. But she felt compelled to explain. Devon wasn't really sure why. "I got caught stealing at school, tried to take money from a teacher's purse. School pressed charges. I ended up in family court. Cyndi and Boyd offered to pay for the damages . . ." Devon's voice trailed off, and she snorted. "Probably because they didn't want anybody poking around. The judge in family court wouldn't go for it. I'd already been in trouble for stealing, for drugs. I think the judge decided I needed to get my act cleaned up. I had to do community service, I was put on probation, and I had to start seeing a therapist."

From the corner of her eye, she saw Luke's face. He had a stony, cold look to his features, and she jerked her gaze aside, staring out the window. Looking at him right now made it worse, made it harder. "The therapist figured out what was going on. I hadn't told anybody. Boyd told me nobody would believe me if I told the truth, and he'd been hurting me for so long, I believed him. But the therapist . . . her name was Rebecca."

The words were coming faster now. Harder. Spilling out of her almost like vomit, and holding them back would have choked her. "He'd raped me the night before. I hurt so much, and all I wanted to do was disappear. Just disappear forever. Rebecca saw it somehow. He hadn't left a mark on me—Boyd was too smart to leave marks where people could see them—but it showed anyway. I guess Rebecca had worked with so many kids, she couldn't not see it." With a shaky hand, she reached up and wiped away the tears from her cheeks, staring down as they sped down I-75.

"I can still remember the look on her face when she sat down beside me and told me I could trust her. Told me she wanted to hear what I had to say—that I mattered. She had the nicest eyes." Swallowing the lump in her throat, Devon whispered, "I believed her. I didn't want to. I didn't like adults. But I liked her, and that made telling her even harder, because if I told her and she didn't believe me, it would hurt even more. But she believed me."

The Jeep slowed, and she blinked, a little startled as Luke took the exit for her house. Already there—it seemed as though they'd just left her parents' house. Yet it also seemed as though she'd been talking forever. "She believed me," Devon repeated. "Took me to the emergency room and convinced me I had to let them do the exam. I didn't want anybody touching me. But she sat with me the whole time, held my hand. Boyd was arrested. I was so naive, thought everything would get better. But the day the jury found him guilty, Cyndi threw me out of the house. I ended up living wherever I could for a while, went back to stealing whatever I could find. After I'd been arrested for stealing at school, I tried to stop the drugs—didn't want to end up in juvie. But after Cyndi threw me out, I just stopped caring. I was almost twelve by then, and I already felt dead inside. I don't remember half of what happened back then. Stayed in homeless shelters, flopped wherever I could. Lived like that for close to a year. I was living in some abandoned dump—I'd been there about two months when somebody reported me."

The car slowed, pulled into the driveway, and stopped, but

Devon didn't climb out. She was almost done. Getting this out now was paramount; nothing else mattered. "That was when Eden found me."

For the first time since she'd started talking about it, Luke spoke. "Eden—the lady who calls you every week."

"Yeah." She glanced at him and gave him a weak smile. "My guardian angel. She hates it when I call her that, embarrasses the hell out of her. But she is. She took me to the hospital, and I had to be admitted. I was malnourished; you've seen the scars on my arms. I'd been using dirty needles, and the tracks got infected. It's a miracle I didn't end up with hepatitis or HIV. Between the infection, me being so malnourished, and my addiction, I had to spend a week in the hospital. I left the hospital, thinking Eden was going to take me back to Cyndi's, and I was ready to run away again as soon as I had the chance. But she took me to the Mannings. And I was still telling myself I'd run, just as soon as they weren't watching me so close. But I fell in love with them. They loved me. I'd forgotten what it was like to have people love me, and they loved me almost from the first. After the first month or two, I stopped thinking about running away. Then I started thinking of the place as home. A little before I turned fourteen, they asked me if they could adopt me. It was the happiest day of my life."

Blowing out a breath, she slid him a deprecating glance and said, "I bet you weren't expecting all of that, huh?" Releasing the seat belt, she opened the door, but before she could climb out, Luke grabbed her. She yelped, startled, as he hauled her across the center console and into his lap. He buried his face in her hair and held her.

He was shaking, she realized. The bag of food was still in her lap. She half tossed it, half shoved it into the passenger seat and then shifted around until she could wrap her arms around his neck.

"Damn it, Devon."

Lifting his head, he stared at her. His eyes were as hot as molten steel—and damp. Like he had to hold back tears—over her. Not too many people in her life had ever loved her enough to hurt for her. "Not the prettiest life story, huh?"

"I want to kill him. I'm going to find him, and I'm going to kill him."

"You can't."

"Wanna bet?" he said, his voice icy and harsh. "I can, and I will, and I'm going to enjoy it."

"He's already dead, Luke. He was killed before he'd even served three months of his sentence. He was sentenced to three years, probably would have gotten out in eighteen months." Snuggling up against his chest, she rested her cheek just above his heart and traced the small American flag he wore on one lapel. "I didn't know anything about it until a few years after it happened. I had nightmares, bad ones, for the longest time, and after one really bad one, Mom and Dad sat me down and told me. They said he couldn't ever hurt me again, or anybody else."

"I hope he suffered." Luke slid a hand into her hair and tugged lightly until she arched her face up to look at him. "Okay. So I can't kill him. Can I go kill your aunt?"

Devon laughed. "No. Because she doesn't matter enough."

"She let him hurt you."

"Yes. She did." Wriggling around, she shifted until she could face him. She ended up crouching on his thighs, the steering wheel digging into her back. "But she doesn't matter enough to me for me to want you getting in trouble."

A mean smile curled his lips. "I can absolutely guarantee you nobody could ever prove I did a damn thing."

Laughing, she leaned in and kissed him. "I'm tempted. But, no. I don't want that between us. Her selfishness has left enough marks on people, Luke. I don't want it affecting my life anymore."

Pressing his brow to hers, he said, "I have to do something, Devon. I fix things. That's what I do, and I don't know how to fix this. I don't know how to make this better for you."

Her heart flipped in her chest. "Oh, Luke. You don't get just how much better you've made everything for me—just by being you." Dipping her head, she pressed her lips to his.

He slid a hand up her back, curved it over her neck, and when she would have pulled back, he held her close. But he didn't deepen the kiss. He just brushed his lips back and forth over her mouth and then slid them up her cheek. "I want to kill anybody who ever hurt you, Devon. I can't stand the thought of it."

The intensity came off of him in waves, hot and thick and powerful. Shivering a little, she pulled back and stared at him in the dim car. "I don't need that, Luke. I don't want that." Then she leaned and pressed her lips to his ear. "You want to make this better for me, then take me inside and make love to me. Hold me all night and keep the nightmares away."

It wasn't enough, Luke thought, as she straightened up and watched him. The faint moonlight shining in through the windows fell across her face, and he could see the need in her eyes, and although his body was already responding, inside, he knew it wasn't enough. Not for him. Although he'd left the military behind, although the wars waged within the world were over for him, he was still a warrior. A fighter. He knew how to find his enemy and destroy him; it was what he did.

But how did he fight this?

He couldn't fight the memories darkening her mind, the memories that still managed to cause her grief and give her nightmares. He'd seen her caught in the grip of them, and he knew they were ugly and vile, but he hadn't expected this.

How could he fight it?

"Take me inside, Luke," Devon whispered again. "Make love to me."

It wasn't possible to get out of the car with her in his lap the way she was, but the moments it took for him to get out of the car and then lift her back into his arms were sheer hell. Not touching her was sheer hell. Not having her in his arms where he knew she was safe, where nobody could ever hurt her, was torture. She wiggled in his arms and gave him a self-conscious smile. "I can walk," she said weakly.

"And I can carry you. I want to."

A faint smile curled her lips. "Put like that, seems kind of silly to argue." Devon slid an arm around his shoulders and snuggled in, rubbing her cheek against his chest like a little cat.

A shy, sweet little cat who had been kicked far too often. *Nobody will ever hurt you again,* he promised silently. He wouldn't let them.

He kicked the car door shut and headed to the front door. Devon smiled up at him, a slow, whimsical curve of her lips. "How are you going to open the door, Luke? Going to be hard to do that without putting me down."

Fighting to push aside the grim fury, he forced himself to smile at her. "I'll manage." Reaching the front porch, he shifted her weight around and then, as Devon squealed, he draped her over his left shoulder in a fireman's hold, one arm over the backs of her thighs to hold her in place. As he unlocked the front door, he slid a hand up one sleek thigh, under the short, flirty skirt of her black velvet dress, cupping it over her rounded ass. "If this skirt was much shorter, we could get arrested for this," he said.

"You're the one carrying me around with my butt up in the air. They can arrest you," she said, her voice muffled against his back.

Opening the door, he toyed with the lacy edge of her panties. "You're wearing a thong, Devon . . . Damn, I spent the whole damn day not knowing you've been wearing a thong?"

"Yeah, well, it's not like you've had a lot of chances to stick your hand up my skirt today," she said. His body went stiff, and he moved so quickly, the world started to spin as he abruptly put her on her feet. Devon wobbled a little and fell against him, reaching out to grab his arm, only to stumble into the hard, ridged line of his back.

"Be quiet," he said, his voice flat, hard. Commanding.

Peering around his arm and up at his face, she stared at him. The skin on the back of her neck started to crawl as she saw the look on his flat, stony features. "Luke?"

"Shhh." Without looking at her, he reached up, laid a finger across her lips. Then he took a deep breath, dragging it in through flared nostrils.

Instinctively, Devon did the same thing, and that was when she smelled it. Her belly rebelled. It was faint, whatever it was, cloying and noxious and foul.

Devon knew that stink. She hadn't been around too much death, although she'd seen more than her share of violence. But death was the sort of thing that only required a brief meeting, and then you never forgot. The stench filled her nostrils, and she reached up, covered her mouth and nose with her hand.

"Go back outside, Devon. Lock yourself in the car and call the police," Luke said, pushing his keys into her hand.

"Oh, hell, no," Devon said, shaking her head adamantly. She took the keys, though, shifting them in her palm so one of the keys protruded out between her first and second knuckle.

"Devon, go outside," Luke insisted.

"No."

He shot her a narrow look, his gaze dropping to her hand. When he saw the makeshift weapon, a slow, faint smile curled his lips. He heaved out a harsh breath and then swore, shifting so he stood in front of her. "You stay behind me. Get your phone; call nine-one-one. Tell them somebody broke in."

How he could know that, Devon didn't know. Her eyes darted back and forth across the anteroom, trying to see whatever he'd seen, but it was too dark. Her own house seemed unfamiliar, terrifying, as she followed him out of the anteroom.

With a shaking hand, she dug her phone out of her purse and punched in 9-1-1. As the operator's voice came over the line, she crashed into Luke's back. He'd stopped in the arched entryway, reached out to flick on the light switch, but no light came on.

"Nine-one-one, what's your emergency?"

"I think somebody's broken into my house," Devon said. Luke started forward again, still moving through the darkened house with a confidence Devon wished she had. The smell was getting stronger. She started to gag and had to force back the bile as they neared the kitchen.

The emergency dispatcher had an annoying nasal voice that buzzed in Devon's ears like an angry fly. Responding to the questions distracted her momentarily as Luke tried another light switch.

This one came on.

Luke swore and spun around, caught her arms. Blinking at the bright light, she squinted up at Luke. "Go to the porch, Devon," he ordered.

But instead, she glanced around his big body.

The phone fell from numb fingers. A scream rose in her throat. Clapping a hand over her mouth, she stumbled backward and spun away, wishing she had done exactly what Luke had said.

Some images scarred the mind: the sight of a mother using the metal buckle of a belt to beat her child, the sight of a child so starved and skinny she could see the outline of bone, the battered face of a girl who was beaten by her boyfriend when she realized she was pregnant—and the bloody mess that lay on the long, gleaming white surface of the island in her kitchen. That sight was going to leave an ugly, nasty scar, and she suspected it was going to be one of the deeper ones.

It didn't make sense in her mind at first. Moaning, she stumbled into the wall and closed her eyes, tried to block out the memory, but her mind kept working away at the puzzle of what she'd just seen. Stupid human mind—sometimes it was better to just not understand.

But the mind couldn't grasp that, and it just kept working away until it made sense of what she'd seen. A dead dog, its golden pelt stained black with old blood. Its face had been turned toward her, soft dark eyes blank with that death stare.

It had been gutted—the only way to explain what had happened—gutted so its internal organs spilled out onto the island's white tiled surface.

"Oh, God . . ." Devon closed her eyes and sank down to the floor, drawing her knees to her chest and burying her face against her legs. "Oh, God . . ."

NINE

"You need to get some sleep."

Devon glanced back at Luke as he closed the patio door behind him. The house was finally quiet. She'd been in a numb haze as the police arrived and started doing their thing. It seemed to take days, but in reality, she knew it was only a few hours.

Too many hours. Although the sky was still dark, she knew morning couldn't be too far away. "I can't sleep."

A warm weight settled over her shoulders, and she looked up at Luke, curling her fingers into the blanket and wrapping it tightly around her frozen body. "Thank you."

"They'll have an official report in a few days," Luke said, wrapping both arms around her and tucking her in closer to his warm body. "The detectives are probably going to have to talk to you again."

"Hmmm. Yeah, I don't think I was a whole lot of help just now." A bitter, ugly smile curled her lips. "I haven't had too many dead dogs break into my house."

"Don't think about it right now," he murmured against her ear.

"Can't help it." She swallowed the bitter taste of fear and anger, tried not to puke. She'd been fighting the need to vomit ever since seeing that poor, dead animal in the middle of her kitchen, and thinking about it wasn't helping her in that fight.

But she couldn't stop thinking about it. "They have any idea what happened?"

"Devon . . ."

Sending him a narrow glance, she said, "I don't need coddling right now. I need to know why in the hell I found a dead animal in my house." A sliver of unease wormed through her belly. "A dead animal. Another one—Luke, that skunk. What if . . ."

She saw he'd already made the connection. A grim look darkened his face. "There's no way of knowing now," he said, restlessly moving his big shoulders, and then he started to pace back and forth, his feet moving soundlessly over the patio. Luke blew out a harsh breath and said, "The dog wasn't killed here. Not enough blood. And the police can't find how the guy got into your house—no busted locks, no broken windows. Nothing."

He shrugged his shoulders again, like he couldn't stand being completely still. "I told them your parents had a key to your place and Danielle across the street. And me."

"Danielle's on a cruise," Devon said, her voice quiet.

"You know where she keeps the spare key?"

Devon nodded. "Yeah, it's in the junk drawer in her kitchen." Absently, she reached up, brushed her fingers over the pearl necklace she wore. Wryly, she added, "Along with keys from every house she's ever lived in. Dani is sort of a pack rat."

"You got a key to her house?"

Devon nodded. "Yeah. We swapped keys so we could get each other's mail and stuff on vacations—and because Dani's a bit scatterbrained, loses her keys all the time."

"Maybe we should check and see if she still has it."

"Okay." Feeling a little scattered herself, Devon started toward the door, only to stop and stare down at herself. She still wore the black velvet dress she'd worn to her parents for Thanksgiving. She'd swapped out the heels for a pair of bunny slippers, complete with floppy ears and bright button eyes, so at least her feet weren't killing her. But she was freezing. So cold she hurt with it. "Maybe I should change."

Luke slid a hand around her arm and murmured, "Maybe you should lie down and rest. We can look for the key later."

"No. I don't want to sleep right now. I couldn't anyway." She shivered, mentally shying away from the idea of it. Every time she closed her eyes, she saw that poor dog, and her belly revolted. There was no way she could sleep just yet.

"Okay. Let's go upstairs."

For some reason, the soothing, gentle timbre of his voice rubbed her raw. She almost lashed out at him, and at the very last second, she managed to bite back the sarcasm burning in her throat. Instead, she tugged her arm away from him and forced a smile. "Luke, I'm okay. I'm not going to break." *I don't think.* "I can manage to go upstairs and change without help."

He stood there, big hands opening and closing into fists, and the impotent anger rolled off of him in waves. "Devon—"

She took one step, closed the distance between them. Laying her finger across his lips, she said, "Luke, give me a few minutes, okay?" She tried for a real smile. "I could use some coffee, though. Would you mind . . . ?"

Coffee, Luke thought, disgusted. He watched Devon walk off, the blanket wrapped around her thin shoulders, her head slumped.

Somebody had gone out of their way to terrify Devon, and he was making her coffee. A nagging sense of guilt ate inside him, spreading like a cancer, and it was getting worse as the night wore on.

It had been nearly six weeks since he and Devon had started sleeping together. That first night, he could recall the whole thing with almost crystalline clarity: all of it, including the weird sensation he'd had of being watched. Six weeks, and that was the only time it had happened.

Luke hadn't said anything to Devon, not wanting to scare her or upset her, but now he wished he would have. Still unwilling to write it off as his own imagination or some weird sense of paranoia, he'd kept his eyes open, checked out things around her house. There was no sign somebody had been watching her and no more repeats of that one strange incident. Although he didn't want to think he was imagining things, after six weeks of nothing else happening, he'd started to write it off as some internal reservations of his own.

Considering the complicated mess between him and Devon, maybe his psyche was conjuring some imagined enemy as a way for him to deal with the intensity of his emotions. Sounded like bullshit to him. He was crazy about Devon, and if he weren't worried about scaring her off, he would have already made sure she knew just how serious he was about her.

But it also didn't make sense that somebody would have been watching Devon, just that one night, the one night she was with him—and then disappear.

But now his mind was working overtime. Brooding, he stalked into the kitchen and got the coffee going. Devon drank too much of it, and she liked it hot, strong, and sweet. Luke normally didn't drink coffee outside of work, but he went ahead and fixed enough for him as well, more to have something to do with his hands than anything else.

Devon had already made the connection to the skunk. He wasn't surprised. She was sharp, and despite being shaky, she was also entirely too rational and logical. She'd made the logical conclusion. Right now, Luke was counting on that logical, rational mind to help him figure this mess out.

A dead skunk. A mutilated animal. There was an escalation of violence there that didn't go with any pattern he could think of.

There had to be more, something he'd missed. Something he didn't know about.

The coffeepot started to steam and hiss. Watching as the dark liquid dropped into the glass carafe, he leaned back against the opposite counter. When he heard Devon's feet on the steps, he shoved away from the counter, crossed the kitchen—it seemed empty without the wheeled island in the middle of the room.

"Smells good," Devon murmured, padding over to him in stocking feet. She'd pulled on a long, bulky sweater over a skinny-legged pair of jeans. Thick gray socks covered her feet. He poured her a cup of coffee and added two heaping spoonfuls of sugar.

He drank his own black and watched Devon from under his lashes. She was pale, but that empty, disconnected look was gone from her eyes. She looked pissed off, he decided. Oddly, that, more than anything else, eased some of the tension in his gut.

He'd take pissed off over scared any day. Pissed off didn't give her that wounded look that made him so sick with fury, he couldn't even think.

"Who in the hell would do something like that, Luke?" she asked abruptly, setting her coffee down and shoving away from the counter to pace. Her feet were soundless on the floor, and she moved around with a restless energy Luke understood all to well.

Better to move than stand still. Gave some small relief to the fury inside. Yeah, he understood restless, edgy energy, although he had learned to channel his. Took a little more effort this time around, though—or actually, a lot more effort.

"I don't know." Setting his mug down, he moved to intersect her as she started back across the kitchen floor. Reaching out, he laid his hands on her upper arms and stroked up and down. She felt so frail under his hands, he thought. But her body all but vibrated with rage. "We need to try to figure that out. Anybody you can think of who would want to scare you like this?"

Her lips curled in a sneer. "There are plenty of people who'd like to scare me, Luke." Then she scowled and added, "But I don't know if any of them would want it bad enough to kill some helpless animal over it."

"Two."

Sliding him a glance, she paused, then nodded, slowly. "Two. So you don't think it's impossible whoever did this killed the skunk, too, right?"

Luke wished he had a concrete answer for her. "Definitely possible, I'd say. Likely?" He shrugged. "I honestly don't know. Has there been anything weird going on?"

She sent him a droll look. "Besides the fact I've got a man practically living with me?" Devon shook her head. "No. Nothing I can think of. Same old cases at work, a few hard-assed teenagers, but none of them strike me as this brutal."

Brutal. Yeah. That pretty much described it. "Come on. Let's go check on that key."

"And if it's missing?" Devon asked, her voice soft, hesitant. "What then?"

Luke was actually more concerned about what it could mean if the key wasn't missing. Somehow, somebody had gotten in and out of her house, leaving no signs. That, even more than the brutality of the dead animal, bothered him—downright scared the hell out of him.

But he didn't let it show. Stroking a hand down Devon's tumbled hair, he responded, "Then we do the same thing we're going to do even if it's not missing. We're changing the locks. I'm going to take a look at your security system and probably going to beef it up a little." *A lot.*

He slid her a sidelong glance and asked, "How do you feel about getting a dog?"

"A dog?" she repeated, her brows going up.

* * *

THE key was still in the drawer.

Devon blew out a sigh of relief and turned to look at Luke. He was studying the kitchen with a weird look on his face.

"When did Danielle leave for her cruise?"

"Last Friday. Flew down to Florida and spent the night." Cocking her head, she peered at his face and asked, "Why?"

Luke shrugged. "No reason," he said.

There was nothing in his tone to indicate otherwise, and nothing in his expression, but he wasn't telling her the truth. Folding her arms over her chest, she said succinctly, "Bullshit."

Gray eyes narrowed on her face. Stomping over to him, Devon pushed up on her toes and shoved her face into his. "Don't lie to me, Luke. I hate lies."

A faint smile curled his lips. "I'm not lying—not exactly." He dipped his head and pressed his lips to hers, fast and soft, and then he stepped away, circled around the kitchen. His head tipped back, and he took in a slow, deep breath, dragging the air in through his nose, holding it, and then releasing it in a slow, controlled manner. "She's been gone a week since Friday, so the house has been empty about a week, right? I haven't seen anybody staying here."

Devon shrugged. "There isn't anybody. I've come over a couple of times to bring her mail in."

His eyes shot to hers, cutting through her like a laser. "When?" he demanded, his voice hard and flat.

"A couple of times. Sunday, to leave her paper. You were already at work. Monday, Tuesday—again, you were at work. I forgot to check on Wednesday. That's the whole reason I have a key to her place, Luke," she snapped, tossing her head back and planting her hands on her hips. "You know, I'm really getting—oomph. Hey!" He grabbed her by the hips and hauled her up, planting her butt on the counter between the stove and the refrigerator.

"You don't come in here alone again, Devon. You got it?"

Devon stabbed her finger into his chest. "I don't like being told what to do, slick."

He caught her wrist, squeezed. "Somebody's been in her house, Devon."

Those words sucked the anger right out of her, and she squirmed around a little as confusion took its place. "Nobody's staying here, Luke. Danielle would have let me know if—"

"Danielle probably doesn't know," Luke said, his eyes grim. "Come on." He tugged her off the counter and laced their fingers. "I can smell food—something spicy, like Cajun. If Danielle's been gone since Friday, I wouldn't be able to smell that. And cigarette smoke, but I don't see any ashtrays."

Automatically, Devon took a sniff. "I don't smell anything. And Danielle doesn't smoke."

"No, but somebody who does smoke has been in here. And pretty damn recently." He led her through the house, checking each room, and making her do the same. They stopped in the bathroom, and Luke examined everything from the shower stall to the sink drain. He treated each room to the same thorough examination.

But whatever he was looking for, Devon didn't think he found it. After nearly an hour, he led her back outside, taking her keys and locking the door. "We need to tell Danielle to get her locks changed. You're getting yours changed today."

Defensively, Devon said, "I'd already figured that much out." Then she felt stupid. Luke was worried. Hell, she was worried. What normal person wouldn't be downright terrified right now?

"Look, can we go back to the house?" Devon said. She shoved her hair back from her face and laced her fingers behind her neck. "I'm tired, I'm freaked out, I can't concentrate right now."

Luke's arms came around her, and she leaned into him, sliding her arms up around his shoulders. He brushed his lips over her forehead and murmured, "It's going to be okay, Devon. I promise."

* * *

FOGGY from lack of sleep, Devon huddled on the couch, her knees drawn up to her chest and her head propped on the well-cushioned armrest.

Luke was on the phone talking to somebody from the hospital—arguing more like it. "Don't give me that shit that this doesn't qualify as an emergency," he snapped into the phone. "My girlfriend is being stalked, some nutcase broke into her house, and until I know she's safe, I am not working nights or evenings."

He was quiet for a moment and then said, "So fire me."

"Luke . . ."

He shot her a narrow look, and Devon rolled her eyes. The man would get his way anyway. He was like a bulldog when he got something in his head. "I don't give . . . Yeah, fine, put her on the phone."

Tuning out the sound of Luke's voice, Devon stared into the fire, letting the undulating flames soothe her, lull her into a state of semiawareness. Focusing very hard on not thinking about anything, she jumped when Luke knelt down in front of her and touched a hand to her thigh. Forcing a wan smile, she asked, "Do you still have a job?"

He shrugged. "Yeah. Talked to Lynette Ransom. She'll cover my shift today and find somebody to cover tomorrow. I'm off Monday anyway, and hopefully by Tuesday, we can work something out."

"Luke, you do not need to rearrange your life over this."

His mouth compressed into a thin line, he said, "If you think for one damn minute I'm not going to rearrange heaven and earth to protect you, then we got a problem." He moved onto the couch beside her and pulled her onto his lap. With his arms looped around her waist and his chin resting on her shoulder, some of the ice inside her thawed a little. Devon relaxed back against him and finally allowed herself to think, just a little, about what in the hell she should do.

"Let me move in."

Startled, Devon straightened up and glanced back at Luke. "Move in?"

"Yeah." He lifted one shoulder in a half shrug and said, "It's not like I'm not here half the time anyway. If I'm here, with you, you'll be safer. I'll feel better."

"You going to watch me twenty-four/seven, Luke?"

"I plan on doing that anyway, even if I have to sleep in my car out in the driveway," he said. He lifted a hand, ran it through her hair, and then curved his palm over her neck, his fingers splayed wide. Using his thumb, he tipped her head back. His eyes, that smoky, sultry gray, bored into hers. "Let me move in, Devon. I'll do what I can with my shifts so I'm not working nights for a while. Don't ask me to leave you here alone at night."

His fingers tightened, and impossibly, his eyes seemed to darken. "Damn it, do you have any idea how sick it's making me, to think you were over at that house while he was staying there, watching you?"

"We don't know . . ."

"I know," Luke said. His muscles bunched with the need to do something, hit something. He needed action, something defined, decisive. Something he knew would keep her safe.

Safe—he had to battle back a bitter, ugly laugh. A fucking Ranger, and he hadn't been able to stop this. That nagging sense of guilt, compounded by his stupidity, was going to eat a hole inside his gut the size of the Great Lakes.

She reached up, laid a hand on his cheek. "Why do I get the feeling you're blaming yourself?"

"Because I am." Closing his fingers around her wrist, he brought her hand around and kissed her palm. "That first night we were together, after you fell asleep, I went outside to get my bag." Luke leaned his head back against the couch and blew out a harsh breath. "I felt somebody watching me, Devon. Watching your house."

Devon squinted at him, her nose wrinkling as she repeated, "You felt somebody watching my house."

"Yeah." Lifting his head, he said, "I'm not the paranoid type, Devon. I brushed it off, thought maybe it was too little sleep, stress, whatever, but now, I'm not so sure."

Shaking her head, Devon said, "I just don't get it. Why would somebody be watching me? Hell, why would somebody leave a dead skunk in my yard, and why would somebody . . ." Her voice broke, and she paused, took a deep breath. "Why would somebody do something like that to a dog and then leave it in here for me to find?"

"Because whoever did it is crazy. Crazy people don't need reasons. They don't need answers or logic." Luke cradled her face. "I'm sorry. I let this happen."

"Oh, bullshit." Devon smacked his hand and shoved off his lap, stalking over to the fireplace. Spinning around, she glared at him. "You didn't let anything happen. And assuming you're right about that night, that somebody was watching me—what in the hell could you have done?"

Luke exploded off the couch. "Damn it, I could have watched you better!"

"Watched me?" she repeated, her brows rising. "Watched me? Luke, I am not some eight-year-old who needs a babysitter."

She started to turn away and then abruptly spun back to him. "Wait a minute . . . is that what the past six weeks have been about, Luke? You're watching me? Trying to take care of me?"

She blinked rapidly, but not before he saw the glimmer of tears in her eyes. "Get out of here, Luke. Now."

"Like hell," he snarled, reaching out and snagging the neckline of her sweatshirt. Hauling her against him, he glared down at her. "The past six weeks have been about getting as close to you as I possibly can, in every way I can."

"Yeah, so you can make sure some nutcase isn't out there who wants to hurt me?" she demanded. "I knew you were a bit of a Boy Scout, Luke, but this is ridiculous." She shoved against his chest but didn't manage to budge him an inch, and that only pissed her off more. "Damn it, let go of me. I don't need a bodyguard. I don't need some Good Samaritan in my life."

"You think that's what this has been about?" Incredulous, Luke stared at her. She struggled to get away, but instead of letting her go, he worked an arm around her waist and hauled her rigid body off the ground. Tangling his free hand in her hair, he said, "You actually think I've been spending every free, waking moment with you because of one occurrence, more than a month ago?"

As if realizing the futility of struggling against him, Devon settled for arching back as far as she could and keeping her body stiff and rigid. "Makes plenty of sense to me."

"That's not what this is about," Luke said, his voice hollow, his heart all but bleeding inside his chest. "I told you that first night, before we made love, before anything weird happened, that you mattered to me. I told you I didn't have any intention of letting you go."

Slowly, he lowered her to the ground and took one careful step away, and then another. "Yeah, so what? I drove by your house a few times after that, just because I was a little worried. I'm crazy about you. Why wouldn't I want to keep you safe?"

"Because you're a decent guy, Luke," Devon said softly. "You've got a do-gooder streak in you a mile wide. You want to help people. Take care of them. Fix them." She shrugged her shoulders, shifted her feet.

"Take care of them," he repeated slowly, trying to keep control of his temper. It was getting damn hard, though. Very damn hard. "Honest answer, Devon . . . Is that why you think I'm here with you? Because I want to help you? You think I look at you and see some wounded soul and feel obligated to make it all better and then pat you on the head and send you off on your merry way?"

He watched her throat work as she swallowed. In a thin, reedy voice, she said, "It makes more sense to me than anything else."

"Really. Well, I hate to smash your image of me, but I'm not into pity fucks. I'm not that nice a guy. Hell, I'm really not that nice at all." Screw being cautious. Screw taking his time. Once more, he reached out, grabbed the front of her shirt, and hauled her against him. This time, when her slight weight fell against his body, he banded his arms around her, lifted her up, and crushed his lips to hers. She opened for him almost instantly, moaning into his mouth. Her arms came around his neck, her hands fisting in his hair. She moved against him, hot and hungry, but Luke wasn't going to lose his head, not just yet. Tearing his mouth away from hers, he fisted a hand in her hair, jerked her head to the side, and raked his teeth along her neck. "Make sense of this then, Devon Manning. I'm in love with you. Been that way for weeks—longer, practically from the first—and I didn't want to tell you because I didn't want to scare you off."

Lifting his head, he stared into her eyes, watching as huge, diamond-bright tears formed. "Can you make sense of that, Devon? Do you believe me, or are you going to find some way to rationalize what I say I feel?"

Stroking one palm down the long, slender line of her back, he slid a hand under her shirt. Her skin was warm, soft satin under his hand. "You think all I see when I look at you is some poor, sad woman in need of a little TLC? Is that what you think?"

She sighed, a soft, shaky little whisper of sound. "Aren't I?"

Luke shook his head. Slowly, he lowered her feet back to the ground and then brought his other hand to her waist. Cupping his palms over the slight curve, he drew her against him. Brushing her tangled curls aside, he dipped his head and nuzzled her neck. "I look at you and see a fighter, Devon. A stubborn, sexy little fighter who won't give up even when all you want to do is quit. I look at you and I see the woman I want to spend the rest of my life with—and if it takes years to make you see that, then so be it."

TEN

"STOP hovering."

Devon met Luke's gaze in the mirror's reflection, watched as he slid his hands into his pockets and rocked back on his heels. "Men don't hover, Devon."

Snorting, she gathered her hair into a loose tail at her nape and started to twist it. "Don't know where that rule is written, but trust me, pal. You're hovering." With one hand holding her hair in place, she grabbed a clip from the top of her dresser and stuck it in her hair. A few loose tendrils escaped, but she ignored them as she turned away and went to dig through her closet, looking for a pair of black boots she'd bought.

It was cold out. The mild fall weather they'd been having was gone, and probably for good, from the looks of things. Outside, there was a hard frost covering everything in a soft, hazy white.

She grabbed the boots and settled down on the bed to put them on. "What are you doing today?"

Luke shrugged. "I was thinking about packing up my clothes.

Bringing them over here." From the corner of his eye, he glanced at her and said, "Although you never really did give me an answer."

She didn't need to ask what he was talking about. Their conversation from Friday had weighed heavily on her mind throughout the entire damn weekend. *"I'm in love with you."*

She didn't see Luke as the type to say something he didn't mean. It just wasn't who he was. Her first instinct was to pull back. Devon had happily gone most of her life without letting people get close. Her adopted parents, Eden, a few select friends, but that was it. Even Luke, although she knew she was getting completely tangled up with him, she wanted to keep him at some kind of distance. Enough so that she still felt in control.

Slowly, not looking at him, she finished putting her boots on, zipping them up, and then smoothing the legs of her wine-colored pants. "This is a big step you're asking me to take, Luke," she said, forcing herself to look up at him.

He watched her with those insightful, intense eyes, arms folded across his chest. "You think I don't know that?" Luke crossed the room and hunkered down in front of her beside the bed. He laid his palms on her thighs, rubbing in slow, gentle circles. "That wasn't exactly the way I'd planned on doing this. But it's something that's been on my mind for a while. Hell, forget about whoever this shithead is, and just think about us—just you and me. Do you seriously hate the idea of me living here? Because if you do, fine—tell me. But if you don't—"

"I don't hate the idea," Devon interrupted, laying one finger against his lips. "I don't hate it at all. This is just very strange territory for me, Luke. I don't know how to handle it."

Luke's lips parted, and he gently nipped her finger. "How about one day at a time? We'll just take it as it goes."

Swallowing around the huge knot that had taken up residence in the middle of her throat, Devon forced herself to go on, to get it all out. "You said you loved me."

He reached up, laid a hand on her cheek. "I do."

Blinking away the tears, Devon said hoarsely, "I don't know if I'm ready to say that to you yet. I don't even know if I'm ready to love you."

"I'm not asking you to. At least not yet." Then he grinned, a cocky, confident grin that somehow managed to lighten the weighted atmosphere. "But you will be ready, Devon. You'll say it back sooner or later. I can wait until you're ready."

"Arrogant."

"Nah. Just confident." Hooking his hand over the back of her neck, he drew her close, pressed his lips to hers. "I know what I see in your eyes when you look at me, Devon. I see it, even if you aren't ready to."

He kissed her again, light and soft, and then he stood up. He tugged on her wrist, and Devon slid off the bed, standing in front of him. "I need to get going," she whispered.

Luke said nothing else, just followed her out of the bedroom and down the stairs. As she got her purse, he took a long leather coat from the closet. "I got your car running for you—should be warm enough by now," he murmured, helping her slide the coat on. "I'll be here when you get off."

Devon nodded, headed toward the door. Luke followed her, sliding the keys from her fingers and using the key fob to unlock the door and open it for her.

She tossed her purse inside and started to slide into the car, but then she stopped. Spinning around, she said in a rush, "If you want to move your stuff over here, go ahead." Without waiting for his response, she climbed into the car and left.

At the end of the driveway, she glanced at Luke. He was still standing in the driveway, that faint smile curling his lips.

* * *

"So how is school going, Tim?"

Devon had to force herself to focus on the boy in front of her.

She'd been working with Tim Wilder since July, and so far, she could measure her progress with him in millimeters.

As in zero millimeters. The follow-up interviews with him hadn't been much fun even under good circumstances. Nothing she'd done the past few days had been under what she'd call good circumstances.

The fourteen-year-old was creative, intelligent, and a fast learner. He also had a world of anger inside of him, as evidenced by the fact that he had been arrested on battery charges back in July. It wasn't the first time he'd been in trouble. Theft, vandalism, and truancy marred his record going back to when he was eleven years old.

But he hadn't ever shown any kind of violence, not until last summer.

It had been an older kid that he'd beaten the crap out of. After reading the arrest report and doing some investigating of her own, part of Devon understood why Tim had lashed out. The sixteen-year-old had spent a great deal of time taunting Tim, making fun of him, and Tim hadn't done much of anything in retaliation. But then, during the last week of the final session of summer school, Bryce Turner had shoved Tim in the hallway at school and sent him flying face-first into the floor.

Tim had come up swinging, and it had taken three teachers to haul him off of Bryce. Bryce was out of school for more than a week healing up, and Tim ended up in court. Since Bryce had set things off, Tim didn't have to serve any time, but the severity of the beating hadn't gone unnoticed. Tim was now under Devon's watch, and he'd stay that way for a good long while.

There were secrets in that boy's eyes, secrets and a fear that made her gut go cold, but all she had were her suspicions. The surprise visits to the Wilder household hadn't given any sign for concern, and none of Tim's teachers had ever seen any signs of abuse.

A troubled kid, she was told.

An angry kid.

A bad kid.

But it was Devon's experience that most troubled, angry kids weren't just born that way. Some were. But most of them ended up that way after years of abuse or neglect—or both.

There were a few rare occasions when she had to deal with kids who just plain and simple were bad, the kind who grew up to be blights on society. But there weren't that many.

"Tim?" she prodded after he didn't answer her question.

He shot her a look from under a fringe of matte black hair and shrugged. "Sucks. Boring."

Typical teenage response. She flipped through the folder in front of her. Most of it held the typical teenage schoolwork. Tests passed with a grade either right at average or just enough above failing to pass. Pop quizzes, the same.

But there was one class where he excelled. She skimmed the essay he'd turned in for a grade in his creative writing class. "You're a good writer," she murmured, more to herself than anything.

"Whatever."

Grinning, she continued to read the short story. "You know, this is proof. You can put together more than one or two words at a time." The story was disturbing, as full of anger as Tim himself was, but it wasn't directed at the world in general. It was all self-directed. Equally disturbing, but for different reasons. "This is a pretty dark story," she said, flicking him another glance. "Who is it about?"

"Nobody. Just made-up crap. Called fiction, ya know?" He smirked as he said it, keeping his chin tucked low so he wasn't facing her.

But Devon saw the look he slid her. It was quick. There, then gone. "Why do you think he hates himself so much?" she asked.

He'd written up a ten-page story about a twelve-year-old boy, the boy's anger, the boy's helplessness, his fear. There were hints of some unknown enemy, somebody who hated the boy, but nothing more than that. "Because he's a loser," Tim said, curling his lip.

"You know, usually when somebody gets called a loser, it's because others just want to make themselves feel better about who they are." She finished the story and tucked it back inside the folder, out of sight. It was very disturbing, very raw—and it rang of an ugly truth. *Come on, Tim. Help me out . . .* That story, if he would just give her something, it might be enough.

"Who says he's a loser, Tim? Who is it that makes him hate himself?"

"He is a loser," Tim muttered, his voice harsh. "Weak, pathetic loser. He oughta hate himself."

Devon shrugged, lifted her shoulder. "Doesn't seem weak to me. Reading it made me think that the boy had some bad stuff happen to him, lived a hard life. But he hasn't given up. That takes strength, Tim. Weak people break."

Slowly, his eyes lifted, and he stared at her. There was a bleakness in those pale brown eyes that cut right through her. "You haven't broken, have you, Tim?"

She watched as his eyes slid away from hers, but he wasn't evading her gaze this time. Keeping her face neutral, she relied on her peripheral vision, watched as he glanced through the glass window of the conference room to the waiting area outside.

Tim's dad. An ugly knot settled in her chest. She felt the weight of Curtis Wilder's gaze cut her way, but she didn't once look at him, didn't ever look away from Tim, didn't let the neutral mask slip away for even a second. "The boy wants help, doesn't he, Tim?"

He slumped farther down in his chair. If he could have disappeared into the floor at will, Devon knew he would have. Sighing, she settled back. *God, let me get through to him . . .* But even as that thought made its way through her mind, she heard a faint whisper. Hardly loud enough to hear.

But she heard it; she'd been listening for that very answer for months; there was no way she'd miss it once he opened up.

"Guess so."

It wasn't much of an opening, but Devon rarely encountered open doors in her line of work. Usually they were more like windows, opened just a crack. That was all she needed.

"I'm good at helping people, Tim." Leaning forward, she willed him to look at her, to meet her gaze. He did, slowly. "Trust me. It's what I'm good at."

He sneered, but it lacked some of his typical anger. "It's what they pay you for; you oughta be good at it."

Devon laughed. "Tim, sweetie, if you had any idea what they pay me, you'd wonder why I bother. It's not because of the money; nobody does this job because of the money."

"Then why do it at all?" he asked, his voice sullen.

"Because I want to help." She licked her lips, weighed her options. "I don't usually tell people this. I was in the system, Tim. Got myself into trouble—even worse trouble than you're in. I would have done worse, too, if somebody hadn't cared enough to help. It was a social worker who cared. She helped me in ways I can't even begin to explain. All because she cared enough to try."

She watched as that crack spread open, bit by bit, widening. Tim lifted his head, looked her square in the eye. His pale eyes gleamed behind a veil of tears, and she watched, felt her throat tighten, as one tear broke free and rolled down his face. "Nobody can help, Ms. Manning."

Although all she wanted to do was cry, she forced a smile. "Tim, I didn't even realize you knew my name," she teased.

A movement from the corner of her eye caught her attention. It was Tim's father, and although his friendly, affable face had fooled the judges, had fooled Tim's teachers, Devon wasn't fooled.

She'd looked into his eyes and saw no soul. Nothing. Looking back at Tim, she leaned forward, said urgently, "Tim, listen to me. I think I understand—a lot better than you realize—what's happening to you, why you're so angry. But I can't help you unless you tell me that you need my help. You don't even have to say why . . . not right now. Just tell me, yes or no, whether you need my help."

Curtis knocked on the glass. It was a polite, friendly tap, and when she glanced up, he gave her that affable smile and pointed at his watch. Slowly, she stood. Technically, their time was up. Tim only spent thirty minutes a week with her, and it had taken the past sixteen weeks to get him to open up this much. Moving around the table, she paused by Tim. "Tim?"

The door opened, and Curtis poked his head in. "Ms. Manning, I'm sorry to interrupt, but we've really got to get going. I've got a conference call this evening that I can't miss. Come on, Tim."

But Tim just continued to sit there. Devon watched as a change went over his body. He went from a sulky, broody teenager to a scared rabbit, all in the blink of an eye. There was a soft, almost soundless whisper. Kneeling beside him, she touched his hand. "Tim?"

"Come on, Tim." Curtis's voice was harder now, and Devon looked up. "We need to get going." His eyes bored into hers, and she could feel the anger inside him, even though no sign of it showed on his face.

Dismissing him, she looked back at the boy. "Tim?"

He glanced at her. In that one brief glance, she saw a screaming, ugly hell, and that was all she needed. But he gave her more. In a low, desperate whisper, he pleaded, "Help."

* * *

THANK God for U-Haul. Luke had spent half the day packing up clothes, the other half boxing up things like dishes, movies, and books. The clothes, he'd take with him. The other stuff, until he had a better idea on where he and Devon stood, would stay here.

His lease was up in another six weeks. He had every intention of figuring out who was trying to terrorize Devon before then. Luke didn't know if he should renew his lease or not. Maybe he could sublet his place or something.

Of course, it might be wise to make sure Devon was okay with it. Might not be a bad idea to let Quinn know where to find him, though. His brother had a habit of dropping in with little or no warning. He needed to talk to him anyway. After that talk with Jeb a few days earlier, he'd been worrying about his brother, but concern for Devon had pretty much dominated his thoughts.

Right now, though, she was safe at work. Which meant he could focus on Quinn for a few minutes. He grabbed his phone with a smirk. "Like a few minutes would *ever* be enough to worry about him."

Quinn answered with his characteristic abruptness. "I was just getting ready to call you. Heading your way. Can I crash with you?"

"I probably won't be around much, but you're welcome to bunk here for a while." Luke grinned. "Where are you?"

"About twenty miles away."

Luke snorted. "Great notice, man."

"Better than just showing up on your doorstep. How come you're not going to be around?"

Luke was quiet for a minute. "I'm going to be staying with Devon. Probably moving in with her."

"For real?"

"Yeah." He closed his eyes, weariness dragging at him. He hadn't had a decent night's sleep since Wednesday. He was used to getting by on little sleep and functioned pretty damn well that way, but he did need some time to recharge, and he hadn't taken it in close to a week. "Talked to Jeb the other day."

Quinn's voice had a weird ring to it when he responded. "He doing okay?"

"Same old, same old. Said he's been trying to get in touch with you."

"Yeah. I've gotten the phone calls. If I wanted to talk to him, I'd answer when he calls."

"So why don't you want to talk to him?" And there was a reason; Luke could feel it. Quinn wasn't telling Luke something. Luke didn't know what, and he also knew that if he pushed, Quinn would just shut down more.

"No reason to. I'm done with that part of my life." His voice was brusque, and the unspoken words came through loud and clear.

Leave it alone.

But Luke wasn't ready to do that just yet. Quinn had opened the door—just a little, but it was there. "You never did tell me why you quit."

Through the phone, Luke could hear Quinn's harsh sigh. "Didn't think I'd need to, Luke. Adam died; everything went straight to hell after you left. I just don't have it in me anymore."

Luke could understand that, and if he didn't know his brother so well, he might have even believed it. But there was a weight in Quinn's voice, something hinting at a bigger story. One that included this still-unknown girl who had died during the same op where Adam was killed.

"Just one day, you go and figure that out? Hell, it took me damn near getting my leg blown off to figure that out," Luke said, trying to keep his voice light, teasing. *Light—keep it light, easy.* Dealing with Quinn was sometimes like dealing with a stray; if he pushed too hard, Quinn would shut him out completely.

Quinn was quiet for a while, almost too long, and Luke started to think he'd pushed too far. But then Quinn sighed and murmured, "Maybe that's what started it, seeing you hurt. I don't know. But I just didn't want it anymore, Luke. I'm tired of it. I didn't think it would ever happen, but it did."

"Something happened, Quinn. I know it. I wish you'd tell me." *Come on, man . . . talk to me.*

Quinn was quiet for so long that Luke didn't think he'd answer. But finally, Quinn murmured, "Yeah, something happened."

"Can you tell me?"

"Can . . . Physically, yeah, I can. Technically, I ain't supposed to. I couldn't give a flying fuck what I'm technically supposed to do—but I'm not going to tell you, Luke. Bad enough I got this shit inside my head. I'm not putting it inside yours."

For Quinn, it was a record. He probably went days on end without saying that much. The underlying throb of anger and helplessness was as clear as crystal to Luke, and he wanted to push, wanted to demand Quinn tell him what was going on.

But he didn't. Not because he didn't want to, but because he knew it would only make things worse. If he pushed, Quinn would lock him out. But if he just waited, maybe Quinn would talk when he was ready. "When you need to talk, I'm here. If it's that bad, you probably *need* to talk."

Quinn snorted. "Yeah, that's what the fucking shrink says."

Warning bells went off. Luke straightened up slowly, tension bleeding into his muscles and tightening his entire body. "Shrink?"

"Didn't Jeb tell you, big brother? I had to start seeing a fucking head doctor. They cut me loose when I told them I wanted out, but they had a couple of conditions—mostly me talking to a psychiatrist until the shrink is satisfied I'm steady."

Slowly, Luke blew out a breath. A fucking shrink. Damn it. Not good. Not good at all. He shifted to the side of the bed, his legs hanging over the side. Under his feet, the hardwood floor felt cold, but it was nothing compared to the ice coursing through his veins. "Why are you seeing a shrink, Quinn? And why in the hell didn't you tell me?"

"Tell you what?" Quinn asked softly. "Tell you that your fucked-up brother is even more fucked-up than normal?"

"You're not fucked-up," Luke snapped. Shoving off the bed, he started to pace the room. "Damn it, Quinn. I want to know what in the hell is going on."

"Nothing." Quinn's voice was flat and level, about as close to comforting as the jackass could probably manage. "I'm fine, okay? Don't go getting freaked out over any of this shit. Hell, I figured since Jeb was calling you to check up on me, he would have let that little detail slip."

"No, he didn't say jack shit about that little detail, but you sure as hell are getting ready to."

Quinn was silent. Through that strange, indefinable bond, Luke could sense his twin's anger, a deep depression, something that until now, Luke hadn't been aware of. Because Quinn had been blocking him out, he realized. When Quinn finally spoke, his voice all but vibrated with fury. "I think I might have loved her, Luke. She . . . she said she loved me, and I think I might have loved her, too, but now I'll never know."

Quinn's voice broke. A spasm of pain twisted Luke's heart—a pain that came from Quinn. "She died, Luke. She died because I fucked up."

"Quinn—"

"Save it," Quinn muttered brusquely. "I need to go."

Troubled but knowing better than to push, Luke asked, "I'm not done with this, Quinn. You and me, we're going to talk more about this when you get here."

"No. We won't."

The finality in Quinn's voice had Luke scowling. "You aren't coming, are you?"

Even without his twin being there, Luke could see Quinn's angry scowl. "No. I got better things to do than have you hovering over me."

"Quinn."

"Damn it, would you stop? I'm not a fucking kid that needs a pat on the head. I've got some shit inside me. I'll deal with it. I got enough people feeling sorry for me or worrying about me. I don't need it from you."

Luke reached up, pinched the bridge of his nose between thumb and forefinger. "What do you expect me to do, Quinn? Not care that you're going through hell?"

"I expect you to let me deal with it." He was quiet for a minute, and then he sighed. When he spoke again, his voice was softer. "Please. Just let me deal with it. I'll be okay."

"You can't expect me not to worry."

Quinn laughed. "You stop worrying about me, that will be the day they bury you—or me. Whichever comes first. I need to go. I . . . I'll call you in a few days, okay?"

"You better."

Luke lowered the phone, started to disconnect. But then he lifted the phone back to his ear, right as Quinn said, "Luke."

"I'm still here."

"That lady of yours . . . you two serious?"

"Yeah."

"You ever figure out if you're in love with her?"

"Yeah. Yeah, I am."

"Good. Good for you . . . Take care of her, Luke." There was an odd note in Quinn's voice, but before Luke could figure it out, Quinn had disconnected, and Luke stood there, listening to dead air.

Closing his fist around the phone, he squeezed; the plastic casing popped. Hurling the phone toward his bed, he leaned forward, head slumped and hands braced on his dresser. Talk about feeling torn.

If it wasn't for Devon, he'd go after Quinn and figure out what the hell was going on. But there was Devon, and the danger to her right now was physical—and possibly imminent.

Quinn could take care of himself. Didn't matter how screwed up in the head he was feeling. Quinn could handle himself.

Whatever demons haunted Quinn weren't a threat to his physical well-being.

At least not yet.

* * *

"You're not home." Luke's voice sounded a bit irritated.

She covered the mouthpiece with her hand and smiled at Tim. "I need a few minutes, okay?"

His only response was a tiny nod. Tim sat on the narrow hospital bed with his knees drawn up to his chest and his face pale. His eyes were wide-open, and he jumped at every little sound.

It had taken her half the afternoon to convince the boy he needed to come to the emergency room. The only thing that had made him follow through was the plain, ugly truth: if he didn't help them, they'd have a hard time proving his father had done a damn thing to him, and they couldn't legally keep the man from taking Tim home.

A series of X-rays had already been done, and now they were waiting for somebody from Psych to come and talk to the boy. The X-rays had told an ugly story, even uglier than Devon had expected. Easily ten different broken bones, all of them old.

"You're not going to leave, are you?" he asked, his voice reedy and thin.

With a gentle smile, Devon promised, "No, Tim. I won't leave."

"Devon."

She grimaced at Luke's hard, flat voice. Slipping outside, she closed the door and leaned back against it. "Sorry, Luke. I'm here."

"What I want to know is why you aren't here."

Glancing over her shoulder, she looked through the glass-windowed door at Tim. "Had a bit of an emergency come up. Can't be helped."

"Where are you?"

"University Hospital." Blowing out a sigh, she shoved away from the door and paced—exactly five steps away and then five steps back. The restless, caged energy in her had Devon wishing she could move farther, faster. She wanted to run. Needed to move, needed some sort of action other than waiting. The legal wheels needed to protect Tim had already been put in motion, but Tim's dad already had his own wheels spinning.

He'd retained a lawyer, and even now, one of the child advocates was in front of a judge, blocking the attempts to have Tim returned home.

"I assume this is one of those things that can't wait and that nobody else can handle for you," Luke said.

"You assume right. It's about one of my kids. He's in a bad place, and he finally gave in, asked for help."

"How long is this going to take?"

Devon pretended to think that over for a minute. In an overly bright tone, she replied, "Hours?"

Over the line, she could hear his disgusted sigh. "Damn it, Devon."

"It can't be helped, Luke."

"Then I'm coming over."

Devon rolled her eyes. "There's no reason for that, Luke."

"Bullshit."

She heard a door slam on the other end of the phone, and then another. "Since you're already in the car, I guess it's pointless to argue with you." She glanced down the hallway and saw a familiar face. "I need to go."

"You leave that hospital before I get there, I'm going to be pissed."

Devon smirked. "Gee, really?" She disconnected before he could say anything else. As she put the phone away, she looked at Dr. Max Schrader. "Please tell me that you're here for me."

He gave her a faint smile. "Unless there's another caseworker by the name of Ms. Manning here, then I'm here for you." He glanced at the chart in his hand and grimaced. "You can't ever come bearing good news and cheer, can you?"

"Sure. At the holidays. I'll drop by with some Christmas cookies."

Max grunted under his breath and flipped through the chart. Considering they'd only been in the hospital for less than two hours, there sure as hell was a thick stack of papers in it. "Looks like this boy of yours has had a number of beatings over the years. Spiral fractures—two of them, one in each arm."

The low burn of fury in her gut threatened to rage out of control, but she kept it throttled down. Years of practice. She'd scream later if she had to, but not now. She'd break later, if she had to—when she had Luke's arms wrapped around her, when he could help put her back together after she fell apart.

But those luxuries would have to wait. "I've talked with all his teachers. Nobody has reported any signs of abuse," she said softly. She glanced back through the window at Tim and sighed. He had his face turned away from the window. The anger inside the boy was usually so dominant, it made him seem bigger, older than he really was. The fear was in control right now, and all she could see was a helpless, scared kid.

She hadn't been wrong. Devon had suspected abuse with Tim almost from the first. The typical physical signs of abuse weren't there, and to be honest, she hadn't gotten that vibe from his dad, either. She hadn't really liked him, but she hadn't pegged him as an abuser, either.

At least not right away.

Because he'd learned to hide it.

Smoothing a stray lock of hair back from her face, she looked back at Max. "I need some concrete information from him, something we can use in court. His dad already has an attorney trying to get us to return the boy."

Max slid her a glance. "I'll do what I can."

Giving him a wry smile, she said, "Take your time. I'm not going anywhere." There was no possible way for things to get wrapped up here before Luke showed up. But even if that impossible miracle happened, and Devon tried to leave without Luke, he'd strangle her.

Considering the time of day, the time of year, traffic in Lexington was going to be slow-moving, and Luke wouldn't make it to the hospital in less than forty-five minutes. More like an hour.

So with time to kill, Devon snagged a chair in the small family lounge just a little down from the exam room. If she was lucky, Tim would bare his soul to Max, and soon. If she wasn't lucky, she was going to be around for a good long while.

* * *

IT ended up being somewhere in between *soon* and *a good long while.* The next morning, she was bleary-eyed as she skimmed the e-mail the child advocate had sent her. Exhausted, but satisfied.

It had been nearly ten before Max got the information he needed, but it had been worth it. Devon had spent the time contacting some of the couples she worked with who would take kids on short notice. Only one family had been able to take the troubled teen, but Devon knew he was going into good hands—a local minister who was used to dealing with abused kids and his wife. The Grants had met Devon at the door with smiles, even though it had been nearing midnight before Devon got Tim to their house—and after midnight before she convinced him that he was safe, and no, he couldn't come home with her.

All worth it, every last sleepless minute. Even with Luke shadowing her every movement. Devon couldn't decide whether to be frustrated or not. Luke had followed her to the Grants' home, he'd followed her home, and it wouldn't have surprised her if he'd decided to follow her to work that morning.

"You look strangely satisfied and totally exhausted."

Devon smiled as Noelle propped a hip on the edge of her cluttered desk. "I'm very satisfied, and I'm very exhausted."

Noelle craned her head around and glanced at the e-mail still visible on Devon's screen. "Tim Wilder." Her brow creased and then smoothed as she managed to assign a name to a face. "One of our budding repeat offenders." She finished skimming the e-mail, and then she sighed. "Damn. Looks like there's a serious history of abuse there—but we've never had any contact with the family until recently?"

Shaking her head, Devon replied, "Nope. But I have a feeling somebody has had contact."

"Speaking of contact . . ." Noelle looked down, studied her nails. They were painted a smooth, glossy pink that matched Noelle's silk shirt and her lips. "I heard you had some unusual contact of your own this weekend."

Tongue in cheek, Devon murmured, "My, you are subtle, aren't you, Noelle?"

When it came to the kids, Noelle was made of pure steel; she never let her nerves show, her anger, or her worry. But outside of the job, when Noelle was nervous, she fussed. She buffed her nails, she smoothed her clothing, she plucked away invisible lint. Right now she was studying her cuticles with single-minded focus. When she spoke, she didn't once look up at Devon. "Cliff and me had a date this weekend. He mentioned he heard your name come up at work. Mutilated pets, Devon . . . that's pretty sick."

Shrugging restlessly, Devon said, "Yeah, I know." She glanced at the opening of her cubicle and then back at Noelle. "You haven't mentioned this to Dawson, have you?"

Noelle lifted a brow. "No. But you need to. Could be related to a case."

Just barely, Devon managed to keep from rolling her eyes. "Yeah, that occurred to me."

Judging by the look on Noelle's face, Devon didn't do a good job suppressing the sarcasm. Noelle made a face at her and then shoved off the desk, slid her hands into the pockets of her black blazer. "I'm worried about you, Devon. This is sick. This is weird. You could be in danger. You live alone . . ."

Devon shot Noelle a narrow look and then wished she hadn't as Noelle's brows arched. "You do live alone . . . right?" When Devon didn't respond right away, a wide grin split her friend's face. "You little tramp. You're shacking up with that gorgeous doctor, aren't you?"

Her face flamed red, and Devon glanced around—like she could see anybody through the cubicle walls. "Would you shut up? I don't want everybody and their brother hearing about my personal life."

With an unrepentant smile, Noelle said, "Hey, you know about everybody else's personal life; now it's their turn." She grabbed the hard, uncomfortable chair from in front of Devon's desk and hauled it around to the side. Perching on the end of it, she leaned forward and said, "So spill. How long have you two been living together?"

Giving Noelle a withering look, Devon said, "We're not exactly living together. He's just staying at my place for a few days." The she blew out a breath and leaned back in her chair. "He went all macho and possessive after Thursday."

Remembering last night, she smirked and said, "I had to make an end-of-the-day run to the hospital with Tim yesterday, and Luke ended up coming out to the hospital and hanging until I was done."

"Man, I knew I liked this guy," Noelle said, shifting on the seat and crossing her legs. "Watching after you like that."

Devon grimaced. "He's worried."

"I'd say he's got reason. Have the cops been able to tell you anything?"

"Nope." She shrugged with a carelessness that she didn't really feel. "I don't think they'll be able to, either. No fingerprints in the house; nobody saw anything. It's like a ghost slid inside."

"You know, if somebody had left a dead animal in my house, I don't think I'd be so blasé about it."

"I'm not blasé." Her lack of sleep and the perpetual knotted state of her gut were plenty proof of that. "But I'm not going to let it control my life, either. That's what whoever is doing this wants . . . for me to be afraid."

Devon had been controlled before—those few years so early in her life had left deep, ugly scars. She wasn't going to let anybody do that to her ever again.

"Devon." Noelle's voice was soft, understanding and compassion glowed in her blue green eyes. Noelle was one of the few friends that knew about what had happened to Devon. Devon could tell by the look on her friend's face that Noelle understood all too well. "I can understand that, but don't go letting that need interfere with your safety. Don't do anything stupid."

"Hey, I like safety. I like safety just fine." Giving Noelle a wan smile, she said, "Don't worry so much. I won't do anything foolish."

Her phone started to ring, the strains of "Brown Eyed Girl" filling the small cubicle. Luke had programmed the phone to play that when he called. With a wry grin, she said, "Besides, I got my own personal bodyguard. He won't let anything happen to me."

"Hmmm. Tell that sexy doctor of yours I said hi. We need to go out sometime, the four of us, get a drink."

As Noelle slipped out of Devon's cubicle, Devon flipped the phone open. "I'm supposed to tell my sexy doctor hi."

"You better not be expecting a phone call from your doctor's office, babe," Luke drawled.

"Nah. Only doctor I expect phone calls from is you. What's up?"

"Just wanted to hear your voice."

"Liar," Devon said, rolling her eyes. "You're checking up on me."

"You make it sound like a bad thing that I want to see if you're okay."

"Not a bad thing," Devon said, shrugging. She spun around on her chair and stared at the pictures tacked to her cubicle wall. "Just a little unnecessary. Luke, I'm at work; nobody is going to try something while I'm in a government building surrounded by several hundred people."

"You probably don't want to be telling me that. That's going to make me think that I need to be double-checking on you once you leave work." His voice was wry, and she could almost see that faint grin that would tug at his lips. "Make me think that I need to see if I can't get a friend to come watch over you while I'm stuck here or maybe figure out a way to not work nights for a while. Hell, I'm already trying to work that out."

"Luke," Devon said. "I don't want you rearranging your work schedule over this, and I damn well don't want you getting somebody to babysit me. I am fine."

"I'm going to make sure you stay that way," he replied, his voice steel-edged.

"Why in the world do I even try to argue with you? You've got a head like a rock. Look, I'm being careful. For the love of God, please don't hire somebody to watch my back. That's a waste of money."

"I wouldn't hire somebody."

Blowing out a breath, she muttered, "That's a relief."

"I'd get a friend to do it."

Her jaw dropped open, then she snapped it shut. She wanted to ask him if he was serious, but she already knew the answer to that. "Don't do that, Luke. Please. Geez, even the thought of that is enough to make me nauseated. I can't have some stranger hovering around me, or even thinking about it. I'd go crazy."

"It would keep you safe."

"I'll be careful. I'm *being* careful, I promise. Hell, you go and do that to me, it's going to make me a nervous wreck, and I'd be more likely to do something stupid. Stupid right now isn't good. I'm already a wreck; don't make it worse."

"How is wanting to keep you safe making it worse?"

"Having some stranger following me would make it ten times worse. I'm already paranoid, and I can't do my job, I can't function very well, if I'm too busy worrying about somebody watching me."

"You've been functioning just fine when I'm doing it."

She huffed out a breath. "It's not exactly the same thing."

He was quiet for a moment. "Devon, I have to know you're safe. The hours the two of us work, I can't be with you all the time, and you need somebody with you."

"I can't live my life looking over my shoulder or being afraid of the dark. I can't live like that. You can't ask me to. *You* wouldn't live like that."

"It's not the same thing."

"Why? Genetics?"

"Ahhhh . . . is there any way I can answer that without sounding completely sexist?"

"Doesn't matter if there is or not, because the fact that I'm female is why you're so worried about me."

"No. The fact that you're *my* female is why I'm worried."

My female . . . Devon closed her eyes and tried not to melt, tried not to notice that her knees had gone a little weak, and she tried really hard not to smile. She didn't completely succeed, but she managed to stay upright and reply in a fairly normal voice, once she swallowed the knot in her throat. "Your female is going to be fine, Luke."

"Damn right."

"So we can table the talk about getting somebody to play watch-dog or you juggling your shifts around so you can play watchdog?"

"For now, we can table the talk about me getting you a watch-dog. But we're not going to agree on my job, Devon. I'm already doing what I can, and I'm not changing my mind about that." His voice was flat.

She didn't bother arguing with him. Sighing, she smoothed a hand back over her hair and rubbed her temple. There was a head-ache of mammoth proportions building there, and she wanted noth-ing more than a hot bath, her bed, and Luke. But she had hours of work left to do and a stubborn doctor to deal with before she could even start on that work.

She figured she could do one of two things: either get irritated over it or accept it. Getting irritated seemed a little dumb, since even Devon wasn't so stubborn that she couldn't deny the very real threat lurking around her. Accepting it wasn't much easier, though. Her independence was a part of her. Besides, he'd backed down on find-ing somebody to tag along behind her like she was still a little kid. That was a step in the right direction.

"You're not going to turn into some Neanderthal over this, are you?"

"I dunno. Exactly what do you consider Neanderthal?"

"Hovering twenty-four/seven, interrupting me at work nonstop, following me home . . . Oh, wait. You're already doing that." Devon smirked. "Just don't start smothering me, Luke. Don't go calling in the cavalry to babysit me while you're working. This is hard enough; I feel like I'm waiting for the other shoe to drop. I don't need a mama hen at my back, either."

He sounded amused. "A mama hen?"

"Complete with the clucking."

Movement caught the corner of her eye, and Devon glanced at the door of her cubicle and saw the child advocate lawyer. Dorrie

Fields gave her a wan smile, and Devon waved toward the chair. "Duty calls, Luke."

"You going to be there late tonight?"

"I have no idea."

"So what else is new?" Luke muttered. Then he sighed. "Call me when you're done there. I want to know when you leave work."

"Okay."

"I love you."

Blood rushed to Devon's face. Averting her gaze away from Dorrie's curious gaze, she squeezed the phone with one hand and worried the cord with the other. "Uh . . ."

Luke chuckled. "I'll talk to you soon, baby." And then he was gone.

She looked back at Dorrie, and Dorrie was eying her with a wide grin. "Was that the sexy doctor I keep hearing about?"

Flipping her phone closed, she leaned back. "The sexy doctor does have a name."

Dorrie shrugged. "Not one of the important pieces of info bandied about. What's important is that he is apparently nuts about you, that he's sexy, and he's a doctor. With all that, how important is the name?" With a wicked grin, Dorrie leaned forward and asked, "So . . . is he sexy?"

Sexy didn't describe Luke. Her mouth went a little dry even thinking about it.

"Damn."

Jumping, she looked back at Dorrie, who was watching her with a smirk. "I'll take that stupefied silence as a *hell, yes, he's sexy.* You were practically drooling there."

Instinctively, Devon wiped her mouth and then scowled at Dorrie. "I was not." Not yet, anyway. She eyed the file that Dorrie held and said, "Don't you have some sort of business to discuss with me?"

"I'd rather talk about the good-looking boyfriend," Dorrie said, making a face. But she sighed and tossed the file onto Devon's desk.

"I had a friend do some digging for me. And there was a decent amount of digging to be done. You're not going to find a whole lot of information on Tim before five years ago. Tim or his dad."

Devon shook her head. "This isn't a new thing, Dorrie. It took years to make Tim the way he is. And some of the abuse . . ." As she spoke, she opened the file.

The first thing on top was a death certificate. Made out for a Linda Waller.

"Tim and Curtis Wilder didn't exist before five years ago, Devon."

Devon looked over her desk at Dorrie and saw a familiar, suppressed anger in the woman's dark brown eyes. Her lips compressed into a flat line as she nodded toward the file. "Before 2003, Tim and Curtis were known as Tim and Curtis Waller. They lived in Greenwich, North Carolina. Linda was Tim's mother; she died in a one-vehicle accident."

Puzzled, Devon started flipping through the file, reading an obituary, finding a birth certificate. It matched Tim's perfectly, except the last name was different. "They changed their name and left the state because the mom died?"

"No. They changed their name and left the state because the mom died three days after she was released on bail for child abuse charges—charges she was adamantly denying." Dorrie pinched the bridge of her nose. "I talked to her lawyer. He wasn't able to tell me much, but he remembers the case. I mentioned that Tim and Curtis were living here, and the first thing he asked me was if Tim was okay."

Devon looked up, met Dorrie's eyes. "You think he had reason to think that Tim wouldn't be okay?"

"I think he expected to hear that Tim wasn't okay." Shrugging, Dorrie said, "There's only so much I can base my opinion on. I've requested whatever paperwork there is on the case, but right now, I'm guessing that somebody found out Tim was being abused, and his mom was the one who got arrested—but Curtis was the one beating the shit out of his son."

"I'm still not getting why the name change, why they moved . . ." Then she flipped yet another sheet of paper. She recognized Tim first—younger, more vulnerable-looking—standing at a gravesite. The man at his side was Curtis, all right, looking almost exactly the same. "Greenwich Mayor Buries His Wife," the headline read. In smaller script, there was a subtitle, "Woman Dies Three Days After Being Charged with Child Abuse."

"Mayor."

"Hmmmm." With a shrug, Dorrie said, "I suppose it's possible the mom was beating Tim, and his dad wanted to leave to protect Tim."

"I bet you believe that explanation as much as I do." Devon snorted and continued to flip through the file. There were a couple of emergency room reports, none of them from the same hospital. Then she came to a background report on Curtis Waller: Staff Sergeant Curtis Waller. "He was in the military?"

"Yep. In the marines—got a few commendations in Desert Storm. Was already married to Linda at the time. Came home a war hero, taught at his hometown high school, ended up running for mayor and winning. Seemed like the perfect family, and he acted like the doting daddy when Tim was born. He was in his second term when a teacher reported to the police that she suspected Tim was being abused."

Devon hummed under her breath. "Bet that went over swimmingly. War hero, local boy makes good, ends up an elected official. And then his wife gets accused of child abuse? Why her, and not him?"

"Because Curtis Waller said it was her. Apparently he got all teary-eyed and confessed to the police that it was his wife—but she needed help, not prison."

Devon flipped the file closed and leaned back in her chair. "This is a mess. Even more of a mess than I'd originally thought."

"Oh, I think I can make it even more interesting." Dorrie shot Devon a humorless smile. "The official report on the car accident was that Linda Waller was going too fast and lost control. Car went off the mountainside, crashed, exploded. The only thing they had to bury was a very badly burned corpse. I have to wonder . . . How hard would it be for a smart man to make something like that look like an accident?"

"You think he killed his wife," Devon said flatly.

"Honey, I'm almost positive he killed his wife. The Greenwich police deny it, claim he was the perfect husband, perfect father, great guy. But I don't buy it."

Dorrie reached down and took one of the newspaper clippings, studied Curtis's face. "I spent two hours in front of a judge last night fifteen feet away from that man. And Devon . . . he's got no soul. His eyes, they are empty."

* * *

"HIS eyes, they are empty."

Dorrie's words still echoed in Devon's head a good five hours later as she pulled into her driveway. Shivering, she sat there staring up at her house and dreaded leaving her car.

Her cute, homey little place seemed dark and ominous now, especially with Luke not being there. "Brown Eyed Girl" started drifting from her phone, and she grabbed it like a drowning man would grab a life jacket.

"Hey, you!" When she heard her bright, overly cheerful voice, she winced.

"Hey back," he replied. "You okay?"

"Why wouldn't I be?"

"Devon."

She made a face and then sighed. "Yeah, I'm fine. Just jumpy—sitting in my car and staring at the house, and all of a sudden, I'm scared to death to go in there."

Luke's voice was gentle, understanding, and for some reason, that made her feel even more foolish. "I wish I could leave—"

"No," she said flatly, getting more irritated with herself by the second. It was sweet of Luke to be that worried, but she could see him telling the hospital to kiss his ass. Luke specialized in emergency medicine. He didn't have an office where he saw patients; the hospital was it, and if he came running every time she got wigged out, he was going to have trouble with his job. "Don't even think about it, Luke. I'm not going to let this mess control my life."

"You've got reason to be worried, Devon. You know as well as I do that only a sick person could do something like that—sick and dangerous. Worst sort of person all around."

A dead dog.

A dead skunk—and they couldn't even be sure the two were related.

Her tires . . . her missing planner. Other little things, all so seemingly random, up until she'd walked in and found that dead dog in her kitchen, cut open and left in the most repulsive manner.

"Damn it, Luke, what's going on?" she muttered, but she was talking more to herself than anybody else.

"You have any luck trying to figure out who could have done this?"

"Specifically? No." Sighing, she brought up her elbow and propped it on the door so she could rest her head on her hand. "The cops came by the office today—the two detectives who were out here Thursday night. Wanted a list from me, difficult parents, any of my kids with violent tendencies."

"You gave it to them, right?"

It wasn't very easy to hedge with Luke, especially when she was talking to him on the phone. If he'd been there with her, hedging would have been easier. She could have kissed him, or maybe just taken her hair down. The man had serious issues with her hair. A time or two, she'd pulled it out of its knot and seen him watching her, a weird, glazed look in his eyes. But on the phone, that wasn't possible.

"Not a list exactly," she said.

"Damn it, Devon, you want them to find that guy or not?"

She rolled her eyes. "No, Luke. I want to come home again and find another dead animal gutted in my kitchen. That was just so exciting." Then she dropped the sarcasm and went for cajoling, hoping he'd understand. "Luke, most of my kids are jumpy enough around cops anyway. Do you have any idea how many cases I've handled in the past six months that involved unhappy parents or violent kids?"

"They've got to start somewhere. It's not like you have a lot of places where you could have come in contact with this fucker."

"I'm aware of that. Geez, Luke, I'm not a moron. I'm not a helpless little kid, and I'm not naive. I realize what's going on, and I know I need to do what I can to help." Irritated all over again, she started getting her stuff together, her bag, her lunch tote, and her purse. Climbing out of the car, she glanced around, checking her environment. That was automatic. But then she slowed, took another look, longer, slower. That second glance stemmed from last week.

Keys held in her free hand, she wedged the phone against her shoulder and headed up the sidewalk. "I gave them a couple of names to start with. Out of all my cases, there are probably less than five that have this kind of stuff inside them. Those names, the cops are welcome to. A cop showing up on their doorstep is a common enough occurrence for most of them, and it's not going to freak them out the way it would with most of my kids."

Headlights splashed across her yard as she climbed the porch steps. She glanced over, watched as Danielle pulled into her driveway and parked her little red Spider.

"Devon, the cops know what they are doing."

"And so do I," she responded. "Look, I know my kids." Unlocking the front door, she paused inside just long enough to reset the alarm, and then she locked the door and dumped her bags on the narrow console table just inside the entryway. "Most of them aren't capable of this, Luke. I know it."

"Glad to hear it. But I'm not worried about the kids, Devon. I'm worried about the adults. If this is related to your work at all, then it's probably a parent."

She kicked off her shoes and wiggled her toes, rotated her ankles before heading into the living room. "I've thought of that, too, Luke. I'm doing what I can to get a list together for that, but that one is going to take more time."

"You don't think the cops can figure out how to narrow down a list?"

Devon sighed. "Luke, the cops don't know the families. They weren't there when things went down. They won't know the details that I know. I know which parents were pissed that I took their kids, which ones couldn't care less, and which ones were mad enough that they would be willing to kill Lassie and leave her body as a message."

"Lassie?"

With a sheepish grin, she replied, "I can't seem to quit thinking about her. Should probably call her something."

"How many parents are on this list?"

A face loomed large in her mind as she headed into the living room. She went to check the wood bin and saw that Luke had already laid logs out for a fire. A goofy, sappy smile curled her lips, and she almost forgot he'd asked a question.

"How many?" he repeated.

"How many . . . Oh. Oh. Um . . ." Devon squinted up at the ceiling and did a quick mental tally. "Maybe eight or nine."

Right at the top of the list was Curtis Wilder/Waller.

"His eyes, they are empty."

Reluctantly, she said, "There's one dad in particular that's right at the top of the list."

"And did you tell the cops about him?"

"Yes, Daddy," she replied in a mocking voice. "I also ate all of my lunch, and I'll wash behind my ears before I go to bed, too."

"Smart-ass."

Devon grinned. "Maybe you'd like to help—" Her voice broke off as she heard his name on the overhead speaker through the phone line. "Sounds like you're being summoned."

"Yeah. I'm going to call again here in a little while."

"You're scheduled to get off at midnight, Luke. There's no reason to call."

"I'll call," he repeated, his voice hard. The line clicked and then went dead. She stood there for a minute, staring at the phone, and then she crouched down in front of the fireplace.

Luke wouldn't be home until midnight, but Devon had a feeling she wouldn't sleep until he was home anyway.

ELEVEN

IT was an uneasy week that passed. When Luke told her he'd cut back to two shifts a week, she'd yelled at him. It ended up being their first actual fight, and for nearly a week, the tension was thick enough to choke her.

They lay in bed beside each other at night, not touching, but come morning, she'd wake up plastered against him with his arms wrapped around her. Embarrassed, aroused, but still too stubborn to back down, she'd squirm away from him the minute she woke up—and spend yet another miserable day wondering if she hadn't bitten off more than she could chew.

Complication: that's what she'd decided Luke was back before they'd started dating. But now she knew complicated didn't even begin to cover it.

Friday rolled around, and she sat at her desk, reading through a couple of reports, brooding, and then tossing the reports down in disgust when she realized she couldn't remember a damn thing of what she'd just read.

When the phone rang, she answered it with a weary, "Hello." Within five seconds, she wished she'd let it go to voice mail.

It was Detective Miranda White. Yeah, white was an accurate description, all right. Snowy white skin, hair so pale a blonde it appeared white, and pale, pale blue eyes with only a hint of color. She was every bit as thin as Devon herself was, but the detective was nearly a foot taller. She looked like a stiff wind would blow her away, and Devon couldn't quite wrap her mind around the concept of the detective arresting some three-hundred-pound drug dealer and manhandling him into a squad car.

That was until Devon had to deal with her.

The woman was a bulldog. A bulldog with a chip on her shoulder and an ax to grind, and she managed to make Devon feel defensive in under two minutes flat—and Devon didn't have a damn thing to feel defensive about.

"I've been going through the names you've given me, talked to most of them. So far, nothing's popped. Wanted to touch base with you, see if maybe there are other people we should look at . . . Perhaps there's somebody not related to your job. Ex-boyfriends?"

"That list would be pretty much nonexistent, Detective," Devon answered. She leaned back in her chair and rubbed her temple. Already there was a headache brewing, a headache of mammoth proportions.

"Come on, Devon. Help me out here."

"I can't," Devon replied. "There aren't any exes out there carrying a grudge, Detective. The only serious relationship I had before Luke was six years ago, back in college, and he moved away and got married. Up until I started going out with Luke, I had maybe two dates a year, and never with the same guy."

"No one-night stands, no affairs gone bad?"

Devon snorted. "You sound like you watch too much *Law and Order*, Detective. I just told you . . . there's nobody. No ugly affairs. There's no furious wife out there plotting revenge, no obsessive, controlling old boyfriend."

"What about your aunt?"

Devon stilled. "My aunt?" she repeated carefully. Hell, she hadn't once thought of Cyndi. She doubted Cyndi would even know where to look for her now. Or that she'd care enough to try.

"Yes. Your aunt. Looks like her last name is Hopkins now . . . She does go through the husbands, doesn't she?" Detective White spoke in a cheerful, almost joking voice as she mentioned, "Looks like the first one ended up going to prison and dying there. Do you remember Boyd Chancellor?"

In a faint voice, she replied, "I remember him."

"You think there's any reason your aunt could be doing this? Holding a grudge against you over something? Maybe something related to him?"

That bitch. She knew. Devon didn't know why she hadn't realized it before now, but White had gone looking through Devon's past, and she'd found out about Boyd. His trial was public record, and now the detective knew. Her gut roiled, and she swallowed back the bile rising in her throat.

"My aunt doesn't care enough about me to hold any sort of grudge, Detective," Devon finally managed to get out.

"Hmmm." It was a noncommittal sound, bland, neutral—and it left Devon totally unprepared for what came next. "What about an ex-john?"

"An ex-what?"

On the other end of the line, Detective White chuckled. "Don't sound so surprised, Devon. I realize your juvie record was sealed, but there's always a way through that. You ran away from home when you were thirteen . . . spent some time living on the streets, doing drugs. Sounds like a hard life. It's forced a lot of girls into prostitution—not like you're the first."

It took a lot to throw Devon off guard. She'd seen too many weird, strange, or just plain evil things. She'd spent her own time in hell when she was a kid, and for the past four years, she'd spent her life trying to save other kids from that kind of torment.

Catching her off guard just wasn't that easy.

But Miranda White had just done it. For a minute, Devon sat there opening and closing her mouth, trying to give voice to the words bubbling in her throat. Scathing insults, derisive laughs, but none of them managed to get past her tight throat.

She managed to squeak out, "Excuse me?"

"Come on, Devon. Don't hand me the innocent, outraged routine. Girls on the streets don't have too many options. It's a sad, ugly fact, but don't worry; I'm not going to share this with your employers or your boyfriend. But you need to be straight with me. You come across any of your former . . . acquaintances? Any of them capable of this?"

Her voice rusty, Devon forced out, "You don't know jack shit, Detective. I lived on the streets, stole money, stole food, went cold more nights than I can count, but I never whored for money. I couldn't stand the sight of most men. There was no way I could let one touch me."

Miranda gave a world-weary sigh, the long-suffering sort of sound that practically every cop practiced to perfection. "You're not helping me out here, Ms. Manning. Don't you want us to find this creep?"

In an icy voice, Devon replied, "Yeah, I want you to find the creep. Preferably before he decides killing animals isn't fun anymore, and he decides I'm next. But if you're looking for an ex-john to investigate, you won't find one. He doesn't exist. Now, unless you have something serious and a little less insulting to ask me, then I have work to do."

She slammed the phone down and sat back in her seat and sent it rolling back two feet until it crashed into the wall of her cubicle. Bringing her hands up, she covered her face and swore.

For the most part, Devon had nothing but respect for cops. They had a hard road, maligned by a huge part of the population, all because a few select assholes popped up from time to time and managed to grab a few minutes in the spotlight. Most of them were decent, hardworking people who just wanted to help in some way, shape, or form.

But in that moment, Devon wasn't feeling too friendly toward cops, and even less friendly toward any cop that was investigating the mutilated animal and Devon's stalker . . .

Stalker.

A chill raced down her spine as the thought circled through her mind. Stalker. Somebody who watched her closely enough to know when she wouldn't be home, somebody who knew how to get into her house.

Her belly cramped. Folding her arms across her abdomen, she leaned forward. "I'm going to be sick." She stayed huddled over like that for what seemed like ages, her blood roaring in her ears, a clammy sweat breaking out over her body.

When a hand touched the back of her neck, she was so scared, she yelped. Without hesitating, she shoved back from her chair, slid out of the seat, and grabbed a heavy marble paperweight from her desk. Then she felt like a total fool as Luke rocked back on his feet and tucked his hands into his pockets. There was a smile on his face, that same gentle smile she'd seen him give to scared, hurt children, but the hard glint of fury darkened his eyes to pewter, and she heard it edge into his voice as well as he murmured, "It's just me, Devon."

Sheepish, she put the paperweight back on her desk. It was about the size and shape of one of those silly eight ball games, and it weighed a ton. It hit her desk with a dull thud.

Giving him a forced smile, she asked, "So what are you doing here?"

He shrugged. "Wanted to see you." He slid her a look from under his lashes. "The past week has kind of sucked."

"Yeah," she murmured quietly. "It has." Sliding back into her chair, she braced her elbows on her desk and dropped her head into her hands, shaking a little as residual adrenaline hit her system.

"Sorry I almost brained you there. I'm a little jumpy," she mumbled into her hands.

This time, when he touched her neck, she leaned into his touch. "You're tight," he said softly. He shifted around until he stood behind her chair and brought up his other hand, massaging her neck.

Devon moaned. Her head dropped down until her chin nearly touched her chest. That was the only noise she made for the next few minutes. It was Luke who broke the silence as he asked, "What's got you so jumpy?"

"It's going to sound a little lame."

She could hear the smile in his voice. "Try me."

"It's been a couple of weeks since we found Lassie," she said, starting out slowly. "And logically, I knew what was going on, but I think I just now admitted it to myself: I've got a stalker. A genuine, bona fide stalker." Ugly images and thoughts circled through her head. "I've worked with a couple of girls who have had problems with boyfriends stalking them. None of them had this same thing happen . . . but one of them ended up in the hospital after her boyfriend beat the shit out of her. Nobody took it seriously. Nobody took her seriously—until he damn near killed her."

Feeling a little disgusted, she added, "And while I am not going to let this bastard control my life in any way, I don't think I've been taking it as seriously as I should."

"I have." Luke's fingers dug into her neck with a little more force, and his thumbs hit a spot just a little to the left, pushing, pressing, kneading. The tension melted away, and as it did, her headache faded. "I'm not going to let anything happen to you, Devon."

Don't make promises you can't keep. She kept the words to herself. Luke would do everything he could to keep her safe, and as of now, Devon was going to stop arguing with him about it so much. "I'm sorry I've been so stubborn about this," she murmured.

"So does that mean you're going to stop fussing if I try to get a friend to come help me keep an eye on you for a while?"

Devon stiffened. "No. It doesn't mean that."

"Somehow, I knew you'd say that."

With a sigh, he bent down and slid his arms around her. The warmth of his body managed to penetrate the chill of hers, and slowly, she felt herself relaxing.

"Maybe I'm being too pushy," Luke murmured. "This just has my head messed up. Doesn't help that the police haven't been able to come up with any concrete information or get any idea who he is."

"Or you?" she asked mildly, sliding him a sidelong look from under her lashes. "I noticed you following me to work this morning."

He gave her an unrepentant grin and then dipped his head, nuzzled her neck. "You've got good eyes, then. I stayed pretty far back." Straightening up, he moved around and leaned back against her desk, studying her with curious eyes. "You noticed me following you?"

"Yeah. And a few times before this. How often have you been following me to work?"

Lifting one shoulder in a shrug, he replied, "Pretty much every day if I'm not working. Just trying to see if I can see anybody else doing the same. Have you noticed anything?"

She made a face. "No. But honestly, I usually don't pay too much attention unless I'm in my neighborhood. I've just been more watchful lately because of everything that's been going on." She slid him another sidelong glance and added, "Besides, I wanted to make sure you hadn't gone and put some bored army buddy on my tail after you'd told me you wouldn't."

He cracked a grin at her. "It occurred to me." He reached up, hooking a hand over the back of his neck. "So you notice anybody besides me?"

"No." She blew out a breath and closed her eyes. "But that doesn't mean much."

Luke shook his head. "You're more observant than you realize, Devon. You notice things. Some of it probably just goes with your job, but I think some of it comes from your past, who you are."

A nasty taste started to climb up the back of her throat, and she swallowed back the bile. Nervously, she picked up the marble paper-weight and started to pass it from one hand to the other. "Speaking of my past, Detective White called me. Turns out she's been snoop-ing around, trying to get some information about me, see if that can give her any leads on who could have done this." She glanced up him from under her lashes and then looked back at the paperweight.

Although she'd never once thought about hooking, shame flooded her. How many people suspected that of her? Did her parents? No. No, they wouldn't. Very, very few people knew. Devon preferred not to tell people. But the few people who did know, had they ever won-dered if she'd gotten along by selling herself?

Luke reached up, covered her hands with his. Gently, he took the paperweight away and then he crouched down in front of her. "You've got a record; I know that. But it's sealed. She can't . . ."

Lifting her head, she met his eyes. "Yeah, it's sealed. But there are ways to get around that . . . talk to people who worked my case, or bribe somebody to let her see the records."

"So she managed to get a look at them?" Luke asked.

Something had happened. Luke doubted that having some cop check out her background would put that dark look in her eyes. She looked haunted, humiliated—and angry. Very angry. Her breathing sped up, and a sneer curled up one corner of her mouth.

"I don't know if she saw my records or not. But she's put enough together to come up with some lame conclusion. A seriously way-off lame conclusion."

"And what would this lame conclusion be?" Luke asked, nar-rowing his eyes. Had to be something—something that would make her look so angry, so embarrassed.

Devon averted her eyes. She licked her lips, ducked her head, and fiddled with the buttons on her dress. It was forest green, and it made her eyes look darker, mysterious. Her pale skin glowed against it; she looked absolutely gorgeous. Gorgeous, furious, ashamed. He reached up, cupped her chin, and forced her face back to his. "Out with it."

"She implied that when I was living on the streets, I got into prostitution. She has this theory that one of my johns or a pimp is behind this." She spat the words out like they were acid.

"She what?" Luke demanded. Involuntarily, his fingers tightened on her face. Swearing, he jerked his hand back and stared at the faint red impressions he'd left on her porcelain complexion. She had baby-soft skin, he thought inanely, and she bruised too easily.

Bile churned in the back of his throat. He shoved to his feet and moved away from her desk. None of the social workers had their own office on this floor, not unless they were in charge. But Devon's cubicle had a small window, facing out on the parking lot. He moved to the window and leaned his head against the chilly pane of glass, tried to cool his anger so he could help Devon with hers.

But the objectivity that served him most of his life was coming up seriously lacking here. Under most circumstances, Luke could be completely pissed off yet maintain his composure. Wasn't so easy this time. Devon . . . a whore. Her youth had been hell. He still didn't have the whole picture. The ugly reality of what her childhood had been wasn't one that Luke liked to think about, yet it was compulsive, something he couldn't stop thinking about.

But even as often as he'd wondered about what all she'd gone through during the time she lived on the street, this wasn't something that had occurred to him. Even if it was something that she'd been forced into as a child, the picture just wouldn't come together for him. He couldn't imagine how anybody could think it of her.

"She's just trying to do her job," he said, forcing the words out through a tight throat. He glanced back at her, forced a smile he didn't feel. "Logically, I know that. You probably do, too."

He waited a beat and then asked, "So did you hit her?"

A faint smile curled her lips. "No. I was tempted." He glanced down, saw her hands, clenched into fists so tight her knuckles had gone white. "But she isn't worth the trouble I'd get into for assaulting an officer." Then she grinned. "Of course, she called—didn't come in person. If she'd been standing here, who knows what might have happened."

Snorting, Luke turned back to stare out the window. He took a deep breath and blew it out. "It's bullshit. I know that. Chances are she probably knows it. But I guess cops have to dig around in bullshit a lot."

"Thank you."

Slowly, he turned back around, studied her pale face. "You didn't have some weird idea in your head that I'd believe that, did you?"

Devon grimaced, shrugged. "No. Not really." Then she looked away, shot him a sidelong look from the corner of her eye. "Maybe a small part of me was a little worried. Just a small part, though." She sighed, reaching up to rub her temple. "You know, I remember when I was in the hospital, a lady came in—it wasn't Eden. I don't even remember her name. But she talked to me, wanted to make sure nothing bad had happened, wanted to make sure I hadn't been forced into . . . that. I was embarrassed, mad, scared . . . but she just wanted to make sure. She never accused me of anything. This was the first time anybody has ever implied that I was a whore."

"Somebody like her, she probably doesn't see a whole lot of the good stuff in life. Probably gets natural for her to assume the worst."

She glanced back over at him. "You saw a lot of bad stuff." With an indelicate snort, she added, "Hell, I've seen a lot of bad stuff. But that doesn't always make me assume the worst. Even when I know the worst is probably the truth, I hate to think it. Leaves me feeling dirty, angry. I can't imagine living my life always thinking that way."

Sighing, she tucked a strand of hair back behind her ear and then touched her fingers to the strand of pearls around her neck. "I hate this, Luke," she murmured. "This entire mess is driving me fricking nuts."

Luke crouched down in front of her, laid his hands on her thighs.

"Yeah, me, too. Since she basically called to dig around in shit, I guess they really don't have a clue about who did it, do they?"

"I'd say they are pretty much clueless."

Clueless. Yeah, that pretty much summed up Luke's state of mind, too. He had absolutely no fucking clue about who had done it, and he'd spent a decent amount of time over the past couple weeks trying to figure it out. But nobody had seen a damn thing, and the times he'd tailed Devon to or from work, he hadn't seen anybody else doing the same.

The only thing that made sense was that it was somebody related to her job. Occasionally Devon had to deal with distraught or out-right pissed parents, but none really stood out in her mind.

Devon was a sharp lady. If something out of the ordinary was going on, she would have noticed. More, he would have been able to tell. They'd spent too much time together over the past couple of months. He knew her; he knew when she was pissed, when she happy, when she was sad.

If something had been worrying her, troubling her, he would have picked up on it.

But there hadn't been anything hinting at something like this. The only moment that stood out in Luke's mind was that first night he'd been with Devon, those few moments when he'd felt like he was being watched. Just that one moment in time, and then nothing.

"It has to be somebody through here, Devon. Either one of the kids or their parents. It's the only thing that makes sense," Luke said quietly.

Her eyes darted off to the side, and he followed her glance, saw a closed manila folder. "I've pretty much come to that conclusion myself."

When her eyes came back to his, Luke asked, "You got an idea about who?"

Devon licked her lips, opened her mouth. Then somebody passed by the narrow door to her cubicle. "Not here," she murmured with a shake of her head. Sliding a hand around the back of her neck, she rubbed the tense muscles there. Already the tension was coming back, even after Luke had worked his magic. "Gee, you think I could be lucky enough that's it over? I mean, maybe it's just some twisted kid, and all he wanted to do was scare somebody for kicks."

"You know better than that," Luke murmured. "A twisted kid is a possibility, but he'd have to be damn smart, damn clever—and damn twisted. More, he'd have to be patient. Whoever is doing this understands patience; most kids don't."

Distracted, he reached up and pushed a hand through his hair. The pale, golden blond locks fell right back into place, shielding his gaze from her as he looked downward. He shifted so that he knelt in front of her, close enough that she could feel his heat. "I'll be honest, Devon. It's not even the dead dog that bothers me the most."

Devon grimaced. "It sure as hell has me worried."

He blew out a breath. For a second, Devon was unaware of anything he did or said as that air caressed her legs. The dress she wore had a full, long skirt that buttoned down the front, but she'd only buttoned it to the knee. Sitting with her legs crossed had the skirt parting a little higher on the thigh than was probably professional, but she hadn't really noticed, not until now. And now? She didn't give a damn. Too aware of the heat of his body, how close he was . . . and how serious.

Yeah, they were discussing something serious. Something important. So why was she suddenly having a very hard time focusing on it?

It had been too long since he'd touched her. How she'd managed to go her entire adult life without feeling him pressed against her, she didn't know. The past week had dragged on, and now it was like her body was reminding her just how long it had been.

Giving herself a mental shake, she tried to focus on what he was saying, rather than his body.

It didn't help, though, that when she licked her lips, his gaze dropped down to her mouth, and Devon felt the heat of that gaze burn through her. His hand came up, rested on her bared knee.

He stroked her skin, his fingers warm and calloused, but as she focused on his words, the heat she'd been feeling melted away into icy fear.

"It takes a pro to get in and out of a house without leaving a sign, Devon."

"A pro . . . ? Like a professional thief?"

Luke shook his head. "Serious thieves aren't into violence. They don't even carry weapons. Increases the penalty if they are caught armed. I don't see a thug doing this without leaving a trail."

Laying his palm flat against her thigh, he flexed his fingers and then squeezed gently. "I'm not talking a professional thief or a thug. Getting in and out of places without leaving a sign requires a lot of focus, a lot of training." He glanced up at her. "Kind of like I had."

Devon blinked. "Kind of like you . . . you mean in the army?"

Luke shook his head. "The typical soldier isn't trained on breaking and entering, Devon. The average cop couldn't do it without leaving some kind of sign. Hell, I bet the average fed couldn't."

"Okay, then who trains on breaking and entering? Doesn't sound like any electives course I've ever heard of."

"Special Forces." He glanced at the files on her desk and asked, "Any of those possible suspects of yours have a military background?"

"Military background?" she repeated faintly.

"It's the only thing that makes sense to me. Yeah, a professional thief could break into your house, but I haven't heard of too many pros with a bent toward violence. The other types of people who can do this, frankly, you wouldn't show up on their radar." With a restless shrug of his broad shoulders, he murmured, "This makes sense, though. If you've been working with a child with a parent who worked Special Forces . . ."

It was like having cold water dumped on her. She suddenly felt chilled, and nausea churned inside her belly. Crossing her arms over her middle, she leaned forward and dropped her head down on his shoulder.

His only response was to curve a hand over her neck, holding her close. His warmth and his strength were a soothing comfort, and for a minute, she relaxed against him.

Once she'd settled, he asked quietly, "There is somebody, isn't there?"

In a stiff voice, she replied, "Yeah. Yeah, there is."

"Are you okay?"

"Oh, sure. I've got some psycho, crazy stalker on my ass, and who knows, he just may be a professional whatever in the hell you call it. I'm fine."

He rubbed his cheek against hers and whispered, "You've also got a professional whatever in the hell you call it watching your pretty little ass, Devon. I won't let anything happen to you. Got it?"

"Hmmm. Yeah. I got it." With a weak laugh, she snuggled in closer. "And as long as I can stay just like this, I think I can be pretty okay."

Luke slid his arms around her, tucking her as close as he could manage. "I got no problems with that."

But life and responsibilities intervened. Her office phone started to ring, and as she reached for that, so did her cell phone. She gave him a wry grin and said, "Break time's over."

* * *

Jumping at shadows . . . seemed she'd been doing a lot of that lately. Once more, Devon sat in her driveway, staring at the garage and wishing she'd gotten around to clearing it out enough that she could park in there. She just hated to do it. It was a small garage barely big enough for her car, and when she parked in there, the few times she had, she ended up overcome with a sense of claustrophobia that had her shaking and hyperventilating.

She couldn't handle small spaces and the garage with a car in it was damn small.

Her nerves were already shot, and the thought of parking in that small garage was even more unnerving. But she couldn't decide what was worse: getting out and walking up the sidewalk in the dark to her house, or parking in the coffin of a garage.

It wasn't even dark now, and Luke was home, no reason to be so nervous, but she couldn't move past it.

It had been one hell of a day, and she hadn't even worked a full day.

Even aside from the troublesome case of Tim Wilder, her day had been crap. She'd talked to a mom who was encouraging her six-year-old to diet—a six-year-old who was small enough to still wear clothes off the toddler rack; she'd talked to three judges, two lawyers, one doctor, and one very insulting cop.

The doctor was Luke, naturally, and he'd been the highlight of her day. After he'd left, it had only gone downhill. Detective White had called three more times but Noelle had fielded two of the calls, and Devon had hung up on the detective the third time. Sooner or later, she'd have to talk to the cop again, but not today. Not until she cooled off.

At three o'clock, she'd gone to her boss and asked if she could cut out early. Normally, as heavy as her workload was, he wouldn't have been happy, but thanks to the office grapevine, he had heard about what had happened and apparently understood the need to cut out for a while.

Cutting out wasn't what she needed. What she needed was Luke. But now she couldn't seem to make herself climb out of the car. Luke was home and probably waiting for her to call and tell him if she'd be leaving work at her regular time, and he'd probably growl at her for not letting him know that she was leaving early.

Fine. He could growl away, and then she could cuddle up against him, and he could make her forget about life, abused kids, crazy stalkers, and cruel parents. "Ain't going to happen until you get your butt in the house," she muttered.

She'd like nothing more than to shrug this whole mess off, forget all about it. Devon had decent instincts, and the few times there had been a client capable of causing serious problems, she'd known. When the threats, thankfully few, were serious, she'd known. If somebody had been following her home or watching her, she would know . . . right?

Lifting her head, she looked into the rearview mirror, tracking a silver Jeep as it headed down the street. She saw nobody. Still, her skin crawled, and she was so damn jumpy, when a squirrel dropped down out of the tree in her front yard, she almost leaped out of her skin.

Uneasy, she grabbed her purse and slid the strap around her neck, adjusting it so that it would lay crossways over her chest, and then she dug the pepper spray out. Holding it in her hand, Devon climbed out of the car and headed for the front door. Her gaze darted back and forth. Her heart slammed against her ribs. Part of her insisted, *Relax. Relax.*

The other part was going, *Yeah, right.* Relaxing was so not going to happen. Her hands shook as she slid the key home, and she breathed out a sigh of relief as she turned the doorknob. Then a hand landed on her shoulder. Yelping, she whirled around, her hand lifting up the pepper spray, pushing down—

Long fingers caught her wrist, jerking her hand aside at the last second. Air wheezed out of her lungs as she stared up at Luke's face. A muscle jerked in his jaw as he studied her face. Almost imperceptibly, his features softened, and he tugged on her wrist, urging her closer. "I was across the street, talking to Danielle again. I'm sorry. I didn't mean to scare you."

Cuddling up against him, she sucked in air and waited for her heart to level out before she even tried to speak. "It's okay. I'm just a little jumpy." Something bit into her fingers, and she looked down, saw that she was holding the little canister of pepper spray so tight, the grooved plastic was cutting into her skin. With a grimace, she murmured, "Okay. A lot jumpy. Second time today."

"Let's not go for a third." Strong, gentle hands stroked up and down her back, and he nuzzled her neck. "It will be okay, Devon."

Turning her face into his, she replied, "I know." Their lips were all but touching, and unable to resist, she leaned in, covered his hard, unsmiling mouth with her own. He opened for her, and she pushed up on her toes, winding her arms around his neck.

He felt so damn perfect against her, warm and strong, his hands cradling her so gently, his mouth moving against hers in a rhythm that felt as natural as breathing. She felt safe with him, but more than that, she felt whole.

Whole—and hungry. All the pent-up adrenaline channeled itself into heat, burning away her fear but leaving her so aching and so empty, it almost hurt.

Wiggling closer, she rocked against him, shuddering as she felt the heat and strength of him through their clothes. Devon forgot where they were, unaware of the cars that moved up and down the street, the retired couple across the street that passed down the sidewalk, their terrier prancing around like he owned the world, the little girl who was riding her bike in the driveway next door.

Nothing seemed to exist but his mouth on hers and his arms holding her close.

Tearing his mouth away, Luke pressed his face against her neck and muttered, "Damn it, girl. You trying to get us both arrested?"

He didn't wait for a response, though. Banding an arm around her waist, he lifted her and carried her inside. He kicked the door shut and then spun around, pressing her back against the smooth wooden surface. Sliding his hands under her skirt, he shoved the loose material upward, higher and higher until he slid his hands inside her panties and cupped her butt. "I'd planned on yelling at you for not letting me know you left work early," he muttered against her mouth.

Then he lifted his head, held her gaze as he closed his fists around the skimpy strings at either side of her hip, jerking. Her panties tore, and he threw them to the ground. "I'll do it later." Still staring into her eyes, he cupped her heated core in his hand and rubbed the heel of his palm against her. "Unbutton my jeans, Devon."

Her hands shook a little as she obeyed, fumbling with the button and then the zipper, easing it down over the massive length of his erection. After dragging the zipper down, she ran the back of her fingers down his hot flesh, a faint smile curving her lips as he jerked in response.

He hissed out a breath and pushed away from her just long enough to shove his jeans and underwear out of the way. Strong, big hands cupped her bottom, boosted her up. "Wrap your legs around me," he rasped, and his eyes burned into hers like molten silver, hungry, intent.

Unable to resist, Devon wrapped her legs around his waist and whimpered as that simple movement opened her folds, exposing her to the heated shaft pressing against her. Sliding her arms around his neck, she tugged him closer.

"It's been too long, Devon. The past week has been hell. Damn it, Devon . . . you're so fucking wet," he crooned as he pushed inside, working past the initial tightness. "So soft . . . relax for me . . . fuck, yeah. That's it."

Arching her back, she cried out as he thrust deep, seating his entire length completely within her. Her lids fluttered closed, and Luke growled—actually growled. One of his hands shot into her hair, dislodging the pins that held it confined in a knot. Tangling his fingers in the curls, he tugged her head back and demanded, "Look at me."

Her eyelids felt weighted down, but she forced them open, staring into Luke's harsh, hungry face. "I want to see you," he whispered, using his hand to hike her hips a little higher, changing the angle so that he rubbed against her clit with even the slightest move. "I want you to see me."

He pulled out tauntingly, teasingly slow. "I want you to feel me."

Letting go of her hair, he laid his hand along her cheek and pushed his thumb into her mouth. Automatically, she opened for him and sucked on his flesh. "I want you to taste me," he whispered, dipping to his head to kiss her neck. "I want to taste you."

When he pulled out of her, Devon whimpered in protest, curling her hands around his biceps and trying to tug him back to her. As he lowered her to the floor, her skirt fell back into place. Luke sank to his knees in front of her, his gaze ravenous and intent. "Taste you," he muttered again. But instead of pushing the skirt up, he reached for the row of tiny little buttons, starting at the bottom. There were probably twenty of them, marching up to the modest sweetheart neckline, and before he even got to the dress's bodice, Devon was ready to tear it off.

She even went to grab the dress and pull it over her head, but he caught her hands and pressed them back down to her sides. "I've been out of my mind this past week, missing you, worrying about you . . . needing you," he said, his voice rough as sandpaper, a sexy little rasp that sent shivers down her spine.

"Shit, I love this dress," he muttered. "Earlier today, in your office, you were sitting there, wearing this pretty dress buttoned all the way up to your pretty neck, and I wanted to rip it off. All I could think about was getting you naked again, getting inside you."

Her knees wobbled, and Devon had to lock them, otherwise she would have keeled over. Even so, she felt like she was melting, melting like wax that wanted to puddle and pool all around him. "So do it, already," she said. He just smiled at her and kept on undoing the buttons, one at a time—slooooowwwly.

"I was tempted to do just that when you leaned back in your chair and crossed your legs. Your skirt fell open. If you'd moved just a little, I would have gone crazy. Just a little, and I could have seen paradise." He reached the last button and then sat back on his heels, pushing the dress open. It parted, the sides falling open to frame her torso, hips, and legs. The bra she wore matched the panties he'd torn off, simple white cotton embroidered with little hearts, scalloped lace edging the cups. Devon squeezed her eyes shut as he stared at her, feeling so inadequate. Too skinny, too short, hardly the pretty, feminine type that threw themselves at Luke on a regular basis.

"You're so damn beautiful," he whispered, leaning in and pressing his mouth to her pubis, then lower . . . lower . . . When he pressed his mouth against her and licked her, Devon thought that she'd die from the pleasure, right then.

Only his hands kept her from sagging to the floor, her knees all but useless and her legs too watery to support her weight. Bracing her hands against his shoulders, she locked her elbows and stared down at his bent head, watching as he licked, sucked, and stroked. Her face flamed red. Watching him like this, as he knelt between her thighs and tongued her, it was too hot, too intimate, too intense.

Wet, suckling noises filled the air, punctuated by her cries and his occasional grunt or groan of satisfaction. "You're sweet . . . Yeah, you like that, don't you . . . Devon . . . damn . . ." He caught her right leg and lifted it, draping it over his shoulder, and shifted his head just a little to the side. Then he sealed his mouth against her and pushed his tongue inside, circling around the entrance to her passage and then pulling back, settling into a rhythm that mimicked lovemaking.

He groaned against her again, and the vibration of it echoed through her, and she came, screaming out his name, fisting her hands in his hair, and holding his head steady as she rocked, wiggled, and squirmed against his oh-so-talented mouth. He worked her through the orgasm, and only after she sagged back against the wall, reeling and gasping for air, did he stand.

Their gazes locked, and he stripped his shirt away, kicked off his boots, then his jeans and underwear. When he came back to her, he was gloriously naked, a faint dusting of gold hair on his chest, his mouth red and swollen from her, and his eyes heavy-lidded. "Good enough to eat," he muttered, slipping his fingers into his mouth and licking them.

Devon blushed hotly.

Luke laughed, dipped his head to kiss her shoulder. She still wore the dress, hanging open, but when she went to shrug it off,

Luke caught it and held it in place. "I want to fuck you like this . . . wearing that dress open. That's how you looked when I was fantasizing about you earlier."

A grin curled her lips. "Really . . . what else happened in this fantasy?"

The wicked, teasing light faded from his eyes, and he shook his head. "Doesn't matter, Devon. Come here. I want to make love to you."

Whether it was the challenge therein or her own curiosity, she didn't know. Backing away from the hand he held out to her, she sidled down the wall and leaned back, tucking her hands behind her. Resting her head against the wall, she turned her head to stare at him. "I'm not fragile, Luke. I keep telling you that."

"You might not be fragile, but that doesn't mean you want to know about some of the things I want to do to you," he said, his voice flat, shutting her out. He thought he was protecting her; Devon knew that.

But all it did was hurt her. She'd spent most of her life afraid of any kind of intimacy, and now that she'd finally found the courage—and the man—to have it with, he wanted to keep bits and pieces of himself locked away from her. "Not good enough," she whispered. Staring at him, she straightened away from the wall and pulled the edges of her dress together. "You figured out my deep, dark secrets, Luke. You know almost everything there is to know about me, but I can't say the same about you. I don't figure this is meant to be a one-way relationship, Luke. It's not fair."

Brushing past him, she started to work on the buttons with hands that shook. Damn it, she wouldn't be able to wear this dress again without thinking—

He tackled her, the weight of his body crashing into hers and sending her staggering. If he hadn't grabbed her waist upon impact, she would have ended up on the ground. Instead, she ended up pressed face-first against the wall. "You want to know my deep, dark secrets," Luke rasped, grabbing her skirt and shoving it up over her waist. He insinuated a knee between her thighs, forcing her to spread her legs.

She started to shake, his intensity bleeding over into her, yet in the back of her mind, fear danced. This was too dominating, too controlling, as he caught one of her wrists and brought it up, pinning it to the wall by her head. The other hand held her skirt out of the way as he pressed against her. He dipped his knees, aligning the thick head of his shaft with her dripping core, and then he pushed, forcing her softness to yield to his length. As he tunneled through her tight sheath, he caught her other wrist and pressed it to the wall. "You want to hear how I think about how much I'd like to push you down to your knees and make you take me in your mouth? You want to hear how I've thought about what it would be like bend you over and take you from behind . . . kind of like I'm doing now? I think about it—a lot. But I don't want to scare you. I don't want to hurt you."

Then he swore. His body tensed, and she knew he was going to pull away. Her heart pounded in her throat, and the terror that was trying to edge in on her paled in comparison to the panic she felt as he started to pull back. "Don't you dare," she hissed, shoving her butt back against him, wiggling and squirming against the thick length invading her. His greater height made it a challenge, but she finally found a rhythm that worked, riding him, clenching down around him, moaning when he jerked and throbbed inside her. "Don't you pull away from me, Luke. I'm not fragile . . ."

For agonizing seconds, he remained still, his rigid length pulsing inside her, his body tense and unmoving, and then he pushed back into her, crowding her against the wall. Letting go of one wrist, he worked his hand between their bodies and tore her dress back open so that her bare torso was pressed into the wood. "I've thought about taking you just like this," he whispered into her ear. "Listening to you scream, knowing that I can do damn near anything to you and make you love it. Tell me I can, Devon."

His voice was a challenge, and she got the weirdest feeling that he wanted to find her limits, to find some line she didn't want to cross. But Devon wasn't sure that line existed, not with him.

If any other man grabbed her like this and held her restrained, she knew she would lose it. But Luke—he wouldn't ever hurt her. In her gut, in her heart, in her soul, she knew it. And she trusted him. Craning her head around, she glanced at his shadowed face from the corner of her eye. "You can make me do anything, Luke. You can make me love it."

"Fuck . . ." The word escaped him on a gasp. His hands tightened and then inexplicably gentled. Plundering and ravishing turned to soft, silken seduction. His lips brushed across her shoulder, a soothing caress that comforted every bit as much as it aroused. "And me, Devon? Could I make you love me?"

Her voice shook a little as she replied, "Luke, you've already done that."

Any other words would have to wait until later. The time for speaking fell away as he stroked, and teased, and caressed her straight into the realm of paradise. His voice became a nonsensical rumble in her ear, and his hands brought her wrists down, his arms wrapping around her so that she embraced herself, and his arms enfolded all of her, holding her steady for his slow, gentle rhythm.

When they came, it was with a mingled groan, her head falling back onto his shoulder, his forward onto hers. It was possibly the most perfect moment in her entire life.

* * *

"DID you mean it?" he asked an hour later as they sat soaking in a hot, steaming tub of water. She sat with her back against his front, drowsy from the heat and the sex.

For a minute, his question didn't register, and then she slid a nervous look at him over her shoulder. "We've only been going out for a while, Luke."

That faint, knowing grin curved his lips, and he said, "That's not what I asked. Did you mean it?"

Blushing to the roots of her hair, she swallowed, squirmed, and finally blurted out, "Would you mind if I did?"

His arms came through the soapy water to band around her waist, tugging her closer. "I'd mind it if you didn't. I think I fell in love with you before I even knew you, before I even saw you," he whispered, kissing her neck. "I feel like I've loved you my whole life, and I've just been waiting to find you."

Tears stung her eyes. Wriggling away, she turned around and straddled his lap, not caring that the water sloshed on the floor, not caring that they didn't really fit like this in the old-fashioned claw-foot tub. "Yeah, I meant it," she said, leaning in to murmur the words against his lips. Then, a giddy smile on her lips, she said, "Never would have pegged you as the romantic type, Luke."

"Hey, I can get plenty romantic." Curving into her body, he rubbed his stubbled face against her neck. Devon squealed and arched away from him, wriggling back and giggling. She ended up with her knees wedged between his hips and the sides of the tub. Curling his arms around her waist, he tugged her close and rested his chin between her breasts, tilting his head back so he could stare at her. His voice went serious and soft as he murmured, "So, can you say it?"

Running a hand through his damp, disheveled hair, she smiled down at him. Something tender and soft moved through her heart as she met his gaze. "Yeah," she murmured, touching a finger to his lower lip. "I can say it." She replaced her finger with her mouth, kissing him gently, softly. Then, easing back, still keeping her lips pressed to his, she whispered, "I love you, Luke. I flat-out adore you."

* * *

"*I love you, Luke. I flat-out adore you.*"

Two days later, her softly spoken words still sent a primitive, possessive thrill through him. In the still quiet of the night, hours before dawn, he lay in bed next to her, unable to sleep. Devon lay cuddled up against him, lost in dreams. Occasionally, she'd make a soft little sound caught between a gentle snore and a kittenish little purr. She muttered something in her sleep and wiggled, pressing her butt back against him.

He pressed his lips to her shoulder and smiled. Even sound asleep and wearing flannel pajamas, the woman managed to turn him on and turn him inside out.

It was the inside-out part that was keeping him awake, though. Damn near three weeks had passed since some sick bastard had broken into her house, but the cops were clueless. More infuriating, Luke was clueless. It was like a ghost had done it; no fingerprints were left, no trail, no sign that anybody was following her or watching her. Luke was good, but shit, he couldn't track a ghost.

It was the complete lack of a trail that had him really worried. Some punk kid couldn't do that, no matter how smart the kid was. Coming and going without a sign was a mark of practice. The vicious nature behind killing a pet was even more telling. Professional thieves could come and go without a sign, but thieves generally weren't violent.

Devon rolled onto her belly and sighed, turning her face toward him. The faint moonlight streaming in through the window cast a silvery sheen to her delicate features and darkened her hair to near black. She looked defenseless, vulnerable.

Luke knew better. The woman had a fighter's heart. And a fighter's stubborn nature. She had an idea who her stalker was—he'd finally managed to pry that much out of her—but she wouldn't tell him who.

"You'll go all postal, Luke, and I won't have it. I'll talk to Detective White. She can handle it."

Postal. Yeah, that pretty much described it. She'd finally broken down and called Detective White about her suspicions, but she hadn't done it while he was in the room, and she flat-out refused to tell him.

Hell. That was fine. He'd figure it out himself. He waited until he knew she wasn't on the verge of waking up, and then he slid out of bed. On the way out of the room, he grabbed his jeans from the foot of the bed and pulled them on. He zipped them but didn't mess with the button as he headed downstairs.

Ever since the break-in, Luke had been existing mostly on combat naps. He was used to functioning on scant amounts of sleep, but not for weeks on end. Plus he was a hell of a lot older than he had been back when he'd still been with the Rangers. He was dog-tired, and some caffeine would be seriously great at the moment, but if he started coffee, Devon would wake up.

And then he'd have a hard time explaining why he was reading her e-mails. Figuring out the password for her work account shouldn't be too hard. Luke had held off on invading her privacy like this, but since the woman was being stubborn as a mule, he'd decided to hell with it. It was either go through her e-mails or sneak into Social Services after hours. He could do either one, but reading the e-mails was less risky.

Making do with a Diet Coke from the fridge, he settled down in her office and went about trying to figure out her password. He got it on the third try, and started going through her e-mails. Most of them were reminders about court dates, psychiatric counseling for her clients, that sort of thing. Some came directly from child advocate lawyers, and there was one name that seemed to pop up quite a bit over the past few weeks. He did a search and found mentions of the boy going back a good four months.

A lot of e-mails regarding him, though, over the past couple of weeks. Most of the e-mails were from a child advocate who was working to have the child permanently removed from the father's care on suspicions of abuse.

There was one that had been forwarded from a cop. A background check on the boy's dad, complete with pictures.

It took Luke less than fifteen seconds to figure out that this was the dad Devon suspected, and even less time to figure out why.

He had empty eyes. He managed to hide it pretty well with a friendly, open smile, but that smile didn't quite reach his eyes.

Luke continued skimming the guy's history, grimacing when he read about the wife's death, her arrest on suspicion of child abuse, the abrupt name change, and sudden relocation to a different state. But it wasn't until he got to the guy's earlier history that alarm bells really started to go off.

A marine. Commendations in Desert Storm. The information in the background check was sketchy, but that sparse information told Luke a hell of a lot. Eyes narrowed, he got his own laptop and got online, going to a different website, another government site and one he technically wasn't supposed to access anymore.

But the technicalities weren't going to keep him out, and neither was an outdated password.

Getting into that website took a little more finessing, but he was inside in under five minutes and reading classified information on one Staff Sergeant Curtis H. Waller.

"Son of a bitch," he swore. He tried to go a little deeper, but a message came up, blocking him from accessing more information. Hunkering over the keyboard, Luke pounded the keys and tried to go around or under the block, all with no luck.

A warning came up, and he shoved back from the desk and broke the connection with the website. The DOD could figure out who he was easy enough, but right now, none of them would throw too big a fit. If he tried to go deeper, though, people would get temperamental. Luke didn't have the kind of equipment he'd need if he wanted to get a little deeper without being tracked, and that was just fine.

Luke didn't need to get to that hidden information to figure out that most of the guy's service history was classified. That, in and of itself, wasn't disturbing. But combined with the lack of soul he'd glimpsed in the man's eyes, it got plenty disturbing.

All of it together was enough to convince Luke that Curtis Waller/Wilder was the man stalking Devon. And postal pretty much described exactly what Luke was going to do.

He shut down Devon's laptop and put it away, but before he could shut down his own, an e-mail appeared in his in-box. From Quinn. There was no message, just a subject line.

Turn on your IM.

Luke almost ignored it. But chances were, Quinn knew he was online—the weird twin connection deal at work. He logged on to the instant messenger service, and there was already a message waiting for him.

Who are you getting ready to kill?

Luke's lips quirked in a grin as he pounded out a reply.

Why do you think I'm getting ready to kill somebody?

Because you are. I can just tell. What's got you so pissed?

Luke blew out a harsh breath, debating on how much to explain. *It's a long story, don't know if I got time to tell it all right now.*

Then tell what you can now and explain more later.

So he did, keeping an ear out for Devon, should she wake early. *You're that sure he's the right guy?* Quinn asked.

Luke grinned. *I'll be more sure once I have him on the ground and I'm beating the shit out of him.*

So what if he ain't your guy? Then you're beating the shit out of the wrong guy.

Guy's been beating his kid. Any beating he gets, he deserves, far as I'm concerned. But he's the right guy. I know it.

There was a lengthy pause, and Luke could feel Quinn's anger as strong as if it were his own. Quinn didn't have many weaknesses, and Luke couldn't exactly call kids a weak point for his twin, but abused kids were one thing guaranteed to flip Quinn's switch.

Finally, words appeared in the window. *You want some help?*

Luke grinned. *Nah. I got this.*

Whatever. You let me know if you need me.

Quinn signed off without typing another word, and Luke leaned back, stared at the laptop monitor. There wouldn't be a reason to get ahold of Quinn. If Quinn was needed, the man would know. Hell, Luke was a little surprised his twin hadn't shown up already. He'd been having an internal debate over whether he should get somebody watching over Devon, and Quinn was the only person he'd trust enough.

The only thing that held him back was knowing that Devon would know—somehow, she'd know. He wasn't so much worried about her getting mad at him. If it kept her safe, she could get as mad as she wanted. But he knew her nerves were shot, and having somebody babysitting her would only add to the pressure. People under pressure too often did things they shouldn't do, and he needed her to be careful right now.

Still, he wasn't ruling the possibility out. Quinn would be there in a heartbeat if Luke needed him. *Two bodies, man. One mind.* It was something Jeb had told Luke way back. The three of them had just joined a unit, out on their first mission. Luke had been injured and his partner killed; their communication had been cut off. Luke had lain in hiding, convinced he was getting ready to breathe his last, and then Quinn, still a new guy at the time, had emerged from the shadows, leading the team.

Eerie as all get out sometimes, but oddly comforting. It was nice knowing you'd always have somebody to back you up in a jam and not even have to worry about getting word to him.

He smiled bitterly as he acknowledged that it wasn't exactly a two-way street. Luke could read Quinn's moods better than any other soul on earth, but Quinn wasn't the open book to Luke that Luke was to Quinn. Just like when Quinn had abruptly left the Rangers after Adam died, left the army, Luke had known there was something wrong, even aside from the obvious. He had felt it.

But he hadn't realized it was something serious enough that it had driven Quinn into counseling. Quinn absolutely hated doctors of any kind, Luke excluded. And head doctors were the absolute worst. He'd only go if he was forced. So, what had forced him into it?

Although Quinn seemed to have some sort of built-in compass where Luke was concerned, Luke couldn't home in on Quinn in the same way. He hadn't ever woken up in the middle of the night and known that Quinn needed to hear his voice.

But on Quinn's side, different story. The guy just knew sometimes—had some hidden knowledge Luke didn't have.

Luke didn't understand why, didn't know if it was something he did, some sort of wall he'd unintentionally built, or what. He suspected it could be. He was aware of his twin, an awareness he didn't have with anybody else, something that surpassed instinct, but he wasn't tuned in to Quinn the way Quinn was tuned in to him.

Probably because Luke had held back from Quinn. For the longest time, Quinn had kept him at a distance, and Luke had done the same thing. All the anger he'd sensed inside Quinn back when they'd first met had done a good job of keeping people at bay—his twin included.

That anger had slowly faded, but it never completely died. Neither did the darkness that lurked just under the surface.

There'd been a woman once, Elsa. They'd met her in Havana and spent four pretty damn fantastic days letting her wear the two of them out. The last day, she'd come to Luke and murmured, "*Watch your brother; he's got a darkness inside him. Something close to cruelty.*"

She'd been wrong. Quinn wasn't cruel. Luke couldn't deny his twin had a mean streak inside him. Mean streak or not, though, it seemed Quinn was the more sensitive of the two.

Smirking, Luke shut down his laptop and stood up from the desk. Yeah, Quinn was more attuned to their unique bond. In a way, that did make Quinn the more sensitive one.

But that wasn't something that Luke would share with his brother. Not so long as he liked his teeth the way they were.

* * *

AN hour later, as Luke leaned back against the wall, enjoying the sight of Devon slowly waking up over a cup of coffee, his cell phone rang.

It lay on the counter next to Devon's and he tipped his head, read the number on the display.

It rang a second and a third time before Devon turned her head and looked at him with bleary eyes. "You gonna get that?"

He shrugged. "Nah. If it's anything an important, they'll call back."

"Not the hospital, is it? Luke, you better not keep blowing them off." She yawned, rubbed her eyes, and then sent him a glare. It wasn't too effective, considering she was still flushed from sleep, her hair tousled around her shoulders, and her lids drooping low over her eyes like she was trying to slip back into sleep.

"It's not the hospital. Old friend from back when I was in the army." He shrugged and took his half-empty cup over to the coffee-pot and added more. He drank it strong and black, and the caffeine was already jumping through his system. He didn't much care for the artificial stimulant, but until he got some serious shut-eye, he'd have to make do. "I'm too tired for casual conversation."

"So what if he isn't calling for casual conversation? Most people don't call at the crack of dawn just to gab."

Crooking a brow at her, Luke reminded her, "I left the army more than five years ago. Not much else he could want besides casual conversation." Well, except to maybe rip his ass for trying to sneak into the DOD's website and access classified information. Chances were whoever caught Luke had figured that going through a friend, somebody from his old unit, would definitely be the friendly way to approach it. And it was friendlier; the other option could be threatening to arrest Luke's ass.

He didn't figure they'd follow through with any threats, and it wasn't like they were going to catch him doing it again. There wouldn't be a next time, because Luke already knew what he needed to know.

If he did by some weird quirk of fate need more information, he'd cover his tail better.

But none of that was exactly something he could share with Devon.

"Ummm." She yawned and rested her chin on her fist, stared into her coffee. "You working today?"

"Yeah." He glanced at his watch and sighed. "I've got to get going here soon. Working seven to seven. I talked to the head of the ER, Deb Reilly, convinced her that I didn't need to be pulling late-ass shifts until we knew you were safe." He shrugged. "Her daughter was the victim of a stalker attack a few years ago, so she understands. Once this is taken care of, I told her I'd put in an extra shift a week for a month or so."

He watched as she slid off the counter and padded over to the sink to rinse out her coffee cup. "You coming straight home after work?"

She shrugged. "I dunno. I need to buy a few more Christmas presents for Mom and Dad." Turning around, she leaned back against the counter and grinned. "I've already bought your presents."

Setting his cup down, he crossed over to her and wrapped his arms around her waist. Nuzzling her neck, he murmured, "I'd be perfectly happy to come downstairs Christmas morning and find you under the tree. Nekkid."

She poked him in the ribs and snorted. "I bet." She snuggled up against him and sighed. "We haven't really talked about what we're doing for Christmas. Do you want to go see your dad? You hardly ever talk about your family."

"Dad's actually going on a cruise," Luke said, smirking as he remembered the e-mail from his dad the other day. Patrick had been seeing a lady who lived about forty minutes away from the ranch. Luke knew it was pretty serious, but still, the abrupt decision to take two weeks off and disappear on some tropical cruise, that had thrown Luke a little. "I'm thinking about taking a week in the spring to go back home." Glancing down at her, he suggested, "You know, you could come with me."

She flushed, shrugged. "Maybe. So your dad is it?"

"Actually . . . no." Luke tugged her back against him, slid a hand down her back. It was awkward, telling her about Quinn, even more so now because he knew he needed to get the two of them together. If he really wanted to spend his life with this woman, then Quinn needed to meet her.

Meet her, accept her.

Waiting hadn't made it any easier, though. It was still . . . just weird. Awkward. He cleared his throat, shrugged, but even that felt disjointed and unnatural.

"I've got a brother. He's kind of a loner, moves around a lot." He smiled a little. Describing Quinn as a loner was like describing Devon as just some lady he knew. Neither description even came close. "Maybe . . . maybe I could see if he wanted to come over for Christmas. Would you mind?"

Devon tipped her head back to look up at him. "You never told me you had a brother."

Luke smiled. "Never really came up."

"Hmmm." Rising up on her toes, she kissed his chin. "Of course you should ask him to come over. That's what Christmas is for, families."

She gave him a winsome smile and asked, "Is he anything like you?"

Luke laughed, a little unsettled. "Yes. And no."

"Meaning . . . ?"

Shaking his head, Luke said, "You'll have to meet him to get the point." The phone rang just as he was getting ready to mention that his brother was actually his twin—identical. Physically, so alike. Emotionally, so different.

Devon grimaced and grabbed her cell phone from the island. "Sorry, Luke. This isn't a call I can ignore." She flipped it open, and Luke watched as the sleep cleared from her eyes, as her easy smile faded, and a grim disgust settled in its place.

It was a short call, mostly filled with terse "Yes," "No," and "What hospital?" When the call ended, he turned and held out a thermal cup he'd filled with coffee and said, "Looks like you're going to have one of those days."

"Tell me about it." Rolling her eyes, she grabbed the cup from him, pushed on her toes to kiss his lips. "I gotta get moving."

"Hmmm." He snaked out a hand and fisted her hair before she

could slip away. "Yeah. Me, too." He brushed his lips against her, lingered for a moment, breathing in the warm, sexy scent of her body. "I love you."

She flushed, a self-conscious grin tugging at her lips. "Yeah, love you, too."

* * *

ONE of those days.

Hell. That didn't even come close to describing the day she'd just had.

She'd spent half the morning at the hospital, where one of the moms she'd worked with off and on for three years delivered a baby that tested positive for cocaine and barbiturates. It was the woman's third child—and the third child born an addict.

Her afternoon was eaten up with a court appearance, a visit to check on how well Tim Wilder was settling in with the Grants, paperwork done in between phone calls, and two more home visits.

By the time she was done, Devon was so tired she couldn't see straight, her feet hurt, her back hurt, and the thought of braving the mall and traffic to get some shopping done was enough to give her hives.

"Done for the day?"

"Yep." Devon smiled at the security officer and had to glance at his badge to remember his name. "Doing okay, Ronnie?"

"Doing just fine." He fell into step alongside her.

Devon rolled her eyes. "My car is in plain view of the door, Ronnie."

He smiled. "Yeah, but if your boss hears I didn't walk you outside when it was getting dark, with all the trouble you've been having, he'd have my hide."

They pushed through the door, surrounded by a throng of people who were also heading out for the day. Devon glanced at the crowd and smiled. "I don't think anybody is going to bother me when I'm surrounded by this many people."

"And he'd still have my hide," Ronnie replied, shaking his head. Then he gave her a somber look. "You know what kind of crazy people are out there. Somebody wants to hurt you bad enough, being surrounded by people won't stop them."

Whether it was his words or the chill in the air, Devon didn't know, but suddenly, she felt frozen to the bone. Sometime during the day the temperature had dropped, and the light jacket she wore offered little protection. Snow flurries were coming down in a soft, steady drift. The flakes melted almost as soon as they hit the ground, but many of the cars had a thin white blanket forming on them, including hers.

"*Somebody wants to hurt you* . . . "

She reached her car and tossed Ronnie a smile. He waited until she climbed inside the car and locked the doors before heading back inside. As she started the car, her cell phone started to ring.

"Hey."

The sound of Luke's voice had her smiling, and she murmured, "Hey back." After starting the car, she leaned her head against the headrest and closed her eyes, willing some of the tension in her muscles to relax.

"You leaving work?"

"Yeah."

"You didn't walk out alone, did you?"

Devon rolled her eyes. "No, Daddy. I had the nice security guard walk me to my car."

"Smart-ass," he grunted.

In the background, she could hear the low hum of voices, punctuated by an occasional angry shout. "Sounds kind of busy."

"Yeah. Pileup on the I-75. I think they're still cleaning up; you probably need to find a different way home."

Devon muttered, "Great." She opened her eyes and looked at the snow falling. The car hadn't warmed enough to melt it. "It's starting to snow, too. People around here drive like morons in the snow."

Luke chuckled. "Baby, that isn't snow."

She wrinkled her nose. "Baby, you've spent a couple of winters here by now. You know how people act around snow; they think even a few flurries equals the blizzard of the century." Her breath came out in frosty little puffs of air, and she shivered. The air coming out of the vent was still too cool, and she cranked it up a little more, wishing she had put on a warmer coat.

"I bet half of you haven't even seen a real blizzard. You still going shopping?"

She made a face. "No. I need to, but I'm too tired. You think you'll be able to get out of there in time?"

"I'll be there before eight." He fell quiet for a moment. "Maybe you could go over and hang at Danielle's for a while. Until I get home."

Grimacing, Devon shifted the phone to her other hand and put the car in reverse, maneuvering out of the parking space. "By the time I get home, it will be less than two hours. I think I can handle being home for that period of time."

"Damn it, Devon." His voice was low, frustrated, and she could practically see his face, could practically see him pushing a hand through already tousled hair.

She almost told him to get back to work, to stop hovering. Remembering what Ronnie had said—"*Somebody wants to hurt you bad enough, being surrounded by people won't stop them*"—it was nothing but a fact. What if whoever it was followed Devon to Danielle's? If somebody else got hurt because of her, Devon would choke on the guilt.

But how likely was it that something would happen in those two hours? Besides, after Luke talked with Danielle back when they first found the dead dog in Devon's house, Danielle had gotten a security system of her own installed. If anybody tried to break in, the alarm would sound. Devon had her own alarm system, nice and beefed up, thanks to Luke, but at Danielle's, she wouldn't be alone, and there was that whole safety in numbers thing.

Sighing, she tucked a strand of hair back behind her ear. "Okay. I'll go over to Danielle's for a while. She'll be home by now anyway." Danielle's job as office manager at a local ophthalmologist generally wasn't one that kept her working late.

The busy sprawl of the county building loomed in front of her. This time of day, traffic was always slow-moving. Add in the traffic for Christmas shoppers, and the street was practically a parking lot. She made a face and added, "Besides, the way traffic looks, it might take me until eight to get home." Catching an opening in the traffic, she zipped out of the parking lot, ignoring the horn blaring behind her. "I better go so I don't cause another wreck."

"Be careful. Love you."

A delighted thrill pulsed through her, and a grin spread across her face. "I love you, too." Then she disconnected and tossed the phone onto the console.

He loves me.

That sexy, smart, considerate guy loved her.

* * *

THE drive took a good forty-five minutes. As she turned down her street, she saw Danielle's car in her driveway. She glanced longingly toward her house, thought of a glass of wine.

But the nagging reminder of common sense sent her across the street instead. Inside the lined leather of her boots, her toes were frozen. As she rang Danielle's doorbell, she wiggled them and waited.

A minute passed, and no answer. She rang the doorbell again and glanced back at Danielle's car. It sat there, covered with a fine blanket of snow. Devon glanced down the street. Nolan and Shara DeVille lived next to Danielle, and they usually got home about the time Danielle did. No snow blanketed their cars; they were still too warm for the flakes do anything but melt as they landed.

A shiver that had nothing to do with the cold raced down Devon's spine. Slowly, she backed away one step, then another. *Paranoia at it's finest,* she thought as she reached for her cell phone.

A flicker of movement caught her eye, and she glanced toward one of the windows. It was Danielle's bedroom. The lights were on, and Devon stared as the curtains fluttered. Just a slight movement, but enough to let light spill out through the pane of glass and let Devon see a swath of red: a bloody handprint, the fingers smeared.

Her throat closed up on her. The skin on the back of her neck started to crawl. There was a quiet snick, and she glanced at the front door, watched as it opened to reveal Danielle.

But she wasn't alone. Curtis Wilder stood behind her, holding the woman upright as he smiled at Devon. Danielle's face was battered, covered with blood, and her eyes were wide and terrified. Curtis held a gun in his hand, the muzzle pressed to Danielle's temple. "Come on in, Devon. You're crashing the party, but that's fine."

Icy fear made her movements stiff, jerky; she felt like a damn marionette as she took one step toward the porch, followed by another. She tried to keep the phone in her hand hidden, but Curtis saw it. He stroked Danielle's face with the gun and said, "Drop it, bitch. Otherwise, I'll drop her."

Her voice shook as Devon said, "You don't want to hurt her. She isn't the one who took your son away."

A queer light lit his eyes. "No. That was you. But that doesn't mean I wouldn't like to hurt her." He shoved Danielle away from him, off to the side like she was just so much trash, and she collapsed, hitting the floor with a dull thud.

Leveling the gun at Devon, he said again, "Drop the phone." When she hesitated, he shrugged, shifted his aim to Danielle. "Me and your pretty friend here had a lot of fun. I've been here with her all day. She could probably use a doctor." A cold smile curled his lips, and he added, "Actually, I'm pretty damn convinced she could use a doctor. But if you don't drop that phone, she isn't going to need one. Corpses don't need much more than burying."

She dropped the phone, and it hit the ground.

Headlights splashed beams of light across the yard, and hope, for two seconds, leaped to life. Two seconds, because she watched as Curtis shifted, lowering the gun so that the driver of the car would see nothing more than a man in the door and Devon on the front porch.

Too far away to see what Devon saw.

He'd kill Danielle without blinking an eye. And then he'd come after Devon. Whether he got her tonight or not, the man didn't care. He'd just keeping coming until he did.

"Come inside and join us, Devon."

On stiff legs, she stepped inside, edging past him, trying not to touch him. The door banged shut. Something beeped off to the side, and she turned her head, watched with dread as Curtis reset the alarm system.

He smiled. "Nice system. Took a few minutes to get around it, but I managed. Not quite as good as the one your boyfriend did at your place."

That one small hope died, even as it tried to flare to life.

As he reached out to stroke the muzzle of the gun down her cheek, she cringed away. Devon sank her teeth into her lip to keep from whimpering as he shifted and grabbed a fistful of her hair in his free hand, yanking.

A soft, pitiful moan escaped Danielle's lips. Devon watched as Danielle forced her hands underneath her body, trying to force herself upright, but she collapsed back onto the floor. Her bright green eyes were hardly visible because of the bruising and swelling. Her lip was split open, nearly twice the normal size.

Around her neck there was a series of dark, splotchy marks—a necklace of bruises. The bastard had choked her. Fury and terror simmered inside Devon's belly, and she jerked away from him, but he wouldn't let go. His hand tightened on the knot of the hair, and then Curtis shoved her, sent her sprawling onto the floor.

She slammed out her hands just in time and shoved to her feet. He let her, but the second she was standing, he backhanded her.

Years and years of self-defense classes sprang into place, and she lifted an arm, trying to block him. All it did was make him laugh as he countered.

He struck again, catching her in the mouth. The metallic taste of blood hit her tongue. She went flying backward, crashing into a wooden table. Devon might have screamed. Pain exploded through her, and there were a couple of terrified seconds when she couldn't get her arms and legs to move.

The sound of his footsteps, soft, almost silent, sent adrenaline rushing through her, numbing the pain and lending her the desperate energy to move. Shoving to her hands and knees, she spied something from the corner of her eye: a bookend, red, shaped like a heart, and heavy. Closing her hand around it, Devon lurched to her feet as Curtis drew near. He glanced at the bookend and smirked. "You planning on hitting me with that, bitch?"

Sidling away, she fought to keep some distance between them. "What do you want?"

He shrugged. It was a careless, negligent move, but it didn't match the hot fury that lit his eyes. "I want nosy little bitches like you to leave me and my boy alone. How I raise him is my business." He jabbed a thumb toward his chest.

"And you think hurting me is going to help get him back?"

Curtis sneered. "They aren't going to give him back. You think I'm stupid? That bitch lawyer did a good job seeing to that. And my son? That whiny little prick ran his mouth the minute he had a chance."

"*Whiny little prick.*"

"If that's how you feel about Tim, then what does it matter if he doesn't live with you?" As she spoke, she backed her way along the hallway, circling away from Danielle. In the back of her mind, she had some dim hope that Danielle could manage to call for help, but it was a very dim one. Devon had seen people beaten nearly to death before, and Danielle was pretty close to that point.

In a silky voice, Curtis replied, "Because he's mine, bitch. My kid, mine to do whatever in the hell I want to. Try to raise him to be a real man, and all he does is sit and write that stupid poetry shit or ridiculous stories. Finally shows a little bit of spine, defends himself, and what happens? Gets arrested for assault, and we get saddled with you. Punk can't do jack shit right."

By this time, she'd sidestepped her way to the stairs; she could go up, or into the kitchen. Danielle's kitchen was a cook's dream, big island, lots of shiny pots, pans—and lots of shiny knives. Her mind rejected that outright. Even if she could manage to get her hands on a knife, he'd get it away from her.

She shifted toward the stairs instead, backing her way up one at a time. "So what are you going to do?" she demanded, her voice rising a little. She hated the panicked, terrified sound of it, but it was taking everything she had just to keep from bolting. Running blindly from a guy like Curtis seemed like a dumb thing to do. Screw false bravado; he already knew she was scared, anyway.

"You and me, we're going to have a little party. I'm going to show you what women are good for, going to teach you not to interfere with a man and his kid."

Devon reached the landing and started to circle around, through the bathroom, through the connecting door to Danielle's bedroom. "And when you're done? You plan on killing me? Don't you think people will check out my cases and work and find you?"

He smirked. "They already know about me, bitch. That lawyer saw to that, with her fucking background checks. But they'll come looking for a man that ain't around any longer. I disappeared once. I can do it again."

"You weren't wanted for murder last time. Cops tend to look for people they suspect of murder."

Curtis smiled. "They'll have a hard time convicting me of murder if they can't find me . . . or you. When I'm done with you, your own mama won't recognize you—and I plan on putting you someplace where nobody will ever find you."

Oh, God.

Adrenaline-fueled panic tried to take over, and Devon battled it back through sheer will. She'd been hurt before and lived through it. She'd been younger, stupider, but the man who had hurt her when she was a child wasn't the same make as the guy in front of her.

Both of them had been predators—that was a certain fact—but Curtis wasn't just a predator. He was a killer. And if she didn't do something—

He echoed her every move, still watching her with that amused smile on his lips. "Are you going to scream? Or maybe I should ask if you'll try. Your friend tried to scream for nearly half the day before she finally gave up. Every time she opened that mouth to scream, she paid for it."

Her mouth was trembling; Devon could feel herself quivering as the terror inside her worked to find some release. Yeah, she could just imagine Curtis going to work on Danielle every time she tried to call for help. The memory of her friend's battered, bruised face and the knowledge of what he planned on doing to both of them finally gave Devon the courage to move.

He planned on killing her anyway; trying to get away now, what was that going to cost her?

Letting the tears flood her eyes, she whimpered, "Please don't hurt me. I swear, I just thought I was doing what was best . . ."

"Oh, so you're going to try begging, huh?" He rolled his eyes, distracted just a second by her tears. She swung out, fast and hard. Curtis saw her swinging, but this time, he didn't react quickly enough. She managed to hit him on the temple with the sharp corner of the bookend. Without waiting to see if she'd done him a lick of damage, she whirled around, running for the stairs.

She reached the bottom before he caught her.

He pounced, taking her to the ground under him, and he flipped her over like she was a rag doll. A big, mean hand closed around her neck when she opened her mouth to scream, closing down, cutting her air off before she managed a strangled, "Hel—"

"Stupid little bitch," he whispered, leaning down and putting his face into hers. Blood trickled from his temple to splash hot onto her face. "I'm going to make you hurt for that."

He squeezed and squeezed, and Devon clawed and tore at his fingers, but his grip was merciless. Darkness danced in around her, and as she swayed closer and closer into unconsciousness, she heard the sound of cloth ripping.

* * *

LUKE lowered the phone back into its cradle with a softly muttered curse. Devon wasn't answering her cell phone. For the life of him, he couldn't remember Danielle's number, didn't even know that he'd ever known it.

Shooting a glance at the clock readout on the phone, he started to stand up and get back to work. A few more charts to finish up, and he'd be out of here.

Half a heartbeat later, he stopped. He was probably going to end up looking like an idiot, and Devon would no doubt would be irritated.

But that didn't keep him from calling the police.

* * *

CRUEL fingers pinched her through the thin silk of her bra. Devon shrank back in revulsion and wished he'd just kept on strangling her, instead of letting her get enough air so she woke up.

Now he had a piece of duct tape over her mouth, and she had to fight the urge to puke as he tore her skirt off. "You're a skinny little bitch. That man you got sniffing around after you, he either likes them skinny as a damn stick, or you give a damn good blow job." Dipping his head, Curtis pressed his mouth to her cheek and licked her. "You give a good blow, bitch? You want to show me? Maybe if I like it enough, I won't hurt you too bad for hitting me."

She gagged, swallowed. Behind the makeshift gag, if she puked, she'd choke. Saliva pooled in her mouth, and she couldn't swallow fast enough, but every time she did, the urge to vomit got stronger and stronger.

Curtis lifted his head and looked at her face. Her disgust and fear must have shown, because he laughed as he shoved a hand between her thighs. "I'll take that as a no. Eh, it's okay. Don't really want to take that tape off, because if I do, and you try to scream . . ." He smiled and stroked his fingers across the abraded, tender skin at her neck. "I'd hate for you to faint again on me. I want to see your face as I—"

In lieu of finishing the sentence, he shoved a hand between her thighs, fingers rough and cruel.

Moaning in her throat, she averted her head. From where they lay in the hallway, Devon could see Danielle; he'd gagged her, as well. Must have done it when Devon passed out. The other woman's eyes were still closed, her hands and feet bound together with the same duct tape that had been used to cover both of their mouths.

In defeat, Devon closed her own eyes.

Luke . . .

"Look at me, bitch." His fingers cupped her chin and jerked her face around to meet his, but Devon didn't open her eyes.

She didn't want to see him as he . . . as he . . . He shoved up, fisted a hand in her hair, hauling her off the floor. "Look at me, fucking whore."

When she ignored his second, and third, and fourth order, he shoved her against the wall and closed his hand around her neck. The need for air overcame the need to escape into her own personal oblivion, and as he choked her again, Devon opened her eyes, closed her fingers around his wrist and jerked, scratched, fought against him.

Panting, he leaned into her. "That's better." He loosened his hold on her neck just a little, and she sucked in air through her abused throat, but just as her breathing leveled back out, he tightened his fingers again.

He kept playing that little game until her throat felt like fire, and even breathing was agony. Eventually, it became harder and harder to struggle back into awareness or even to try to breathe. She was only dimly aware as he dropped her to the floor again. From the corner of her eye, she saw the red bookend again, thought of reaching for it.

Luke . . .

There was a crash.

Luke.

Dimly, almost dreamily, she turned her head toward the sound. Luke? The dreamlike state persisted, and she felt like she was moving through quicksand as she lifted her head, tried to focus.

Curtis was on the floor beside her, facedown. Blood flowed.

"Luke," she tried to whisper, but no sound came out.

Red and blue lights splashed through the small windows that lined the front door. But by the time the cops broke down the door, Devon was already unconscious.

TWELVE

Two Weeks Later

Sᴛᴀɴᴅɪɴɢ at the window, Devon stared at the For Sale sign in Danielle's front yard. The other woman had lived through the attack, and after spending ten days in the hospital, Danielle had been released three days ago.

But she hadn't come home.

Devon couldn't blame her. Every time she looked across the street at Danielle's place, fear, nausea, and a disconnected sense of disbelief overtook her.

Curtis Wilder was dead.

Luke had tried to keep her from reading the details, but she'd had Noelle get her a copy of the police report, detailing how her attacker had been found lying on the floor next to Devon's unconscious body, the back of his head bashed in.

His blood and bits of his hair had been found on the marble bookend lying by his body. The exact details of how he'd died were a mystery to Devon, to the cops, to Luke. She didn't remember killing him, didn't think she could have, not at that point.

But nobody else had been on the premises when the cops arrived.

Luke arrived less than three minutes later, and as they'd loaded Devon onto a stretcher, he'd been by her side.

Most of the night was a blissful blur, but she still couldn't go to sleep without seeing Curtis's face.

"You ought to be sitting down. Resting."

She looked over her shoulder at Luke. The past two weeks had been hell on him; Devon was pretty sure they were just as awful for him, in a way, as they were for her. He'd lost weight, and although he smiled at her, it always seemed strained.

"I'm fine," she said quietly, resting her head against the window. The cool chill of it felt good. She hardly ever felt anything anymore. Not hunger, not pain. Her bruises were fading, but she still looked like she'd gone a few rounds with a heavyweight boxer.

Physically, the pain was there—sort of, and she was aware of it—sort of. But it wasn't like she really felt it, more like she was experiencing somebody else's pain.

"Are you hungry?"

Devon shook her head.

"You hardly ate anything at lunch."

She shrugged. "I'm tired of soup." For a while, it was all she'd been able to get down through her throat. Now that she could actually swallow without pain, there was no reason she couldn't eat.

She just didn't want to.

"We could go out to eat. Do some Christmas shopping." He tried to smile, and it fell flat. "Only have three more days."

She cringed inwardly. Out. Around people. Shaking her head, she whispered, "No."

"Devon . . ."

Looking back at him, she waited. Luke stared at her, and in the misty gray of his eyes, she saw the hell he was going through, and distantly, she hurt for him.

She couldn't work up the energy to find it in herself to care. But if she kept standing there, staring at Danielle's empty house, he'd just keep hovering. Turning away from the window, she gave him a vacant, halfhearted smile. "I think I'm going to lie down."

She passed by him, and from the corner of her eye, she saw him reach out to touch her. She paused, froze inside, and then shame flooded her as he closed his hand into a fist and let it fall back to his side. "Try to get some sleep," he said hollowly.

Sleep. No, she didn't want to sleep.

When she slept, she dreamed. And only in her dreams did she really remember much of what happened.

It eluded her almost the moment she surfaced, but whatever happened in her dreams was enough to have her fearing sleep almost as much as she feared everything else.

* * *

LUKE dropped into a seat across from Quinn and signaled the waitress for a beer. The steakhouse was as crowded today as it had been the night he'd run into Devon, and for a few minutes, he was glad of the noise, glad of the distraction. It drowned out the ugly, ridiculing voice in his head.

You failed her.

Yeah. He'd failed her, thanks; he didn't need the glaring neon reminder. It was a fact he was going to have to live with—and worse, one that Devon had to live with.

"You look like shit," Quinn said without preamble.

Luke didn't bother with a pretense. With Quinn, it wasn't necessary. "I feel like shit." When his twin had called that morning to say he was in town, Luke had to admit, he was a little put off. He couldn't leave Devon alone; he knew he was hovering, as she called it, but he couldn't stop.

But then Devon's mom had shown up and browbeaten Devon into some Christmas shopping. It was interesting, the way a mom could make her child do something she definitely didn't want to, even as a grown-up. Luke's experience with having a mom was nonexistent, and he'd watched the exchange with something akin to fascination and envy.

Liz alternately bullied, chided, and dared Devon, until Devon gave in and agreed to do some shopping. On their way out, the older woman had paused beside him, patted his cheek. There was a world of understanding in her eyes, even though she didn't say a single word.

So while Devon was out shopping, or pretending to, Luke called his brother and asked where they could meet up. The restaurant wouldn't have been his choice, because Devon might end up at that mall. But Quinn was already at the mall, checking out the bookstore, and Luke wasn't about to explain why he didn't want to be there.

"What do you think about Dad heading down to the Bahamas with Carrie Moorehaven?" Luke asked, trying hard not to think about Devon and failing miserably.

His brother shrugged, but there was a ghost of a smile on his face. "Figure it's about time. She's only been trying to get his attention since I met her."

Luke laughed. "She's been trying to get his attention for as long as I can remember." Closing his fingers around his beer, he lifted it, but instead of taking a drink, he just stared at the brown bottle.

Feeling Quinn's eyes on him, he lowered the beer back down and tried to focus on his brother. Focus wasn't his strong point lately, and he couldn't make himself relax worth anything. "You going to be around here for Christmas?" he asked, even though he hoped Quinn said no. He wouldn't let his brother spend the holiday alone, but maybe Quinn had plans . . .

"Nah. Jeb called me a few days ago, asked me if I wanted to meet up with him, do some skiing. Might do a little hunting." Quinn rolled his eyes, smirking. "I still don't see the appeal of shooting deer, but I could go for some peace and quiet."

"His cabin in Vermont?"

Quinn nodded. "Yeah. Thinking I might try to find some work

in the town near the cabin, maybe spend a while up there. Jeb's talking like he might be up there for a few weeks at least."

"Weeks?" Luke repeated. "Why weeks? He didn't get hurt, did he?"

"Nah. Just taking some downtime." He shrugged and added, "God knows he probably needs the downtime." Pausing, he took a drink of his beer. "Actually, I think he's pulling out. Not altogether, but . . ." Quinn stopped in midsentence, blew out a hard puff of air. "Jeb said they disbanded the unit. Reassigned Brandon and the younger guys to different teams. Offered reassignment to Jeb, but he didn't want to start over again. Said he might think about teaching or training or some shit."

Brows drawing together over his eyes, Luke said, "Are you serious?"

"As a heart attack."

"Damn." Then he cocked his head, eying Quinn curiously. "You said Jeb and the younger guys. What about Tony?"

"Beats the hell out of me," Quinn said, his voice sharp as a blade. Anger throbbed there, but it was an icy-cold rage. His eyes cut to Luke's, and he shook his head before Luke could even form the question. "Don't. Okay? Just don't."

Quinn lifted his hands, scrubbed them over his face. When he lowered them, the harsh, angry features had softened just a little.

"Everything okay, Quinn?"

Smirking, Quinn lifted his bottle and saluted Luke with it. "Right as rain."

Leaning back, he studied Luke. The look in those familiar gray eyes was one that Luke knew spelled out trouble. "So when do I get to meet this girl of yours?"

He'd wanted to have his twin meet Devon on Christmas, but now . . . now it didn't seem like such a good idea. Quinn wasn't the easiest person to handle under ideal circumstances. The past few weeks? Not ideal in any way, shape, or form. "Sometime." He shrugged. "Soon. Maybe."

"Why not now?"

Thinking back to the past few weeks, Luke shook his head. "Bad timing, Quinn." Seriously bad timing. Hell, he had his concerns about introducing them period, although he knew he needed to. But Quinn would home in on Devon's past; somehow or other, something she did, something she said would clue him in, he'd see her scars, and Quinn would make a quicker jump than Luke had. Luke needed to prepare Quinn first, but now was definitely *not* the time.

"Yeah, I figured something like that. You've been in a bitch of a mood the past few weeks." He lifted his beer to his lips, took a drink. "Been waiting to hear why, but you ain't called me. It's about her."

Luke heard the undercurrent, heard Quinn's need to know what was going on. Sighing, he rolled his shoulders, tried to ease some of the tension inside him. "Devon was attacked a few weeks ago," he said quietly, passing his beer from one hand to the other. "He hurt her pretty bad, scared her to death."

Luke trailed off, his mouth going dry as he remembered rushing inside Danielle's house to see the paramedics hovering over Devon's still body. The hours that followed had been the most awful hours of his life. She'd briefly come to in the ambulance, but her battered throat had made speech impossible.

Even now, her voice had a husky, rough quality that Luke wasn't sure would ever go away. A permanent reminder of his failure. "Some bastard had been stalking her," Luke said brusquely. "You remember that guy I told you about?"

"The one you wanted to kill that morning. Yeah."

"He'd been stalking her. I didn't want her home alone." His voice cracked, and for a moment, Luke didn't think he could do this. *Shit, shit, shit.* Squeezing his eyes closed, he whispered, "I asked her to wait across the street at her friend's. But he'd been over there, waiting for her. Just waiting. He beat the shit out of the girl, and then he went and did it to Devon."

Quinn was silent.

For that, Luke was thankful. Words were pointless by then. They did nothing to ease his guilt, and they did nothing to bring him comfort, either. But Quinn slid his hand across the table, closed his fingers around Luke's wrist. Like grabbing onto a lifeline, Luke turned his hand over and clutched his brother's. "I failed her. I knew something would happen, kept telling myself I should call you, have you come watch her for me while I was at work, but when I mentioned doing something like that, it freaked her out. I didn't want her more nervous, figured that wouldn't help, but I knew I needed you there, and I didn't call you. I fucked up, and she damn near died because of me."

"That isn't true," Quinn said. He glanced around the crowded steakhouse with a scowl and then slid out of the seat, threw a twenty on the table. "Come on. You and me don't need this shit right now."

On stiff, wooden legs, Luke got up and followed Quinn out of the steakhouse. Quinn walked in silence, and Luke followed aimlessly behind him, uncertain where Quinn was going and not really caring.

"How do I live like this, Quinn?" he asked raggedly. "How do I live knowing that I failed her? I was supposed to protect her."

Quinn took his time answering. "How did she get away?"

"Get away?" Luke shook his head, not understanding the question at first. "She didn't . . . She—the cops think she killed him when he tried to come at her. He'd already beat the hell out of her, kept choking her until she passed out, then letting her go until she woke up and he could do it again. Looks like he was getting ready to rape her, and she got ahold of some bookend, brained him with it. He was dead, and she was unconscious when the cops found them."

"How did the cops know to go check things out? Neighbors?"

Shoving a hand through his hair, Luke answered, "I was worried. She didn't answer her phone. So I called—"

"And they found her. Even if the guy wasn't dead, they would have found her."

"Not soon enough," Luke said harshly.

They stopped in front of a big, mean-looking Harley. It had lots of chrome and lots of black paint. Quinn rested a hip against it, folding his arms across his chest and leveling a steady gaze at Luke's face. "They found her alive, didn't they? Luke, that's better than what could have happened." A grimace twisted his lips, and he muttered, "Believe me, I know."

"That's not good enough." Luke shook his head, his eyes burning. "It's not. I can't live with that."

"You have no choice," Quinn said, in an oddly gentle voice. "You can't undo what's happened."

"You think I don't fucking know that?" Luke demanded. He spun away and started to pace, ignoring the ebb and flow of holiday shoppers who rushed out of the mall to shove last-minute gifts into their trunks and then go back inside for more. A car paused by the spot where Quinn sat on the bike, waiting to see if they were leaving, but the twins ignored him, and the man finally drove off.

"It's over. It's done. I get that. What I don't get is how I'm supposed to live with this guilt choking me. I don't know how I'm supposed to act around her, if I'm allowed to touch her, if I should hold her when she's having nightmares. I don't know what to do, Quinn."

Quinn waited a beat and then drawled, "Well, that's gotta be new territory for you." Shoving off the bike, he moved to intercept Luke, blocking his brother's ceaseless pacing. "You really think you feeling guilty is helping her at all?"

Luke shook his head, hardly able to breathe past the knot in his chest. "I can't not feel guilty, Quinn. I sent her over to that house, because I thought she'd be safer there."

"Since when were you a fortune-teller, Luke?" Quinn shook his head. "Safety's an illusion half the time anyway. We both know that.

But whether you get it or not, you did save her. Now finish the job; save her from letting this destroy the rest of her life. And yours."

"*Finish the job.*"

* * *

"*FINISH the job.*"

Luke paced the living room floor for the hundredth time and then stopped, swore out loud. Quinn made it sound so damn easy. "*Finish the job.*"

Never in his life had Luke left a job unfinished, but Devon wasn't a job. She was the woman he loved, a woman he hadn't protected.

Stop it. Coming to a halt in the middle of the floor, he pressed the heels of his hands to his eyes and muttered out loud, "Just stop. You can't help her with this if you let the guilt eat you alive." Logically, hey, he knew that. But putting it aside was going to be harder. Luke knew he'd be fighting this guilt for the rest of his life.

But if he didn't do something, he'd be spending that life alone.

In his gut, he knew it.

Devon was drifting away from him, slowly, bit by bit. Every day she became a little more distant. He had to get her to forgive him for failing her, had to convince her that she could trust him to take care of her. Had to convince her that he loved her more than anybody else ever would.

"*Finish the job: save her from letting this destroy the rest of her life.*" Damn Quinn. His twin had a knack for pointing out what should have been obvious.

There were times when it astounded Luke just how clearly Quinn saw things. Quinn kept himself so far apart from people, and most people were more than happy to let him keep that distance. Including Luke, at times. As much as he hated it, there were times when the storms he sensed raging inside his twin left Luke feeling so damn tangled inside, it was a relief when Quinn pulled back.

Maybe it was that distance that let Quinn see things so clearly. Whatever it was, Quinn was right.

If Luke let this take over, then it wouldn't matter all that much that Devon had escaped with her life, that Curtis Wilder or Waller or whoever in the hell he had been, it wouldn't matter that he hadn't raped her, hadn't killed her.

She'd retreat back inside her shell, that safe, lonely place where people couldn't hurt her and where she'd slowly die inside. Where nobody could touch her—including Luke.

On leaden legs, he moved to stand in front of the window, staring across the street at Danielle's house. He wanted to burn the place down. Wanted to get rid of any physical reminder of what had happened there, but he knew it wouldn't solve anything.

Physical solutions weren't going to fix emotional hurts. He couldn't erase the memories, even if he burned Danielle's empty house to the ground, and it was nothing more than cinders and ash. Fisting his hand in the soft, thick curtains, he leaned his head against the icy windowpane.

Closing his eyes, he whispered, "God, what in the hell am I supposed to do?"

How could he help her now, when he hadn't helped her then? Like a ghostly whisper, he heard Quinn say, *"But whether you get it or not, you did save her."*

Luke didn't get it. He didn't see it. If he'd saved her, he would have gotten to her before she'd been beaten, strangled, almost raped.

"But you got to her before he could rape her. Before he could kill her."

Luke shook his head, mumbled, "But she stopped him. It wasn't me. Wasn't the cops."

She stopped the attack by killing Wilder. Now she had to live with the memories as well as the knowledge that she'd taken a life. Wilder deserved to die—there was no doubt of that—but Luke hadn't ever been able to kill without feeling the loss of each life somewhere deep inside him. Terrorists, drug lords, murderers, he'd taken those lives during his time in the Rangers, but each death had marked him.

This would mark Devon, and that was another way he'd failed her.

"Stop it," he snapped, jerking away from the window and pacing. "Put it away, damn it. Put it away." He closed his eyes, a ragged sigh escaping him. Luke knew how to live with guilt. He'd lived with it for years, guilt that Quinn had been a punching bag for their mother while Luke was happy, safe, and loved with their dad. Guilt that he hadn't even known about his twin until he was older. Even if he'd grown up feeling like some part of him was missing, he hadn't known. Guilt over not being enough of a brother to Quinn, enough family to make the sad, quiet loner happy.

Luke wasn't a stranger to guilt, but it hadn't ever swamped him quite like this. It hadn't turned his heart into ash and cast a gray pall over everything he did, everything he said, everything he felt and thought. Forcing himself to take a deep breath, he focused his mind, tried to distance himself.

If this wasn't Devon, if it wasn't a woman he loved, but somebody he had seen in the hospital, or the wife of a friend, somebody, anybody but Devon, how would he handle it? How would he suggest others handle it?

He couldn't even think in terms of *How would I handle this if I had shown up in time to keep her from getting hurt?* He'd been playing that song and dance for two weeks, and all it did was add the weight of guilt.

No, he had to take a step back, force himself to think about this like it had happened to somebody else.

Give her time.

That would have been his first suggestion. Although two weeks wasn't much time at all, Devon wasn't getting better. She was getting worse, becoming more and more reclusive. Before today, she hadn't left the house for anything except a follow-up doctor's appointment he'd dragged her to and to go see Danielle at the hospital. She hadn't left for work, she hadn't left to go to the store, she hadn't left to go to church, she hadn't left the house to even check the damn mail.

Time wasn't helping her.

Get back to life. That was what she needed to do. What they both needed to do. He'd taken the first week off, but this past week, he'd gone back to work. Just two days this week, and next week, he had three shifts down. Easing back into it, even though he felt guilty as hell for leaving her alone in the house.

The first few days, her mother had come by, but yesterday, Devon had been alone in the house. Alone all day and when he got home, she'd been sitting on the couch in almost the exact position she'd been in when he'd left, still wearing her pajamas and staring at the TV with a glassy, fixed gaze.

He'd gently bullied her into taking a hot bath, had fixed her a bowl of chicken noodle soup that she hadn't touched, hot cocoa that she only sipped from two or three times, and then he helped her get ready for bed—babying her. She hadn't said anything, hadn't seemed to mind or care.

Hell, she didn't even seem to really notice him.

Okay. So he'd start there. Not with making her notice him, but with the rest of it. He couldn't keep coddling her. Even though that was what he wanted to do, what he needed to do, he had a feeling it wasn't what she needed.

She needed from him what her mother had done.

Forcing her to get up, get out. Get back to life.

Blowing out a breath, he muttered, "Yeah. That's what I need to do."

Of course, saying it, thinking it, and actually doing it were very, very different things.

*   *   *

"Oh, that was fun," Liz said, her voice just a little too bright. Her smile, although as sweet and warm as ever, was forced, and Devon saw right through the cheerful pretense.

But Devon didn't want to hurt her mom's feelings or make her worry any more than she already had. Forcing a smile of her own, she said, "Yeah. I'm glad you talked me in to it."

They worked their way through the crowded restaurant, following the hostess to a booth way in the back. They'd only waited thirty minutes, nothing short of a miracle this time of day. P. F. Chang's, as always, was seriously busy, and with the holiday shoppers descending on the mall en masse, it was a stroke of luck the two women had gotten to a table in under an hour.

As they settled down at a small table, Liz smiled at Devon. But this smile, though sadder, seemed more real. "You never were a good liar, baby," she said softly. She reached out, tucked a strand of Devon's hair back from her face, and said, "But you needed to get out of the house. You can't stay inside forever."

Shrugging, Devon opened the menu and tried to concentrate on it. But her mother's insightful, knowing stare never wavered, and finally, she looked up and met that stare. "I was going to get out . . . soon."

"Oh, really? When?" Liz asked curiously, bringing up her arm and propping her elbow on the table. She rested her chin in the cradle of her hand and waited.

Devon shrugged again. "I don't know. Maybe this week . . ."

"And maybe not. Have you called your office about coming back?"

She shook her head. "My boss told me to take all the time I need. They'll do okay without me."

"But will you do okay taking all the time you need, Devon?" Liz sighed and shook her head. "You do need time, Devon. Time doesn't heal all wounds; you and I both know that. It does help . . . but not if you just sit around and watch the hands on the clock tick away your life."

Squirming on the hard seat, Devon tried not to hear the truth in those words. She didn't want to hear it; she didn't want to face reality, face life. As long as she just kept floating through the days like she had been, it was easier not to think.

Not to feel.

Warm hands covered hers. She blinked and looked up to meet her mother's concerned gaze. "Baby, you can't keep going like this," Liz said. "Not you. You have to fight this back; otherwise, you'll lose yourself again." She reached up with one hand, stroked Devon's inner arm, touching the faded scars.

Devon tried to jerk away, but Liz wouldn't let her. "You've lost yourself before, baby. And you and I know that it wasn't easy to come back. You get lost like that again, there's no guarantee you'd make the trip back this time."

Defensively, Devon jerked her arm and wrapped it around herself, hiding the scars. "I'm not going there again, Mom. I wouldn't . . ."

Sighing, Liz leaned back. "I'm not talking about the drugs, Devon. I'm talking about you. When you first came to us, you didn't care if you lived or died. That's what I'm talking about. You're falling back into that hole again, and if you hit rock bottom this time, it's going to be every bit as hard, if not harder, to climb back out. You really want that fight?"

"I'm not . . ." She blinked, cleared her throat. Tried again. Her voice shook as she said, "I'm fine, Mama. I'm getting better."

"You're not fine. You're losing too much weight; you're drifting away . . . That man of yours? You barely even looked at him the entire time I was at your house." Liz leaned forward, reached out, and laced her fingers with Devon's. "You're pushing him away. Don't think I don't see it. Don't think he doesn't see it. You're pushing him away . . . and he made you happier than you've ever been."

This time, the tears weren't so easy to control, and Devon turned her head aside as they started to fall. "I know he made me happy." *Made . . . past tense.* Even she heard the finality of it. And it hurt. Hearing that hurt.

The pain hadn't been absent after all. Just hiding. And for some reason, acknowledging that she didn't want to let Luke make her happy anymore was the key to opening that gate. Tears burned her eyes, and sobs threatened to choke her. She battled it back through sheer will, but even so, when she looked back at her mother, it was through a veil of tears.

"Don't you want that back?" Liz asked.

Devon shook her head. Her voice trembled as she whispered, "I don't know, Mama. I don't know anything anymore."

"Is it because you blame him?"

Devon stilled. Blinked back the tears. Her mother's hand tightened around hers in a comforting squeeze, but it didn't give her comfort. Jerking back like she'd been scalded, Devon said stiffly, "I don't blame him. He didn't do it. He didn't make it happen."

"But he wasn't there to stop it, either."

Shaking her head, Devon said, "He did stop it. The police came . . ."

"After that bastard was already dead. Why not sooner?" Liz countered.

"And what if he hadn't called them at all? What if he'd waited until he got home to find out why I wasn't answering the phone?" Devon shook her head, scrubbed the tears from her face. "No. I don't blame Luke, and I sure as hell hope you aren't."

A slow, pleased smile bloomed on Liz's face. "Good. I'm glad to hear that." She opened her menu and started to study it.

But then she lowered it, glanced at Devon over the top edge. "You know, maybe you should let Luke know you don't blame him. I haven't ever seen a man so eaten up with guilt, Devon. This is killing him. Seeing you hurt is killing him."

Quietly, Devon whispered, "He loves me."

Liz nodded, lifted the menu back up. "Yes. He does. You don't really want to lose that, do you?"

Devon closed her eyes and swallowed. Made herself think. Made herself feel. The sweet, blissful fog of the past few weeks was slipping away, faster and faster, and she knew she couldn't bring it back, couldn't lose herself in that oblivion anymore. Thanks to her mom. Grimacing, Devon tried to decide if she wanted to thank her or stomp off in a sulk.

But then she made herself think about Luke. The important thing.

You don't really want to lose that, do you?

The answer, once she let herself think about it, was simply there, no waiting, no searching, no introspection. Simply there, like it had been waiting for her to look.

"No. I don't want to lose him."

Her mother's only response was a noncommittal "Hmmm."

Rolling her eyes, Devon muttered, "You should have gone into psychology."

"I did, baby. But I only use it with you." She glanced over the menu and grinned. "Is it working?"

Flipping the menu open, Devon replied, "What do you think?"

She skimmed the entreés, tried to think of something that sounded good. Actually, the longer she looked at it, though, the more all of it sounded pretty damned good. Her belly rumbled demandingly, and she was still weighing her options when the waitress arrived with ice water.

"Are we ready to order?"

Devon gestured toward her mom and continued to ponder. Finally, she decided on the orange chicken. Closing the menu, she asked for a bowl of hot and sour soup. As the waitress took the menu, Devon reached for her water.

But as she lifted it to her lips, a shiver raced down her spine. It had nothing to do with the cold, though. The skin on the back of her neck started to crawl, and her gut went hot and slippery with panic.

Lifting her head, she glanced around, trying to pinpoint what was wrong.

Somebody . . . it felt like somebody was watching her.

"Baby? Is something wrong?"

The sound of her mother's voice jerked her back to the present, and Devon swallowed, shook her head. *Nobody is watching you, Devon. He's dead. Dead. Buried.*

She forced another smile at her mom and shrugged. "No. Just a case of the heebie-jeebies for a second."

* * *

WHEN the car pulled in the driveway a good five hours after they'd left, Luke heard it. Gut instinct was to go outside into the soft drift of snow, open the door for Devon, hold her elbow as she walked up the icy sidewalk.

Second instinct was to just wait in the living room.

He went with the third one, moving to the door and opening it, waiting there as Devon and her mom climbed out. As they moved to the back of the Subaru, he headed outside. "Anything left to buy this close to Christmas?" he asked.

Then he took a look in the trunk and blinked. It was literally filled with bags. "Uh . . . guess so."

Devon glanced at him, then away. But she had a small smile on her pretty mouth. A real one. Not that blank, empty smile she'd been giving him for the past two weeks. "You know how I am about shopping." She nodded toward her mom and added, "She's worse."

In a breezy voice, Liz said, "I am not. I'm better. Shopping is an art, sweetheart. You know that."

"An art?" Luke repeated.

"Hmmm. And Mom's a master. I'm her fledging protégée." She grinned at her mom.

For a second, just one split second, Luke's heart lodged in his throat. He made himself talk, almost afraid of bursting the bubble, but he wanted to see her look at him with that smile on her face. "I don't know, sugar. I've seen you shop. I wouldn't call that fledging."

Liz chuckled. "Obviously you haven't seen me shop."

Devon smiled and reached for some of the bags. Luke went to take them from her, but Liz intercepted him and dumped several more boxes and bags into his arms. "Be a dear, Luke. Can you carry these inside for Devon? I really do need to get home."

She waited until Devon had the rest of her bags, and then she brushed a kiss over Devon's cheek, waved at Luke. "You kids get inside now where it's warm."

Luke glanced down at the load in his arms and then stepped aside, let Devon head up the walkway first. The walk inside was completed in silence. Although Luke still wasn't sure, it seemed this silence was different, though. He couldn't explain how, but something seemed different.

Her eyes, maybe. They didn't have that flat, vacant stare, and she actually looked at him of her own volition a time or two. Her face wasn't as pale, either, and while she still hadn't said much of anything, she didn't seem so withdrawn.

Following her into her office, he waited while she stowed her bags in the closet and then did the same with the ones he carried. As she tucked one last box away, Luke tucked his hands into his pockets and waited.

He wasn't sure what he was waiting for, though.

At least not until Devon took a deep breath, bracing herself, or at least it seemed that way to Luke. She slid the pocket doors shut and then turned around to look at him, leaning back against the doors. "Hasn't been the best first Christmas season the two of us could have had, huh?" she said into the silence.

"No." In his pockets, his hands clenched into fists. It was hell, he'd discovered, having a gut full of fire-hot fury and no place to direct it. The only target that deserved the kind of fury he had trapped inside was dead, dead and cold in the ground. There was no way to make Wilder pay for what he'd done to Devon.

"I'm not real sure how to get things back the way they were." Her voice was sad, soft, and wistful. Her lids lowered over her eyes, and the look on her face added just one more jagged tear to his heart.

"Is that what you want?" He had to know. The distance between them, the pain inside of her that he couldn't ease. He kept thinking that Devon would decide she'd deal with this better if she just wiped the slate clean and started over. Away from him.

"Yeah." She lifted her lashes and stared at him. Her voice was different now, and Luke suspected it wouldn't ever be the way it used to be. The whiskey-rough timbre would most likely sound sexy as hell to a lot of men. But Luke couldn't hear it without recalling the ring of bruises around her neck and how her throat had been so swollen, she hadn't been able to swallow even a spoonful of water for two days after the attack. It was a miracle her throat hadn't been permanently damaged, that her airway hadn't been crushed.

Her head cocked to the side, the long, russet red sweep of her hair framing her face. "What about you? Do you want that, or are things too different now?"

In a rusty voice, Luke whispered, "Things are different—and they aren't. I fucked up, Devon. You got hurt because of me." So much for putting it aside, he thought bitterly. But the words had escaped before he could stop them, and it was too late to take them back.

He stared at her from across the room and wished he could go to her, wished he could hold her. But he wasn't so certain he had the right.

"I got hurt because that of that crazy bastard. Not because of you." Pushing off the wall, she started toward him, and when she stopped, she was so close, he could smell the warm scent of honeysuckle on her skin and see the faint discoloration that still marred the creamy flesh of her neck. "And, if we really want to be honest here, how much worse could it have been if you weren't around, Luke? Would he have gotten to me before? Done worse?"

Her voice hitched, and she broke off, swallowed, licked her lips. When she continued, her voice was just the slightest bit uneven. "And we both know it could have been worse."

Although neither of them said anything, they were both thinking of Danielle. The other woman hadn't just been beaten and terrified. Wilder had raped her repeatedly throughout the day. Broken ribs, a concussion, a shattered cheekbone—plastic surgeons had been called in. The physical damage could be fixed; Danielle would heal.

On the outside.

But the rest of her was a different story.

"Have you talked to her any more?"

Devon shook her head. She'd gone to see Danielle in the hospital exactly one time. Luke had been with her, and when Danielle had looked at Devon and started to panic, they'd left. "I left a message with her mom. If Danielle wants to talk with me, she'll get in touch." She grimaced and added, "But I'm not expecting to hear from her."

"I'm sorry."

Tears glinted in her eyes, and when she blinked, one broke free, spilling over to roll down her cheek. Luke reached up, slowly, waited for her to flinch away. Instead, as he wiped the tear away with his thumb, she turned her face into his palm and kissed him. "I hate him for what he did to Danielle, more than any of this. She wasn't anything to him, an innocent bystander, and he damn near killed her."

When she stepped forward and pressed her body against his, Luke swore the earth shifted and moved. And as she slid her arms around his waist and settled against him, rubbing her cheek against his chest, he all but heard the little click as everything in his world settled back into place.

Well, not quite. He still had the rage eating away at his gut like acid, and he didn't dare do more than hold her for fear of scaring her.

But this? This was a start.

* * *

MORNING dawned, and Devon found herself wrapped in Luke's arms. The faint, silvery light of early morning streamed in through the slit in her curtains, but she had no desire to move.

Against her back, she felt the warm, long length of Luke's body. Against her bottom, she felt another warm, long length—no, not warm. Hot, throbbing.

Ever since the attack, Luke had been treating her like spun glass. He always woke before she did, leaving the bed in silence, although it was usually the absence of his warmth that woke her. He didn't seem in any hurry to move this morning, though, and Devon was glad of it.

Mostly.

When he slid a hand over her hip, she held still, almost afraid to let herself react in any way. She didn't want to go back to being scared to death of a man's touch, especially not Luke's touch. Yet she knew that was an unrealistic expectation, and she'd been dreading this on some level.

The part of her that hadn't completely shut down, that is. Dreading anything sexual, yet also regretting the knowledge that it would hurt Luke when she pulled back.

But as he stroked his hand up and down, slow and gentle, all she felt was warmth. It spread through her lazily, need easing through her instead of exploding. The bed shifted under him as he pushed up onto his elbow, lowering his lips to brush them over her shoulder.

"Morning." His voice was husky and soft, and it sent shivers running down her spine.

"Hmmmm. Morning."

He kept up the slow, lazy caress on her hip, but his touch was light, almost impersonal. "Don't suppose you're in the mood for breakfast, are you?"

"Uh-uh." Closing her eyes, she focused on his hand and wished he'd touch something beside her hip. She bit her lip and wiggled, pushing back against him.

Luke, nice and casual-like, eased backward, breaking the contact between their lower bodies. Smoothed her hair back from her face and asked, "Was that *uh-uh* a yes or a no?"

Rolling onto her back, Devon smiled up at Luke. "It was a no. Or least a no, not right now. Right now . . ." She reached down and closed her fingers around his wrist, tugging his hand upward, guiding it to her breast. Her face flamed hot, and she knew she was probably blushing to the roots of her hair, but she didn't look away from him. "Right now, I'm in the mood for this."

Like a flash, heat leaped into his eyes, but then it was gone, tucked away and hidden. He dipped his head and rubbed his lips against hers. "Devon . . ."

She narrowed her eyes at him and then let go of his hand, shoving at his chest until he fell back—humoring her, no doubt. She could shove on him all damn day and she wouldn't budge him until he let her. That was fine, though. Just fine. As he settled down beside her, she threw one leg over his hips and straddled him.

Luke's breath blew out of him in a huge rush, his chest expanding, the muscles in his belly rippling. She stared into his misty gray eyes and rocked against him, watched as the misty gray deepened to smoke. "This, Luke. I don't want you patting my back, soothing me, feeding me . . . I want you touching me. I want your hands on me." Bending down, she pressed her lips to his, keeping the contact quick and light. "I want to forget about anything and everything but us."

His hands, strong, hard, yet so gentle, slid down her sides, cupped her hips. His voice was hoarse as he asked, "You sure?"

Giving him a wide grin, she settled back on her heels and grabbed the hem of the T-shirt she'd slept in. Pulling it over her head, she tossed it to the side. "Very sure." She reached for his hands and brought them up, pressing them to her breasts. "I told you before, Luke . . . I'm not fragile. I won't break."

A grim look crossed his face and he trailed his fingers up over her collarbone, brushing the tips against the fading, yellowed bruises at her neck. "Maybe you won't break. But I'm terrified I'll scare you, hurt you."

She caught his hand, brought it to her lips. Pressing her mouth to his palm, she kissed him and then, letting go of his hand, she slowly stood. His eyes burned as his gaze slid down her body. For a minute, she had to wonder what it was he saw that made him want her so much. She was even thinner now than she'd been before, and what few curves she had were slight at best.

But when he stared at her, it made her feel beautiful.

Even more so as she dropped her hands to the waistband of her panties and started to push them down in a slow, teasing move. Luke watched her with wide, unblinking eyes, and his chest rose and fell in a fast, erratic rhythm. A light film of sweat gleamed on his skin, and twin flags of color rode high on his cheeks.

It was a heady, almost drugged sensation, and if she didn't ache to feel his hands on her, fast, she might have drawn the moment out. She shifted her stance, bracing one foot on either side of his hips, and when his gaze lowered, focused on her core, a spasm of need tightened her belly. As he continued to stare at her, she knelt back down. Luke still wore the boxer-style briefs he'd slept in, and through the thin barrier, she could feel him.

"Touch me," she whispered, skimming her mouth down his jawline. "Please, Luke. I need this . . ."

She was killing him, Luke thought, dazed. She moved her hips in slow, sinuous circles against his, and he could feel the soft, wet heat. The dark, snug briefs he wore were suddenly sheer hell, too tight, too rough, too confining.

"*I need this . . .*"

Her whispered plea echoed through his mind. *Fuck it,* he decided. They both needed this. Wrapping his arms around her waist, he rolled to the side, putting her body under his. Levering up onto his elbows, he stared down at her, watched for some sign that he needed to stop and either back off or let her run the show. But all she did was smile at him, a sleepy little cat's smile with her eyes half-closed and her hands stroking down his shoulders.

Without waiting another heartbeat, Luke shoved his underwear out of the way. Her knees came up, her legs wrapping around his hips, pulling him closer . . . closer . . .

When he brushed against that silken wet heat, they both moaned. As he pushed inside her, they stared at each other, eyes rapt on the other's face. Luke held back, for fear of scaring her, hurting her, marking her in some way.

But the only thing that showed on her face was that faint feline smile that soon faded away, replaced with husky whimpers, moans, and pleas. Hunkering low over her, he kissed her. Her nails bit into his flesh, her mouth greedy and demanding under his.

That desperate hunger did a wicked number on his self-control, and when she started to move under him, she smashed that iron self-control like it was made of paper. Growling, he buried his face against her neck, kissing each and every last visible bruise. Her hands dipped into his hair, fisting there and clutching him close.

Stroking a free hand up her thigh, he palmed her butt and canted her hips upward. The slight change of position took him deeper, and he felt her reaction all the way to the soles of his feet as she clenched around him and started to wail out his name.

Greedy need filled him, and he shoved up, bracing his hands on the mattress beside her head and holding his upper body up.

He wanted to slow down.

Wanted to pull out, pull away, get his breath, and then start over again. Slower. Sweeter.

But leaving her would be as easy as walking on water . . . unnatural, impossible, unthinkable. There was no stopping this storm, and the only thing he could do was make sure she came with him. He slid his fingers through the curls at her sex, seeking out the sensitive bud there.

As he stroked her, Devon gasped. Within thirty seconds, she was whimpering, rocking against him, and keening out his name with every breath. She started to come, and as she shattered under him, he sank down onto her soft, sleek body, his eyes closing as he lost himself inside her. With rhythmic milking caresses, she emptied his body.

And as she wrapped her arms around his shoulders and whispered his name, the huge, gaping hole in his heart shrank down . . . just a little.

*   *   *

IN the silence, Devon lay curled against his chest and listened to his heart as it slowed down.

"I think I need to get back to work."

Luke grunted.

Lifting her head, she watched his face. One lid popped open, and he peered at her through the veil of his lashes. "You don't need to go back yet."

Making a face, Devon muttered, "Wish I could agree with you."

Now Luke opened his other eye and studied her face. "You've got the time coming, Devon. You need a break; you deserve this."

She shook her head. "I don't need it. Actually, I think staying inside as much as I have, practically from the first, has done me more harm than good." Turning her head, she rubbed her cheek against his shoulder. "The real world is still going on outside, Luke. Hiding away from it won't change what happened. And . . . and I think it's making it harder on me."

"Maybe you're not giving yourself enough time."

Devon wished she could believe that. But she knew from experience that time didn't heal all wounds. At least not completely. In her case, the longer she waited, the more time it took, the harder it was going to be for her to go back out there. "I think maybe I took more time than I should have." She wiggled and shifted until she could sit up on the bed and meet his gaze levelly instead of looking up at him.

"Sooner or later, I have to deal with the fact that I've got to go back outside, climb into my car, and go back to my job. I've got to deal with the fact that I still have cases and kids that need me . . . including Tim."

Tension arced through him, and Devon met his gaze, saw the

turmoil there. Softly, she said, "You know this has nothing to do with him. It's not his fault, what happened."

A grimace twisted his lips. He sat up and shoved a hand through his hair as he said, "Yeah. Yeah, I know that. But what do you think it's going to do to you to look at him? Hell, I remember seeing him in the hospital that night you took him to the ER. He looks like his dad. No, he can't help that. But what's that going to do to you?"

Shaking her head, Devon said, "I don't know. But I can't just not go back to work over that." With a shrug, she added, "Besides, chances are he'll already have been reassigned. And I'll be good with that. It's better for both of us. But . . ." she blew out a breath, closed her eyes. "I do need to see how he's doing, maybe just talk to him once more. It isn't his fault; he deserves to know that I don't blame him."

Silent, Luke reached over and slid his arms around her waist, tugging her into his lap. "Definitely not fragile, Devon," he whispered, brushing his lips against her bare shoulder.

Leaning back against him, she laid her hands atop his and squeezed. "I keep telling you that." Then she sighed, tucking a lock of hair back behind her ear. With a glance over her shoulder, she smiled at him and only hoped it looked a little better than it felt. "Hiding from it doesn't make it go away."

He looked like he wanted to say something else . . . argue with her. Squirming around, she straddled his lap and gazed at him. She pressed her fingers to his lips and whispered, "Don't. Don't give me a reason to just keep staying home, to keep hiding away. If I want my life back, then I have to take it."

Luke had already learned that look on her face meant she'd made up her mind, and nothing he did, nothing he said, would change it. But even as a huge part of him heaved out a sigh of relief, another part of him was icy with tension.

"Are you really sure you're ready to do this?"

Her head fell forward and rested on his shoulder as he looped his arms around her waist. "No," she replied honestly. "I'm not. But

I'm going to do it anyway." Her voice trailed off as a loud, demanding grumble emerged from her belly. Lifting her head, she grinned at
him. "Did you say something about breakfast?"

* * *

As it turned out, Luke was easier to convince than her boss. She'd
expected the reticence from her boyfriend, but not the guy who au-
thorized her paycheck. When she walked into the chaotic office, the
insane cacophony of voices, ringing phones, the copy machine, and a
crying infant had her smiling.

Until one by one, her coworkers caught sight of her, and the
noise, bit by bit, faded. The fax machine continued to spit out what
looked to be one long-ass report, the annoying squeak of the an-
cient copier droned on, and the phones still rang, but even the baby
sniffled once or twice and then curled up against a welcoming
shoulder and drifted off into sleep.

Eyes drifted her way, then skittered off as though looking at her
made them uncomfortable. Pity, sympathy, and curiosity appeared
on a few of the faces, only to disappear when she met their gazes.
Abruptly, there was a squeal, and out of Dawson's office came a
little towheaded boy, holding a cell phone in his small hands and
laughing as a woman came out after him.

It was one of the foster mothers, a favorite in their office, and
she smiled at Devon as she passed by in hot pursuit of the phone
thief. As though that had been some sort of signal, the chaos re-
sumed. Although people continued to send her weird glances, some
subtle, some not, the rhythm of the office fell back into place.

When Dawson appeared in the doorway, he gave her a familiar,
world-weary smile and beckoned to her. But if she thought he was
going to welcome her back with open arms, it took less than two
minutes in his office to get disabused of that notion.

"Absolutely not. You're not ready." Dawson folded his arms
across his beefy chest and shook his head.

Devon didn't bother trying to cajole him or charm him; under the right circumstances, both could work. But this wasn't the right circumstance. He stared at her with bulldog obstinance. Logic probably wasn't going to work, either, but maybe a bit of logic, a bit of compromise . . .

"Dawson, look, I understand that you want to be cautious, but I'm fine."

"The hell you're fine," he muttered, retreating back behind the scarred, beat-up wooden desk that was overrun with charts, reports, and what looked like a thousand sticky notes. "Do I have to remind you that somebody tried to kill you two weeks ago?"

Grimacing, Devon touched her fingers to her bruised neck. It didn't hurt to swallow anymore, but she wouldn't ever forget how it felt to have hard, cruel hands closing around her neck and choking the life out of her. "I don't need a reminder, Dawson. It's not something I'm going to forget, and believe me, I'd love to do just that. I need to get back to work."

He nodded, ran a hand over the grizzly gray stubble on his chin. "Yeah, I get that. But this can't be your therapy, Devon." Awareness lit his eyes, and he sighed, leaned forward, braced his elbows on the surface of his desk. "A lot of us go into this as some screwed-up kind of therapy. You did. I did. I know that. But this is a little too close, Devon. A little too recent. You have to take more time."

A slick, icy ball of fear formed in her belly. "How much more time?" she demanded.

Dawson's face softened. "Just a few more days." He grabbed a piece of paper and jotted a number down. "You need to talk to somebody before you come back."

"Somebody," Devon muttered. She recognized the name on the slip of paper he held out toward her, and she scowled. Lydia Marsh was one of the therapists they often referred adults to, particularly battered women. Yeah, Devon figured that what had happened certainly filled the battered requirements, but she wasn't so sure she wanted to stretch out on a couch and prattle on about it.

She wadded the phone number up in her hand. "Dawson, I've

had my share of talking to shrinks and therapists and counselors. I've done that before; I don't want to do it again."

He smirked at her and started to dig through his desk. Finding a half-empty bag of red hots, he leaned back in his chair and popped a couple into his mouth. "Yeah. I guessed as much. But you can't come back until you talk to somebody."

Planting her hands on her hips, she glared at him. "What are you going to do, make me bring in a doctor's note?"

"Damn straight." He shook a few more pieces of candy into his mouth, and she caught a whiff of cinnamon. "Look at it from where I'm at, Devon. You had a shitty ordeal, and if you didn't ever want to come back to this, nobody would blame you. A lot of women wouldn't want to."

Lowering her eyes, Devon thought of Danielle. Danielle had left her home for that very reason. A home was generally harder to replace than a job, but Danielle had done it without thinking twice. "I'm not a lot of women, Dawson. I'm just me."

"Yeah. And you're a hell of a lot stronger than most people would ever guess." He poured more red hots into his hand and dropped the bag onto his desk. Instead of eating them, he made a funnel out of his hand and let the candy fall into his open palm.

He repeated that over and over, and Devon was about ready to go over there, grab the candy, and throw it away before he finally spoke. "Social workers have a high burnout rate, Devon. Most of us, we just quit and go on to something else. We go back to school, go into counseling. Or we become alcoholics." He grinned a little, as though he'd told a joke that only he understood. Then his face sobered, and his gaze came back up to meet hers. "But then, some of us don't have the sense to get out while we can. People break under pressure. Under pressure, they can do some really awful things they'd never do otherwise. If you're not under a lot of pressure right now, I'll eat my hat."

"You're not wearing a hat," Devon muttered, wishing she could be furious at what he was implying. But she couldn't. "Dawson . . ."

He gave her a gentle smile. "Devon, I know you. I trust you, You tell me that you're steady enough to come back, that's good enough for me. But it can't be good enough for this office. It can't be good enough for those we're supposed to help." Nodding toward the phone number she still held crumpled in her fist, he added, "Seeing Lydia will be. And getting that note."

* * *

"Is your brother coming over?"

She stood in front of the mirror, her hair twisted up off her neck so she could admire the earrings Luke had bought to match the pearl necklace. She stroked her fingers over the necklace and decided that most of the bruising was gone.

The few bruises that remained, although they still looked pretty damn noticeable to her, were so faint, most people probably wouldn't even see them. Sighing, she reached for a clip to secure her hair.

Luke appeared in the reflection as she started to pin her hair into place, and after she fastened the clip, he reached up and took it down. As her hair came tumbling down her shoulders, she glared at him. Luke tossed the clip over his shoulder and then slid his arms around her waist, resting his chin on her shoulder. "Leave it down; I love it down," he said softly. Then he sighed, and she could feel the warm whisper of it caressing her skin. "I never got around to asking him."

"You didn't get around to asking him? But . . ."

The question never formed, but it didn't have to. His gaze dropped to her neck, and when he stroked his fingers over her skin, Devon swallowed. He pulled his hand back almost right away, but Devon caught his wrist and lifted it, kissing him. "You ever going to stop beating yourself up over this?"

Luke snorted. "Yeah. Sooner or later. I'm thinking the day after Armageddon."

That weird, alert tension had crept back into his body, his eyes taking on a glitter that reminded her of some big predator on the prowl. A shiver raced down her spine. But as quick as it came on him, it was gone, draining away as if it had never even been there. When he met her gaze in the mirror, he smiled ruefully and shrugged. "I'd meant to call him before it happened. After . . . well, just didn't seem right."

She took a minute, finger-combing her damp curls back from her face, adjusting her necklace, fiddling with the neckline of her sweater. Part of her appreciated his consideration, but another part of her hated to think that Luke had a brother out there spending Christmas alone. "I can't help but think that him being alone instead of with family isn't right, either."

Luke shook his head. "He isn't spending it alone. I talked to him a few days ago. He was heading up to Vermont with a friend of ours. Staying at a cabin somewhere." He grimaced and added, "I wasn't real hot on the idea of him spending it alone, either. Not an issue, though. Quinn's not much on the family get-together thing, anyway."

"He doesn't live around here, does he?"

Luke shook his head. "Quinn moves around a lot. Doesn't care for staying in the same place."

Lifting a brow, she asked, "Exactly what does he do that lets him move around?"

"Do?" Luke repeated. He grinned and shook his head. "Quinn does pretty much whatever he wants to. He takes odd jobs here and there, and when he's ready to move on, he does just that."

He turned her around and hooked his arms over her shoulders. "Stop worrying about Quinn, Devon. Like I said, I talked to him a few days ago, and he's got plans—and he'll probably enjoy that more than some Christmas deal where he almost feels obligated to behave himself."

"Any reason why he wouldn't behave himself?"

"With Quinn? Always." He dipped his head and pressed his lips to hers. "You know those loner types? Quinn makes the typical loner look social. He's not much for people, especially people he doesn't know."

Rising on her toes, she pressed a kiss to his chin. "Still . . . he's your brother, Luke. Wouldn't he want to spend the day here?"

Restless, he shrugged. "With Quinn, it's hard to say." Silently, though, he couldn't help but think he'd screwed up on that front . . . even if he was trying to be considerate of Devon, he'd messed up. Blood mattered; he'd let his worry about her override that simple fact. But it was a little too late to do anything about it now.

"Go call him. Even if he's out roughing it in the wilds of Vermont, you can at least tell him *Merry Christmas.*"

Luke lifted his head. She smiled up at him, her hair hanging long and loose, and her eyes so deep, so dark and soft, he could drown in them. "Hmmm." He covered her smiling mouth with his and kissed her lightly. "Yeah. Yeah, I think I'll do that."

THIRTEEN

THE bed shifted just a little as Luke rolled out of it. Devon opened one eye to glance at her clock, and then she rolled onto her belly and groaned. Five a.m. Luke wouldn't leave home until six, but she imagined he would go for a run and then shower, some coffee . . .

Burying her face in the pillow, she drifted back into sleep. Not even the thought of a naked, wet Luke and a steaming-hot cup of coffee was enough to entice her out of her bed or into anything other than sleeping. She was too damn tired.

Time drifted by, Devon caught in those moments between awake and asleep. A warm hand stroked down her back, and she arched, smiled. His mouth touched hers. Humming under her breath, she opened for him. His taste . . . damn, but she loved his taste. Sliding a little more into wakefulness, she curled her arms around his neck and wondered if maybe she was interested in a wet, naked Luke. Except he wasn't naked anymore. She ran her fingers through his hair, and the damp strands curled around her fingers. His lips slid over her cheek. "You're not naked," she whispered.

He chuckled, nuzzled her neck. "Am I supposed to be?"

"Ummm. I was thinking that maybe I'd like to wake up now if you were wet and naked."

Lifting his head, he smoothed her hair back from her face. "I can get wet and naked real quick."

She glanced at the clock. "You'll be late for work."

Grimacing, he muttered, "Yeah, there is that." His lips brushed against her once more, and then he settled back on his heels. "Speaking of work . . . today is your first day back. You sure you're ready?"

Lifting a brow, Devon said, "I've been off for three weeks, Luke. If I don't go back to work soon, my kids might forget what I look like."

He sighed and laid a hand on her cheek.

In the dim light, she could see the concern on his face. "Luke, I love you." She reached up and hooked her hand in the neckline of his shirt, tugged him close. "But if you don't stop hovering, I'm going to scream. I have to get out of here. I'm going stir-crazy."

Grinning, he dipped his head and kissed her, quick and hard. "Well, that's a huge improvement over the girl who didn't even want to leave the house to go Christmas shopping not too long ago."

In a lofty voice, she reminded him, "I made up for it on the after-Christmas sales."

He winced. "Don't remind me. I still haven't recovered from that." He pressed his lips to her cheek and then straightened. "I better go. I love you."

He turned, and she sighed, tugged the blankets around her, and snuggled into the pillow. "You have a good day."

From the doorway, he smiled back at her. "You, too."

Rolling onto her side, she stared out the window, watching until his headlights splashed beams of light on her wall as he pulled out. The sound of his car faded, and she closed her eyes and slid back into sleep.

Back into dreams. Luke was back in the bed beside her, his body hard and strong against hers, his hands sliding and stroking. The dream changed, faded, and realigned; they weren't in bed anymore, but walking through the mall. An empty mall. None of the stores was familiar, and Devon found herself wandering through a huge room filled with freestanding doors. The doors led nowhere, she discovered as she opened one and peeked through. She stepped through, looked around, and saw she was still in the same room. Another door, another . . .

"What are you looking for?"

She looked behind and saw Luke standing there, his hands jammed in his pockets and his head cocked. He looked . . . different. His eyes were different. "You."

He glanced at the doors and then back at her. "I'm not inside any of those."

Devon shrugged and continued to open the doors, one after the other. Then she came to a door that wasn't like the rest. It was set into a wall, and when she opened it, a huge dark maw awaited her—seriously dark, so dark that the light shining over her shoulder couldn't penetrate the darkness.

She looked back at Luke.

"I'm not in there."

But she stepped inside anyway. Of its own accord, the door swung shut behind her, and that huge darkness was suddenly stifling, pressing in on her. She sucked in a desperate breath of air and turned, searching for the door. But her hands encountered blankets. Endless swathes of cloth that wrapped around her body.

Back in bed—she was back in bed. And she wasn't alone. He watched her face as he reached for the hem of her nightshirt and stripped it away. Then he came to her. The body pressed to hers wasn't familiar, although the eyes that glittered down at her were Luke's eyes. His hands were hard, strong, and cruel. They closed around her neck and started to squeeze.

Terror exploded through her, and she fought, struggled, and beat against his chest. The air supply in her lungs dwindled, and in a panic, Devon opened her mouth to try to scream. He was kissing her, though, and her scream was muffled against his lips. Kissing her, choking her, killing her—

"Killing. It's what I'm good at."

His words were spoken so casually, so easily, as he squeezed and squeezed . . . Then there was something covering her face, something that blocked his face from view, pressing tighter . . . tighter . . .

Devon came awake with a scream, jerking upright in the bed and huddling in the middle of the bed with her face pressed against her knees. There was a nasty, noxious taste in her mouth, and her throat hurt.

Early morning light shone in through the window, and a quick glance at the clock told her she must have been sleeping for a good hour. Felt like longer. Her skin was all sweaty and itchy, and her head had a weird, muffled feel. "Oh, shit," she muttered.

Fighting her way free from the sheets and blankets tangled around her, she sat on the edge of the bed and scrubbed her hands over her face. Talk about a bitch of a nightmare. It clung to her like an oily film, and she shoved her hair back from her face, grimaced at the sweaty tangles. When her alarm clock went off a few minutes later, she reached over and shut it off, standing with a sigh.

But she hadn't taken more than two steps before the chilly air on her bare flesh registered. Her mouth went dry, and she stopped in her tracks, staring down at her bare body.

A whimper escaped her.

Her eyes raced over the room, but she stood completely still, terrified to move.

There. Hanging over the doorknob of the closed door was her nightshirt.

Spooked didn't quite describe Devon's state of mind. There were logical reasons for what had happened . . . right? Maybe she'd forgotten to put it on. Or maybe Luke had stripped it off of her before he left. It wasn't like she'd been completely awake.

Rationalizing it away, or trying to, didn't do a damn thing to make her feel better, though. She kept feeling that hand on her throat, squeezing not quite hard enough to bruise. More like the promise of a threat than an actual one.

I can hurt you if I want to . . . See how easy?

No words had been spoken, but in that weird, terrifying dream, that was the message she'd gotten.

Part of her mind insisted, *Not a dream.*

But the logical part denied even the possibility. Luke wouldn't hurt her. Curtis Wilder couldn't hurt her, not when he was dead and cold in the ground.

That part of her mind that was almost frozen with fear rebelled as she went through the motions of getting ready for work, showering, getting dressed. Every few seconds, even when she tried not to let herself, she realized she was searching the room, peeking around the corners, listening for footsteps that would fall so very softly on the stairs.

By the time she was dressed and ready, she was strung so tight, her hands shook as she made herself a pot of very strong, very black coffee. It hit her empty stomach like she'd just taken a couple of shots of espresso. "Ick," she muttered, pressing a hand to her belly.

Instead of trying to sweeten it or cover that bitter taste with milk, she dumped the coffee and grabbed a Diet Coke from the fridge. It wasn't a huge improvement, but at least she managed to drink some of it without feeling like getting sick.

With a headache pounding behind her eyes, her hands trembling ever so slightly, she finished getting ready to leave. Coat, bag, purse. Keys in hand, she headed outside, shutting the door behind her with a sigh of relief.

"That's seriously messed up," she muttered, shaking her head. People were supposed to be relieved when they *came* home, not when they *left* home. But as she walked toward her car, she had to restrain herself from looking backward.

Back at the house.

The skin on the back of her neck crawled. She walked faster, climbing inside the car, locking it—and then she looked back at the house, the windows dark, the lights off. The thin winter sunlight shone down on the house, but she couldn't dispel the dark, ugly fear sliding through her veins.

"Nerves. That's all it is. Just nerves," she said, closing her eyes. Her attempt at a few calming deep breaths failed miserably. Her hands still shook, her belly was still all slimy cold with fear, and when she tried to swallow, the memory of the hands closing around her throat had her wincing.

Three days ago, she'd left Lydia Marsh's office after brushing the receptionist off when offered another appointment. Devon had no plans of going back to see Lydia, not since the counselor had spoken with Devon's boss. Lydia couldn't see any logical reason why Devon shouldn't be back at work, if Devon felt ready.

She could have kissed the counselor at the time.

But now . . . now, as she sat shivering with fear in the driveway of her own house, she wondered if maybe she tried to rush out of the counseling too soon. Under her breath, she swore. Then, resolute, she shoved it all to the back of her mind and started the car.

She had a job to get back to, and she wasn't going to let the memory of some dead psycho keep her from that one more minute.

* * *

LUKE pulled into the driveway just as Devon climbed out of her car. She gave him a wan, distracted smile as he came around the car.

"Hey."

"Hey back." He studied her face and didn't like what he saw. She was pale, tired, and there were little lines fanning out from her eyes. "Looks like you had a bad first day back at work."

She shrugged her shoulders. "Not bad, really. Average. I'm just . . . I don't know, Luke. Edgy." Her lips curled in a wry smile, and she added, "Plus, I didn't sleep worth a damn once you left."

Sliding a hand around the back of her neck, he tugged her close. He pressed a kiss to her lips and whispered, "I'm sorry."

"Hmmm." She pulled back a little and licked her lips, smiling at him. "I feel better now."

Wanting to keep that smile on her face, he grinned down at her. "That was easy. And here I was thinking that maybe I should make us something to eat while you took a bubble bath or something."

He hooked an arm over her shoulders, and together, they walked toward the house. Devon slid away while he unlocked the door, and when he glanced back at her, he saw her staring at Danielle's house. "Hey."

She started. When she looked back at him, her face was even paler than before.

"Are you okay?"

Giving him a weak smile, she said, "I'm fine. Just tired. Edgy."

Luke glanced at the house over her shoulder and thought once more about burning the damn thing to the ground. "It's just going to take a while, baby." He linked their fingers, lifted her hand to his lips. "Come on inside."

* * *

"It's going to take a while."

Two weeks later, Devon was still telling that to herself, but now, it was more mocking than encouraging.

Yeah, getting over an attack would take a while, but she'd started to get better. And then, with one dream, she went crashing back to rock bottom.

No. This was worse. She'd hit rock bottom when she was a teenager, and she hadn't thought there was anything lower than rock bottom, not until now. She'd sunk to an all new low, and it was sheer hell.

Climbing out of the shower, she went to stand in front of the mirror and stare at herself. Much worse. She was so damn skinny, her hip bones jutted out. She could see her ribs.

Her appetite had dwindled back down into nonexistence, and

although she knew she needed to eat, she was existing on coffee, Diet Coke, and what little food Luke could coax her to eat.

The only time she was able to sleep was when Luke was with her. Up until a few days ago, it hadn't been too bad, but this week he was on night shifts. No matter how hard she tried, Devon couldn't get much more than a catnap in here and there.

It wasn't just the dreams, though. She was hearing things, seeing things. From the corner of her eye, when she knew she was alone in the house, she'd see a shadow. But when she turned to look, it was gone. Driving to work, she'd see a car behind her, following her—speeding up when she did, slowing when she slowed—but then, it was gone. Hell, poor Noelle probably thought Devon had gone off the deep end. They'd been riding out together to visit a child both of them had worked with, and Devon had thought they were being followed. She'd seen the car three times, but when Noelle had looked, the blue sedan hadn't been back there.

On her way in to work, she'd get a crawling sensation along her spine, like somebody was watching her. At night, she heard strange noises.

As each day passed and she slept less and less, she started to question her sanity.

Grimacing at her rather pathetic-looking reflection, she grabbed a towel and started to scrub her body dry. She tried damn hard not to think, but the ugly nightmare from the past night lured her like a moth to a flame. She'd fallen asleep on the couch. She didn't even remember sitting down, much less lying down, and when her eyes opened, at first, she hadn't realized where she was or that she was dreaming.

He appeared. Luke—only not. Luke didn't have that malice in his eyes or that cruelty. He looked just like Luke, sounded just like him, but he didn't feel like him, didn't smell like him.

The dream had ended abruptly, too abruptly, but not before he'd touched her everywhere, leaving her feeling dirty and in desperate need of a bath. Worse, when she climbed off the couch, her head all muffled and thick, her shirt had been tangled and twisted up under her armpits, exposing her breasts.

"This is getting ridiculous."

No, it had gone beyond ridiculous a week or so past.

As she'd stood in the living room, fighting to straighten out her shirt and still the tremor in her hands, Devon had known it was time. More than time. Staring at her shaking hands, she'd told herself she'd call Lydia come morning.

She hated the thought of going back to a counselor. She'd seen more than her share growing up, and going back to one was at the very bottom of her list of things to do.

But lately, she was starting to question her sanity.

Worse, she was starting to question Luke.

* * *

WHEN Luke came home from work, he found Devon already up and moving around. Standing at the new island her dad had given her for Christmas, she huddled over a cup of coffee. Her skin was paler than normal, and there were bags under her eyes that she'd tried to hide using some makeup. She rarely wore any, but she'd done a decent job covering up the signs of her exhaustion.

Luke saw beneath it.

Concern and that nagging, restless sense of guilt and anger kindled inside him, She smiled at him, and he pushed his worry aside, moving up behind her and wrapping his arms around her waist. "Hey, beautiful," he murmured, nuzzling her neck.

At first, she didn't react, holding herself still, stiff. Then, almost like she had to consciously force her body to relax, she leaned back against him and laughed. "You need to get your eyes checked. I look like a hag."

"Nothing wrong with my eyes." Not one damn bit. Devon had always been delicate, almost too slim. But she shouldn't feel so frail in his arms. Over the past few weeks, she'd lost more weight, and it wasn't like she had any to spare in the first place. But Luke knew better than to mention that to her. She'd get self-conscious, and there would be no way in hell he could get her to eat anything for breakfast.

She'd been living on coffee and soft drinks ever since she'd gone back to work. When he wasn't around, he suspected she didn't even attempt to eat. But he was here now, and she didn't need to leave for work for another hour still. She usually wasn't up and ready so early.

"I'm starving," he said, resting his chin on top of her head. "Think I'm going to make some waffles." He squeezed her waist gently and then moved away, digging out a mix, the waffle iron. As he made the batter, he asked, "You eaten anything?"

He already knew the answer.

Devon gave a halfhearted shrug. "Nah. Not hungry."

"I'll make some for you anyway. If you don't eat them, I might eat them later."

"Maybe a couple bites. I need to go in to work a little early today."

Glancing at her over his shoulder, he asked, "Anything wrong?"

"With work?" Devon shook her head and folded her hands around the thick white mug, staring into the coffee. "I just need to leave early, and I want to get everything done."

"Why are you leaving early?"

She looked away.

With slow, precise movements, he set down the glass bowl and the batter. After he wiped his hands off on a towel, he crossed the kitchen to stand next to her. Reaching out, he caught her shoulders and waited until she looked up at him. "What's going on?"

Her tongue slid out, damped her lips. "I . . . uh." She blew out a breath, focused her gaze somewhere in the vicinity of his throat. "I'm going to see Lydia."

The counselor. Okay. He'd figured she should have gone to talk to the woman for a while longer anyway. But something was off. Luke couldn't quite put his finger on it. Devon had made her dislike of counselors and the like clear. Damn clear. Part of him understood it. He knew she'd spent a great deal of time in counseling when she was a teenager, and she'd been more than glad to leave that behind.

"Probably not a bad idea." He smiled at her, ran his thumb across the delicate skin under her eyes. "You're not sleeping well."

Her gaze darted off to the side. Something cold skittered through his belly. That look in her eyes, on her face, it bore a rather strong resemblance to guilt. "Harder to sleep without you here," she said, shrugging. Then she made a face. "Forget I said that. I don't expect the hospital to work around my neuroses."

"You're not neurotic," Luke said darkly. Cupping her chin, he forced her gaze up to his. Squeezing gently, he repeated, "You're not neurotic. Shit, Devon, do you have any idea how many people would have snapped if they went through what you did? A lot of them."

Her smile was brittle, false. "Snapped." She shook her head. "Don't be so sure I haven't snapped, Luke. Sometimes I think I'm going crazy."

"You're not going crazy."

In a small, haunted voice, she whispered, "Don't be so sure."

*　*　*

"You're not going crazy, Devon," Lydia said, her voice gentle, calm, and confident. The perfect response for a counselor.

Smirking, Devon replied, "And if I was, would you tell me?"

Lydia laughed. "In those words? No, probably not." Then she leaned forward and took one of Devon's cold hands. "But you're not going crazy. You're just having a bad time. That's natural."

Linking their fingers, Lydia squeezed and waited until Devon looked up to meet her gaze. "You realize that so much of this can be attributed to the attack, don't you? The sensations that you're being watched, followed . . . You were being stalked, and it was going on for months before you knew. It's natural to feel this kind of apprehension."

Tears burned her eyes. Lydia's voice was so gentle, so understanding. The compassion on her face, in her manner, was real. It was genuine. Lydia was good at her job, and she believed in it. She'd helped a lot of people, but Devon had a feeling this was a waste of time. No matter what Lydia said, Devon was terrified that her grasp on reality was slipping.

"I do know that. But what about these dreams? Why do I keep having these dreams about Luke? He wouldn't hurt me; I know that." She tucked her chin against her chest and wrapped her arms protectively around her body, unaware that she'd started to rock, ever so slightly, back and forth. This morning, when he'd touched her, it had taken everything she had not to pull away.

She wasn't afraid of Luke, but part of her didn't seem to understand that. "Why do I keep dreaming that he hurts me? Why does part of me want to hide from him?"

Lydia squeezed Devon's hand. "Perhaps, on some level, you blame him. After all, he'd promised he'd take care of you. You let yourself believe that, even though you knew it would be impossible for him to stay by your side twenty-four/seven. When Curtis Wilder attacked you, nearly raped you, it wasn't Luke who stopped him. It was you."

Devon cringed. Yeah, that part was really weighing on her. She'd killed a man. No, she didn't remember it, and no, she wasn't sorry he was dead, but to know that she'd taken a life, even in self-defense, that knowledge was a leaden weight inside her. Shaking her head, she said, "It's not that. It's not."

"Are you sure?"

Swallowing, Devon tried to say, "Yes. Yes, I am sure."

But the words wouldn't come. As fucked up as it was, something about Luke . . . no, something about those insane, horrifying dreams had her so scared, she couldn't even breathe past it at times. It was like her throat was closing up on her, like some invisible band was squeezing the air right out of her.

"It's natural to want to blame somebody. You know that."

Devon scowled. Shoving out of the chair, she started to pace Lydia's office. It was done in soothing tones of cream and blue, but it might as well been bloodred for all the good it did her. *Blood . . . no.* "Don't think about blood," she muttered, rubbing the back of her hand over her mouth.

"Yeah, I want to blame somebody." Spinning around, she glared at Lydia. "I do blame somebody. I blame that sick fuck for hurting his son, for forcing me to take a boy away from his only parent. I blame him for being a cruel monster and for having that kind of evil inside him. I blame him, Lydia. Curtis did this to me, not Luke. Luke didn't do a damn thing wrong . . ."

Her voice broke, and her knees started to give out. Collapsing onto the floor, she whispered, "So why am I so scared of him?" Burying her face against her knees, she whispered, "When Luke's there, after he's been around awhile, it's like that scared part of me relaxes, realizes he wouldn't hurt me. But after he's been gone, or I have, or after one of these dreams . . ."

"The mind can play tricks on the body, Devon."

Lydia's voice was closer, and Devon lifted her gaze to watch as the counselor settled down on the floor next to her, smoothing down her burgundy skirt with an automatic gesture.

The woman probably spent half her time here either on the floor or standing in the corner by one of her scared, screwed-up patients. Devon absolutely despised the fact that she'd become that again: a scared, terrified, screwed-up victim.

"You don't get it," Devon said hoarsely. "It's not my mind that's afraid of him. It's my body. My head tells me to stop it, that Luke wouldn't hurt me. But my body wants to run. Especially . . ."

"Especially after one of these dreams. It's your subconscious mind, Devon. Somewhere inside you, I suspect you have a great deal of pent-up anger, rage, and blame. We have to deal with it."

Bitterly, Devon said, "Isn't that why I'm here?"

With a sympathetic smile, Lydia replied, "You tell me. Is that why you're here?"

"Why else would I be here? It sure as hell isn't because I want to be."

Chuckling, Lydia patted Devon's shoulder. "Oh, I'd pretty much figured that out." Cocking her head, Lydia pinned Devon with a direct, honest stare. "Tell me, though, why did you come back? What do you expect to get out of seeing me?"

Devon swallowed. Lydia wasn't asking because she didn't know the answer; she was asking because she wanted Devon to understand the reasons, to acknowledge them. To stop hiding. Damn it, she hated therapy sessions. Hated therapists, counselors, psychiatrists— all of them. Hated that she had to be here. "I want these dreams to stop. I want to understand why I'm having them and figure out how to make them go away." Closing her eyes, she added, "And I want to stop feeling so scared when Luke touches me."

She opened her eyes and looked at Lydia. "I want my life back."

"And are you willing to do what you need to do to get it back?"

"I'm here, aren't I?" Rolling her eyes, she moved to her knees and stood up. Lifting one hand, she shoved her hair back from her face, but as she lowered her hand, she stopped, stared. Startled, she stared at her bony wrist. Damn it, she looked like a skeleton. She knew she'd lost weight; she'd seen it in her reflection that morning after she'd climbed out of the shower, and she could tell by how loosely her clothes fit.

But for some reason, it really hit home just how thin she'd become. Luke had called her beautiful that morning, and she'd laughed, told him he needed to get his eyes checked. But maybe Devon should as well, because although she'd looked, had seen, she hadn't seen enough to make her do something about it.

If it wasn't for Luke, she wouldn't be here.

But that was a skewed way of looking at things. Trying to fix it because of him wasn't the way to fix things. She needed to fix things for herself.

Fisting her hand, she lowered it back to her side and looked up, watched as Lydia stood up. "I'm scared. All the time, I'm scared. I can't eat. I can't sleep unless Luke's with me. When he's gone, that's when the dreams happen. It's like my body, my subconscious realizes he isn't there, that he can't hold me and keep the dreams away. And when he comes back . . . Is this some weird way of punishing him for not being there all the time?"

Lydia lifted a brow. "Entirely possible. Do you expect that of him?"

"No, I don't expect it. But part of me, a huge part of me, wants it." She shivered, suddenly cold. Rubbing her hands up and down her arms, she moved to stare out the window. Night was falling. She'd been in Lydia's office for more than an hour. When she'd called to set up an appointment, Lydia had rearranged her schedule so that Devon would have the last appointment of the day, giving her as much time as needed.

Devon suspected she could stay there until midnight every night for weeks, and it still wasn't going to be enough.

"I don't feel safe when he isn't with me." Looking back at Lydia, she asked, "But isn't that a weird way of blaming him? If I blamed him, if I held him responsible, couldn't it be interpreted that I don't trust him to keep me safe?"

Lydia made an incomprehensible little "Hmm." Then she answered Devon's question with one of her own. "I'll ask you again. Do you blame him, Devon?"

In a whisper, Devon replied, "I don't know."

"Then I'd say that's a question we need answered." Lydia settled back in her seat and smoothed her skirt down.

"And if I find out that the answer is yes, that I do blame him? What then?" She closed her eyes, thought of all the times she'd seen such guilt on Luke's face, all that self-directed anger.

He was dealing with his own guilt, his own self-blame. But could he deal with it if she threw her blame onto the fire, as well?

"Then we work past it. If you love this man, and I suspect you do, isn't he worth it?"

"He's worth it." She opened her eyes and looked at Lydia, a sad smile curling her lips. "But I have to wonder, am I? I've already put him through hell."

"No." Lydia shook her head, her gaze sympathetic. "You didn't put him through hell, Devon. A brutal, cruel man did that. He did it to both of you, and it wasn't your fault, wasn't Luke's fault."

But even as she left Lydia's office a few minutes later, Devon had doubts. So many of them, she could feel their weight pressing down on her, weighing heavier and heavier as she went.

* * *

SWEARING, Luke lowered the phone back into the cradle and leaned back against the wall in the doctors' lounge. It was nearly eight. He still had nine hours left in his shift, and he was so damned anxious to see Devon that it had become a chore to focus on the job.

He'd thought maybe if he could talk to her, he'd feel better.

Hear her voice. That was all he wanted. All he needed.

But she wasn't at home, and her cell phone had directed his call into her voice mail. A call to Lydia's office didn't tell him anything. The counselor's phones had been turned off, and all Luke could do was leave a message with her answering service.

She shouldn't have gone back to work so soon.

A very large part of him, the macho, possessive, protective part, kept telling him he should make Devon take more time off. The slightly saner, slightly more rational part of his mind guffawed at the idea of telling her that.

Devon needed her work. While he suspected she didn't love her job, it was cathartic for her—or rather, it had been. Helping kids escape hellacious lives was her way of dealing with the hell her own childhood had been. She was good at it. She got through to kids, and Luke had no doubt that a lot of that was because of her own experiences.

She'd been doing okay. The week after Christmas, she'd seemed happier. More at peace. Like she used to be. Even though she'd hated it, she'd made the appointments with Lydia, saw her three times. Devon had admitted that the counselor suggested a few more sessions, but Lydia hadn't insisted, and she'd given Devon the all-clear to return to work.

Then she returned to work, and that was when all hell broke loose. That was when she'd stopped sleeping unless he was with her. That was when she started jumping at shadows and starting at every sound. That was when she'd started to pull away from him again.

She tried to hide it. But Luke was a trained observer, and he'd seen it clearly enough. It wasn't all the time. And there were times when she seemed just fine. The past few days had been the worst. The nights he'd been working.

This morning, although she'd said nothing, although she'd done nothing, he'd seen it. The signs of another sleepless night and the stiff way she'd stood in his arms before finally leaning back against him.

It was normal, wasn't it? Being scared after what had happened. She'd been like that the first couple of weeks after the attack, and it shouldn't send alarm bells screeching when it happened.

Except why had it stopped . . . then started again?

Why did he have this gut-deep dread that it was him that Devon was afraid of? As much as he'd like to write it off as his own imagination, he couldn't do it. His gut wouldn't let him.

The door to the nurses' lounge swung open, and one of the other physicians came in. A new guy whose name escaped Luke, followed by one of the residents. Reluctant to get into a conversation, he slid past them and left the lounge. He wasn't in the mood to talk to anybody other than Devon, especially not some enthusiastic resident eager to impress or a new guy equally eager to impress the cute young resident.

The door swung shut behind him as he headed down the hall. He spared another glance at his watch, even though he'd just checked the time.

8:01.

Great. He'd managed to pass a whole four minutes.

When a nurse called out his name, he was almost relieved. That tone of voice, followed by the ensuing tension as other nurses started to rush around in a familiar fashion, meant only one thing. A trauma en route.

Before he had another chance to kill a few more minutes and check the passage of time, his gloved hands were covered with blood, and he was too busy barking out orders for the nurses to think about Devon.

That trauma was followed by another one, this one a self-induced. The patient had gone up on the roof to take down Christmas decorations and had slipped, fallen. In addition to the broken arm, he'd also managed to break his ribs when he landed on a small lawn statue. The broken ribs had punctured a lung, and the guy's wife, trying to help him, had wasted precious time.

Getting him stabilized wasn't too hard, but Luke got the short end of the straw and was elected to go out and talk to the hysterical wife. The teenager with her was in better control than her, and it took a good twenty minutes before Luke could get her to calm down and listen.

That was how the rest of the night progressed: a drunk driver involved in a one-car accident, a possible suicide attempt, three kids with fevers, ranging from 100 degrees to 104.3 degrees. Ended up that the one with the lower temp was the troublesome patient. The toddler with the 104 degree temp had a nasty case of strep. The older child with the 100 degree fever was asthmatic, and what had started out as a mild cold ended up putting him into a full-blown asthma attack. By the time his mother had realized he needed to see a doctor, it was late, and she'd thought the boy could wait until morning.

No. Instead of a trip to the doctor's, the boy was getting admitted.

The asthmatic was followed by a false labor, and when Luke finally convinced her she wasn't getting ready to have the baby, she'd broken into tears.

By the time his shift ended, Luke was dragging. He hadn't slept worth shit the past couple of weeks, and he didn't see that changing anytime soon.

Traffic was light, and when he pulled into the driveway, the lights in the house were still off. He found Devon asleep in the living room, cuddled up on the couch with her head pillowed on the over-stuffed armrest. He dropped his coat right where he stood and went to her, settling down behind her.

Devon started a little. "Shhh," he murmured, nuzzling her neck.

She hummed under her breath and then sighed, settled back against him.

Wrapping an arm around her waist, he closed his eyes. Sleep dropped down on him like a leaden weight.

* * *

SHE was surrounded by warmth.

At her back, there was a plush wall, and along her front, a hard, warm body. She recognized his scent even in her sleep, and with a happy sigh, she snuggled against him. His hand stroked down her side, and it never occurred to her that maybe she should be afraid.

Content, warm, safe, she settled deeper into sleep. And that was where fear waited to strike. In reality, she lay on the couch, wrapped in Luke's arms, but in her dreams, she wasn't pressed up against Luke but pinned under him. His voice, familiar but not, was a low, ugly whisper in her ear, and when he told her what he planned to do to her, she wanted to scream.

The only sound she made was a whimper.

Hard hands came up, wrapped around her throat. Choking, struggling to breathe, she swung out.

"Hey!"

She jerked away, tears stinging her eyes and panic crowding her throat. Confused, still tripped up by the fear, she tried to pull away, but firm hands held her in place.

Through her tears, she saw Luke's face. Her heart skipped a beat or two. Then her mind started to work, and she saw the concern, the worry in his gray eyes. The hands holding her in place were strong but not cruel. His grip was firm but not tight, and as she stared at him, his thumbs started a slow, gentle sweep along the inside of her wrists. "It's just me," he said quietly. Slowly, he sat up, pulling back and holding up his hands.

Her mouth trembled. She tried to keep from crying, but the sobs burned in her throat, and when she opened her lips to try to get a breath, they spilled out of her. Deep, ugly sobs and tears that burned like acid spilled out of her. Without realizing it, she reached for him.

Luke's arms, warm, protective, came around her, and she buried her face against his chest. Pent up for too long, the storm inside her raged on for what seemed like hours, and when the tears finally passed, her throat was raw from crying, and her head ached.

Luke still held her. Under her cheek, the soft, worn fabric of his T-shirt was soaked with tears. She sniffled and pushed against him gently. Without meeting his eyes, she sat up. Still sniffling, she looked for a box of tissues.

They appeared in front of her eyes, Luke holding them out in silence. Taking one, she mumbled a thanks under her breath and blew her nose. She scooted off his lap, but when she would have stood up, Luke reached out. Gently, almost carefully, he stopped her, his fingers wrapped loosely around her wrist. "This has gone on long enough, hasn't it?" he asked quietly.

Yes. Yes, it had.

Swallowing the knot in her throat, she glanced back at him over her shoulder. He watched her with those amazing eyes, that beautiful face of his etched with worry and exhaustion. *This isn't fair to him,* her mind whispered.

Devon licked her lips and wondered just where she should start. She was so tired of being scared all the time. Scared when he wasn't there, but scared when he was.

You're not always afraid of him.

No. But a lot of the time, I am.

Until she could work past that ... *Oh, God, I'm not thinking* ...

But as she shifted around on the couch, turning to face him, she knew she was. She had to get away from him, had to, before she ended up hurting him more than she'd already done.

He won't leave ... It was a sad, certain truth that he wouldn't leave for that. Not for him. He'd take whatever pain she heaped on him and never let it show when she hurt him; he'd keep taking it and taking it, and knowing him, even if he ended up hating her for it, he wouldn't leave.

Not for him.

Then make him think it's for you. If she told him she wanted him gone for *her* sake, not for his, he'd do it. That would hurt him, too. She didn't doubt that, but better to get it over and done quick than to just keep torturing him like she had been.

Her throat burned, and although nothing touched her, she could all but feel an invisible hand wrapped around her neck, squeezing ... squeezing ...

He could see her turmoil. It was written on his face, in the compassionate, loving depths of his gaze, in the way he reached out, cupped her cheek. "What's going on, Devon?"

Her mouth had gone dry, and it took two tries before she could even put words together. "I think I need some time by myself, Luke."

A muscle twitched in his jaw, but that was the only reaction. The hand cupping her cheek remained gentle, and his eyes were unreadable. "Where's this coming from?"

She turned her head, pressed a kiss to his palm, and then slowly curled her fingers around his wrist, tugging until he was no longer touching her. He watched with wary eyes as she stood and started to pace. Words were a jumbled mess in her head, and she couldn't focus on any one word in particular. "I don't know, Luke. Everywhere. Nowhere. I just ..." Stopping in midsentence, she turned and stared at him, tears blurring her vision. Desperate not to cry anymore, she blinked them away.

"I'm scared. All the time, I'm scared, and I'm tired of it. I don't even know who I am, what I want; half the time I can't tell if I want you with me or not."

He flinched, the color draining from his face. Devon pressed her lips together and spun away. *I didn't just say that!* But she had. The words were out there, and she couldn't take them back. "I'm sorry," she whispered in a reed-thin voice. "I didn't mean that the way it sounded. I do want you with me. I love you. But . . ."

"But what?" he asked woodenly.

"But . . ."

"Look at me." His voice was flat, but the command came through loud and clear. "If you're throwing me out of your life, the least you can do is look at me and tell me why."

She turned on stiff legs. When she met his gaze, he shoved up off the couch and shoved his hands into his pockets. Staring at her with turbulent eyes, he demanded, "But what?"

Devon shook her head. "I can't explain this very well, Luke. I feel like I'm going crazy. I need to get my head on straight. I have these dreams, crazy dreams—dreams where you look like you, but . . . well, you aren't. Your voice sounds the same, but it isn't. When you touch me, your hands feel like yours, but they aren't. And you hurt me."

Licking her lips, she turned away from him so she didn't have to see the pain in his eyes. So she didn't throw herself at him and hold on to him, beg him to just stay right next to her. Always. Couldn't do that—had to get him away, before she hurt him more.

Even though the words burned in her throat like acid, she didn't mention the rest of it, the bizarre, terrifying sensation of being watched . . . followed. He'd worry, and he'd stay. If he stayed . . .

"Look, I just need some space. Some time. I don't even know who I am right now, Luke."

"And you think getting rid of me is going to clear that up for you?"

"I'm not getting rid of you." When her voice broke, Devon closed her eyes and turned away. She took a deep breath. *You have to do this. Get it over. Get it done.* "Luke, I'm not getting rid of you. I love you. But . . . I can't breathe anymore. I can't think. I never sleep. I need to get myself together and deal with this."

"And you can't do it with me here?"

Devon gave a watery laugh. "Don't you think I've been trying?"

For the longest time, all Luke did was stare at her. Her breath froze in her chest as he took one step toward her. He saw it, that tiny, imperceptible action, and Devon watched as a look flitted across his face. There, then gone, but she'd seen it; she'd seen the pain she caused him, and she hated herself for it.

He took another step, and another, watching her face, and Devon forced herself to hold still, to not look away from him, not even allowing herself to blink as he lifted a hand and cupped her chin, arching her face up to his. His voice was hoarse as he whispered, "I love you." Then, his touch as gentle as a breeze, he kissed her.

The tears she'd been fighting to hold in check spilled over as he lifted his head. He brushed one away with his thumb. Devon swallowed, the knot in her throat huge and painful. He moved away in utter silence, and Devon, unable to watch him go, turned away.

She didn't even hear the front door open or close, and she hadn't heard the sound of his car starting, but she knew in her heart when he left anyway. It was like the light had just gone out of her world.

And she was the one responsible.

Numb, she sank to her knees in the middle of the floor, staring off into the distance. Now that he was gone, she wanted to cry, wanted to throw herself down on the floor and scream, rail, and curse at the sucker punch that fate had sent her way.

But she couldn't. All she could do was sit there and ask herself, "What in the hell did I just do?"

FOURTEEN

LUKE wanted to call her. That first day, he found himself reaching for the phone almost every twenty minutes, from the time he left her house a little before nine, to one o'clock, when he finally fell into a restless sleep. For two hours, he catnapped on the couch in his old condo, and when he awoke, he was stiff, sore, and mad as hell.

It was his Saturday to work, and he was as enthusiastic about dealing with people as he was about moving off the damn couch. A glance at the clock told him he had less than forty-five minutes to shower, get dressed, and get something to eat if he wanted to get to work on time.

His black mood wasn't improved by the fact that there was nothing to eat, nothing to drink in the whole damned place. Up until a few weeks ago, dealing with the condo had totally slipped his mind.

Now he had somebody interested in subletting it from him, Luke was going to have to call the mess off. He took a shower and got ready for work, leaving just in time to avoid being late. But there was no time to grab a sandwich or even a damn cup of coffee. Eyes gritty with fatigue and his head hurting like a bitch, he made it halfway through his shift before he let himself slow down for more than five minutes.

But five seconds was all it took to start thinking about Devon. Locking himself in an empty office, he dropped down behind a desk and found himself staring at the phone. He'd finally managed to grab a few cups of lousy coffee, and the strong brew had left a nasty, bitter taste in his mouth. Between the headache and the heartburn, it was a wonder he could even feel the pain in his chest.

But the heartache was worse than the other two combined, hitting him with an intensity that had him staggering from the pain.

She didn't want him around.

She was afraid of him. Having nightmares where he was the one who hurt her.

She'd shoved him out of her life and hadn't so much as said good-bye when he left. He'd seen the look in her eyes when he went to kiss her, and he'd almost left without touching her. That look, it was one he'd seen in her eyes too many times, one he hadn't let himself acknowledge.

Fear. And it was of him, not just left over from the attack, and not out of some deep, hidden instinct. But fear of him.

"You fucked it up," he told himself, tearing his gaze away from the phone and propping his feet on the edge of the desk. Where he'd messed up, when, how, none of those were questions he had any answers for, but somehow, he'd messed up.

A slimy, insidious voice inside him whispered, *You know damn well where you fucked up, Rafferty. You didn't protect her.*

He'd tried to deal with the guilt over that, and he'd thought maybe he'd even started to manage it. But that ugly reminder undermined all of it, and the guilt came crashing down on him.

Memories of how she'd looked that night were forever burned on his mind, and now they played before him in a sickening display. Devon strapped to a stretcher as they loaded her into the ambulance, bruised, battered, and struggling to breathe on her own. Her pale face splattered with blood. Lying on a narrow hospital bed as a monitor ticked away every beat of her heart.

Yeah, he'd fucked up, all right. Fucked up in the worst way possible, failing to protect his woman. Maybe this was right. Maybe this was fitting that she kick him out on his sorry ass.

She sure as hell deserved better.

* * *

MINUTES turned into hours, which turned into days. By the time Monday rolled around, and Luke had a few days off, he was still fighting the urge to call her every few days, and as five o'clock approached, he found himself sliding into his Jeep and heading toward her office.

He wasn't going to talk to her or even let her see him.

He just needed to see her. Needed to make sure she was okay. He turned into the parking lot of the government building where Social Services was located, riding the bumper of the blue sedan in front of him. Impatience ate at him, and when the sedan finally turned left, Luke laid on the gas and sped down around the building until he came to the part of the building where Devon worked.

Her car was still there. Parking a few rows down, he turned off the ignition and leaned back in the driver's seat, prepared to wait all night if he had to. He just wanted to see her.

That was all.

He'd just do it today.

And maybe tomorrow.

* * *

AFTER Luke had left her house in silence, Devon felt like she spent the weekend in hell. The walls seemed to close in her. She couldn't eat. What little sleep she'd gotten happened in front of the TV, wearing one of Luke's shirts and breathing in his scent, pretending he was there with her.

By Monday morning, she was so damn eager to get out of the house, she got to work more than an hour early. It ended up being one of those days, too. Missed appointments, a runaway, bureaucratic bullshit that was going to delay the medical treatment that a disabled foster child desperately needed. Still, she wasn't ready to go home, and she made the drive from work to home in a state of dread.

As she pulled into her driveway, her cell went off, and one look at the display had her backing out of the driveway and stifling the urge to sigh in relief.

Getting called to the emergency department at University wasn't an escape, and she shouldn't see it as one. While she listened to the doctor explain why Social Services had been called, guilt darkened her mind. She rounded out her night by taking three children, all under the age of five, away from their mother. The mom, restrained to the hospital bed, had been shouting and spitting, half out of her mind from whatever drug cocktail she'd taken before she took a header down the stairs in her apartment building.

All three of the kids showed signs of neglect and abuse, and Devon knew she'd be talking to a judge about temporary placement for the kids while the mom made an attempt to get her act together.

By the time she was back home, it was after midnight. Too tired to even try to eat, she'd listened to her messages—and the one from Luke had damn near broken her.

She wanted to grab the phone, wanted to call him, screw how late it was. But she couldn't make herself pick up the phone. Couldn't make herself call him.

Instead, she went to the closet and grabbed his coat. He'd left it behind, and although she knew he probably needed it, she couldn't make herself take it to him. Burying her face in it, she breathed in the scent of Luke and leather. She slid it on, held it closed across her chest, and the warmth of it surrounded her.

Pretending it was Luke, she went to the couch and settled down, prepared for another long, sleepless night . . . or worse, one filled with those damn dreams. Surprisingly, she fell asleep easily enough.

She even managed a couple hours of deep, dreamless sleep before waking in stark, utter terror. Uncertain of what had woken her, she'd sat there in the darkness, so scared she didn't even want to breathe. From the corner of her eye, she thought she saw something move, a darker shadow lost among the shadows, and then a sound, almost like a sigh.

Vaulting out of the chair, she grabbed a poker from the fireplace and turned on the lamp—to find the room completely and utterly empty. Going through the house room by room, she turned on every light, searching behind doors, inside closets, even under her bed.

Feeling very much the fool and very much in doubt of her sanity, she'd turned to leave her room when something caught her eye. Not in her room, but outside, across the street. A light on in Danielle's still-empty house.

But when she'd gotten to the window and peered through it, Danielle's house was dark, and the curtains were drawn.

Icy chills wrapped around her like a shroud. Even after drinking nearly a pot of coffee, and one very long, hot shower, taking the poker into the stall with her, she still couldn't dispel the chill.

Tuesday morning dawned to find her dressed and bleary-eyed as she brewed a second pot of coffee and forced herself to swallow a couple bites of bagel. And yet again, she left home so early, she got to work an hour before she was scheduled to clock in.

Working off the clock—a big no-no—and hoping her boss didn't show up, she finished up the paperwork from the previous day.

Devon spent the day buried in work, getting the approval for temporary placement for her three newest charges, busting her tail to find a decent set of foster parents who could take on not one new child but three.

Midafternoon, she finally forced herself to do what she'd been dreading, and that was make a quick visit to see Tim, riding along with his newly assigned caseworker. It was every bit as awkward as she'd expected.

Most of the visit, she stood off to the side, staring anywhere and everywhere but at Tim. Near the end of the brief visit, Tim finally blurted out, "Don't you hate me?"

If her heart hadn't already been broken, that would have done it. Turning her head, she looked at him, tried to smile.

It fell flat, though. Instead of trying again, or looking for some trite line, she said, "What happened wasn't your fault, Tim."

"Isn't it? He did it because of me."

"No." Sighing, Devon reached up and rubbed the back of her neck, trying to ward off the tension headache. "He did it because he was a sick man, Tim. It's the same reason he hurt you. None of it, and I mean none of it, is your fault."

She saw the doubt in his eyes, but Devon knew there was nothing else she could do or say, not at this point. With one more forced smile, she excused herself and spent the rest of the visit huddling in her coat out on the wraparound porch.

Near the end of the day, she had an appearance in court where she got to witness the formal adoption of Ellie by the Parkers.

As the judge signed off on the adoption, Ellie had launched herself at her new mom, and Devon found herself sniffling and blinking back tears of happiness. The one highlight in her day. Seeing Ellie reminded her of Luke, but Devon shoved it out of her mind, determined not to let her own depression darken that moment.

But now, nearly an hour after Ellie had skipped out of the courtroom holding her parents' hands, Devon couldn't keep herself from thinking about him, wondering yet again if she'd made a mistake.

She'd only asked herself that ten thousand times since Saturday morning, and she was no closer to an answer now than she had been then.

Brooding, she gathered up her things and got ready to leave. Caution had her slowing down as she reached the main entrance, and when Ronnie offered to walk her to her car, she jumped at his offer with relief.

The parking lot was still full, people coming out in small groups of two or three. Surrounded by people, she felt it ripple down her spine, that certainty that somebody was watching her.

Somebody. But who?

Surreptitiously, she glanced around, tried to see who it could be, but she saw nothing. All around her, she heard laughs, good-natured complaints, and some not so good-natured as a lawyer griped about a cop he'd had on the stand, but it all fell on unhearing ears.

It was background noise and nothing else as Devon fought to pinpoint where it was coming from. She'd been fighting this bizarre, paranoid sense of being watched, being followed, for weeks, and she'd yet to actually see anybody. A blue car every once in a while—and how many blue cars where there in Lexington? A ton. It was a college town, and half the people here probably bled blue.

But it was strange. Although she could feel eyes on her, she didn't have that overwhelming sense of fear. Preoccupied, when Ronnie touched her shoulder, she jumped. Feeling like an idiot, she blushed when she realized they'd passed her car.

"Sheesh. Sorry, Ronnie." She gave him a sheepish grin as she backtracked.

He just smiled. "Everything okay? You've been so quiet since . . ." His voice trailed off, and he winced. "I'm sorry, Ms. Manning."

"Devon," she corrected automatically. She'd been telling him that for the past two years and knew she'd be doing the same in another ten years. "It's okay, Ronnie. And yes, I know I've been quiet. Just—I don't know, trying to get my head back together."

Ronnie was quiet as she opened the driver's door and slid inside, but before she could shut it, he reached out and laid a hand along the top. Pausing, she looked up at him. In a soft, almost hesitant voice, he said, "Maybe you came back just a little too soon, Ms. Manning. Awful thing that happened. Taking a little more time . . ."

But Devon shook her head. "Time isn't going to help what's going on right now. Right now, I just need to get my head together, and taking off from work isn't going to accomplish that." With a bitter smile, she added, "Right now, work is the only thing keeping me halfway sane."

But just barely.

Closing the door, she gave him a wave before she started the car. Ronnie waited until she pulled out before he headed back inside.

His words echoed the sentiments of Noelle; her boss, Dawson; and the few casual friends that had been concerned enough to approach her about it. Everybody thought she'd come back to work too soon, including Luke. She couldn't tell any of them how much worse it was when she sat home by herself.

Memories of her miserable weekend still loomed large in her mind, and she knew no amount of time spent at home was going to help her. Not one bit.

She had hopes that the upcoming session with Lydia might help a little, that she might find some as-yet-undiscovered answers, but she wasn't going to hold her breath.

Exhaustion pulled at her, and if nothing else, she knew the session would leave her feeling emotionally and physically drained. Hopefully, by the time she got home, she'd be so tired, thoughts and fears wouldn't have room to intrude.

Wishful thinking.

The session with Lydia was every bit as exhausting as Devon had expected, but it also left her twitchy, edgy, and filled with adrenaline that was probably going to keep her awake half the night.

Trying to work some of it off, she shoved out of her chair and began to pace Lydia's office. The therapist watched her with calm, unreadable eyes. Devon really hated that expression, hated the professional calm that therapists projected, and she hated that she couldn't find any semblance of calm within herself.

"How did you feel after he left?"

Shooting Lydia a dark look, she said sourly, "How do you think I felt? I went dancing." Groaning in frustration, she turned away. Abruptly, she reached up and pulled the clip out of her hair. The weight of it fell down her back, and her scalp had that weird, tingly pain. Running her hand through her hair, she finger-combed out some of the tangles and stared off into the distance. "I was miserable, Lydia. I wanted to call him, tell him to come back. I still do."

Shrugging, she said softly, "I don't know what I want, other than to stop feeling so scared. And him. I want Luke back with me."

"Then perhaps you should call him. Having him leave, did it help you at all?"

She gave up fiddling with her hair and wrapped her arms around her middle. Unconsciously, she rocked herself back and forth. Inside, she was miserable, aching, and so heartsick, her chest hurt with it. Desolate, she replied, "Him leaving didn't help at all. But . . ." Devon closed her eyes. "I'm a mess right now. How fair is it for me to expect him to hang around while I try to get my head on straight? I keep doing things, saying things that hurt him. That isn't fair."

"Let me ask you a question, Devon. And you need to answer honestly. Do you believe that he loves you?"

She opened her eyes and turned around, staring at Lydia. "Yes." Plain and simply, yes. She didn't just believe Luke loved her; she knew it. Right down to her bones, she knew it.

"Then reverse the situations. If he was the one dealing with some inner turmoil, wouldn't you want to be there and help him through it?"

Scrubbing her hands over her face, Devon whispered, "It's not that simple."

"But it is." Lydia leaned forward, and for once, the look on her face wasn't one of calm professionalism or nonjudgmental understanding. It was earnest concern, more the kind a friend would give a friend than that of a therapist to patient. "It is that simple, Devon. If the two of you are going to have any chance together, you need to accept that you don't have to work through things on your own anymore. You don't have to handle every hurdle, every obstacle alone. That's part of being in a relationship."

Settling back in her chair, Lydia sighed. "Devon, we both work in a field where we see some of the shittiest people imaginable." She gave Devon a wry smile and added, "Friend to friend here for a few minutes, Devon. Friend to friend. I've always admired you for your professionalism, the way you are with kids, the way you can relate to some of the older kids, the ones a lot of your coworkers have already written off. You connect with them, and you've helped so many. But with jobs like ours, it's hard to be an island. You need an escape from it, somebody to lean on after you've had a particularly bad day, kids to remind you that not every child is neglected, abused, or unloved. Hobbies, friends . . . something. But you shut yourself off and trudge along on your own. There's nothing wrong with strength, Devon. But standing on your own two feet isn't going to keep you warm at night. It's not going to make you laugh, and it's not going to help ease the pain and the heartbreak we encounter in our professional lives."

Lydia looked down, and Devon watched as she touched a finger to the ring on her left hand. The diamond caught the light and sparkled. When Lydia looked up, she had a smile on her face that had an ugly knot of envy forming in Devon's chest. "I love my job, Devon. I love knowing that I can help people. I love knowing that some of the people I see here eventually go on to live stronger, better, happier lives and that I had some small part in it. But there are days when I know I'm not getting through, when I know that nothing I've done or said will make a whit of difference—and there're some days when I realize that I failed. That a battered woman goes back to her abuser, and then I get a phone call that she'll never have the chance to find that safe, happy life, because she's dead. On days like that, I wonder if I'll have the strength to keep doing this—and then, I go home. I see Alan at the stove making lousy spaghetti while our kids are at the table doing their homework. I see them, and I realize that I do have the strength. They give it to me."

Devon turned away, unable to stare at the happy, content look that was even harder to face than the calm, professional mask. Staring back out the window, she said softly, "I know I'm stronger with him in my life. I could feel it. The heartbreaks in the job didn't weigh down on me as heavily; they still hurt, and I don't want to get to the point where those heartbreaks don't hurt. I stopped expecting them to break me, though. But . . ." She closed her eyes and leaned forward, resting her brow against the icy glass. "I'm not going to put him through hell just because some hidden part of me blames him. I need to get past that."

"Hmm. Well, Devon, tell me, do you honestly think he's not going through hell now?"

When she left Lydia's office, instead of going home, she found herself driving toward Luke's condo. She didn't even know if that was where he was staying. A couple of weeks ago, he'd made an offhand mention that he might try subletting it out. For all she knew, he wasn't even there.

What if he decided to leave?

It was a nasty, ugly fear. When she drove through the parking lot and found the reserved space in front of his condo empty, Devon grabbed her phone to call him.

Staring down at the black RAZR, she muttered, "What in the hell are you going to say? 'Luke, I just wanted to make sure you weren't leaving town. Just in case, well, you know, I can decide not to be a total basket case.' Shit, Devon."

Tossing the phone back down on the seat, she pulled out of the parking lot. Dread curdled inside her as she headed home. Dread, fear, and paranoia that once more started to work on convincing her that she had no right to resume a relationship when she was falling off the deep end. Working to get a handle on it, she tried to battle all those fears into submission. It even felt like she was making some headway.

Then she saw that damn car again. Just a flash, as it turned onto Nicholasville Road and fell into place a few cars back. The thick flow of traffic made it impossible for her to look for the car and still drive without having a wreck.

She bypassed the road she usually took to get home, going the back way, a trip that took a good twenty minutes longer. The entire time, she kept an eye on her rearview mirror, and every time a pair of headlights drew close, she braced herself, certain she'd see that blue sedan one more time.

Her skin crawled, and she knew, just knew, it was back there. Her imagination kicked into overdrive, and she imagined a car that was piloting itself, following her to and from work, shadows that moved on their own and lights that went on and off of their own volition.

But during that drive home, not once did she see the car again, and when she turned down her street, there wasn't another car coming from any direction.

Nobody had followed her. Nobody had been following her. Her hands shook as she turned off the ignition and climbed out of the car. Her gaze jumped all around, searching the shadows, eying the corners of the house as though they hid some hideous monster. A voice whispered, "You're losing it . . ."

But for the life of her, Devon couldn't tell if it was her own voice or somebody else's.

* * *

THE nights had gone and gotten long on him.

Luke lay in bed, staring up at the skylight overhead. He'd kicked the sheets and blankets down to the foot of the bed, hot and irritable, but even the cool air dancing over his flesh aggravated the hell out of him.

Physically, he was tired. The full moon was affecting people early or something, because it seemed half the crazy people in town had descended upon the emergency department at Rudding Memorial, and it seemed like half of them ended up getting referred up to Psych for evaluation—or admitted.

Luke had been forced to physically restrain three patients, and one of them had managed to sucker punch him. All the combat training in the world wasn't enough to prepare a person for a face-off with a schizophrenic who was convinced the medicine the nurses held was actually acid.

But as exhausting as the day had been, as heavy as his eyes were, he couldn't sleep.

It had been four days—come nine, it would be five days—since he'd seen Devon. Oh, he'd swung by her work Monday and Tuesday, and if he hadn't been scheduled to work, he would have gone by her work Wednesday afternoon as well.

He was pulling days the rest of the week, and he wouldn't have another off day until Saturday. He had to work the seven a.m. to seven p.m. shift Sunday through Wednesday of the following week, so he wouldn't be able to park himself in the lot by her office and hope he could catch a glimpse of her on the way to her job. Oh, he'd swing by her house on the way home, but usually by that time, she was settled inside, unless she'd been called out for one of her kids. Little chance of seeing her then.

He needed to see her, though. Wanted to hear her voice, talk to her . . . just to make sure she was okay.

Rubbing a hand over his face, he muttered, "Of course she's okay. Devon's a big girl; she doesn't need you."

Hell, she'd made that more than clear when she kicked him out. He'd called Monday while she was working and left a message that he'd come by Tuesday to get his stuff . . . unless she didn't want him to. All night, he'd waited for a call that he didn't need to, that it wasn't necessary, but the call didn't come.

He took that to mean she wanted his stuff out of there, and as long as she didn't have to see him, she didn't care when he came and got it.

But when Tuesday rolled around, instead of going to get his stuff, he left a message that something had come up. He'd just wait until he heard from her before he did anything—okay? Even as he left the message, he felt like a fool. But at least he was still a fool who could cling to a few illusions. For a little while longer.

And when she didn't call, Luke let those illusions grow.

Deep inside, though, Luke knew he was deluding himself.

Her words from months earlier came back to haunt him. *"But I'm a mess. You need to know that. I can't do casual, but I don't know if I can handle not casual, either."* No way he could say she hadn't warned him, but he hadn't expected it to end quite like this.

He hadn't been expecting the attack on Devon, either, and he hadn't counted on his abysmal failure to take care of her. Looking back at all of that, was it any wonder she needed to get away from him?

There was a logical voice left inside him, one that patiently reminded him that she hadn't dumped him, hadn't told him she didn't love him. She just needed a little bit of room. If he could have found it in himself to be objective, maybe he could have even understood it a little.

But objectivity, something that had always been easy for him, totally eluded him. He couldn't be objective, and he couldn't convince himself that he needed to give Devon some space, and maybe, after some time passed, they could try this again.

Hell, who knows . . . maybe it wasn't over. Maybe.

That was what the logical part of him kept trying to tell him.

But if that hated, logical, rational, calm voice didn't shut the fuck up, Luke was going to strangle it. How he'd strangle the voice of his conscience, he didn't know, but he'd figure it out.

When his cell phone rang, he almost ignored it. Even if he hadn't recognized the ring, he knew who it would be. Not too many people would call at this time of night. He wasn't on call, his dad wasn't much for phone calls, especially not late-night ones, and it wasn't like he'd have a girlfriend calling him who would just want to hear his voice, right? Self-pity had an ugly, bitter taste to it, but Luke was just fine wallowing in it.

Talking to Quinn wasn't what he wanted or needed at the minute. After three rings, the phone stopped ringing, automatically going to voice mail, and Luke closed his eyes, told himself Quinn was better off not talking to Luke right now anyway. His mood was lethal.

But then the phone started to ring again. Snarling, he grabbed it and flipped it open, and growled into the mouthpiece, "It's late, I'm tired, and I'm in a shitty mood, Quinn. Call back some other time."

Quinn's voice came back over the line, oddly raspy. "A shitty mood. Yeah, I can tell."

His twin's bitterness, always simmering just below the surface, seemed a little less hidden. Not that Luke gave a flying fuck at the moment; he had his own anger to deal with. Luke pinched the bridge of his nose and blew out a harsh breath. "Trust me, Quinn. I'm not safe for public consumption right now."

"Your brother ain't exactly public consumption," Quinn drawled. His voice was slow, lazy, and Quinn's characteristic sarcasm was there, but still . . . something was—strange.

Strange enough that it managed to penetrate Luke's fog of anger, loneliness, and self-pity and jerk him back into awareness. So what if it felt like he was bleeding to death inside, his heart oozing out something black and bitter?

"No. No, you're not." Slowly, he sat up and swung his legs over the edge of the bed, planting his feet on the floor and resting his elbows on his knees. Forcing thoughts of Devon, self-disgust, and self-pity out of his head, he focused on his twin, focused on their weird, tenuous connection. Tenuous but strong. Luke might not be as attuned to it as Quinn, but when he reached out, when he focused, Luke could home in on Quinn. Usually.

Quinn did a good job keeping Luke from picking up random things here and there, much better than Luke could do. It was how Quinn always seemed to know when Luke was pissed, moody, miserable, and why Luke couldn't quite pick up on the same things from Quinn.

But when Luke focused, it was a different story. He wouldn't ever read Quinn as easily as Quinn could read him. He didn't need to go deep to feel his twin's inner turmoil, though.

What he found now when he focused was a dark, deep, ugly mess of pain, guilt, and rage. A lot of rage. Even for Quinn, and Quinn was almost always pissed about something. "What's going on, Quinn?"

"I fucked up, man. Fucked it up all to hell and back." Quinn was quiet for a moment and when he spoke again, his voice throbbed, shook. "Too late to fix it now."

A sliver of unease settled inside Luke's heart, blooming into a ugly, raw mess. Shoving off the bed, he started to pace. He rubbed at the knotted muscles in his neck as he said, "There's no such thing as too late, Quinn."

Quinn laughed. The ugly, bitter sound hit Luke like acid, burning, eating away at him. "Ever the optimist, aren't you? With your nice, normal job; nice, normal woman; nice, normal life; it's easy for you to think there's no such thing as too late." Quinn was quiet for a second, and then in an ugly, hard voice, he asked, "How's that nice, normal woman doing, Luke? Your nice, normal life treating you well?"

"Go fuck yourself, Quinn. You calling to give me shit or because you wanted to talk?"

"Talk." Quinn gave a bark of laughter. "I don't call you to talk, do I? I call you because you're feeling sorry for yourself, or because somebody got you to thinking you needed to worry about that head case brother of yours. Hell, you didn't even want me around your pretty lady for Christmas. Nobody—" Abruptly, his voice ended.

The line went dead.

But Luke heard the words loud and clear: *Nobody really wants me around.*

As far as Quinn was concerned, that was a fact of his life. Their mother sure as hell hadn't wanted Quinn. She told him, often enough, that she should have left him in the hospital. Although Luke hadn't met the woman, he knew she probably regretted the impulse that had made her grab one of her newborn sons and disappear.

She hadn't wanted a son; she'd wanted to make her husband suffer. Then she passed that on to Quinn, and by the time she died, Quinn was already convinced of his complete lack of worth.

Those first few months had been awful, the two of them trying to adjust to each other. Hell, having this other half you didn't know existed dropped into your life. It had upended Luke's happy, carefree existence, but he hadn't cared. He'd loved his brother from the first. It had been like pieces of some unknown puzzle had fallen into place.

But loving his brother meant hurting for him, because Quinn had been a mess of pain, anger, and grief. Over time, a lot of it had lessened, the pain fading away, the grief dying once he figured out there was really nothing worth grieving about, and the anger becoming a bitter cynicism that had made the boy seem much older than he truly was.

Nobody really wants me around. It wasn't something that Quinn had ever given voice to, but Luke had heard those unspoken words loud and clear. He'd thought he'd managed to convince his twin that wasn't true.

Obviously not. He'd made the right choice—he knew he had—not dropping Quinn on Devon at Christmas. She'd been too fragile, and Quinn was an abrasive bastard by nature. Luke loved him, but he was under no illusions as to how Quinn came off to people in general.

Devon hadn't needed that.

But Quinn hadn't deserved to be shut off from his family at Christmas, either. Even if he hadn't ever seemed to give a damn one way or the other. Luke had called Quinn on Christmas, but a damn phone call didn't mean much.

The two most important relationships in his life were seriously fucked up. He'd failed Devon, and he'd failed his brother.

"Fuck this shit." He punched in Quinn's number and held the phone to his ear. Yeah, he'd screwed up with Devon; he'd failed her. He couldn't fix that, and he couldn't undo the damage he'd done to Quinn over the past few weeks, either. But that didn't mean he couldn't reach out to his brother.

Quinn didn't answer the first time. Or the second. On the third call, Quinn finally answered, his voice a rough, hoarse growl. "Just lemme alone, Luke. I'm all fucked up right now, and you clucking over me ain't going to do a damn thing to help me."

"If you didn't need to talk to me, why did you call?" Luke demanded.

"Beats the hell out of me. Look, I'm drunk, I'm exhausted, I'm pissed—but none of that is really anything new."

There was a pause, and through the connection, Luke could hear his brother swallowing. "Since when did you start drinking?"

"Since I stopped being able to sleep at night," Quinn replied. "You should give it a shot, man. Maybe then you wouldn't keep me awake at night feeling sorry for yourself over whatever petty shit is wrong in your life."

Luke narrowed his eyes. *Petty shit?* He lost the one woman he'd ever loved, and it was *petty*? "Kiss my ass, Quinn. You ain't the only man in the world with problems."

"Yeah, well, what in the fuck kind of problems can you have? You got a woman who loves you, you got a nice, normal job, and all sorts of nice, normal people in your life that respect the hell out of you."

"You're talking out of your ass, Quinn. Wake up, sober up, whatever in the hell you need to do, but I got plenty of problems of my own, and they are all centered around that woman."

Quinn snorted. "Uh-oh, trouble in paradise?"

"You know what? I don't need this shit right now. When you decide you want to talk instead of just rip into me, call. Until then, you keep crying into that bottle." Swearing, he disconnected and lowered the phone, staring at it.

For the longest time, he didn't move. When he did, it was to settle his back against the wall and slide down to the floor, staring off into the darkness as he wondered who else he was going to fail in the near future.

At this point, it seemed like he was batting a thousand.

FIFTEEN

H ER head hurt.

Devon climbed out of bed on shaky legs. It had been a bad night, the worst yet, and the nightmares had seemed to drag on forever.

She shivered as the fading memories danced through her mind. An evil, ugly whisper in her ear as cruel hands touched her body, something over her face cutting off her air.

"*I could kill you without leaving a mark.*

"*You think getting raped is bad? You have no idea the things I can do to you.*

"*Go ahead . . . try to scream . . . Nobody would hear you anyway. And if they did, nobody would care.*"

It lasted forever. No wonder she felt like shit, after a night like that. No woman could come through that and feel anything close to human.

But as her legs continued to wobble and quake under her, she wondered if maybe this wasn't more than a case of a bad, no . . . make that a horrible night. She stumbled into the bathroom and hit the light, flinching at the brightness. It made her eyes hurt, added to the agony inside her skull.

Out of self-defense, she reached out and smacked the light off. In the dim bathroom, lit only by the early morning light filtering through the curtains, she could see that her face was far too pale and her eyes were glassy.

Shit.

This was so not what she needed. Getting sick on top of everything else.

The only comfort was that it was Saturday. At least she wouldn't have to call in sick to work, not that she'd been much good there the past few days. She shuffled and stumbled and wobbled her way back to bed, falling facedown lengthways across it. Her body didn't even feel like her own, her arms and legs clumsy, slow to respond to her commands. Needles of pain jabbed her skull from the inside, threatening to split her head wide-open.

Too weak, too tired to move around, she just reached out a hand and tried to snag the blanket at the foot of the bed. Her hand touched something soft and fluffy, but as she dragged it up over her, she knew it wasn't the blanket. It smelled of Luke. A thick fleece robe. Every day she'd stopped and reached out, touched her hands to it and wondered if she shouldn't put it up.

When he'd left a message on her machine a few days ago about picking up his stuff, she hadn't been able to return it; she didn't want him coming to get his things. But she hadn't been able to call him and tell him not to come, either.

Just the sound of his voice on the machine had been enough to turn her inside out.

She didn't want him taking his stuff. Made it seem too final, and she didn't want this to be final. So when she'd gotten home Tuesday and seen one of his jackets still hanging on the hook by the door, a rush of relief had left her weak-kneed. And she'd welcomed the message on the machine, too, listening to it a good five times, feeling a little more lame each time.

"I'll just wait until I hear from you before I do anything, okay?"

Okay? She was pretty sure nothing was okay. Nothing ever would be . . . unless it included him calling her, showing up at the door, and insisting that this was a mistake.

A mistake—yeah. She'd been slowly coming to that conclusion for the past week. She wanted him back. Right here with her, right now.

Get up. Call him. She started to do just that, but her throbbing head, the weakness in her arms and legs, kept her from doing it. "Later. Get some sleep. I'll call him later."

Tears burned her eyes, and she buried her face in the robe, whimpering as his scent surrounded her.

"I miss you."

* * *

IT was a low, ugly laugh, the first sound she heard when she opened her eyes. She could see nothing, could hear nothing beyond that laugh.

But she could feel. The soft, warm weight that had covered her as she slept was gone. Cool air drifted across her flesh, and Devon realized she was naked. She tried to lift her arms, but she couldn't move.

She wasn't restrained, at least she didn't think she was, but she couldn't move her arms, her legs—she couldn't even lift her head to look down at her body.

Not that she would see a damn thing in the thick, oppressive blackness.

A hand touched her, and she couldn't so much as cringe away.

Devon opened her mouth to scream, but all she managed was a pitiful whimper. The sound was obscenely loud, all but echoing back at her, bouncing off the walls.

"Cry, little girl," a voice whispered—that voice. Deep inside, she sensed there was something different this time about this dream. Totally paralyzed, unable to move—that hadn't happened before.

This felt too real, but then, these crazy dreams had always seemed too real, dreams that terrified her even as they faded away with the morning light.

"Cry all you want; nobody will hear you . . . Nobody will believe you."

Oh, dear God. That voice. Hated, nearly forgotten memories rushed back at her. All the time Boyd Chancellor had touched her, how he'd laughed when she cried the first times and said that she'd tell.

"Nobody will believe you." The voice came again, and this time, she recognized it. It was Boyd's voice.

"De—" She tried to say, *You're dead*, but she couldn't speak, either. It was like whatever held her body immobile had also paralyzed her vocal cords, and those pathetic little whimpers were all she could manage.

But he knew. Somehow he knew. "Dead. Am I dead?" He laughed, and laughed, and laughed—and all the while Devon lay there unable to move, cold and terrified.

Abruptly the laughter stopped. "Am I dead, too?" But the voice was different this time. This time, it was Curtis Wilder, and when he touched her, it was to put his hands around her throat and squeeze. "I spent too much time playing with you. Should have just given you the fuck a cold-ass bitch like you needs—and then snapped your skinny neck. You're a sad, pathetic waste of space, bitch. Just like that whiny kid of mine. Useless."

He squeezed, squeezed . . . . Devon gasped for air, still unable to move. But finally, she managed to get her tongue moving. She rasped out, "What do you want?"

"I want you—dead. That's where you belong."

The hands fell away, and a dim light appeared from nowhere. She screamed when she saw the face only inches above hers. It wasn't Boyd; it wasn't Curtis; it was Luke.

Luke, with cold, hard eyes and a mouth curled in disgust as he stared down at her. "Cold-ass bitch. You just going to lie there and whimper? Or do something? Scream for help. Go ahead." He dipped his head a little closer and licked her cheek. Then he pressed his lips to hers, a macabre mockery of a lover's kiss. "Scream—and if anybody cares enough to do anything, what are you going to say?"

A strange smile, one that didn't look like Luke's smile at all, curled his lips, and he added, "Nobody will believe you."

His face changed. Once more, it was Curtis. "Nobody will give a damn."

And then Boyd. "You're worthless. You were then. You are now."

"Leave me the hell alone!" she tried to scream. But the words lodged in her throat, choked her.

He laughed and grabbed something from beside her. The robe. That warm, soft weight she had curled up with as she drifted back to sleep. He pressed it down on her face, blocking out her sight, and pushing.

Through the thick fabric, she could barely suck air into her lungs. She struggled, using up what little air she had. Her strength dwindled, and her chest felt like it was going to explode, desperate to breathe—and then, everything stopped. In her sleep, she moaned and rolled over, still holding the robe clutched in her arms.

As she settled into a deeper sleep, tears slid out from under her lids to soak the blankets beneath her.

SIXTEEN

AFTER a restless night, Luke rolled out of bed and spent a good ten minutes in the shower trying to clear his head. Lack of sleep had his thoughts muddled, but as tired as he was, as much as he needed to just lie back down and try to get more rest, he couldn't.

He was edgy. Uneasy, although he couldn't explain why, just that it had to do with Quinn. But whether it was from the weird call last night and Quinn's unexpected, unexplained anger or something more, he couldn't tell.

It was almost a relief to have his brother weighing so heavily on his mind; kept him from brooding over Devon. Hell, maybe that was why he'd fixated on Quinn; maybe all this restless, edgy energy was brought on in some unconscious attempt to think about something, anything, other than Devon.

Maybe. And Luke didn't give a damn, either.

Focusing on his brother, he thought, *I need to talk to you.* It usually worked. Neither Luke nor Quinn would consider it any kind of psychic gift, their ability to sense each other. Luke suspected it came from their being formed from one single embryo, two halves of a whole.

From the time they'd first met when they were eleven, they could do this, and Luke suspected even before that. There had been times when he awoke from nightmares, times he stopped doing whatever he'd been doing, absolutely certain, absolutely convinced somebody had called him. Without saying a word, or name, but looking for him nonetheless.

Quinn hadn't ever totally ignored Luke, but he was doing it now. Whatever he was doing, wherever he was, Luke couldn't pick up on anything more than Quinn's general state of mind, which was pissed.

When Quinn failed to contact him, Luke spent most of Saturday morning trying to get hold of his brother. His calls were ignored, rolling over to Quinn's voice mail. The e-mails and instant messages went unanswered.

A few minutes on the phone ascertained neither their dad nor Jeb had talked to Quinn for a couple of weeks. Quinn may as well have dropped off the face of the earth. After spending an hour wearing a path on the gleaming hardwood floors, Luke found himself standing at the counter in the kitchen and staring at the phone.

Something was wrong. It wasn't just his imagination, and it wasn't some fucked-up distraction conjured up by his bruised, battered heart.

Something was wrong, and it could only be connected to Quinn. Luke wasn't attuned this way to anybody else but his twin.

Everything had just gone straight to hell. Devon, there wasn't much he could do about that. She had to decide whether she wanted him back in her life, or maybe she already had, and this *I need some space* line was just that. A line. A gentle send-off.

But whatever was going on with Quinn, Luke was going to find out. Find out, and fix it. He wasn't going to fail somebody he loved again.

He thought back to Jeb's weird call back in November, the bad vibes he'd picked up on, and his own internal alarm that things were seriously messed up with Quinn. But then he'd talked to Quinn, and Quinn had seemed fine—or at least he'd seemed his normal self: edgy and caustic. Nothing that had added to Luke's mental alarms. When he'd called him at Christmas, Quinn had seemed level, steady.

Then the call from last night . . .

"*I fucked up, man. Fucked it up all to hell and back. Too late to fix it now.*"

What exactly had Quinn fucked up?

Voices started to whisper inside his mind, words of possible warning that he'd heard, then dismissed.

Quinn's own caustic voice: "*That head case brother of yours.*"

Elsa, the woman whom both Luke and Quinn had spent four days with, living out lurid sexual fantasies, letting her touch and the endless flow of liquor dull the ugly memories from an op that had taken their unit straight through hell. Elsa had come to him, warned him: "*Watch your brother—he's got a darkness inside him. Something close to cruelty.*"

Jeb: "*Everything okay with him? He ain't answering when I call him. He ever tell you why he got out?*"

No. Quinn hadn't ever told him, and for some reason, in that moment, Luke realized he needed to know. Had to know. His mind kept churning as he reached out and grabbed the phone.

Luke had defended Quinn, like he had always had: "*It got to all of us, Jeb. No way it couldn't.*"

Jeb's calm, compassionate reply: "*You know that ain't what I'm talking about, Luke.*"

Luke was certain—or at least he had been—that everybody was getting worked up just because Quinn had that effect on people. He unsettled them and didn't give a damn. He had a mean streak in him, but not a cruel one. Luke had always been so certain of that, so convinced.

Quinn was a decent guy underneath that hard-ass exterior.

A good guy. A strong one, too strong for what Jeb had insinuated.

Staring at the phone, Luke tried to calm the wash of emotions rushing through him. Fear, doubt, disbelief, coupled with the embers of rage that would explode into an inferno.

"*I fucked up, man.*"

"How, Quinn?" His voice echoed in the quiet kitchen. The silence weighed down on him as he struggled to think beyond the mess of information and memories clogging his mind.

The memory of another voice came to him, whispering soft and low, so tortured, so scared. Devon's voice, soft and shaking, as she stared at him with desolate eyes: "*I have these dreams, crazy dreams—dreams where you look like you, but . . . well, you aren't. Your voice sounds the same, but it isn't. When you touch me, your hands feel like yours, but they aren't. And you hurt me.*"

Out of the blue, he found himself thinking about the night back in the fall when Devon had shoved up her sleeves and showed him the scars left on the smooth inside of her forearms.

"*You just seem so . . . I dunno, steady.*"

"*I am steady. Now.*"

Steady. Devon was that. She was rock steady, so much that even a stalker on her ass hadn't deterred her from doing what she intended to do. Steady enough that less than a month after a whisper-close brush with death, she'd gone back to work, settled back into her life.

A life that had come crashing down on her

"*I feel like I'm going crazy.*"

A muscle throbbed in his jaw as he punched Jeb's number into the phone and held it to his ear, waiting for an answer.

Jeb's familiar voice rasped out, "Hey, Luke."

"What happened on the op when Adam died?" Luke demanded, bypassing any attempts at polite conversation. He didn't have time for polite conversation. Stalking through the house, he grabbed a pair of shoes from his closet and wedged the phone between his ear and shoulder as he put them on.

"You know I can't—"

"Don't give me that fucking shit," Luke snarled. "I need to know what in the fuck happened, and I need to know now."

Jeb was quiet for a minute. Then, his voice quieter, farther away like he'd moved the phone away from his mouth. The words were indistinct, followed by a weird clicking sound, like footsteps, then another, a door closing. "They disbanded our unit."

"I heard about that. I don't give a flying fuck, and that's not what I asked you."

Jeb's harsh laugh seemed to speak volumes. "Yeah, I bet you don't give a flying fuck, but that's part of the answer. The unit got disbanded because the higher-ups started questioning the stability of a couple of the boys . . . namely Quinn and Tony. Quinn's out now, and they pulled his shadow. They figure he's about as stable as he's ever been. But a few months ago, they decided against replacing him and just split the rest of us up."

The one thing that stood out in Luke's mind was the reference to Quinn being stable. Under his breath, he muttered, "I don't know about that."

Standing, he left his room and headed into the foyer. There, he grabbed a coat from the hook by the door, his wallet and keys. "Something's not right with Quinn, and I got a feeling it's ugly."

Ugly.

The deepest part of him didn't want to believe what the rational side of his head was telling him. The picture it was painting. *Not possible*, he thought. *No way, no how.*

"*I keep having these dreams—dreams where you look like you, but . . . well, you aren't.*"

Again, Quinn's bitter, angry voice from last night. "*How's that nice, normal woman doing, Luke?*"

"Tell me what happened, Jeb."

"Damn it, Luke, I don't know all of it." Jeb blew out a breath. "I thought there was something between him and the woman who died last spring. I was right; he finally spilled that when he was at the cabin with me last month. Her dying fucked him up something bad."

"*I fucked up, man. Fucked it up all to hell and back. Too late to fix it now.*"

Dread was a slimy, ugly weight in his chest as he headed out to his car. "I get that, but why was it decided that Quinn might be a time bomb?"

Jeb was silent for so long that Luke wasn't sure he'd answer. Then, finally, in a soft, quiet voice, he said, "Because he went back. We were in South America, trying to track a new player on the drug scene—you don't need to know any more than that. But suffice it to say, the whole damn op went to hell in a handbasket, and not just because of Adam or the girl. They knew we were coming, knew who we were. Best thing we could have done was get the hell out and stay out. But after we got to a secure area, while we were waiting to be evacuated, Quinn disappeared. Like a fucking ghost. Two days after we pulled out, there's this rumor that this new player was found gutted in his bed, along with the other men that were in the house. All dead. And there was a woman . . ."

Luke's stomach dropped to the floor. *God, no.* "Please tell me he didn't . . ."

"No. She wasn't hurt. But she was terrified. Saw the whole damn thing." Jeb broke off, sighed harshly. "He went back, like a raving lunatic, alone, and gutted a man. Hell, we don't even know for sure that man was the one we were looking for; we were just down there gathering intel, looking for evidence. This guy wasn't even the only one we were looking at. For all we know, Quinn killed an innocent man."

Luke closed his eyes. Silent, he stood in the bitter cold, trying to absorb what he'd just been told. He knew Quinn could kill; they'd all done it, and while it didn't settle well on him, Luke knew they hadn't been killing at random. They'd always had targets, and they'd always had a reason. Didn't make it any easier, but he could live with it.

But if what Jeb was saying was true . . . God. Had Quinn killed some innocent guy? Did he even care that the possibility existed?

Worse, if he didn't care, what else had shattered inside him?

His voice gritty, he said, "I gotta go, man."

"Luke, wait."

"No time, Jeb. Something's going to hell in a handbasket." He disconnected, and when the phone started to ring a few seconds later, he just ignored it.

* * *

BACK in Fort Bragg, Jeb Gray stared at the phone in his hand and had to resist the urge to throw it. Damn those two Raffertys to hell and back. Neither of them could ever do a damn thing the easy way.

He tried once more to call Luke, but there was no answer. There wasn't much point in leaving a voice mail, but he did anyway, keeping his voice low and hoping like hell nobody overheard him. Not now, and not earlier.

"Listen, Luke, I don't know what in the hell is going on, but Quinn ain't the man you need to worry about." Then he disconnected and glanced around the hallway one more time.

He could get in serious shit if he got involved in this. In any way. He'd been told time and again to let it go when he had tried to get somebody to listen to him. They couldn't be blind to it, not totally. They'd split the unit up, right?

But that wasn't going to fix the problem, and damn but was there a problem. A problem that seriously needed help, if Jeb's gut was right. He'd gone as high as he could manage on his own, but nobody seemed to want to listen.

There was no proof. No signs of trouble. It ended up that Jeb was told he could either let it go or risk ruining his career.

It didn't make a lick of sense to Jeb, because they'd gone and stuck a tail on Quinn, hadn't they? But just Quinn. Yeah, Quinn seemed like the one more likely to go postal with that cold face of his and his knack for saying the wrong thing to the wrong person, his knack for pissing people off and not giving a damn.

After leaving Luke that short, terse message, he paused and

silently asked himself if he wanted to get involved in this. Hell, even he had his doubts about whether his fears were founded or not.

But he hesitated only few seconds, long enough for his questions to form and then fade away. Whether or not he should get involved was a moot question at this point. He already was involved.

From memory, he punched in another number. A headache throbbed at the base of his skull, and he smoothed a hand back over his naked scalp, hooked it over the back of his neck, digging his fingers into tight muscles.

There was no answer here, either, and Jeb swore.

As the phone rolled over to voice mail, he snapped, "Get off your ass and call me. There's trouble." He disconnected and closed his eyes and muttered, "Talk about going to hell in a handbasket."

Luke had been determined to find some kind of normal life for himself, and after the past year, Jeb had begun to understand why. But if this was anything even close to normal, he wanted back out in the field.

Out there, he could at least pretend he was in a position to help people. Now he was in a position to sit on his ass and hope like hell some of his friends didn't wind up making some seriously bad mistakes.

Footsteps echoed down the tiled hall. Tucking the phone away, he started back toward the computer lab. Inside the lab were a bunch of hopeful would-be Rangers, guys who looked tough as nails yet were entirely too young in Jeb's eyes.

Whether or not they had what it took to make it in Special Forces, it was now Jeb's responsibility to find out. It was one that was weighing heavily on him, and he wasn't so sure he was cut out for teaching.

Of course, he wasn't sure he was cut out for much of anything other than what he'd always done.

SEVENTEEN

H ER house was quiet.

Luke had parked his car one street over. But even as he took that precaution, he hoped he was wrong. Hoped that maybe he was the kind to see monsters where there were none, after all.

Maybe he was imagining some unseen, nonexistent enemy now, just as a way to deal with being dumped. Fighting, he could handle. Having the woman he loved push him out of her life, that was harder.

But every step he took closer to Devon's house had his skin drawing tighter and tighter. The front door was locked, and he used the keys he hadn't returned to unlock the door, grimacing at the quiet, almost imperceptible sounds as the tumblers fell into place.

Easing the door open, he listened for some sound as he slid inside and reset the alarm. Devon's car was in the driveway. If she was here, she'd have the radio on, the TV, something. She hated utter silence.

But that was what greeted him.

Complete, utter silence. No, not complete.

Just faintly, he heard a voice. Indistinct, deep, and rough, the voice of a man talking low and soft. Luke's lip curled, rage setting vicious, cruel hooks inside him.

Making his way through the house, he relied on the knowledge picked up after living there for the past couple of months, avoiding the middle plank in the hallway. It always squeaked when it was stepped on.

As did the fourth and seventh stairs. Keeping his back pressed to the wall, his ears pricked, he listened.

Whoever it was, the man was quiet, too quiet, and it wasn't until Luke was a few feet away that he could pick out individual words.

The voice, he knew that voice. Familiar, but not the one he'd expected. It wasn't his own voice, and Quinn sounded just like Luke. As they should. Twins, identical on the outside . . . and maybe not all that different on the inside.

It wasn't Quinn.

Relief hit like a tidal wave, but he didn't even have time to wallow in it as the voice raised, calling out to him. "Come join the party, Luke. After all, your little whore is the guest of honor."

Shoving off the wall, Luke entered Devon's bedroom and faced Tony. The past few months had worked some serious changes on the other man. Tony's large, powerful frame had become gaunt, big hands attached to bony wrists and too-skinny arms.

Big hands that were even now petting Devon's tangled hair. A grin appeared on Tony's face, and he shook his head. "You figured it out too quick, man. I'm not quite done with my game. I didn't want it to end so damn fast."

From the corner of his eye, he could see Devon's face. Her eyes were wide-open, stark with terror, the pupils so dilated, he couldn't even see the soft green gold of her irises. Her body lay limp on the bed, too damn limp. She made a weird gurgling sound in her throat as she breathed out.

She'd been drugged.

Tony had fucking drugged her. What in the fuck had he given her? Damn it, it could have been any number of things.

Luke's hands closed into fists, and he had to fight to keep from lunging for the other man. And he would have. Except the hand that wasn't stroking Devon's hair held a gun, and the muzzle of the Beretta was nestled in the soft underside of Devon's chin. One little twitch, and she was gone.

"What kind of game is this, Tony? Terrorizing women . . . drugging them? Not the kind of game you used to play."

"Too damn bad, too," Tony replied, his voice cheerful. "It's a fun game. Especially when it's your woman. It's your damn fault, you know."

"Yeah. Yeah, I know that." He'd failed her. Again. Once more, Devon was in the hands of a lunatic, and Luke, sorry-ass bastard that he was, hadn't figured it out in time.

"No." Tony's voice went hard, harsh. "You don't know, man. You fucked it all up. You leave, go after your nice, normal life, and all of ours go straight to shit. Adam dead, Carpenter dead, Elena . . ."

Tony's voice broke, and he bent down over Devon, pulling her limp body close and cuddling her like a child seeking comfort from a teddy bear. "Elena's dead."

"Elena . . ." But Luke didn't have to ask who Elena was. He already knew. Jeb had told him before. Quinn had feelings for the woman who had died during that last op, but he'd suspected Tony had as well.

Her death had pushed somebody over the edge, all right. Luke had suspected just that earlier as Jeb told him about Quinn's little disappearing trip down in South America. Yeah, somebody had gone fucking nuts.

But it wasn't Quinn. Not Luke's twin.

It was Tony.

"I'm sorry about Elena," Luke said quietly, edging a little closer.

He shook his head and said, "I can't undo what happened to her. But neither will this."

Looking up, Tony smiled. It was a smile that totally lacked anything remotely human, anything remotely sane. "It won't undo it, but it's justice. You cost me the woman I loved; I'll do the same for you." He slid a hand down and cupped one of Devon's breasts in his palm. She gurgled but didn't move.

Luke didn't think she *could* move. Whatever drug Tony had given her had worked to paralyze her muscles, keeping her chemically restrained, and that was every bit as effective as if the man had chained her to the floor. It was the only thing that made sense, because if Devon could have moved, there was no way she would lie there without struggling like a wildcat, whether or not there was a gun at her throat.

Trying to keep from howling with the rage inside him, Luke asked, "What did you give her, Tony?"

With an ugly sneer on his face, Tony asked, "What the fuck's it matter?" Then, with another abrupt mood shift, Tony smiled. "Can't really hurt to tell you, can it? You already know the basic *what* . . . a doctor type like you can tell when somebody's been chemically restrained. Atcatamin—picked up some of the cat down in Colombia, figured it would come in handy."

Cat . . . son of a bitch. Cat, or atcatamin, was a powerful muscle relaxant, so powerful it wasn't even legal, due to the risks. It had killed plenty of people just because they'd received one cc too much. "You trying to kill her?" Luke rasped. "That shit will shut down the heart, the lungs."

Tony simply looked bored. While Devon lay there, struggling to breathe, he looked *bored*. "Relax, man. It's diluted. I wanted to make sure she was good and awake for this. No fun if her lungs shut down because of a drug, ya know. And man . . . has this been fun. The past few weeks? Watching her? She went and turned into a scared little girl." Tony's eyes glinted like broken glass. "Elena was no girl. This little bitch cried herself to sleep, whispering your name, and when I was there, she never even knew. Nice and normal . . . If she's what nice and normal is, I don't want it. I want my Elena back."

"Tony, let her go. You want to make me suffer, that's fine. You and me can take her car, get the hell away from here, and you can do whatever in the hell you want. Just . . . just let her go."

"Whatever I want?" Tony smirked. "Luke, what I want is you dead. Half my team is dead because of you. Then they go and tell me that maybe we should have my men reassigned. That it's best I find something else. Like *I'm* the fucking problem . . ." His voice dropped to a ragged growl, and he spat, "*You* are the fucking problem. Walking away from us like that."

He stopped in midrant, took a deep breath. He pushed the muzzle of the Beretta a little harder against Devon's neck. "You know what I want, buddy? I want to put a bullet between your eyes and watch as you hit the ground. And I almost did that a time or two." He fisted a hand in Devon's hair and jerked, grinned as Devon made another one of the weak, strangled sounds in her throat. "But then I saw you with her. Started watching you two . . . saw that I wasn't the only one watching. That night when he attacked her? She isn't the one that killed him. I did. Because when he was done, he was going to do her, and I didn't want you to get off that easily. She dies, and the game ends. But as long as she's alive . . . as long as I make her suffer, I get to see you suffer."

"You've done that," Luke said, trying not to let his desperation, his rage, show. He didn't so much as have a damn knife on him. He no longer even owned a fucking gun. "You think I'm going to go a day without remembering this?"

"But this . . ." Tony acted as if he didn't even hear Luke speaking to him as he lifted one of Devon's arms and watched it fall slackly to the bed. "This isn't even half of it. She's been a lot of fun to play with, Luke. And now . . . it's time for more fun."

He stood up. Tony lowered the gun, but he kept his eyes on Luke. There was a look in his eyes, a silent dare: *Come on, buddy. Rush me. Try to save her.*

Luke knew better. It might only take him a second or two to get to Tony, but Tony would already have a round chambered in that fucking Beretta, and it would take the other man even less than a second to put a bullet in either one of them. He'd willingly take that bullet, but not if it meant leaving Devon alone with one very dangerous man who'd lost his damn mind.

His tone casual, Tony moved around the bed, settled on the other side. "I kept asking myself how I needed to end this game. A few days ago, I figured it out. All I've done until now is watch her. Slip her a bit of ketamine every now and then. You know what that shit does to the mind, buddy, don't you? Makes you wonder what's real . . . what isn't . . . Makes you wonder if it really happened or if it was some bizarre nightmare. And shit, is she easy to control. All I had to do was whisper what I wanted her to think . . . and she thought it."

Shit. Ketamine, too. Damn it all to hell, no wonder Devon had thought she was going crazy. The dreams that shit could cause, that alone could be pure hell. But somebody purposely drugging her, toying with her vulnerable mind while she was under the influence . . . *Shit, shit, shit.*

Devon stared at Luke, her drugged, glassy eyes wide and terrified, as Tony reached out and ran his hand down her midsection, from her breastbone to her pelvis. "They cut Elena open, man. From her neck down to her belly, they cut her open. She was alive when they did that, and she died covered in her blood, their semen. They raped her, beat her, sliced her up like some animal, and left her to die."

With a laugh, he reached out and flicked one of Devon's nipples. "The pretty Lab came right to me, Devon. And when I cut her open, I was thinking of you and wondering if you'd whimper and whine while you died like the dog did."

"You," Luke said through stiff lips. "You're the one who killed the dog."

Tony snorted. "Of course it was me. You didn't really think it was that dumb-ass, psychotic leatherneck, did you?" He knelt down on the bed beside Devon, and Luke felt his muscles coil and tense, his body prepared to lunge, capture, destroy. He was going to kill Tony. It was simply fact, and because he had every intention of seeing it happen, he didn't let his body respond as Tony trailed his fingers down Devon's rib cage, circled her belly button and then lower, brushing the tops of her thighs. "I knew what he was doing. It was fun to toss a few things in here, there, watch the cops stumble around like some shit-faced teenagers who can't figure out which way is up."

Tony brushed his knuckles against the russet curls between Devon's thighs, but then his hand moved back up. "It's even more fun now." His voice was a low, insidious whisper that burned a hole inside Luke's gut. "Watching you put it all together. You ought to be happy, buddy. She wasn't alone all those nights you were at work. I was here with her."

A grin split his face, and he shrugged. "Of course, she thought it was you. Every time she screamed, every time she said your name and begged you not to hurt her . . ." His lids drooped, partially shielding his eyes. "And now you're wondering what all I did. Did I fuck her? You wouldn't ever know, not unless I tell you. And neither will she."

"You didn't." Forcing the words out was like vomiting up acid, painful and unending. "You wouldn't do it without making sure I knew exactly what you were doing, or what you planned to do. That's what this is all about. Punishing me for something."

"No. It's not about punishing you for something. It's about punishing you for everything." Tony shook his head.

The humor, that sly, amused smile, so terrifying because it seemed so normal, faded from Tony's face, and he shoved to his feet, pointing the gun at Luke. "Everything, you dumb fuck!" he bellowed.

"You take a damn bullet in the leg, and then you decide, 'That's it, hey, I'm done.' What about the rest of us? You left your team, you left your brothers out there, and when we started dying off one by one, you showed up at the funerals like it was nothing. Like you didn't have a damn thing to do with it."

His voice dropped. "But you did. It all started when you left. It's your fault Max is gone. It's your fault Adam's gone. Collins. You fought with them, side by side, and then you just walked away." Tears glittered in his eyes, but Tony wasn't even aware of them as he whispered, "And Elena. She's your fault, too."

Luke knew better than to try reasoning with somebody who had so clearly lost his grasp on sanity. Staring into Tony's pale blue eyes, he tried reason anyway. "Yeah, it's my fault. Mine, not hers. You're a soldier, Tony. You don't punish the innocent—you protect them."

Tony's lip curled. "She's your little slut, Luke. That makes her not one of the innocent." He stooped down by the bed, grabbed something from the floor.

"Get that chair and pull it closer to the bed."

Glancing back at the overstuffed chair by the window, Luke looked back at Tony and then turned, grabbed the chair, hauled it until it was close enough that his feet would touch the bed if he sat down in it.

No. Not if. When. He had a sick feeling he knew what Tony was planning. Stall.

Stall somehow. It was the only thing he could do. The atcatamin was short-lived. Powerful shit, but short-lived. And thank God, Tony hadn't given her too much, because if he had, Devon would already be dead. But maybe, just maybe, if Luke could stall long enough, the drug Tony had pumped into Devon would wear off.

God, please, God, he prayed in desperate silence as he turned to look at her again.

If he could stall long enough, maybe the cat would wear off, and she could get the hell out of here. If she got away, Luke didn't give a shit what happened to him. So long as he didn't fail her again, so long as he took Tony with him.

"How long have you been planning this?"

Tony smirked. "Long enough. I knew back when we buried Adam that you'd have to pay for his death, for Elena's, for Carpenter, for Collins. Been watching you, off and on, ever since then." A disgusted look entered his eyes, and he shook his head. "You went and got soft, man. Six years ago, there's no way somebody could trail you without you realizing it."

"The man who helped train me could have."

With another one of those eerie laughs, Tony said, "Oh, now you're going to flatter me. You're stalling . . . Don't think I don't know that. But it's a waste of time. The drug won't wear off in time for her to stop me." He tossed a black duffel on the bed and nodded toward it. "There's some more atcatamin in there. I only used a couple of cc's on her, but you'll need more. You do the math, Dr. Rafferty; figure it out. But I'm watching you."

"What am I drawing it up for?" Another pointless question that he knew the answer to. But he'd be damned if he'd stick that needle in his flesh, damned if he'd let Tony do what he was planning.

"You know what it's for. This stalling tactic is lame, Luke, and you really ought to know better. You can stall all damn day, and it won't matter. Nobody's coming to help you, Luke. There's no team hiding in the shadows to back you up. You damn well saw to that. It's just us.

"She can't scream for help, and you know that if you try, I'll put so many holes in her, she won't even look human when I'm done." Then Tony smiled at Devon and asked, "Or do you want me to say it out loud for her benefit? You want her to know how I'm going to paralyze your ass, then tie you upright to that chair so you can watch me fuck her raw?"

Devon moaned. Maybe it was Luke's wishful thinking, but the sound wasn't as strangled and choked as before. A little clearer.

He watched her from the corner of his eye as he pretended to fumble through the contents of the bag. Yeah. Her chest was moving better. Drugs like these were dangerous; they could paralyze the diaphragm and stop breathing if too much was used. Atcatamin was even worse; it wasn't regulated, tested. Nothing. The unlabeled vial could have God knows what else inside it.

But if her chest was moving better with her breathing, then the effects were starting to wear off.

More, when he'd turned to grab the chair, he'd seen something else from the corner of his eye.

Taking his time, he filled the syringe, draining the vial. "Leave some extra in there for your bitch, Luke."

"I'm twice her weight," he said, staring at the murky white fluid in the syringe's barrel, flicking it a few times. Air bubbles drifted to the top, and he eased the plunger up a little to get rid of them. "You want me out of commission; you won't be able to give me any less than this."

"Oh, thanks for being so cooperative, Dr. Rafferty," Tony said mockingly. "That's okay. It's not like I'd need much for her anyway. Would have thought you'd go for a real woman, Luke, not some whiny bitch who's scared of her own shadow."

He smiled and leveled the gun at Devon's head. "Do it, man."

A muscle jerked in his jaw, and he lowered his gaze to Devon's, stared into her terrified gaze for a long moment. *I'm sorry,* he mouthed. He jerked his gaze away, as though he couldn't stand to see her pale, scared face. Glanced at the window.

"That's sweet, Luke. Tell it to God, though." Tony squeezed, ever so slightly, on the trigger of the Beretta in his hand.

Luke tore his gaze from Devon's face, looked at Tony. "Okay. Just don't . . . don't kill her."

Tony laughed.

Luke dropped the syringe, faked a fumble-and-grab, and went to his knees. As soon as he dropped, glass exploded. Taking advantage of the few seconds of distraction, Luke grabbed Devon and hauled her off the bed, thanking God for her slight weight. Shoving her under the bed, he paused only long enough to grab the syringe from the ground, and then he pivoted and braced himself as Tony lunged.

Lifting his forearm, he blocked the first wild swing. There was blood on Tony's face, probably from the glass that went flying when Quinn had shot out the window. Whatever happened now wouldn't matter. Even if Tony killed Luke, it wouldn't matter.

Because Tony had been wrong. Luke had backup, and he hadn't even realized it. Quinn had been crouched on the roof of the house next door, and it wouldn't matter if Tony managed to take Luke down or not.

If Luke died, Quinn would kill Tony.

Devon would be safe.

That was all that mattered.

The blood dripped into Tony's eyes, blinding him. Sliver-thin cuts marred the right side of his face, and like most facial and head wounds, those cuts were bleeding like a son of a bitch. With a mean grin, Luke dodged another jab, this one a little bit closer to home. "Don't you hate trying to fight with blood in your eyes, man?"

"Going to gut you," Tony rasped. "Gut you and while you lie dying, I'm going to do the same to your bitch."

He swung again, this time with the hand that held the Beretta, and although the punch went wide, the muzzle caught Luke's cheekbone. Pain flared, his eyes watered, but he ignored it. He didn't need to see all that well to grab Tony and beat the life out of him. With all the rage and adrenaline fueling him now, he could find the man blindfolded.

He brought his foot up and out, hitting Tony's weapon hand. The gun went flying. Tony roared and lunged. Luke, still holding the syringe, met him head-on and wrapped one arm around the other man's waist, hooking his foot behind Tony's. Once, they'd been a spot-on match for height and weight, but the past few months had eaten away at Tony, and although the bastard was strong, he didn't have the weight behind his strength anymore. They crashed to the floor, Luke riding Tony down. Lifting the syringe, he stabbed it into Tony's neck and pushed the plunger down.

Tony's head smacked up against the floor, and he bucked, dislodging Luke before he'd emptied the syringe. Luke rolled to the side, searching for the syringe as Tony came up, swinging. That was when Luke saw the syringe; it was still buried in Tony's neck.

Luke watched as Tony took another swing. This one wide, erratic, and wild.

The third and the fourth punches were almost comically slow. Tony staggered to a halt and gave Luke a dazed, confused look.

Luke watched as Tony reached up, touched his fingers to the syringe protruding from his neck, wrapping his hand around the barrel and jerking it free.

It fell to the floor. "You sorry fuck." Tony's words were slurred, his voice thick. He weaved on his feet, stumbling back and crashing into the wall. "You . . ." He stopped, rubbed the back of his hand across his mouth. "You can't have it. Can't—ain't right. Your fault."

From the corner of his eye, Luke saw a flash of white flesh. Devon. Relief crashed into him as he realized she was moving around a little. But he didn't go to her, not yet. Not until he knew she was safe. Knowing the drug would most likely affect Tony's coordination and his sight, he edged away from the bed, keeping Tony's attention focused on him. "Why is all this my fault, Tony? What in the hell did I do?"

Tony licked his lips and swallowed, watching Luke as though he couldn't quite understand what Luke was talking about, or even where they were. He closed his eyes for a second, rested his head back against the wall. "You left. Left the team. Everything—" He stopped, once more licking his lips.

As Tony's eyes remained closed, Luke took one step, then another toward the other man. But on the third step, Tony's eyes flew open, and his rage had managed to penetrate the drugged fog. "You left us. It all went to hell because of you. Elena's dead because of you. You don't get to have a life."

Tony reached behind him, his reflexes slowed by the drug, but still, he moved too damn quickly. Quickly enough to draw the gun he must have tucked inside the back of his pants. Luke lunged for him just as Tony lifted the gun to aim.

Tackling him, Luke sent both of them crashing to the floor. He grabbed Tony's wrist, slamming it into the floor, struggling to get the gun. Although Tony's reflexes were hampered and his movements stilted, almost jerky, the bastard was strong.

Too damn strong. Snarling, Luke finally managed to wrench the gun away, reversing it in his hand and bringing the butt down, clipping Tony across the temple. His eyes rolled back, but Luke hit him a second time, not quite trusting the man to stay down.

There might have been a third time, a fourth, a fifth, if a hand hadn't caught his wrist, stopping Luke in midstrike. He snarled and jerked without recognizing Quinn, but his brother didn't let go. "Enough, Luke."

"Can't be." Luke's voice was hoarse, reedy. Shaking his head, he repeated, "It can't be enough."

"Has to be." Quinn squeezed Luke's wrist once more and then reached for the gun.

He let his twin have it, and then he shoved to his feet as fast as he could, desperate to get away from Tony. "He moves, shoot the fucker."

A mean smile curling his lips, Quinn said, "Happy to." Then he glanced down, the smile fading as he looked at something on the floor just beyond Luke.

Devon.

* * *

SHE was imagining things again; Devon knew she was.

Except she hadn't been imagining anything. Her head ached, throbbed. Felt like her head was stuffed with cotton, too, and thinking hurt. But she hadn't imagined all the stuff that had been happening.

She wasn't going crazy. She really wasn't.

She wasn't going crazy, and she wasn't dreaming, she realized, as Luke helped her out from under the bed. As he settled on the edge of the bed, cradling her in his arms, she saw the man lying on the floor, his face battered, his eyes closed. It was a man she didn't recall ever seeing before.

A total stranger.

A stranger who was responsible for terrorizing her for months. A stranger who had killed a dog and then killed Curtis Wilder during the assault on her. But not out of an altruistic moment. He'd done it because he couldn't fuck with her, and thereby fuck with Luke, if Devon died.

Licking her lips, she lifted her head, tried to focus on Luke's face, but her vision blurred, danced around like a ballerina on speed. Instead of trying to see his face, she leaned into him. Shivers racked her body, and she started to quiver and shake. Why? She needed to know why. But all she could manage was a hoarse, "Wuh—" Her mouth, her throat, they were so dry.

"Not now, Devon," he said softly, shaking his head. He grabbed something soft and warm, wrapped it around her shoulders, tucking it around her. As the scent drifted up to surround her, she realized it was his robe again.

The warmth of his body pressed against her, his scent surrounded her, and she told herself again that she was safe.

Safe. And as she sat on his lap with his arms holding her close and tight, she didn't feel afraid. Not once. Not even when she could find the strength and control to lift her head and look at the other man, a man who looked like a mirror of Luke.

Except the eyes. The eyes were cooler, harder, cynical. A twin. A twin who had appeared out of nowhere and was now standing over the body of a total stranger, holding a gun in his hand.

Different, but not.

In a flash, all the ugly, hated dreams rushed at her, and as she stared into eyes that were so similar to Luke's, Devon waited for panic to set in. Waited for some bizarre sense of déjà vu. It was like looking at a nightmare come to life, somebody with Luke's face, Luke's eyes; even their hands looked the same to her. Inside that man, Devon could sense a darkness, an icy anger that was capable of nearly anything.

But the panic never came. Slumping against Luke, she closed her eyes and sighed. Whatever drug had been pumped into her had worked to freeze her vocal cords as well as her muscles, effectively silencing her.

But now she could breathe again, maybe even talk. Her heartbeat sped up, and she welcomed it. For a while there, her heart had felt heavy, leaden within her chest.

Luke's hands stroked up and down her back, his voice a soft, nonsensical whisper in her ear. Devon felt herself relaxing back against him, no longer fearing that she was going to die, trapped inside her body like a prisoner at the hands of some madman. She opened her mouth, wondered if she could finally speak.

She managed a raspy, weak "I . . ." and then she grimaced at her painfully dry throat.

"Shhh." Luke lowered his head and kissed her head. "Don't try to talk yet. The drug he gave you is going take a while to wear off all the way." He eased her a little bit away from him, cupping her face. The robe covering her gaped a little, and gently, Luke tucked it back around her. "Does anything hurt? Can you breathe okay?"

Blinking back tears, she shook her head. "Not hurt. Breathing's easier." Her voice was still harsh, stilted, and sounded nothing like her.

"We'll get you to the hospital." He shifted around, reaching for his phone.

From across the room, the other one spoke up. "I already called nine-one-one. Cops and an ambulance are already on the way." At his feet, the third man groaned, shifted around a little.

Devon involuntarily huddled against Luke, while the twin kicked the man on the floor and added, "Maybe we should tell them to bring a hearse, too. Save a trip."

The calm, casual tone didn't fool her one bit. That one could kill without blinking an eye. Then she glanced up, saw the look on Luke's face.

No. Not so different. Luke had murder in his eyes. But then he looked down at her and wrapped his arms around her. "It's okay, Devon. You're safe now."

Safe: it seemed like even more an illusion now than ever. But she nodded. A shiver racked her body. Without saying a word, Luke grabbed a blanket and added it to the robe she had tucked around her. "Will you stay with me?"

He threaded his fingers through her hair, cradling her head against his chest. "You know I will."

EIGHTEEN

BUT for how long?

How long would she want him here? How could she even look at him again without thinking about the hell he'd brought down on her life?

Luke stood in the hallway, hands jammed into his pockets while one of the other doctors looked Devon over. So far, they'd run pregnancy tests, drug tests, checked for evidence of intercourse, checked for STDs.

Nobody knew what kind of drugs Tony had pumped through her system, and Luke knew Tony wouldn't tell them. He'd like nothing more than to beat the answers out of his former commander, but he suspected he'd end up beating the man to death.

There had been a second vial in the duffel, another unlabeled one. It was probably the ketamine Tony said he'd dosed her with. Ketamine abuse was getting to be a big problem, very popular with date rapists. It distorted reality, could cause amnesiac effects. Because of that, nobody was taking a chance. They were treating her exactly as they'd treat a rape victim, and Luke couldn't imagine the hell that was causing her.

So far, it didn't look like she'd been raped, and in his gut, Luke suspected the same. Tony, whatever his fucked-up logic meant, wouldn't have done it without either making sure she'd remember or that Luke was there to see it.

Although he didn't hear Quinn's approach, he knew he wasn't alone anymore. Slowly, he turned and stared across the hallway at his twin.

Quinn's hair was growing out. Wouldn't be too long before it was as long as Luke's, now, and there was a heavy growth of stubble on his face. Quinn's features looked a bit worse for wear, haggard and edging on too thin, like he'd been eating a diet similar to Devon's: a nonexistent one.

"Hell. I thought I looked like shit," Quinn said.

Guilt choked Luke as he stood there and faced his brother. Dear God, how could he have thought . . . ?

"I don't have the words to thank you enough." Luke's voice was harsh, hoarse.

Quinn shrugged. "Fuck that, man. You think I want thanks?"

No. Quinn wouldn't want thanks. Wouldn't want much of anything except just to get back to doing whatever it was he did with himself anymore. Luke realized abruptly that he didn't even know. His twin had retreated so far inside himself that Luke hardly knew him anymore. "What were you doing around here? How did you know?"

"Jeb." Quinn turned away, shrugging his shoulders restlessly and studying a big poster featuring a pregnant woman holding a pack of cigarettes in one hand while the other rested on the ripe curve of her belly. But Luke was under no delusion that Quinn was looking at the poster out of interest. It was just a way to keep from looking at his brother.

"When I called you last night, I was drunk out of my mind. Been drinking a little too much," Quinn said abruptly. "Had a bad night. Bad few nights . . . a bad few months."

Shit. Luke narrowed his eyes and shook his head as Quinn turned to face him. "Don't you dare apologize, Quinn. Don't. I won't hear it."

That caustic smile appeared on Quinn's face, but Luke didn't know if it was directed at himself or at his twin. "I was in Illinois. Had been half thinking about going back to the ranch for a while. Stopped to get something to eat and saw a girl." His gaze fell away, big shoulders rising and falling on a sigh. "She looked like . . ."

"Like Elena," Luke said quietly when Quinn fell silent.

"Like Elena." A snarl twisted his face, his hands clenching into fists. "Put me back. Saw her face again, saw what they'd done to her. I got drunk. So fucking plastered I don't even remember how much I put away. First clear thought I remember was calling you . . . not sure why. Or what I wanted."

"Quinn, stop."

But Quinn didn't listen. Of course, he never had. "Woke up thinking I needed to get here. I'd done something, said something. Needed to fix it. Jeb called. I didn't answer. He kept calling." Quinn's eyes slid over, met Luke's, and then slid away. "Finally answered, and he said something was up with you, but by then, I'd already started figuring that out."

"He tell you—" Luke stopped in midsentence, uncertain what to say, how to say it.

"Didn't have to," Quinn said, his voice soft. "I don't remember much of what I said last night, but I do know I'm a fucking basket case right now. Not that I've ever been a picture of stability."

He rolled back on the heels of his feet, rotated his head. "I've done seriously fucked-up things, Luke. You know it, even if you try to excuse it or ignore it. Hell, I *am* fucked up."

"No, you're not." Tears burned his eyes, and Luke averted his gaze. "Hell, you never would have thought what I was thinking."

"You've never gone after a man and killed him in cold blood, gutted him in front of his mistress." Quinn's voice was emotionless, but the screaming hell in his gaze told Luke just how much torture that was. "I have."

"I could." Glancing toward the curtained window that hid Devon from him, Luke shook his head. "Maybe I haven't, but I could. I'm tempted to do it right now. Doesn't change the facts, though. There's no excuse, and I can't get—"

"Save it." Quinn shifted around, leaning a shoulder against the wall. He shoved his hands into his pockets, and unconsciously, Luke echoed him. "I don't need you apologizing to me. I don't need you thanking me."

A couple of residents passed by, and the brothers fell quiet until they passed out of earshot. "I can't be okay with this, Quinn." Shoving off the wall, he started to prowl back and forth across the hall. "I can't. I was this close to losing her, this close to seeing her killed right in front of me—and I would have, if you hadn't shown up. And I'd gone there thinking it could have been you. I'm not okay with this. I can't be."

Quinn reached out and grabbed Luke's arm, jerking him to a stop. "Then that's your problem, not mine. Shit, Luke. You remember how many fights I got into before we enlisted? A guy even looked at me wrong, and I put him in the hospital. I did it more than once when we were school. Dad spent half the time getting me out of trouble and the other half, he was trying to keep me out of trouble. If it wasn't for the two of you, I probably would've done something bad enough to land in juvie after she died and gone on to only God knows what after I got out. Probably would have ended up in jail before too long, and don't tell me that's bullshit." Quinn broke off abruptly and turned away.

Yeah. Quinn hadn't been the ideal teenager, if such a thing existed. He'd come close to getting his ass locked up more than once. But a reckless, hotheaded boy with anger issues didn't make for a killer.

He didn't say it out loud. But Quinn heard it loud and clear. He turned around and faced Luke. His voice was a harsh whisper as he said, "Don't you get it, Luke? I am a killer. And I'm not talking about the shit we had to do on the job. I can deal with that." He closed his eyes, rubbed his hands against his face. "I can even deal with the fact that I killed that fuck in Colombia. He was guilty."

Sighing, Quinn lowered his hands and met Luke's eyes. A bitter smiled curled his lips. "He was. I saw it in his eyes. He knew why I was there, and he laughed, called out for his men. But I'd already killed them. Five men. In one night. When I went in there and he called for his men, and they didn't come . . . he panicked. I grabbed him when he ran for the door, and right there, while she was watching, I killed him. She was so scared, terrified she was next. And I didn't give a shit."

Shoving his hands deep into his pockets, Quinn gave Luke a baleful glare. "I've spent the past six months seeing a fucking shrink who keeps trying to convince me to get on medicine for depression. I killed a man in cold blood, and I wake up feeling that blood on my hands, and instead of being sorry, I wish I could do it again, and again. Anything to make him pay for what his men did to Elena. I deserted the team while they were trying to get Adam out of there. I was this close to deserting my team in the middle of the jungle a few months after that, even though I knew we had hell breaking loose around us. I got men shadowing me, making sure I don't go crazy and kill somebody. And you feel guilty for wondering if I've lost it?"

Abruptly, Quinn laughed, a harsh bark of laughter that echoed down the hall. "Half the time, I'm pretty sure I have lost it."

Through gritted teeth, Luke snarled, "That doesn't make it right! Me thinking that. Me actually being so fucking stupid that I could think it for even a minute—" His voice broke.

Quinn reached out, hooked his arm around Luke's neck, and hauled him in close, hugging him tight. "You need to give me some lame-ass apology, do it. It doesn't mean shit to me, because I can see exactly why you might have thought it could be me. Hell, I can see me slipping over the edge. There have been times . . ."

His voice trailed off. "No. I'm not going there. You don't need to hear that; I don't need to say it. But it's not like I've worked hard to convince people I'm even remotely steady. So say you're damn sorry, if that's what you need, but get it over with already."

But the words lodged in Luke's throat. Tears blurred his eyes, and for just a minute, he let them fall. Then he pulled back, rubbed the back of his hand over his eyes. "I'm not much of a brother, am I?" he whispered hoarsely.

"Yeah, like I'm any kind of poster child." Quinn smirked, but then it softened into a real smile. "You're the best friend I have, Luke. Only decent thing Mom ever did was give you to me."

Luke would have said something else. There were words he needed to say, whether Quinn wanted to hear them or not, but he couldn't find them, couldn't give them voice.

Before he had the chance to work at it, the door across the hall opened, and they turned as one to watch as the doctor slipped out of Devon's room. A nurse followed a minute later, stripping gloves off her hands and disappearing down the hall, her shoes squeaking on the tile floor. Deb gave Luke a tired smile and gestured to the small waiting room across the hall. Luke didn't want to follow, didn't want to get that far away from Devon.

Deb gave him a weary smile. "Come on, Luke. Give me a break. I'm exhausted, and you don't look too steady on your feet."

If Quinn hadn't laid a hand on Luke's shoulder, urging him forward, Luke probably would have just stood there. Quinn shadowed them, and Deb paused, looked between them as though debating on whether she should ask Quinn for a few moments of privacy and then dismissing it. "You realize I'm breaking several major laws here, talking to you about this," Deb said, settling on the chair in the small cube of a waiting room.

There were two other chairs, a TV, and a coffee table that had seen better days. Neither brother made an attempt to sit. Deb leaned back. She studied one face then the other before looking back at Luke. "Can the world really handle two of you?"

She didn't wait for an answer, and Luke figured she hadn't been expecting one, either. "Physically, Devon's fine. So far, all of the tests are coming back clear, although some take longer than others." She didn't elaborate, but Luke didn't need her to.

Something hot and sick settled in his gut, but he shoved it aside. Those tests would be clear, too. Tony hadn't raped Devon. He would have—he would have done it right in front of Luke, but he never have the chance, thanks to Quinn.

The strength drained out of him, and he ended up dropping his butt down on one of the hard chairs and resting his head in his hands.

Deb mistook his relief for fear and rushed to offer reassurance. "From all our exams, it doesn't appear that she was assaulted." She shot Quinn another look, swore under her breath. "Damn it, Luke. Don't ever think I don't like you. I can't believe how many ethical codes I'm breaking here, not to mention laws. From everything we can tell, she wasn't raped."

"I know that." He lifted his head and looked at Deb, shrugging his shoulders. "He . . . he was waiting until he had an audience. He was after me the whole damn time. Devon was just the means to an end."

"That doesn't make this your fault," Deb said gently. Her brown eyes were soft with compassion, and she leaned forward, looking like she was going to offer some comforting touch or gesture, but then she stopped and decided better of it.

Settling back in the seat, she sighed. "You know the story about my daughter. It was her boyfriend, you know. I'd always liked him, and when she told me she was breaking up with him, because he was too jealous, too controlling, I tried to talk her out of it." Cocking her head, she asked him, "Does that make what he did to her, what he tried to do, my fault?"

Scowling, Luke shook his head. "I don't need any psychobabble shit, Deb."

"And I don't have any for you. The answer is no. You know it as well as I do." Then she shrugged and added, "But knowing it and believing it, we both know those are two very different things. But don't let this eat you up inside, Luke. She needs you—not your guilt, not your regret. But you."

With a sigh, she stood up and smoothed a hand back over her graying blonde hair. "Considering we still don't know enough about the drug he gave her, it would be best if she stays here for twenty-four hours." She paused, gave Luke a measuring gaze. "Is there any way you can find out if he gave her anything besides atcatamin?"

Luke curled his lip. "I was willing to beat it out of him, but that idea got vetoed."

"You aren't going to be much good for your woman if you're stuck in jail for murder," Quinn said.

Something about the way he said it sent a ripple of foreboding down Luke's spine. He shot Quinn a look, but the other man's face was smooth, blank; even his eyes reflected nothing back. Not his normal cynicism, not humor, not boredom. It was disconcerting. Like looking into a doll's eyes and then having that doll speak to you.

Luke narrowed his eyes and wished he did have some genuine psychic ability that would let him communicate silently with his twin, so he could tell Quinn to stop thinking whatever he was thinking.

A predatory smile lit Quinn's face, his teeth flashing white against his golden skin, and for just a second, the hot light of anticipation lit his eyes. Then it was gone.

Deb, unaware of the silent tension between the brothers, sighed. "He does have a point," she murmured.

It took Luke a minute to figure out what she was referencing. "I wouldn't have killed him."

"Uh-huh. I'd practice saying that in front of a mirror if I were you."

When he said nothing, Deb smiled and shook her head. "All in all, I have to say that physically, she's fine. For whatever reasons, her attacker didn't physically cause her any harm. In most assault cases, the lingering damage tends to be emotional, though." She made a face and added, "And you know that as well as I. I do have to say, emotionally, she's doing a lot better than I think I'd be doing in her place. She's an amazing woman, Luke."

"I know."

Deb passed by him and patted him on the shoulder. After checking her watch, she glanced from one brother to the other. "I'm having her moved up to the third floor here in the next few minutes. Luke, you're welcome to stay, but . . ."

Her gaze slid over to Quinn, and then she glanced back at Luke with a shrug. "Probably not the best place for a visit."

"I don't plan on visiting." Quinn barely glanced at her as she nodded and then walked away.

Moving in tandem, they crossed the hallway, stopping just outside Devon's door. Angling his chin toward the door, Quinn asked, "Is she going to be okay?"

"I don't know." He closed his eyes and said a silent prayer and then looked back at Quinn. "I hope so. Pray she is. But . . ." His voice trailed off, and he realized he couldn't find it in himself to say it.

Saying it made it real—a mantra from childhood. Acknowledging a monster might live in the closest, bringing it to life within nightmares. Giving voice to his fear that Devon would be better off without him in her life would make it so.

Bitter, he let himself admit, in silence, whether he said a damn thing or not, it was probably going to happen. At this point, it should happen.

"You're not helping things."

The words were quiet, spoken with a compassion Quinn rarely showed. Sliding his brother a glance, Luke said sourly, "At this point, there's nothing I can do to help things."

"Sure there is." Using a booted foot, Quinn nudged the door open a little more, keeping his body off to the side so the wall prevented him from seeing inside, or Devon from seeing out. Lowering his voice, he said, "Go on. You really think she wants to be alone right now?"

She lay on her side, facing away from the door. She was covered head to toe with blankets. He'd gotten them for her himself and tucked them around her shivering body. Although he knew Deb and the nurses would have taken them off for the physical exam, they'd replaced them, making sure every inch of her body from below the neck was covered.

But still, she shook. He could see the trembling of her body from here. He couldn't go to her, though. It was like he was rooted in place, frozen. "Why in the hell would she want me with her?" he asked, his voice quiet, lips stiff, hardly able to form words.

"Because she loves you. You love her. Any blind idiot could see that. And trust me, Luke, being alone sucks." On the last word, his voice wobbled. Without saying another word, he reached up and placed a hand between Luke's shoulder blades and shoved, hard.

Luke stumbled into the room, thrown off balance by both Quinn and his own fucked-up mental state. He shot Quinn a glare over his shoulder as Devon jumped. She fought free of the blankets to sit up, her face as white as the bed linens that now lay piled around her waist.

For a moment, they both were still, Luke once more frozen in place, and Devon staring at him with wide, turbulent eyes. His heart sank down to about the level of his feet; he could feel it sinking down out of the protective barrier of his rib cage, his gut, all the way down until it hit the floor. That look on her face, that fear, he was going to see it every day for the rest of his life; he'd see it every time he slept, every time he thought about her.

But he'd be damned if he gave her reason to keep looking so damned afraid. He'd brought this mess into her life.

"You're a complication I don't need." She'd said that to him, and he'd argued, told her he was exactly the kind of complication she did need.

Devon had been right.

He'd brought complication, heartbreak, and fear to her life, and it wasn't like she hadn't already had more fear than any one woman should know.

Yet as he tried to tell his body to move, tried to tell his feet to take him out of the room, Devon cocked her head to the side. A slow smile bowed her lips upward.

Then she held out a hand, reaching for him.

Behind him, voice pitched low and quiet, Quinn said, "Stop being such a chickenshit."

Reluctantly, Luke grinned. And then he did just that, crossing the room to settle down beside her. Nervous . . . hell, screw nervous, he was terrified as he laid his hand in hers, squeezed. She wiggled around in the narrow bed, climbing into his lap and wrapping her arms around his neck. "What took you so long?" she asked, rubbing her cheek against the front of his shirt.

"Sorry." His voice was hoarse, and he had to clear his throat before he could say anything else. "Just needed a few minutes to get my head on straight."

"Hmmm. Trust me, that's an idea that's overrated." She yawned, reaching up to rub her eyes. "I'm tired. Kept waiting for you to get in here. I . . . I don't think I want to sleep unless you'll be here when I wake up."

She tipped her head back, and Luke lowered his eyes, meeting her gaze. "Got your messages."

Luke felt blood rush to his cheeks. "Ah . . . yeah. I couldn't come by Tuesday. Figured . . ."

His voice trailed off, and she grinned, dimples appearing in her cheeks. "You said you'd just wait until you heard from me before you did anything. Does that include coming back?"

Everything in the world faded into the background as he stared at her. *Come back* . . . ? Threading a hand through her tangled hair, he asked, "Should I come back? Is that what you want?"

"Yes." Her eyes skittered away, and in a softer voice she said, "Unless that's not what you want."

Relief crashed into him, and he lowered his head, pressing his forehead to hers. "If I had what I wanted, I never would have left."

"Hmmm. Then you'll come back?"

Pressing his lips to hers, he said, "I was just waiting to hear from you before I did anything."

NINETEEN

"You sure you want to come back here already?"

Devon held Luke's hand as she climbed out of the car. He wasn't looking at her, though. He was staring at the house with grim eyes. The cops had given them the okay to come back, and although Luke had tried to talk her into staying at his condo for a little while longer, Devon knew that wasn't the way to handle it.

Only three days had passed, and she still jumped at every strange sound, still flinched when somebody got too close. Well, somebody besides Luke. It was as though her bizarre fear of him had never existed.

"If I don't come back now, it may never happen."

"Nothing wrong with that," Luke said.

"Yes, there is. This is my home, Luke. I love . . . I loved this house. I want to love it again. I want it to feel like home again."

He blew out a breath, ran a hand through his hair.

She'd been right, she decided. She remembered thinking back in the summer if his hair grew out enough, it would curl. It did, just a little, the thick strands winding around her fingers when she played with it.

"Okay."

Once inside, she had to remind herself to breathe. Her chest ached from holding her breath. Behind her, Luke shut the door. "You okay?"

"It's just a house . . . It's my house, and I'm not going to be afraid of it." Still, apprehension had her body tense as she left the hallway and went into the living room.

"Just take it slow," he said softly.

"No." Turning to face him, Devon held out a hand. "I want you to take me upstairs, Luke."

Brows dropped low over his eyes, Luke shook his head. "Not a good idea. Let's just do it a little at a time."

"No." *Just do it. One step at a time.* So, doing just that, placing one foot in front of the other, she went to Luke. She had more ghosts to face than just the house itself, besides her bedroom. And there was only one way she could think of handling it: all at once, with him.

Rising on her toes, she wrapped her arms around his neck and leaned into him. "I don't want to do it a little at a time. I want to go upstairs with you, and I want you to make love to me."

His breath hissed out of his lungs in a rush. "Devon . . ."

"Luke," she mimicked. Rubbing her lips against his, she said, "Stop worrying, Luke. I know what I want. I know what I need."

His eyes burned into hers, and then he stooped, sliding an arm behind her knees. He lifted her, and cradled in his arms. Devon traced the outline of his lips with her fingers and watched his face. "I love you."

Luke didn't even remember the trip up the stairs. He didn't remember carrying her into the room or putting her on the bed. He couldn't think of anything beyond the sight of her face and the soft, gentle touch of her fingers on his mouth.

Cupping her face in his hands, he dipped his head and kissed her. She felt almost too fragile under him, and Luke went to roll off of her, but she slid her arms around his neck and muttered, "Uh-uh. Like this. Touch me, Luke. I need it."

She didn't have to ask him twice. Curving one hand over the slight flare of her hip, he stroked up, taking the hem of her shirt up, baring her belly, her torso, stopping only when her shirt was tangled under her arms. Levering up, he settled back on his heels and reached for the hem, watching her face closely as he stripped it off. Her hair floated down around her shoulders, curving over her breasts and spilling out over the white sheets in a russet banner.

"Too slow," Devon muttered, and she sat up, reaching for his shirt. It soon joined hers on the floor, and then she reached behind her, unhooking her bra. She tossed it to the floor, but as she went to work on the snap of her jeans, Luke brushed her hands aside.

"I'm supposed to be touching you," he reminded her, and he did just that, unsnapping, unzipping her jeans, easing them down and brushing kisses against her navel, her hip bone, the silk-covered mound of her sex, as he moved. They hadn't taken their shoes off, and he had to leave her jeans tangled around her ankles as he tugged hers off.

She sat on the bed, covered by the heavy veil of her hair, watching him as he climbed off the bed. His body, all golden skin and sleek muscles, made her mouth go dry. He reached for the button of his jeans but paused. Devon tore her eyes away from his hands to look at his face. "You sure about this?"

In response, she slid off the bed and dealt with his jeans herself, crouching down in front of him to push them all the way off. On her knees, she looked up at him as she reached up and wrapped her fingers around him, dragging them up and down in a slow, teasing caress. "Moving slow isn't always the answer," Devon whispered. "I don't want slow, and I don't want to think."

Then, as he continued to stare at her, she eased forward and pressed her lips to the silky hard length in her hand. He groaned and bucked against her. Opening her mouth, she took him inside.

His hands shot up, fisted in her hair, tugging her back. Wild-eyed, he stared down at her. "Damn it, Devon."

She grinned up at him. "It's more fun when we aren't thinking." But then something dark and ugly entered her mind. "Unless . . . well, maybe you don't want . . ." She hadn't thought of that. Maybe he wasn't ready. Hell, the doctors and nurses had been very clear about why they were doing a physical on her, why they were drawing all the blood work, every last humiliating thing they'd pushed on her.

Although Devon knew their precautions were unnecessary, maybe Luke wasn't so sure. Or maybe it had nothing to do with that. Maybe he was mad at her for not believing in him. For telling him to leave. For a hundred little things.

Suddenly chilled, she brought her arms up, wrapping them around herself in an effort to warm up.

"Stop." Luke sank to his knees in front of her and caught her wrists, easing them back down to her sides. "Stop. There's no unless. There's no maybe. I want you. I love you." He dipped his head and pressed his lips to hers.

Opening for him with a moan, she arched against him. Big, hard hands wrapped around her waist and lifted her, holding her. "Wrap your legs around me," he said, his voice guttural and harsh.

She did, and it brought her lower body in direct, close contact with his. Between her thighs, he throbbed, hard, hot, and silky. Wiggling, she rubbed herself back and forth against him, desperate. He reached between them, wrapped a steadying hand around his length.

"Look at me."

The sound of his voice sent shivers down her spine, and when she lifted her gaze to his and saw the naked emotion, the desire burning there, everything inside her went all hot and liquid.

As he entered her, they stared at each other. Luke's lids drooped down, and he muttered, "You're so damn hot. Melt for me, Devon."

She was already doing that—had already done it. She felt like a hot, drippy pool of wax, hardly able to move. Looping her arms around his neck, she rocked against him.

Pressing her brow to his, she stared into his eyes. Nothing else existed. Not for her. Not for him. Just the pulse and slide of flesh, the soft whimpers and harsh groans drifting, the stroke of a hand, the brush of lips.

It was hot, sweet, and perfect—and it ended entirely too soon. Luke worked a hand between them and touched her, whispering dark, erotic words into her ear, teasing and stroking and working her closer and closer, until the climax exploded through her. As she came, his arms went tight around her, and beneath her body, he bucked and arched.

He buried his face in her neck, growling out her name as he lost himself inside her.

"Much better when you don't think," Devon mumbled, dropping her head down and resting it on his shoulder.

His chest moved against hers as his breath sawed raggedly in and out of his lungs. "Definitely."

Then he tightened his arms around her and shoved to his feet with a groan. "On the bed next time, though. Then we can just go to sleep."

Still holding her in his arms, he flopped down on the bed and rolled to his side. He reached out and snagged a blanket. It was a bright, vivid blue, new. Tears burned her eyes as she realized that even the comforter they lay on was new. Luke had seen to that, she knew, doing whatever he could to make coming home easier, even when he hadn't wanted her to do it so soon.

The shattered glass in the window had already been replaced. The curtains were also new, made of the same silky, vivid blue as the decorative blanket Luke had pulled over them. Sniffling, she snuggled against him and told herself she wasn't going to get all weepy.

At least not yet.

It was easy, almost too easy, to drift into sleep, Luke's weight pressed close to hers, his hands stroking up and down her back, his lips pressed to her temple. She was almost there when a harsh, shrill sound jolted her back into wakefulness.

She jolted, and then blood stained her cheeks as she realized it was just the phone. Luke pressed a kiss to her brow in wordless under-standing and then rolled away, grabbing the phone by the third ring.

Rolling onto her belly, she pushed up on her elbows and stared at him. Listening to the one-sided conversation, she watched Luke. His long, nude body was a work of art, she decided. Too scarred to be considered perfect, she knew some people would probably see the myriad scars on his body as a flaw.

Devon didn't, though. She loved everything about him.

"She's doing okay." Luke's eyes met hers, and he smiled.

"I'm better than okay," she drawled. "Who is it?"

He mouthed, *My brother.*

"Where is he?"

Luke rolled his eyes and then said into the mouthpiece, "Where are you?" Then he shifted the phone away from his mouth and said, "Getting gas."

"Here?"

Luke nodded.

Rolling to a sitting position, she grabbed the blanket and wrapped it around her. "Tell him to come over."

Luke frowned and then said into the phone, "Hold on." He low-ered it, his hand over the mouthpiece. "Why?"

Devon smiled at him. "The two of you saved my life . . . and he saved your life. It wouldn't matter if he was a stranger neither of us knew. I'd want to meet him for that alone. But he's also your brother. I think it's time I meet him."

Luke didn't say anything right away, and when he did, his words were slow, almost reluctant. "Quinn's not the easiest person to know, Devon. He can be an ass."

Devon's eyes dropped to the phone, and instinctively she flinched, although she knew the man on the other end of the line hadn't heard.

Luke, knowing exactly what she was thinking, laughed. "He can be an ass, and he knows it. Devon, Quinn is . . . complicated."

Grinning at him, she said, "Hey, not all complications are bad. Didn't you tell me that?"

At first, he didn't respond. And when he did, it was just a slow smile. Then he lifted the phone up and said to Quinn, "Why don't you come over here?" He paused, shook his head. "Doesn't matter if it won't take long. Devon wants you to come over."

Another pause. A short, "Yeah," and then Luke disconnected. "He'll be here in a little while." His gaze dropped to her naked body. Her blanket had fallen off one shoulder and gaped in the front, exposing most of her lower half. "Maybe you should get dressed."

"Hmmm. Yeah. Didn't think about that."

After a rushed shower, Devon dried off and grabbed a pair of jeans and a T-shirt. Weaving her wet hair into a braid, she tossed it over her shoulder and dragged her clothes on over her damp body.

Luke was standing in the doorway, watching her and smiling. Caught off balance, she stopped in the act of zipping her jeans and said, "What?"

He just shook his head and said, "I was just thinking about calling Quinn and telling him to take a little more time getting here."

The doorbell rang, and Devon finished zipping her jeans. "Too late."

She started to go by him, but he reached out an arm, blocking her. "Nah. He'd understand."

"Understand you calling him while he's on the front porch and telling him to take more time?"

He hooked a hand in the front of her royal blue sweatshirt and tugged her closer. He glanced down the neckline, eying her naked breasts, and then grinned at her. "Yeah. He'd understand." He dipped his head and kissed her before letting go.

She was nervous, she realized, walking down the steps and down the hall. Her palms were sweating, and her heart was racing. Hell, she was more nervous now about meeting some guy than she had been about coming back to the house where she'd almost died.

But it wasn't just some guy. It was Luke's brother. His twin. And a man who had saved Luke's life, helped save hers. No, definitely not some guy.

She opened the door with Luke standing at her back, a hand resting on her shoulder.

Quinn stood on the other side, his face unsmiling and his eyes unreadable. Unable to stop herself, she glanced back at Luke and then at Quinn.

Physically, the resemblance was staggering.

But Quinn's features were colder. He wouldn't smile often. That coldness was echoed in his eyes, but it wasn't an expression Devon hadn't seen before.

That kind of ice was almost always a shield. A barrier built out of self-defense, the kind erected by people who had way too much bad shit happen. It was a look Devon had seen on her own face a time or two.

Slowly, a smile curled her lips, and she held out her hand. Quinn dropped his eyes, staring at her outstretched hand for a minute. Something weird flickered in his eyes, and then a small smile appeared on his lips, softening the harshness of his features. He reached out, closed his larger hand around hers. He squeezed and then let go.

"Come on in," she said, stepping back. As Quinn passed by her, Luke slid an arm around her waist and dipped his head, kissing her shoulder.

"Can't stay," Quinn said, turning to face them. He glanced at Devon but focused his attention on Luke. "Have you heard from the detectives investigating what happened? They called?"

"We just got home," Devon said. "I haven't checked . . ." Her voice trailed off and she walked past them. As she drew near to Quinn, she sensed a tension in his body, watched from the corner of her eye as he moved back a little, giving her a wide berth.

Smiling a little, she went into the kitchen and checked the machine. The little digital readout read three. "There are a few messages."

"Probably them. But I wanted to tell you." A harsh smile appeared on Quinn's face. He started to say something and then he stopped, looking back at Devon. "Ah . . ."

Luke shook his head. "Whatever it is, just say it. She won't break."

Devon smiled and went to him, wrapping an arm around his waist and hugging him before looking back at Quinn. The other man shrugged. He stood in the hallway between the kitchen and living room, wearing a beat-up leather jacket, worn jeans, and leather boots that had probably seen better years. He didn't much look like anybody's idea of a savior, she knew. Then again, sexy as he was, sweet as he was, Luke didn't much look like a savior, either.

But they were.

And she suspected if she voiced that opinion to either of them, she'd be met with utter resistance, outright laughter—or on Quinn's part, that icy silence. It seemed to be a part of him. "What is it, Quinn?"

When he spoke this time, his voice seemed a little softer, almost gentle. "It's about Tony Malone."

A shiver went down her spine, and she tensed, unable to stop it. "What about him?"

Behind her, she felt Luke's reaction, a reaction that spoke of hot fury; fury so hot, she could feel it without even looking at him.

"He's dead. Cops found him in his cell a couple hours ago. Used a handmade shiv and cut his wrists. Bled out." He eyed Devon's face warily, as though he wasn't sure how she'd react.

She was uneasy, but Devon couldn't tell if it was because of what Tony had done, or because Quinn didn't seem the type who related with others well—and not the type to care. She swallowed the bile rushing up her throat and tried to think. "Dead?"

"Yeah."

He turned on his heel, headed for the door. But before he could open it, Devon went after him and grabbed his sleeve. Quinn went still, and automatically, Devon let go. The guy had *Don't Touch* written all over him. In blinding blue neon.

He turned to look at her, and she forced a smile. "Luke had planned on inviting you over Christmas before things got . . . complicated . . ."

Her voice trailed off as Quinn stared at her with hard, cold eyes. The ice she saw there softened a little, and he said quietly, "You don't need to explain that, Devon. I get why he didn't. Hell, what person would want to have some stranger dumped on her lap after what happened?"

Shaking her head, she said, "You're not a stranger. You're his brother."

"Yeah. Yeah, I am, and I know what the bastard's thinking better than he does sometimes," Quinn said, shooting Luke a smirk. Then, watching Devon's face, he took a step forward and held out a hand.

She knew if she so much as breathed wrong, he'd jerk away. Slowly, she reached out and laid her hand in his. When she did, he turned her arm. Instinctively, she tensed, would have jerked away, but Quinn's firm hold, while gentle, didn't let her. He reached up and touched the faint, faded scars on her inner forearm. "At some point, Luke, man . . . you need to tell her about our mother."

When he let go, Devon instinctively backed away, settling in against Luke and leaning into him.

Quinn slanted a look at Luke and then met Devon's gaze again. "Luke's probably already warned you I'm not the easiest person to deal with. I can be an ass, and trying *not* to be is something I have to work at—and I rarely see the point. I don't like many people; they don't like me. I'm cool with that. Luke's real good about protecting people. He's kind of a Boy Scout."

Unable to help herself, she smiled and glanced up at Luke. "Yeah. He can be that." Looking back at Quinn, she wondered where he was going with this.

"I kept wondering why in the hell he didn't introduce the two of us early on," Quinn said, shaking his head. "I knew this was coming for him, got it the first time he mentioned you. Kept waiting to meet you . . . but now I know why he waited."

Luke went stiff. Easing away, she studied his tense face for a moment and then looked at Quinn. "And that would be . . . ?"

Quinn's lips curved upward in another faint smile. "Ask him."

Devon shot Luke a puzzled look, watched as he shoved his hands deep into his pockets and averted his gaze. His face had flushed a dull, ruddy shade of red. Lifting a brow, she simply stared at him and waited.

Luke blew out a breath. "Mom was a drug addict, Devon. I don't think about it much, because I never knew her. Never once met her. But she wasn't a nice woman."

Quinn snorted and muttered something under his breath that Devon couldn't quite make out. Ignoring him, Luke shrugged his shoulders in a stiff, jerky motion. "I was worried about introducing you to Quinn because of that . . . Sometimes he . . ."

Luke's voice faded away, and Quinn finished up, a weird, unrehearsed sort of rhythm that made her wonder how often the two finished each other's thoughts. "I tend to recognize addicts on sight." This time, when she looked at Quinn, she saw that he was now blushing red and looked damned uncomfortable under her gaze. "Even recovered ones. I don't always give people the benefit of the doubt . . . and Luke wouldn't want me to dislike you, so he was waiting to explain things."

Unsure how that open, honest response made her feel, she frowned. Slipping her hands into her back pockets, she shifted a little farther away so she could see both of them before her. She watched as Quinn looked from her face to Luke with that faint, sardonic smile on his lips. "I don't give people the benefit of the doubt, Luke . . . but she isn't just people. She's yours . . . and you, I trust."

Luke sighed and ran a hand through his hair, nodded stiffly. "Yeah, I should have realized that. I'm—"

Cutting him off, Quinn said in a flat voice, "I'm tired of the *sorrys*, Luke. They aren't necessary."

arm around his waist. Automatic   , glanced down at her face.

She smiled, reached up, and touched a finger to his lips. Then she looked back at Quinn and said, "Since we never got around to having you over for Christmas, maybe you could come over in a few days."

Quinn looked at her, looked back over her shoulder to Luke, and then shook his head. "I'm heading out of town."

"Going back home?"

Quinn shrugged. "Don't really have one." Then he scowled. "Well, yeah, I do. Where we lived with Dad. But I haven't decided where I'm heading."

"You could stay in the condo." Luke grinned a little. "I don't need it. Hang around awhile, Quinn."

He didn't agree one way or the other, just gave another one of those restless shrugs. He left without saying anything else, and as the door closed behind him, Devon turned to face Luke with a smile. "Well, it's obvious which one of you was the social one."

Watching her, a little uneasily, she thought, Luke shrugged. In that moment, the resemblance to Quinn was even stronger: eyes icy and unreadable, face a mask. "Quinn's not much for people."

Nodding, Devon replied, "Yeah, I figured that. I think there's probably a story about why . . . and I imagine it has to do with your mom."

The ice in Luke's gaze thawed a little. "Yeah. A long one. It's . . ."

"Complicated?" she offered.

"Yeah." He grinned sheepishly. "I was . . . I dunno."

"Yeah, you do. You were worried he'd freak me out or something." Slipping her arms around him, she smiled up at him. "I keep telling you not to worry so much. I don't break."

Luke draped his arms over her shoulders, lowering his head so he could press his brow to hers. "So you keep saying." He paused, the silence heavy and tense. "About Tony . . ."

Devon shook her head. "There is no about. He's dead. He doesn't about complications . . . You know, they aren't always a bad thing. You certainly weren't."